# THE
# REPOSSESSION

# THE
# REPOSSESSION

## SAM HAWKSMOOR

Hodder
Children's
Books

A division of Hachette Children's Books

# SPURLAKE GAZETTE
## COMMUNITY NEWS

Thirty-four children are now missing from the Spurlake/Cedarville area over a two-year period. Are you being vigilant? Are you able to recognize the signs of a teen in trouble? Do you know where your child is after school? Need help?

Come to the town meeting led by the Reverend A C Schneider – 7pm Princeton Park, Fir and Geary Streets. Prayers and parental advice from the Mayor's Office.

All concerned families welcome

# Have you seen this child?

## Denis Malone

DOB: Aug 8, 1996

Missing since: Oct 16, 2009

Sex: Male

Race: Caucasian

Hair: Brown

Eyes: Blue/Green

Height: 4'8" (146.3 centimetres)

Weight: 90 lbs (40.8 kgs)

Missing from: Spurlake, BC

Possible abduction.


**ANYONE HAVING INFORMATION**

**SHOULD CONTACT**

Royal Canadian Mounted Police

National Missing Children Services

Toll-Free: 1-555-318-3576

Telephone: (555) 993-1525

Facsimile: (555) 993-5430

# Have you seen this child?

## Denis Malone

DOB: Aug 8, 1996

Missing since Oct 16, 2009

Sex: Male

Race: Caucasian

Hair: Brown

Eyes: Blue/Green

Height: 4'8" (142.3 centimetres)

Weight: 90 lbs (40.8 Kgs)

Missing from: Spuzzlake, BC

Possible abduction

**ANYONE HAVING INFORMATION
SHOULD CONTACT**

Royal Canadian Mounted Police

National Missing Children Services

Toll-Free: 1-555-318-3576

Telephone: (555) 903-1525

Facsimile: (555) 903-5430

# 1

# The Munby Girl

Six weeks, four days, sixteen hours and twenty minutes since the jail door had slammed on Genie. Seven weeks since the school broke up for summer. God had got her into this room but it would take more than prayers to get her out. How do you pray against God? Reverend Schneider with his snake-oil hair came every day and prayed for her soul. Her mother, the grand inquisitor herself, had drugged Genie and had the Reverend carry her up to her room after they had installed the jail door. It was all for her own good, they said, the devil had possessed her, taken her, duped her, and the great and wonderful Reverend was going to cleanse her, drive him out. The Church of Free Spirits was going to send an army of the devout to make sure of it.

Three specific events precipitated this cataclysm in Genie Magee's short life. It all happened with a relentless logic and there was nothing she could have done to prevent it.

The first, and most important in her calculation, was

1

that she discovered that she had fallen for Rian Tulane in the first year of high school. Fifteen, with beautiful eyes and a lopsided grin that just made her heart beat like a hummingbird. Quiet, bright, kept to himself a lot and always scored the highest grades in her year. No one bothered him; he could talk to a geek without being labelled and laugh with the jocks without being one. You could tell from just looking at him that he had a lot on his mind. He was already planning which university to apply for and he took knowing stuff really seriously. Sure he tried out for the ice-hockey team to make himself look more normal, but they rejected him after only one trial. She had watched the game from the bleachers and made some soothing remarks to him as he limped towards the locker room after. He actually stopped to look at her. He'd never said a single word to her in his entire life, but there he was looking all dejected and sorry for himself and she had to say something.

'They should've taken you. You were real fast out there.'

He shrugged, embarrassed. 'I was kinda hoping there wouldn't be any witnesses to my shame, but thanks, Genie. I guess not fast enough, huh?' He pointed to his swelling bruises. It had been brutal out there. Boys with their sticks. 'Basketball is more my game I think, at least no one is carrying a lethal weapon.' He smiled at her, then just turned on his heels and went to change. He probably had no idea of the devastating effect his smile had made on her.

She hung around for him, hoping that this wasn't as stupid as it looked. He'd most likely just walk right by her when he came out. But when he finally emerged, he smiled shyly, genuinely surprised she'd been waiting for him. He walked her home in the rain that evening and she realized that he liked her. He'd noticed her watching him in class and admitted he'd been too shy to say anything to her. Today somehow was different. Her being there in the ice rink for one thing. She didn't seem to mind that he'd been turned down by the team and they shared so many classes it was stupid they never spoke to each other. Nothing else was said as they walked, but that September evening, when he finally took her hand at the junction of Waterfall and Fraser Avenue, she fell in love, and he with her. Not even a kiss was exchanged. But she knew. And then every day from that moment on, each morning he would be waiting for her at the corner of Fraser and together they walked to school, and back home again in the afternoon.

They spent every moment they could in each other's company. She didn't even mind when he made her read the set books and talk about what they were learning. Her grades leaped up. She'd gone from ditzy low achiever to genius and done nothing extra but actually read the books.

Her old school friends fell by the wayside. Genie was no longer 'fun' and Genie thought that was kinda odd since she'd never been allowed any 'fun' anyway. It was the rule in her mother's house that she went to school and came home. So many kids were going missing now they were talking of making them wear electronic tags. The epidemic of crystal meth dropouts in Spurlake and other nearby towns had parents scared enough without them worrying their kids might disappear entirely. Even though Genie's mother had little liking for her daughter, apparently she didn't want her abducted. So, no deviations on the way home, no visits, no hanging out at the DQ, absolutely no parties. No nothing. The Church of the Free Spirits forbade it and even though Genie never actually attended the church, she had to abide by God's rules. God's stupid petty rules. Naturally she never mentioned the existence of Rian to her mother. God forbid she'd have an actual boyfriend.

And then came the fatal moment whilst preparing lunch on a Saturday when she turned to her mother and said: 'Grandma's dead. She just died. I know it.'

It was a normal sunny morning, but it was as if a bolt of lightning had pierced her mother's heart. Her mother screamed at her, yelled every horrid thing she could think of and told her to get to her room for disrespecting the living.

Sure enough, an hour later they got a call from a doctor's clinic in Hope and Grandma was dead. Fallen over in Cooper's Foods and her heart expired.

Her mother went crazy. Claimed Genie had killed her, had always hated her grandmother and sent evil spirits to kill her. It was even more puzzling for Genie because her mother and grandmother weren't even on speaking terms. They had only ever visited her three, maybe four times, in the log cabin by the old railroad where she lived. She made her living by telling fortunes in the orange CNR Caboose abandoned on the rails. Built in 1917, she'd converted it to a magical place filled with First Nation rugs, wind chimes, cedar baskets and art objects that dated back hundreds of years. Grandma Munby was half-Stó:lō herself and she was always saying that it was the better half. The trains had stopped running thirty years before on this spur line and she had walked Genie along the rusting rails one spring, picking wild flowers that grew beside them. She seemed to know the name of every single one and what they could cure. False Solomon's Seal (not to be confused with poisonous Hellbore), Fireweed, Indian Paintbrush (the bright red flowers were used for warpaint dye), Lady Fern, Oxeye Daisy (interlopers from Europe, she discovered).

Genie had loved learning the names and her quaint cabin. She desperately wanted her own fortune told, but her mother forbade it. Grandma's home was filled with feathers, strange unrecognizable objects, rocks bearing gold she'd found by the river and hanging crystals; almost fifty wind chimes noisily swung in the breeze outside. She dressed like a rodeo queen, was loud and laughed, drank homemade wine, smoked a cigar and was never embarrassed by anything.

She had taken Genie's hand, held it hard and told her immediately that she was unique and special and should never ever be afraid of her gift. Genie had no idea what she meant at the time. Her mother wouldn't let her discuss it and never talked about Grandma if she could help it, as if she was ashamed of her. Genie remembered staring at the big red ruby Grandma wore around her mottled neck and the way she seemed to make you feel warm and safe. The exact opposite of her cold and anxious mother. But now Grandma was dead, it was seemingly all Genie's fault. Her mother had fled to the Reverend Schneider's church to pray for her soul. Pray for help to deal with the evil daughter who'd killed her grandmother.

Thus began a month of craziness. She was banned from the funeral. Then the people from the church started coming and kneeling outside her bedroom door at night to pray for her soul. Genie was amused at first. She had no idea that there were so many crazy people in the world, besides her mother. Reverend Schneider, with his comb-backed hair and pimp moustache, was the craziest of them all. He had all these women seeing the devil in *everything*. Every time another child disappeared from the town, the Church of the Free Spirits would be outside the parents' house praying for the kid's safe return. Whether they wanted them there or not. Genie's mother kept saying the devil was coming for his own, meaning her. She was terrified that the devil was coming to take Genie for his 'bride'. Genie, the fifteen-year-old bride of the devil. Some days Genie couldn't wait for him to come – anything had to be better than staying in this crazy house.

The only thing that had kept her sane in this world was Rian, who, before this madness had begun, had taken her hand, held her tight, promised faithfully that he would take her out of there if it got too bad, and when he kissed her, which he did often, she felt as though she was going into outer space. Rian always laughed about it, he could see her float off, always knew when she had gone, but he still held her tight and instinctively knew that this was Genie's way of being happy.

Sometimes the trance would last as much as ten minutes, but he loved her for it. Adored the way she trusted him completely. He loved her deeply, but knew that he had to deliver her home by five every day or else there would be trouble. They never had an actual date, not once in nine months. No movies, no ice-skating. Genie was never allowed to do anything, but he didn't care. As long as she was there every day and her hot hand placed in his as they walked to and from school, they were happy. He planned out a whole life with her and she with him. Neither spoke of it to the other for fear of being mocked, but that is what each was thinking.

And then, on the last day of school, Reverend Schneider struck with the jail door. The devil had sent him a message, he told Mrs Magee. It troubled him deeply and seared a terrible scar upon his heart. The devil had told him Genie was possessed. She was the one he was going to take next. A day later, her mother, in complete hysterics, imprisoned her in her bedroom.

For the first two weeks they maintained a twenty-four-hour watch, shouting abuse to drive the devil from her soul. Took away her laptop, her phone and her sketch pad and pens. The one pleasure Genie had was sketching

8

and even that was now an instrument of Satan.

On the first day Genie tried to escape out of her window, despite a sheer drop, but discovered it had been nailed shut. A day later they fitted bars to make sure. Teams of rabid women came to her jail door spitting and screaming a torrent of foul language. One woman brought food, then grabbed her through the bars as she handed it over, tried to burn a red-hot silver cross on to Genie's bare arm. She held on, hysterically screaming about 'Satan's bitch' in Genie's face and saying that she should be burned like the witch she was. Genie wrenched free, wishing she could retaliate – but the bars got in the way. She nursed her wounds for a week, hoping it wouldn't scar. She couldn't but help take this personally. She watched the hate in the worshippers' faces, wondered how anyone, any so-called 'Christian' human being, could believe this stuff they screamed. Had any of them ever seen the devil? No. Had Reverend Schneider? She severely doubted it. But Genie had, every day, in the faces of these disciples. She had never seen such evil, as if snakes were crawling out of their eyes. All this because she had somehow known her Grandma had died.

That was her mistake. Telling her mother. The image of her fallen Grandma had caught her by surprise, that was all, and she hadn't thought to suppress it. Wasn't the first time it happened, either. When she was six, she'd known that Henry, next-door's Doberman, was about to die. 'I'm going. I'll miss you,' Henry had told her. She hadn't told anyone about that. Who'd believe a dog could talk, let alone know when it was about to die? Or that time when Rian was in danger. She knew he was supposed to go with his uncle to Kamloops for a week and that there would be an accident. She made Rian stay, fake the flu. He didn't understand at first. She had to demand it and she didn't like to stress their relationship because it was so fragile. But he'd gone to bed with a fever as she asked and the uncle went on his own.

The uncle made it to Kamloops safely and Rian was pissed at her for a few days, but at school on the Monday his mother called him on his cell, totally distraught. His uncle's car had been hit by a truck on the way home, just outside Spuzzum, and he was dead. Rian was shocked. He would have been in that vehicle too if he'd gone.

Genie said nothing and they didn't discuss it – not properly, because Rian was a little scared of stuff like that, but he did write in her notebook when she wasn't looking: *I will always remember that you saved my life*, and that was enough for Genie.

* * *

Six weeks, four days, sixteen hours and forty minutes imprisoned in her room, practically the whole summer. They fed her, passed barely edible food through the bars. She left most of it. She lost a lot of weight, which was cool at first because she knew she had to, but now she knew she was too skinny and so very pale, since the sun never came into this room. Fortunately she had her own tiny bathroom and showered more often than she used to, out of sheer boredom. She had no TV – the devil ran the networks apparently, the only true thing her mother ever said, Rian had joked. All she had was an old AM radio permanently tuned to some angry talk-show jock who ranted and raved even worse than her mother. Everything in Spurlake seemed to be about spewing hate. *'Bring back the noose for those monsters selling drugs to our kids! What was wrong with frontier times when a few burning torches and a mob made townsfolk safe in their homes!'* shouted some guy. She was learning a lot about lynch mobs listening to the radio. She wondered when they'd come for her. They burned witches, didn't they? She had regular visions of her mother leading the angry mob down the street baying for her blood. She was glad when the batteries died.

Not long now before school began again. She speculated as to whether she would be as crazy as her mother by then. She often wondered if she should kill herself, as the praying ladies suggested she should, so the devil couldn't possess her, least ways, not in the 'flesh'. They seemed to be obsessed by that. Genie figured that not a few of them probably wanted Satan to take them when their husbands weren't looking and were almost jealous that Genie had been chosen instead. But that was the road to insanity, even thinking it was possible. All she longed for was to be in Rian's arms, feel his lips on her own and hear his reassuring voice say, 'When we graduate, Genie, we'll quit Spurlake and never, ever come back.' Had he meant it? Did he still mean it? Couldn't they go now? Graduate some other place? 'Cause one thing was for sure, the moment they opened that gate again, she was out of there forever and she'd never speak to her mother again as long as she lived.

She wished every day for Rian to come and rescue her, but how? Metal bars on the windows, strong steel bars on her door. He'd have to demolish the whole house to get at her and they kept watch, all the time. She still had faith he loved her. There would be temptations out there, all summer long, as all the girls flaunted their brown bodies down by the river and the swimming pool. But Rian would resist, would wait for her and for school to start. She was *almost* confident about it. But then some days she imagined she saw him in the arms of another. Slutty Sylvie, for example, who was always flaunting her boobs and saying that Rian had a cute butt. Some days she lost all faith, all confidence, and knew he was kissing someone else and had completely forgotten her. These were the days and hours when she wanted to kill herself. They occurred more often now. Time in this house moved in slow motion. Ice Ages could come and go and she would still be in this room waiting for the devil to show up. She would be the winner of Spurlake's Young Miss Havisham award for patience.

Somewhere outside she could hear a young girl was laughing, riding a bike up and down the street, like she was just learning to ride and couldn't get enough of ringing that bell. A dog was barking some place further up the road. Wind rustled through the fir trees in the backyard. Somewhere out there, people were alive.

# 2

## Bunk Science

Rian passed the salad and tore off a piece of the French breadstick to eat. He wasn't hungry but had to make like he was. At his mother's insistence the Tulanes ate together at the table. The last family in Spurlake that still communicated, his mother often boasted, even though it was just the circumstance that forced the issue. Her being in a wheelchair following the road accident. There was no Mr Tulane at the table since last winter. His father had been driving fully loaded when he was hit by another vehicle on the highway in snow. He'd walked out of the wreck unscathed. His mother broke both her legs and was still in a wheelchair most of the day. The insurance paid out. By sheer luck his father never got tested for booze – at least not within forty-eight hours, as he had wandered off and found a doctor who said he'd had amnesia caused by the crash. By the time he showed up he was sober and clean and no one was any the wiser, except Rian's mother who blamed him entirely.

They had moved to a better, more suitable house where

his mother could run her life and her insurance business without feeling anyone had to help. Mr Tulane was not needed on voyage and he'd gone. Rian wasn't sure he missed him, or his drinking. The house was quieter without the shouting. Mr Yates was his father's replacement. He was there for dinner Monday to Friday, some nights too. He was an accountant, and quite what his mother saw in him, with his red face and weight problem, Rian wasn't sure. He had contrary opinions about everything, but his mother needed him and his 'many kindnesses'. Few other men, she told him, would have such patience with her in this situation, so Rian accepted that he was a fixture. At least he didn't drink. But he always had to have the last word.

'All I'm saying, Rian, is that just because someone thought of it, it doesn't mean it will come true. Teleportation is bunk. Pure bunk. No one will ever beam up Scotty. It's impossible. The future never happened. There are no aliens and we don't commute in flying cars. *Star Trek* is rubbish science. Bunk.'

The usual dinner conversation. Rian would say something and Mr Yates MBA would pounce on it, try to make himself look clever, and his mother would eat it up. Nevertheless, Rian defended his position.

'I'm just saying that if we accept climate change as

inevitable then teleportation would eliminate air travel and that's a whole lot of pollution that goes with it. We could save the polar ice caps and the bears.'

Mr Yates stared at Rian a moment and Rian could see the muscles in his thick red neck pulsating as he sought to deliver a withering reply.

'You shouldn't bait Mr Yates, Rian,' his mother said. 'You know science fiction is just that – fiction.'

'The problem with science fiction,' Mr Yates finally barked, 'is that it makes people believe that there are solutions for everything. There aren't. Take teleportation. What you envisage is just magic. It can't happen. The amount of energy needed to deconstruct a human made up of trillions upon trillions of atoms would be equivalent to the energy output of ten nuclear reactors, at least. Plus, reassembling those same atoms back in the right order is a monumental logistical task. Way beyond what any software program could do. We are talking turning your whole body into digital form, into photons, and sending them across town by light waves, then putting it back together *exactly* as it is now. Your clothes too. Impossible. One slight wrong calculation or dropped piece of code and your arm will come out your head or you'll just collapse into a heap of jelly. It would have to reassemble skin, bone, and eyes.

'It would need the basic carbon raw materials to generate it at the end destination. Any idea how complex your eyes are? Hell, just putting your feet back together would be beyond the power of any machine for decades ahead. Decades.'

'Scientists say—' Rian began again, but Mr Yates interrupted.

'Quantum physics states that you cannot say for definite the position and velocity of any single particle. More importantly, Rian, for teleportation to work – and let's assume someone actually has all the computer power in the whole world at their fingertips to store a trillion, trillion atoms – in order for you to be "transmitted", much like an email with an attachment say, you, in the process of being disassembled would be destroyed. The *new* you across town would be a copy and each time you moved you would be another copy. Can a computer also deconstruct and store your memory? Your imagination? If it can't, you would be a sixteen-year-old baby with no memory of anything. Your memory would get wiped every time you teleported.'

'Never mind losing your soul, Rian,' Mrs Tulane interjected.

Mr Yates beamed at her 'Quite. Every human is

unique – I'm telling you it will always be totally impossible. We should not play God.'

Rian looked at him, his fat fingers and smug expression.

'But *if* you could do it,' Rian insisted. 'You could add DNA, like a smarter memory. People could use it to make themselves brighter, better, fitter.'

His mother smiled. 'Well, that might be popular.'

Mr Yates frowned. 'Don't encourage him. Rian, it can't be done. Consign it to the dustbin along with time travel and men on Mars.' He took a mouthful of food and chewed. He looked out of the window as the curtains flew up momentarily from a gust of wind. 'Better get the shutters fastened and the windows closed. They say there's quite a storm coming up tonight.'

The conversation was over. Rian looked at them both, so smug, so happy to be smarter than him, but all they were good at was imagining how nothing could happen, never what *might* be possible. One day he'd find someone with whom he could discuss Genie's amazing pre-cognitive abilities. He was wasting his breath here. Mr Yates would say it was all bunk. Everything was bunk. Rian checked his watch. An hour to go. Everything was going to change. He'd never have to watch Mr Yates eat ever again, or suffer his mother's despair that he was never going to make it, never going to amount to anything, just like his father.

He nibbled on his food and smiled to himself as he imagined teleporting out of there.

'Another child disappeared today,' his mother suddenly stated. 'It was on the news. Boy from your school again. Anwar – such an odd name. Sixteenth child missing since school broke for the summer, they say. Reverend Schneider is leading a prayer group tonight for him in Princeton Park.'

Rian frowned. Reverend Schneider was always first one there leading a prayer group and speaking on local radio about the tragedy of Spurlake that the kids seemed so desperate to leave. Well, just ask Genie if the Reverend was the saint everyone thought he was. Get *her* on local radio and she'd open a few eyes.

His mother was still talking.

'I can't believe how many are missing now. There's a pile of flowers left beside the community noticeboard on Geary Street and countless candles burning. I just don't know what's going on in this town. If parents ate with their kids like we do, maybe they'd know what they're thinking. It's just so scary. If I hear of one more 1-800 number to call if you know anything, I'll get hysterical. I keep hearing about Mr Harrison out with his flashlight.

19

He's been roaming the hills for a year. That boy of his is gone and he isn't going to call. None of them are coming back, get used to it already.'

Mr Yates helped himself to more cheese.

'You're right, m'dear. Those kids have gone. The town just can't hold them. Happening right the way up to the Okanagan. They just up and go with no thought to the pain their families must feel. I blame crystal meth. It's destroying our society. Once those kids get their hands on it – their lives are already over. There's talk of a government task force coming in to control it, but you think it will stop the kids disappearing? I don't.'

'I don't know any kids doing meth,' Rian said.

His mother looked at him with relief in her eyes. 'Well, I for one am glad about that, Rian. I don't know what I'd do if you started taking drugs.'

'You'd throw me out, just like all the other kids who've been thrown out of their homes in this town for doing something their folks didn't like.'

'And you'd deserve it,' Mr Yates said, pointing his knife at Rian.

Rian glared at him, but let it pass; no point in arguing, he'd be gone soon enough. He'd never heard of Anwar, but then again there were hundreds of kids at his school he didn't know. Tonight he and Genie would be joining those names on the community board if everything went to plan. He briefly wondered if his mother would set up a 1-800 number herself and make Mr Yates comb the hills at nights. Almost made him laugh to imagine it.

He'd started making plans the moment he realized that Genie was being held prisoner. He'd arranged to see her the day after school ended but she didn't show. Then he'd heard about the girl possessed by the devil on Maple Street and knew the moment he walked over and saw the Reverend Schneider's car that they had Genie. Genie's mother had turned her water hose on him. No boy was coming near her house and that was that. The language she used certainly wasn't Christian.

It had taken weeks of organization, but this was the night Genie would be free and they would leave, start a new life somewhere. Everything was prepared.

'Your mother was talking to you,' Mr Yates informed him.

Rian focused on his mother. She was looking at him oddly. 'Sorry.'

'I was asking if you knew any of these missing children?'

Rian shook his head. 'No. But I guess some are pretty desperate. They don't have a choice I guess, some

21

families are pretty messed up.'

His mother looked at him sharply. She knew about Genie and how he liked her. Never met her of course, but a mother can tell when a son is distracted. 'That poor girl. I know you miss her.'

'The Magee girl?' Mr Yates asked, like he knew something about her.

Rian was surprised they knew he liked her, let alone seemed to have discussed it.

'Mother got her locked up in the house, believes she's possessed,' Rian explained.

Mr Yates looked exasperated. 'There is no such thing as possession. God, we might as well live in the middle ages. The County should take her into care.'

'Reverend Schneider sits on the Board of Governors,' his mother informed him. 'He sees Satan's hand in everything. That unfortunate girl.' She looked at Rian with pity. 'Poor you, finally got a girlfriend and she's possessed by the devil.'

Rian heard the sarcasm in her voice.

'Poor family stock. The father was a lawyer but her mother is a Munby and y'know . . .' Mr Yates declared.

Rian didn't know. 'Munby?'

'Not here. Not at the table,' his mother insisted. But then she said, 'Shame, a Munby. That's a special curse all of its own. Poor thing.'

'Genie *isn't* crazy. She *isn't* possessed. She's the only sane person in that house,' Rian declared, trying to control his anger.

'And you're going to save her?' his mother cooed, definitely mocking him now. 'You can't save a Munby girl.'

The wind slammed a window shut upstairs. Rian stood up sharply. He wanted to be far away from this table before he exploded. 'I'll get it.'

'Don't forget the shutters,' Mr Yates called after him. 'I'd better get going. If a storm's coming, I don't want to be on the road.'

Rian stomped up the stairs. This would be the last time he would go upstairs, he was thinking. In just one hour he and Genie would be free of this town forever. This particular Munby girl was going to be saved.

# 3

# A Warning

The lights played on the wall beside her. Genie was sitting at her dressing table in her boyshorts, rubbing antiseptic cream on to the burn on her arm. The blisters were taking a while to heal, leaving a distinct outline of a Celtic cross. Her feet rested on broken pieces of wood hidden by her old clothes. She'd begun this breakout plan, already broken off enough of the panelling on the wall to wiggle her feet through to the next room, but discovered the hole she'd made came up behind one of Grandma Munby's heavy oak chests. It was never going to shift and now she had a problem of how to hide the hole. She'd be beaten for sure if her mother found out.

The evening was warm; the breeze outside was growing louder. Bad weather was coming. She didn't mind, it would be something to listen to at least. The house was already creaking. She looked again at the bobbing shadows on her wall. She could make out the reflection of a tree and something else, like a face but in the negative. She tried to make it into Rian's face, his fine nose, the wild eyebrows, tried to give it the last smile he gave her as she promised to meet him the day after school ended. Rian, her only hope, and she didn't know for sure that he even missed her.

The shape on the wall changed again. She blinked. A chill swept across her, giving her goosebumps. The image looked back! It was no longer indistinct. It was a human face, a real human face and she thought she knew who it was, a kid from school.

'That's so weird,' she was thinking. Then the eyes opened. She was transfixed, her palms began to sweat and she was a little scared. The shimmering image on the wall was staring at her, the lips began to move, soundlessly, but she knew exactly what he was saying. It was impossible. She had finally gone mad like Granny Munby. The face faded a moment as the sun went in, then came back fiercely. It was Anwar somebody, Anwar from Palestine or some place. He'd been in her Forces and Energy class . . . He was staring at her and his lips moved again. 'You're next,' he was saying. 'You're next.'

There was a whoosh as the wind swept up through the side of the house. The sun went in and the image on the wall abruptly vanished.

She tried to remember Anwar. A bright kid, lonely, third from the left in class. Arrived suddenly in the middle of term the year before. No one ever talked to him. His English was perfect, he had polite manners and, fatally for him, a glass eye from some explosion in his hometown of Gaza. You could hardly tell, but that's all the excuse anyone needed to shun him. A freak in a school of anti-social freaks. Anwar had been on her wall and he'd definitely said, 'You're next.'

Genie continued lying there, chilled to the bone. 'Next what?'

She looked out of the window and saw that the trees were now swaying in the stiff breeze. The sky was darkening. She had that prickly feeling she always got when the weather changed.

She urgently needed to talk to Rian. Something was happening out there. Something bad. High school would begin in September. She would leave this room, leave this house. Leave this town. She would leave a note for her crazy mother. Scrawl it right across the living room wall if necessary. 'I am not possessed. You are. I am not evil. It's *you* who's full of hate. You're the devil. It's you he came for and already took you away.'

Yes, Anwar was right. She *was* next. Damn right. 'I'm next!' she shouted to the room. She threw her book against the wall. She really had to get out of here.

# 4

# Freedom

Tunis drove by and flashed his lights. Rian grabbed his backpack, jumped out of his window and dropped with practised ease to the ground below. He ran silently towards Tunis' pick-up truck, flung his backpack in the back before climbing in.

Tunis was driving away already. Slightly nervous about what they were about to do this night. He brushed his dark floppy hair out of his eyes and looked at Rian and nodded. 'You heard?'

'What?'

'Anwar, the Palestinian kid. He's disappeared. It's on the radio, got a CTV crew here and everyone praying again over on Geary Street. So many flowers left there now it's getting to be a hazard. He was in your year?'

Rian shrugged. Couldn't put a face to the name. 'I don't know him.'

'Police definitely going to start tagging the kids now. Sixteen kids in like six weeks. I mean, that's over thirty kids disappeared from this area alone this

27

year. Four brothers vanished from Hope, one after the other, and I heard they got a child watch thing going up in Lytton and Lillooet to make sure no kid leaves – they all have to go around in pairs, they're so spooked. I'm *so* glad I ain't a kid any more. Where the hell do they all go? How come none of them ever come back, or even call?'

Rian shrugged. 'Mr Yates blames it all on crystal meth.'

'No way. Those losers just turn up dead in doorways. They don't have the energy to move, let along run away. Something else is going on here. Maybe this.'

Tunis handed him a printout.

'You think this is for real? Denny sent it to me. He says this is what the missing kids are going for. You think they're that crazy?'

Rian read it. Tunis was always getting crazy stuff from Denny who was always looking to make a quick buck, preferably without any effort.

Want to make $2,000 cash? Participate in a simple experimental trial that could help us cure one of the world's most pressing problems. We need healthy young people, 14 to 17, willing to put their survival skills to the test. We are a non-profit organization with brilliant green credentials.

All applicants apply in total confidence. No adult/parent need be notified. Sign up now and we will give you directions. (We regret that due to the nature of this trial only able-bodied volunteers fit enough to get to us under their own steam can participate.) (Yes, this is part of the test.) We reject many applicants. Call us toll-free and see if you qualify. (North-West Pacific Residents only.)

Call us and change your life forever!

Rian frowned looking at the toll-free number printed at the bottom.

'You're kidding, right? Denny sent you this? Tell me you're not going to do it. Where did he find it?'

'He was on some chat forum. You know, he's always online talking to crazy people and there was this suicide link he found.'

'Suicide link?' Rian queried.

'Y'know. Are you lonely? Getting bullied at school, contemplating suicide – there's tons of stuff like that out there.'

'And he found this there?'

'I called the number.'

'What?' Rian couldn't believe him.

'It's toll-free. Denny tried to backtrack the IP address of the web-link and it sort of vanishes some place in Eastern Europe.'

'But it's talking about the North-West Pacific. That's us, not Europe,' Rian said frowning.

Tunis grinned. 'I know. Cool huh? Two thousand dollars cash, Ri. Probably a cure for the common cold. I heard there was a place out in the Cascades where they pay you to get flu and they pump you full of drugs to see if they can cure you.'

Rian despaired. 'Promise me you won't do anything stupid. You didn't give them your number, right?'

Tunis grinned. 'Gave 'em yours. You think I'm crazy.' He laughed.

Rian shook his head. 'You should send this to the cops. Maybe they should investigate it. Denny could be right, that's exactly where all the missing kids are going.'

'Oh sure. All of them,' he said. 'As if. They're long gone, well out of this town. Living the good life in Vancouver or whatever. It's like you turn thirteen, someone rips a mask off your head and says, "Behold you have been living in a town of monsters! Flee, flee, before it's too late".' He laughed and turned to Rian. 'You're fleeing. You've seen the light. Reverend Schneider will be praying at your door by the morning; your ma will be all teary-eyed and suddenly miss you. It's like a ritual. Cops go search, but they're always one day or one week too late. It's the curse of Spurlake, the dying town in the mountains. I heard the Ski Lodge might not open this winter and so they won't be hiring snow-board instructors. Only places left to hang out are the DQ and McBean's Pancake House.'

Tunis graduated the year before. Worked for a lawn company in summer and taught snow-boarding in winter. He'd never been much of a scholar or anything but he'd been Rian's neighbour for the last four years and they'd struck up a friendship. Mostly playing basketball in the yard or talking about cars. Tunis was a Ferrari fanatic and the only kid in town who followed Formula One racing. He was always making Rian wake up at four o'clock on a Sunday to watch a race from Europe or some place thousands of miles away. Formula One was his religion.

Rian let Tunis rant. Some of what he said was sort of true though. He looked into the back of the truck. 'You got the hook?'

'Rope, hook, everything,' Tunis responded. 'You know where you're going to go? I mean, you got no money now, right?'

Rian shrugged. He'd given Tunis every last dime he'd saved from his summer job. 'We can work. Pick fruit. They always need people to pick fruit.'

'Well, I heard there's someone paying $2,000 for scientific experiments,' Tunis remarked.

'Very funny.'

Tunis laughed and turned right on Fraser on to Maple Street. 'Cops will go crazy when you two disappear as well.'

'They don't give a shit about us kids. If they could ship us all to the next county they would,' Rian said.

'My dad reckons it's all mass hysteria,' Tunis said. 'Trying to arrange a meeting at the school for parents.'

Tunis was adopted; his father was deputy-principal at the middle school. Everyone believed Tunis was a big disappointment to him. But Rian knew this wasn't true. His dad encouraged him all the time. Was proud he was working.

Rian grinned. 'Mr Yates will probably throw a party when I go. He left me a recruitment brochure for the navy yesterday. Wants my mother all to himself and me out of that house sooo bad . . .'

'I'm joining the cops. Decided. Mom's against it, Dad is worried it'll be dangerous, but soon as I'm nineteen, I'm going for it. You get a gun and there's a terrific pension plan. And shit, I'd know exactly who to arrest in this town. I'd make detective grade pretty damn quick.'

Rian smiled. Tunis would probably make a great cop. He had a strong sense of what was right and just, something pretty rare in Rian's experience of people so far.

Tunis slowed the truck to a stop across from Genie's house. 'We're here. What now?'

'We wait. Watch the front door. As soon as her mother leaves for church we go to work.'

Tunis grinned. 'I changed my licence plates. Let's hope Reverend Schneider doesn't get stopped for any violations tonight.'

Rian laughed. 'Rev Schneider? Genius, pure genius.'

Rian kept his head down below the dash as Tunis watched, picking at his teeth with a toothpick. Tunis suddenly remembered something and pulled out a picture from his inside jacket pocket. 'Cute, huh?'

Rian studied the almost-naked blonde girl staring out of the picture. It was signed, *Your bunny girl*. Rian looked at Tunis with surprise. 'You have a bunny girl?'

'Met her on Facebook. Angie lives in Vancouver.'

'And she's your bunny girl?'

'Will be. Going to drive down there on the weekend. She's hot, right?'

Rian was studying the picture more carefully. 'No wonder you suddenly need money. You think she's real? I never saw anyone that perfect outside of a porn site.'

Tunis was offended and took the picture back. 'She's real. We spoke. She sends me pictures every day.'

Rian still doubted Tunis would get a girl that good-looking, even though he was pretty smooth. 'Girl like that is going to be expensive, Tun. Sure she isn't Russian or something? I heard there was a scam. You turn up there and they put a gun to your head and make them marry you for the visa.'

Tunis snorted. 'As if. Nothing but the best for Tunis. She's real, believe me. Studying for her bar exam.'

'That girl's a lawyer?' Rian protested.

'No. She's studying to tend bar. She could make a fortune in Hooters.'

'You actually sent her your picture? Does she know you only turned eighteen last month? Did you tell her what you earn?'

'She knows everything about me. My truck, everything. Angie wants me, man. Badly.'

Rian smiled. Well Tunis was definitely going to get his heart broken but at least he had ambition. Vancouver girls were always so . . .

'We're in business,' Tunis hissed, ducking down suddenly. A cab pulled up outside the Magee house. They heard Genie's mother slam her front door shut, then walk over to the cab and climb in. They waited, keeping low, giving time for the cab to pull away. Tunis looked at Rian and winked.

'Devil's work to do. You sure Mrs Mackie is out?'

'Runs the pet shop. She's there like twenty hours a day.'

Tunis grunted. He remembered Mrs Mackie and all the lectures he'd got about feeding his hamster right when he was a kid. The woman was obsessed. Never seemed to leave that store.

'One weird woman. OK. Out, Ri. Let's do this.'

Rian smiled. Yeah, time to do it. He opened the door and dropped down to the road.

Tunis fired up the engine. He was excited but controlled.

Rian ran across the road to the bushes at the edge of Genie's property and waited for Tunis to get the truck in position in Mrs Mackie's yard next door. Genie's window was at the side of the house, which made it hard to get leverage.

Tunis drove over and backed up at a forty-five-degree angle on to the driveway next door. Rian ran over, grabbed the hook and rope from the back of the truck and draped it around his shoulders. The light was fading; it wasn't as dark as he would have liked. He hoped the neighbours across the street weren't watching. Even if they were, by the time they could do anything about it, everything would be over.

He was up on the garbage bins, hauled himself up on to Mrs Mackie's garage roof where he'd placed a long plank of wood the week before. He was relieved to see it was still there. Genie's room with the barred windows was right opposite, about a head higher. The only detail he hadn't been able to do anything about was to let Genie know he was coming.

Rian lifted and swung the plank across the void between the two houses. It was steeper than he expected and he nearly lost his balance as he ran up it, grabbing the bars to stabilize himself at the window.

Inside he could see Genie was asleep. She looked beautiful lying there in her briefs and torn T-shirt, curled up on top of the blankets. He tapped on the window but she didn't stir. He had a horrible moment of doubt. What if she didn't want to come? He should have prepared her somehow.

'Genie, wake up,' he called, but still she didn't stir. Was she drugged? He wouldn't have put that past her mother.

He wrapped the hook around the bars and turned to signal to Tunis, who waved, gingerly moving the truck forward to take up the slack.

As soon as the rope was taut Rian stepped back, ran back down the plank and pulled it away. Tunis was watching him in his rear-view mirror. He gunned the engine and went for it. At first nothing happened and Rian was afraid the rope would snap, but then suddenly the whole metal window frame came tearing out of the wall bringing some of the siding out with it. It shot forward, narrowly missing Rian and crashing loudly on to Mrs Mackie's roof. The noise would be enough to wake the whole neighbourhood. Tunis was already out of the truck and untying the rope.

Rian got the plank up to Genie's window again and ran up to the gap. She was sitting up in bed, totally spooked. Rian smiled, then he saw the bruises on her face and arms and felt a surge of anger.

'God, Genie, what the hell?'

Genie just stared open-mouthed.

'Ri, you came. *You came.*'

Rian was in the room, grabbed her, and hugged her tightly. 'Grab stuff, we have one minute, babe. Now!'

Genie was just dazed. Rian had really come to rescue her. Took the whole window out and everything.

Rian was throwing stuff at her. 'Dress. Tunis won't wait.'

Genie got the message. She pulled on a sweater, jammed her legs into her jeans.

'Get your shoes on in the truck. We got to go! No time.'

Genie grabbed a plastic bag and crammed some underwear into it and other stuff. Her favourite bunny – childish, but nevertheless couldn't be left.

She ran to the window, careful not to place her bare feet on the broken glass.

'Jesus, Ri, I can hear sirens.'

'Go, go on,' Rian urged.

Her legs were sluggish. She'd been trapped in the room for so long it would be some time before she got back her strength. Rian was right behind her, kicking the plank to the ground as he reached the garage roof.

'Drop down to the garbage bins,' he instructed her.

Genie practically bounced down, heart in mouth, tense, scared the cops would get there before they could go. She ran like the wind for the truck, her legs like jelly, Rian close behind.

Tunis began to move and they had to jump up on the back and flip over to land on the rolled turf stacked there. As soon as they were safe aboard Tunis floored it. Someone would have called 911 and they would have given a description of his truck. So he took the narrow alleys behind the houses, keeping it slow until they reached the far end of Maple Street. Cops, he figured, would only look for a speeding vehicle.

Genie lay shaking in Rian's arms. Still astonished at her escape and how cool Rian turned out to be. If ever a girl needed proof a boy loved her . . . .

Rian was concerned at her bruises. Her eyes were puffy and bloodshot; there was a nasty burn in the shape of a cross on her arm. He knew they had held her prisoner, but they beat her? Burned her? Her own mother had done this?

'She hurt you?'

Genie shook her head, her eyes shining. 'I'm OK. I'm fine, Ri.'

But he was angry. This was his Genie and they'd disfigured her. She was so thin, so unbelievably thin. He couldn't believe what he was holding in his arms. Reverend Schneider was the most evil man on earth. He would have to pay for this.

'Get me out of here, Ri. Take me away,' Genie whispered. 'We have to go far. Reverend Schneider will send people after us.'

'We're leaving tonight. We ain't ever coming back. Get your shoes on. We got some running to do.' He kissed the top of her head. Her heart was beating fast, like a wild animal, as she clung on to him.

Tunis halted at the crossroads at Fir and Geary. People were gathering in the community square by Princeton Park to pray for Anwar. Genie quickly slipped down out of sight below the sides. The shrine to the missing kids was lit up like Christmas and messages to the disappeared were pinned to the community notice board, fluttering in the wind. Heaps of half-dead bouquets of flowers littered the ground and someone had lit candles, which flickered in the blustery weather. Rian stared at the scene with sadness. So many kids gone from Spurlake, and now, perhaps, someone would add their names to it. Well, maybe not their respective mothers, but perhaps one of their friends at least.

Tunis turned off the road and took the unpaved track down by the river. There was good coverage from the forest there. He was confident no one had followed them.

He stopped by the old landing where the gold rush museum had burned the year before. By the time he got out of the truck Rian and Genie were already on the ground. Tunis lifted out the backpack and her bag and handed them to them. 'You need to get going now. I got to change the plates back before he notices anything.'

He saw Genie's face and was taken aback. 'Jeez,

girl, what did they do to you? Hell, man. If I ever see Reverend Schneider or your mother crossing the road, I swear I ain't going to brake. That's a promise, girl.'

Genie broke free of Rian and smiled, wincing slightly from a cracked lip. 'You do that, Tunis, and back up on them in case you didn't do it right.'

'Git going,' Tunis told them. 'Good luck. You're gonna need it.'

They ran.

Tunis quickly wiped down the surfaces of his truck with cleaning fluid. He didn't want their fingerprints found on his truck. The cops might never check, but you couldn't be too careful. He'd miss Ri. Had a very bad feeling that he'd never see him again.

'Where are we?' she asked moments later, as they ran along the riverbank.

'Just beyond the old railroad bridge. Got a boat ready.'

He hushed her a moment and made her squat down. Headlights suddenly swept across the trees as a car turned. Lovers used this area for trysts. He didn't want anyone to see them if they could avoid it.

She took his hand and squeezed it.

'Thanks for coming for me, Ri.'

He said nothing but squeezed her hand back. He

stood up again, pulling her after him, and they continued running. It was dark now and he wanted to reach the boat before the moon rose.

'Where are we going?' she asked after a while.

'Remember the guy from Calgary who fixed our roof?'

She vaguely recalled him. He worked on the oil pipeline. They had met him at McBean's. He told them he made nearly three hundred thousand dollars a year. Was going to retire at forty-five. Had a plan. More importantly, he had a boat on the river. 'We're going to steal his boat?'

Rian shook his head. 'Not a yacht or anything. It's a houseboat. Doesn't go anywhere. Had me varnish it this summer. We're going there first. He's back in Calgary now till the winter.'

She followed him with wonder. How long had he been planning this? She'd thought he'd forgotten her. She suddenly had a rising wave of nausea. She had to stop a moment. Rian held her as she threw up. She was pale and shaking. He dug in his rucksack, found a bottle of Coke. He unscrewed the top and it fizzed from all the jogging. 'Here. Stops me feeling sick.'

She took the bottle. It wasn't cold, but she drank the whole thing quickly, and then burped loudly. She grinned at him. 'Thanks. Needed that.'

'Didn't they feed you?'

She put up her hands. 'Don't even go there. Got any chocolate?'

He plunged his hands deep into the backpack and his fingers closed on a Kit Kat. She seized on it and tore open the wrapper. 'Haven't eaten in a week.' She looked guilty. 'Sorry. I think I was trying to starve myself to death. I didn't think . . .' Tears suddenly rolled down her cheeks. 'Didn't think you'd come. I mean, I prayed you would, but I didn't think . . .'

Rian held her tight. They weren't on the water yet, but he'd let her rest a moment. Get her strength. He wouldn't be happy until he'd got her on to the houseboat downriver. He waited until she finished crying and then he moved them on. He wouldn't feel safe until they were on the water.

# 5

# An Officer Calls

The cop, RCMP Officer Maxwell Miller, was standing looking at the damage with a neighbour from across the road. First time for everything, he guessed. Tore the whole window out and driven off. The neighbour was keen to tell him what she saw.

'This happened thirty minutes ago now,' she explained, the reproach clear in her voice. 'I dialled 911 the moment I saw it happen.'

'Ma'am, there was an accident at the mall. Can't be everywhere now, can we? Did you see who did this?'

'They stole the girl. That's what they did. Everyone knows Genie Magee is possessed by the devil. I don't hold with keeping her prisoner behind bars and everything but . . .'

Miller looked at the woman with her grey hair and hooded eyes and wasn't sure he was hearing right. 'They stole a girl who was possessed by the devil?' He stepped back a little to get a better look at her. 'Ma'am, have you been drinking?'

'I'm just telling you what happened. Aren't you going

to write it down? Genie, that's the girl, she was locked in her room. They put bars up and—'

'Who locked her in her room? You didn't think to call 911 when that happened? Why call it in now? Don't you know it's a felony to imprison someone – put bars on their windows? I don't care if it's family.'

'Reverend Schneider said she was possessed. I told you I don't belong to his church, but he should know.'

Miller wanted to arrest this woman for being so utterly stupid, but he had to listen to her. Sometimes you got the feeling that people didn't deserve protection. And Reverend Schneider was a menace. Blocking the streets with his prayer groups every time a kid went missing. Miller sighed.

'What actually happened?'

'They drove off. A red truck. I saw the boy climbing down from Mrs Mackie's garage roof, but my dog was barking and—'

'You can describe this boy? Did you see the girl?'

'The boy was white.'

Miller looked at her, waiting for more detail. It didn't come. 'Anything else?'

The neighbour thought hard. 'The driver was black.'

Miller took a deep breath. 'Any other details other than white and black?'

'My dog was barking and I thought he'd get loose,' she began again. 'Aren't you going to see what they've done?'

'Ma'am, I can see what they've done. They've torn a window out the side of the house.' He was thinking he should call the fire department or something.

'Mrs Magee belongs to the Church of the Free Spirits. She goes every night at this time to pray. You can set your watch by it. Of course she was a Munby before she married that lawyer. Always going to be trouble if there's a Munby in your street.'

Now Miller had some interest. 'Munby? That's this house?' Everyone knew about the night Grandma Munby had shot the lawyer Magee in the ass. Killed him outright. Claimed he was trying to rape her, but no one believed it. Must have happened twelve years ago, no, more. He remembered that Grandma Munby used to tell fortunes in a caboose down by the railroad.

'And they locked the girl up you say? Any reason?'

The neighbour looked at the cop as if he were a cretin. 'I told you. She was possessed. The devil knows a Munby when he sees one.'

Miller called it in. He wondered what the captain would make of this.

'I got the licence number,' the neighbour reminded him. 'Red truck. It's a Spurlake plate. You'll find them.'

# 6

## *River Run*

The boat rocked gently as the little outboard motor propelled them along the narrow river. Clouds of midges hovered over the water, which was annoying. The moon was rising but they wouldn't see much of it this night. Rian was staring at the tall threatening black clouds stacking up over the mountain. 'Doesn't look good. They said there'd be a storm.'

Genie had one hand trailed in the water as she sprawled in the boat. She was over being nauseous, but was inexplicably tired. Couldn't remember a time when she had felt so exhausted. But she was happy. She studied the sky. It certainly looked ominous. Nevertheless, it was so good to be outside, in the air, under the clouds; she didn't care what the weather was like. She was with Rian and free. She had all she ever wanted right here, right now. She wanted the moment to last forever.

'You OK?' Rian called.

'Where are we going after? We got a plan?'

Rian smiled. 'Yeah. I got a plan. We'll need money. Figured we could head up to the Okanagan. Pick fruit. Lots of kids do it. They need people right now before the season ends. It's hard work but there's a place to stay and we can do it for six weeks or so.'

'Won't they look for us there?'

'Sure. But I got an ace, Genie. New ID. Found a website. You just upload your photos and they mail you new ID. We are going to like totally vanish. We are going to be John and Jasmine Briar.'

Genie looked up at him sharply. 'Married?'

'Brother and sister. No one would ever believe we were married.'

'Brother and sister? Eew. That won't be suspicious. I mean, if I kiss you or something. You are planning on kissing me, aren't you?' She was teasing but it was a serious question.

'I had to get something. Couldn't discuss it with anyone.'

Genie looked at him and nodded. 'No. You did right. No one will be looking for a brother and sister. Be weird though. Weird for other people.'

'I don't care. As long as I'm with you.'

Genie smiled, then leaned over and splashed her face. The water was cool. She wanted to swim. She

48

dunked her head in the water and pulled back quickly, tossing her hair back, spraying Rian.

'Hey.'

She laughed. Was surprised at the sound of it. Surprised she could laugh again.

'Much further?'

'Five minutes. It's a floating palace. You'll love it. Got six bedrooms and the state room is like some old movie with stuffed animals and ivory and—'

'Don't spoil it. I'll see it when I get there. What you do with the money he paid you for varnishing it?'

'Gave it to Tunis. He needed tyres. You any idea what new tyres cost on a truck?'

Genie looked sad. Poor Ri had worked all summer just to give the money away to get her free. She would have to pay him back one day. Somehow.

'Did I say thanks yet?' she asked.

'You just did, Genie Magee.'

'Well thanks again, Ri. And for the record, I know it'll kill you, but I love you and will always love you for what you did for me.'

Rian just smiled. She didn't have to say thanks or that she loved him. He knew that already.

It was steadily growing dark. The ever expanding clouds were rapidly obscuring the stars and the moon.

49

You could feel the atmospheric pressure changing and the midges gathering everywhere was a sure sign that a storm would break soon.

'There it is,' he said. 'Our new home. For a couple of weeks anyways.'

Genie studied the houseboat as they drew closer. It was moored by an old landing right beside the northern tip of Blacksnake Forest. It was an excellent hiding place. There wasn't even a road to it. You could only get to it by river. Rian had thought of everything.

'How the hell did they get a boat that big up this shallow river?' Genie asked.

'Same way they got the theatre up the mountain in 1890, dragged it all the way. Must have been something. I still can't figure out how there were once ten thousand people in Spurlake. They cleared the forest and built the entire town from scratch, didn't even stop when it snowed. My great-grandmother emigrated here from Bordeaux to work in a bank. Gran told Ma that there were thirty banks here in 1915 and it was one of the richest towns in BC. Only two left now.'

Genie smiled, looking back at him. 'Must have been exciting, coming all this way to dig for gold and silver and think you were going to get rich. You think there's any left?'

Rian shook his head. 'Panned out. Tunis and me went digging about two years ago by the river, fancied we'd find gold easy. Gave up after a week and a lot of blisters. Only later did we discover we'd been digging in a place called Sucker Creek.'

Genie laughed. She could see him digging and growing all disappointed as they piled up rocks.

They both heard the roll of distant thunder. They glanced back to the looming mountain. Lightning momentarily illuminated dense clouds. It was going to be real bad up there. Spurlake's street lights twinkled in the distance. They'd get the worst of the storm. That was the problem of living next door to a mountain. Probably why most sensible people left so quickly when the gold ran out.

Reverend Schneider held Mrs Magee's hand as they prayed in Genie's bedroom. The shock of seeing the hole in the wall and the presence of police and firemen outside her home had now passed. The anger that Genie had escaped was still present and it was all Reverend Schneider could do to contain it, keep her calm and just pray for the soul of her wayward daughter. The devil was strong here. He had found a weakness and exploited it and whoever was responsible was clearly resourceful. The girl was out in the world and there was nothing they could do now but pray that when the devil came for her, he would take her quickly and painlessly.

'She can never return to this house. Genie Magee is no daughter of mine. I will never have her back,' Mrs Magee declared to no one in particular.

'She needs our love,' Reverend Schneider told her, but without any sincerity.

'She gets none from me,' Mrs Magee spat. 'That girl is dead to me – forever. I swear it. I never had a daughter.'

RCMP Officer Miller was on the stairs suddenly. 'Reverend Schneider? Can I speak with you a moment, sir?'

Reverend Schneider let go of Mrs Magee's hand and got up off his knees. Mrs Magee remained where she was, staring at nothing, consumed by her anger.

Miller met the Reverend outside on the stoop. Both men could see the wind was gathering strength. The trees shook and swayed, but the rain was holding off for the present.

'Any news on the people who did this terrible thing?'

Miller nodded. 'Witness got a licence plate number. Is that your car there, Reverend?' He pointed to the silver Mercedes Benz parked in the yard.

'Yes, Officer.'

Miller was a tad confused. The witness had described

52

a red pick-up truck. The licence plates she had remembered were now attached to the silver four-door sedan outside.

'Is there a problem?' Reverend Schneider wanted to know.

'You don't happen to own a red pick-truck by any chance?'

Reverend Schneider looked confused. 'No.'

Miller nodded and put his notebook away. 'I guess someone has a sense of humour in this town.' He looked at the Reverend and back towards the Mercedes. 'Looks like God is a paying business, Reverend.'

'The Lord is generous and helps those who do his work, Officer. Now if we are done, I have a distraught mother inside who is missing her daughter.'

'About that girl, Reverend. My report will show that you encouraged Mrs Magee to cage her daughter up for the summer. Copy goes to the welfare officer. You can advise Mrs Magee that she can make a fuss that the girl is gone, but no one is going to be sympathetic, given the situation. You make a song and dance about all the kids that go missing from this town, but in my experience, problems begin at home.'

Reverend Schneider ran a hand through his oil-slick hair and narrowed his eyes.

'You have no idea what situation was going on in this home, Officer. You are not the judge and jury of home life in this town.'

Officer Miller pointed at the badge on his sleeve. 'Serve and protect, Reverend. That's what we do. What is it *you* do exactly?'

Reverend Schneider turned away without a word and went back inside, slamming the door behind him.

Miller walked back to his car. The girl would be long gone by now. Good luck to her. Spots of rain were spitting on to his windshield. Not a good night to be out there, wherever. When that storm broke it would be pretty treacherous. What kind of mother was it that couldn't even produce a photograph of her child? He'd been shocked by that. Something bad had gone on in this house. This wasn't like the other kids who'd gone missing in Spurlake and God knew there had been enough of them lately. This girl had been rescued; he had no doubt about that. He hoped the boy who'd set her free would take better care of her than her mother.

He looked back at the house a moment. Thought he glimpsed Reverend Schneider and Mrs Magee staring at him from a darkened bedroom. He didn't know why exactly, but it made his flesh crawl.

# 7

# Save the Pig – Save the World

Genie watched Rian make pasta with sauce out of the bottle. He'd stashed food and got at least two of her favourite DVDs to watch. He'd even brought cute blue cupcakes from the bakery. She was amazed at how organized he was, how good he was at looking after her.

The houseboat really was like a palace. Well, perhaps not a palace, but maybe like an old fashioned railcar, like one she'd seen in a museum once, with thick upholstered furniture, lit by gold-tipped Tiffany oil lamps and leather armchairs and a wood and steel kitchen and bar that was so elegant it must have been built for a ship's captain.

'This is like a room out of the *Titanic*,' she told Rian. 'I've never been anywhere like it.'

'It once belonged to Premier Maclean. Used it for hunting trips up the river. Wait till you see our four-poster bed.'

Genie smiled. *Our bed,* he'd said. The very idea tingled every fibre of her body.

'Of course it's got all these stuffed deer and bears on

the walls,' Rian was saying, pulling a face as he glanced at a bear's head on the wall. 'People shot anything that moved back then, I think. No respect for wildlife. This was their floating hunting lodge.'

'Well, it's our palace and I love being here with you.'

Rian smiled.

'Food's ready.'

He turned with a steaming bowl of pasta and placed it on to the redwood table. 'It's hot, Genie. Eat slow.'

Genie stood up and promptly sat back down again. She didn't seem to have any balance.

'You're not well,' Rian said, concerned. 'You have to eat, though.'

She made a greater effort and moved over to the chair by the table. Something was clouding her mind, she felt dizzy, but Rian was right about the food, it smelled delicious and she needed it. Rian opened the cabin door to cool the room down and Genie inhaled the fresh air as it rushed in and rustled papers. She wrinkled her nose. 'Going to rain, Ri. Close it again. I can smell it.'

He was standing by the door a moment, amazed at how black it was and how silent. There was no breeze at all now, no sound. As if the birds and creatures were holding their breath. It was uncanny, eerie.

Suddenly an enormous crack of thunder and simultaneous lightning forked right across the river. It lit up the whole world for a fraction of time. A second later the rain fell. Not just any rain, it was as if the whole Pacific Ocean had been scooped up and dropped from the sky. Rian slammed the door closed as it thundered down, drumming on the roof with a deafening roar.

Genie grinned. 'I said it would rain.'

Rian laughed. 'Hell, yeah. You ever hear anything that loud before?'

They just listened to the pounding rain and started eating. Somehow the thunder, lightning and heavy downpour made the whole place more special, as if the storm was just for them.

'Tastes good, Ri.'

'Send a letter to Ragu and tell them.'

'I wish I could cook. Can't even boil pasta. Last time I made anything it was oatmeal when my mother had the flu. Best forty-eight hours of my life. She couldn't move. I was nine, I think. She stayed in bed for two whole days and I could watch TV, eat what I liked and . . .' She sighed. 'I should have run away then.'

Another crack of lightning outside, filling the whole cabin with an intense brilliance. The thunder instantly rolled in on top of them, shaking the whole boat. They exchanged glances, a little afraid – they'd never experienced a storm this loud.

'I blame climate change,' Rian stated, then laughed. 'Glad we're in this old tub. It's ninety years old or more and the steel's thicker than a tank.'

Genie drank some of the apple juice Rian had provided. She stretched out a hand to squeeze his. 'Ri?'

'Yeah?'

'I know why I'm leaving Spurlake. But why are you? I mean, you don't have to. Not for me. Don't want you to ruin your life for me. You wanted to go to university and everything. I'm not worth it, honest. Might never be worth anything.'

Rian blinked, slightly hurt, but saw she was trying to give him a way out. Genie was like that. He understood she was trying not to be selfish.

The rain grew heavier, the noise intensified on the roof; some water was leaking down one wall. Rian thought about trying to stop it, but it would dry once the rain eased off. Nothing was designed to withstand this much rain.

'The day I realized I couldn't see you this summer, I made a decision, Genie. I was going to get you out of there. No matter what. I knew if I got you out, then we'd have to go some place to be safe where she couldn't get to you. You won't be safe till you're eighteen.'

'She won't . . .' Genie began, but Rian shook his head.

'I can finish high school somewhere else. Hell, we aren't stupid, Gen. We're in the top five per cent of students in our year. We can pass the test anytime. My dad took out a university fund when I was a kid and it's all paid up. I can access it when I'm nineteen and it will pay all my tuition. So don't feel guilty. I want to be with you. You're worth the world to me.'

'But your mother relies on you so much. You know she does.'

'She can rely on Mr Yates. Mr Yates is sooo wonderful. She tells me how great he is every day. She won't miss me one bit. I promise, and I'm not a child. I made this decision and we're going through with it.'

Genie sat back in her chair and took a deep breath. 'Wow, Mister. You must have been thinking about this stuff for a while.'

'And you weren't?'

Genie smiled, finishing up her pasta. 'I was going to kill myself if you didn't come and rescue me by the end of summer. I had it all worked out. Half starved myself to death already. It was a plan, right?'

Rian pulled a face. 'Sucky plan. Glad I got there first.'

'Me too.' Genie drank off her juice and slammed the

glass down on the table. 'Me too.' Suddenly the room was going around. 'Ri?'

'What?'

'I feel sick. I haven't eaten so much food in a month.'

'Don't you dare . . .'

But she ran for the toilet. It was all going to come up. Nothing in the world was going to stop it.

'Sorry,' she bleated, between bouts of nausea. 'Sorry.'

A few minutes later, she lay down on the bed, feeling guilty. He'd been such a sweetie for cooking for her and she'd ruined it by throwing up. This whole thing was doomed. He'd get tired of her fast. She knew it. He'd get moody and one day, without warning, he'd be gone, back to his home and she wouldn't blame him one bit. Not one bit.

She watched him cleaning up and being 'sensible', wondering how exactly she scored him and why he stuck with her, knowing that she was a bunch of problems. He saw she was watching and flashed her a smile. It struck her like a missile, lifted her one, two metres off the bed. He could still smile at her. What was it about his smile that made her feel so light, so happy? She didn't deserve it, didn't deserve to be loved at all.

Rian busied himself cleaning up. You didn't live with someone in a wheelchair any length of time without learning you had to clean up 'accidents' and say nothing. He was still in shock about how ill Genie looked. He believed her when she said she'd tried to starve herself to death. They'd done horrible things to her. She'd tell him when she was ready. All he knew was that this was his decision. They had to protect each other, forever. That was the plan. It wasn't going to be easy. How many kids ran away with nothing and survived? Where were all the other kids who'd gone missing this summer? Tunis said they were living in city doorways, pan-handling for food, maybe even prostituting themselves to eat. No one really knew what happened to any of them, they never called home. Well, if determination was worth anything, they'd make it.

'It's getting colder,' Genie remarked. 'You feel it?'

Rian thought about it and sensed she was right. 'Maybe it's because we're below the waterline?'

Genie crawled off the bed and went into the tiny bathroom again. Glad he had cleaned it and guilty all over again she hadn't been able to help. 'Got to brush my teeth.'

'Yeah. You want anything?'

Now she had moved, Genie discovered she needed to pee as well. Suddenly shy, she shut the door. First time she had ever peed so close to a boy. She shrugged. He'd heard her puke her heart out; he wasn't going to be embarrassed she had to pee.

'I'm OK. Really,' Genie told him, looking up at a faded 1973 Canadian Tire calendar on the door. She remembered something suddenly. 'Ri, you ever hear of a kid called Anwar? He was in a class I went to.'

Rian frowned. Third time that name had come up tonight. 'What about him?'

'Promise you won't freak out on me?'

Rian smiled. 'I won't.'

'I was staring at my wall. Earlier, before you came. Suddenly his face appeared and he was staring at me and he said, "*You're next*".'

Rian said nothing for a moment.

Genie didn't like the silence. 'See. You *are* freaked. I knew I shouldn't have told you.'

He sat on the end of the bed looking at the closed door. 'Anwar went missing today. Ran away. It was on the news. You must have heard it on the news.'

Genie pursed her lips. 'News is forbidden in my house, remember? I haven't heard anything or spoken to a single normal sane human all summer.' She flushed and went to wash her face and hands.

'Well. We already know you're kinda spooky. And, well he was right, yeah?' Rian was saying. 'You *were* next.'

62

Genie thought about that. She found a toothbrush and put the paste on it. 'Well yeah, but . . .' She had been next, but instinctively she didn't think that was what Anwar meant. Couldn't exactly say why. Poor kid. She wondered why he'd run.

The rain fell even harder then. She thought of Anwar out there in this rain and felt really bad for him.

Rian was lying on the bed with his shoes off when she came back. He smiled when he saw her. She blushed. No reason. Suddenly shy.

'Don't look so scared. This is me. Mr Knight in Shining Armour.'

She laughed and jumped on the bed, curled up beside him. 'You *are* my knight in shining armour. Always will be, Ri.' She looked up and he kissed her. She felt the familiar tingle and it spread out right across her body, head to toe. She felt his arms go around her, pull her closer, her lips burned under his touch . . . .

She saw it then. A wall crashing down. Saw them gasping for breath, seconds from death. It was so vivid she must have cried out. Rian was looking at her with astonishment.

'What? What did I do?' Rian asked.

Genie was trembling. 'It's bad. Something coming. I

don't understand. We're in danger, Ri. Terrible danger. It's real close.'

At that precise moment the rain stopped, as suddenly as it had begun. The silence was sharp, uncomfortable, uncanny. They both heard the bells at the same time, felt the ropes straining as the old boat moved. The boat was like a rock out in this water. Hadn't moved, except up and down with the water levels.

Rian reluctantly extricated himself from her arms and sat up. 'I'd better check.'

Genie rolled over to the corner, grabbed her bunny. Rian saw her do it and smiled. 'Bunny's not going to save you.'

Genie pulled a zip down in the bunny's back and pulled out some cash. 'This is everything I ever saved.' She stuffed it down her pants. 'If we have to run, I'm ready.'

Rian was astonished, but impressed. He went to inspect the outside. The bells were down by the landing and they were installed to warn of gales, but strangely he couldn't hear any wind.

Genie was getting clothes together. They'd be running soon. The danger was coming and she didn't understand what it was, but experience told her to heed the warnings well.

Rian went to the hatch and flung it open. Outside was

still, water dripped from the canopy, but it had certainly stopped raining. He could even see some stars as the clouds parted. The ropes strained again and he looked down at the water. It was moving fast. As fast as the spring melt. No way it should be going this fast in summer. He squinted as he looked upriver towards town. As he did so he could hear a noise, akin to thunder, but steady and growing louder all the time.

Genie popped up beside him with his backpack. 'What is it?'

Suddenly he understood exactly what it was.

'Hell, Genie. Flash flood. It's a flash flood!'

And now he didn't know if it was safer to ride it out in the boat or run for high ground. But there was no high ground nearby. This was the widest part of the river. Any flash flood would just roll in and . . . .

'Close the door. Fasten it,' Genie told him. 'This boat's been here ninety years. You said so. It can survive this.'

Rian wasn't so sure. Wasn't sure of anything any more. A wall of water was coming downriver and there was no way they could outrun it. No way.

'Inside,' Genie yelled. 'Now.'

Her guess was as good as any. He followed her back inside and pulled the old oak doors shut. They weren't by any means watertight, but they were tough and could withstand some force.

'Genie, check the portholes. Screw them shut. Close cupboard doors.'

Genie was on it, running from cabin to cabin to check the windows. Only one was slightly open and there was no way she could tighten the brass fittings. It was stuck fast. Water would get in for sure.

They could hear it roaring now. There'd be debris, trees, logs, boats, anything that got in its way would be coming round that bend and on top of them in seconds. Rian followed her, grabbed her arm and dragged her to the stern, trying to figure out where the safest place would be.

Genie clung on. Not shaking now. She'd already seen the danger. She already knew what was going to happen. Her job now was to get Rian through it.

'We'll be fine. Just never let me go, Ri. Never let me go.'

The noise was deafening and then they were flying through the air, crashing against the bulkhead as a whole tree smashed through the upper structure and ripped away the roof. A wall of water crashed down, scoured out everything in there and Rian and Genie were scooped up, sucked in and spat out, joining everything else that tumbled in the debris of the first wave.

Genie felt something scrape her arm. Rian was hit hard by something as they somersaulted, breathless, swallowing water, desperate to hang on to each other, stay as one as they flowed along with the torrent.

'Got to grab a log,' Rian yelled. 'We'll go under if we—'

They went under as the water turned, sluiced by rocks in a different direction. Genie clung to Rian, he to her, both hardly able to see anything. Another huge tree crashed into the water ahead as the riverbank gave way and the water piled up behind it momentarily. Rian lunged for a branch and got a hold. Genie emerged, gasping for breath, and grabbed a branch. This river wasn't stopping for any tree, the surge of cold river water continued to swirl and churn. The tree began to roll.

'Let go, let go,' Rian shouted to Genie, but she was gone already.

'Genie? GENIE?'

He let the current take him again. He had to find her. The speed of the water was amazing. Now he was desperate. 'GENIE?'

Genie was spinning as the water propelled her ahead. She couldn't believe they were separated and she knew that if she didn't get something solid to hold on to real soon, she'd flounder. The water wanted to pull her under and it was so very cold.

'Genie?' She heard his cry, thought it was to her left. More in the middle.

'Ri. Ri, I'm over here. Ri!'

She felt something bump her. She grabbed it and it wriggled. She could see nothing but it was strange to touch and it moved again. Suddenly its head surfaced.

A pig! It was alive. Must have swallowed a ton of water, but it was alive and she grabbed its head to keep it above the water. The pig struggled a little but she kept a firm grip and talked to it. 'Keep breathing. You'll be OK. We'll both be OK.'

Just saying it calmed her, the weight of the animal slowed her down and made her think *survival*. She could swim. She'd learned first aid and she knew how to save lives in a pool. The flash flood was crazy but she leaned back into the flow and pulled the pig with her, got her arms under his forelegs and kept both their heads out of the water. No one would ever believe it, she realized. There wouldn't be anyone to tell either. She was gone from Spurlake forever. The flood was her parting gift from a place that had given her years of misery. The pig squealed, but she gripped it tight and it must have sensed that she was helping. She hoped so at least. A surge of water took them forward again and they moved at speed out of the main stream where the riverbank had given way.

Lightning struck a truck nearby and it burst into flames. For one complete second she could see everything. Fifty metres away, damaged cars were all piled up against the walls of a giant glass tower, like so many broken toys, two vehicles burning brightly now, helping her get her bearings.

Lightning exploded to her left again, momentarily illuminating the glass building. Genie frowned. Where? How? This was the middle of nowhere; who would want to build an office tower here? Men in fire uniforms with intense bright flashlights were running everywhere inside it trying to stop the water from flooding the building. She shouted out but no one was listening. Dangerous showers of sparks were spilling down from overhead power cables. Genie and the pig were spinning around now, both spitting out foul-tasting water and then abruptly they found direction again and moved on, swept away into darkness.

Rian found himself among huge floating logs. This was dangerous. Hold on too tight and another log could roll on to yours and crush you. 'Genie?' he yelled again, growing hoarse now. It began to rain again. Lashing it down like before and visibility completely disappeared. He felt despair. He'd lost her. He'd saved her and lost her in one night and he'd live with the guilt for the rest of his life.

There were huge bright sparks up ahead and the lights on the hills blinked out. He suddenly knew exactly where they were. Up ahead somewhere was the hydro power station on a river bend. Half the water would go to the power station; the rest would be diverted by way of a channel to the lower level. There were giant metal grilles to divert debris and keep the logs to one side on their journey to the coast. Now Rian was worried that a whole lot of stuff was going to pile up in one place and they would be caught up in this heap and crushed.

Something crashed into the log he was holding and he was submerged again. He tried to swim back up, but his way was blocked by another log. He tried going another way and that too was blocked and he was rapidly running out of air. He urgently struggled to get to the surface again, his lungs bursting.

Suddenly the water flowed sideways and he found himself pulled along with it. He surfaced, took in a huge gulp of air. He was moving rapidly again with nothing to hold on to. The rain obscured his vision but he knew instinctively he had been diverted – not to the regular channel; this had to be a breach in the riverbank. As the river was squeezed through it, the water flow speeded up. A narrow canyon would take some of the runoff and then a couple of kilometres after it lay orchards and fields. If he wasn't knocked out cold by a dead tree, he'd be OK. But what about Genie? Where would she wash up? Was she even still alive?

She had no idea how long they had been floating but Genie and the pig were both choking. She and the pig had been bowled along for what seemed like forever, until quite unexpectedly the water had finally run out of puff and spread out as it had found open fields to flood. Now the pig was struggling to stand on the mud, whilst Genie was on her knees, throwing up river water and God knows what else she had swallowed. The pig had noticed the change first and violently twisted out of her arms. It stood rather uncertainly near her, resentful and angry. There was a light from a wrecked truck's headlights pointing at the trees on the slope beside them and she could see that the pig was one big animal, like her, covered in sludge. She couldn't believe that she had saved such a huge creature. She had no idea where she was, but it wasn't near the river. Even the river probably wasn't near the river either from the sound of water rushing by below her. She shivered and coughed, glad she was alive. But Ri? What had happened to him? She shouted his name but realized it was pointless.

The pig wandered off, steering well clear of the water. Genie thought she had better do the same, find somewhere dry on higher ground. She stood up and shouted Rian's name for luck once more, but of course, he wasn't there. Her voice came out all strained and hoarse. She turned and followed the pig up the hill. It seemed to instinctively know where to go.

Out of the water, gasping for breath, Rian saw a truck set off ahead, its lights sweeping across the water before turning and heading up a track. He shouted and was running as fast as he could, but the ground was muddy and he saw it pull away and dip out of sight over a ridge. He stopped to catch his breath, turned as he saw a burning car about two hundred metres below him. Thunder rattled overhead and the rain grew more intense. He had to find Genie and shelter. She would be somewhere out there, dead or alive. He tried to block out visions of her body floating along the wild river. He uttered a short prayer for her and grimly smiled to himself; it was the first prayer he'd ever said and ever meant. God save Genie – *please*.

But that awful vision of her floating dead body stuck in his mind and wouldn't leave.

She had walked for hours up the hill and then through the forest, following an old narrow track. Genie had lost the pig or the pig had lost her, but at least she had found an old barn. It never stopped raining and the thunder was still audible in the distance. The barn was dry at least and there were straw bales stacked on one side. She would be safe here. Rain drummed on the tin roof. There was a strong smell of apples and that was comforting in some way. Many farmers grew apples around Spurlake. Everyone said Spurlake apples were the best in BC. Thinking of this, she slept.

She woke suddenly aware that her chest hurt real bad and her eyes seemed swollen. Slowly she realized why she'd woken, the rain had abruptly stopped. She stirred. She was snug under the straw but there was something outside the barn and she felt tense and afraid. She hadn't thought to grab a weapon, a spade or something, and regretted that now. The sound came again and she was glad she had climbed up to the top of the straw bales. She was afraid of rats mostly, in her mind she could see them swarming in the darkness below.

There was a snort then the unmistakable sound of an animal urinating. The pig had found her again.

'Eew, Pig!' she exclaimed. 'Couldn't you do that outside?'

The pig responded with another snort and walked to the bottom of the straw bales and plonked itself down.

'Glad you made it,' she said. Weirdly she felt a whole lot safer now the pig was with her. It was irrational, but strangely comforting.

She was about to settle down again when she heard another sound. What now? She tensed. Didn't anyone get any sleep in the countryside? She saw another figure standing in the barn entrance.

'Eew,' a voice rasped. 'What's that smell?'

'Ri! Ri! Is that you?'

'Genie? I don't believe it. Genie?'

'Don't move,' Genie warned him. 'There's a pig in here and he's huge. Don't scare him.'

'A pig?'

'Keep to your left and there's a short ladder at the end of the hay bales.'

Rian followed her instructions as his eyes adjusted to the darkness. He could definitely smell wet pig, even if he couldn't see it. 'Hell, I can't believe you're in here. I can't believe you're alive, Genie.'

'Pig saved my life, I think.' Genie moved to the end of the hay bales to greet him.

His head appeared and suddenly Genie was on him, arms around him hugging him. 'You're freezing, Ri. Freezing.'

'You're so warm. God, I'm just . . .' He was stunned they had both ended up in the same place. Fate or magic. Clearly they were meant to be. 'I just followed this old track and . . .'

'Hush, come here . . .'

He climbed up beside her and they fell back together on to the hay, holding each other tight. Rian was still wet but Genie planned to hug him dry. 'Pull the straw over you and stay close. I'm never letting go of you again.'

He kissed her and she kissed him back, still stunned he had come back into her life. Below them the pig snorted, and they laughed.

'There's a pig in here,' Rian stated. 'There really is a pig in here.'

The rain began again and the thunder rolled overhead once more, closer than before, but both of them knew that they were safe and dry in here and snuggled up close under the straw, hands and arms and legs entwined. Nothing was going to pry them apart. Moments later, exhausted, but utterly happy, they were both asleep.

# 8

## Finding Denis

The building was bright. Glass walls and huge banks of computer servers, thousands of them, throwing off a massive amount of heat. This was a secret place, she knew that. The building literally hummed with all the power it consumed. She had no idea how she'd got here, but she knew she was trespassing. She was stood barefoot in a corridor unable to decide which way to go. Someone was coming and they meant her harm, but there was nowhere to hide. She saw movement, half turned and saw it again. Untamed ginger hair bobbing on the periphery of her vision.

'Genie?' a voice said, urgent, scared. 'You shouldn't be in here. Go, before they get you.'

She turned and there he was. Denis Malone, the boy who'd disappeared two years before. He looked just the same, which was impossible. She remembered him now, messing about in class and making stupid jokes. He was almost naked save for some scraggy underwear and green socks. There was a livid scar on his left shoulder that looked a lot like the cross burned on to her own arm.

'Denis. I can't believe it's you. You haven't changed—'

'Go, Genie. They'll come for you and you'll never leave. No one who enters here ever leaves.'

'Where are we? How did I get here?'

'You don't want to know. But they're going crazy right now. The storm came, some people fried and it's—'

An automatic door whooshed open somewhere. The atmosphere in the room altered as cool air flooded in. She looked for a place to hide. She had so much to discuss with Denis. What had happened to him? Where had he been? How did he end up here? Why wasn't he wearing any clothes? Denis ran behind a huge computer bank but when Genie rushed there to join him he wasn't there. There was nowhere to hide at all. It was impossible Denis could have hidden here. Impossible. 'Denis?'

She heard footsteps, turned and saw a reflection in the glass wall – a uniformed security guard creeping along the bank of computers. Her throat began to constrict, she felt sick with terror. She suddenly saw Denis was at the other end of the room, behind her now, trying to get the attention of the guard.

'Run, Genie, run!' Denis shouted as he ran the other way. The armed man spun around to follow him. Genie dashed for the double doors at the end of the room hoping they led somewhere. She heard a gunshot behind her. Glass shattered. She burst through the end doors and her feet found nothing. She began to fall, fall and fall into black nothingness. She screamed as young, scared faces stared at her from the blackness. She felt them reach out for her. Heard them call her name. Was this what death felt like, as it sucked the life out of you?

She bounced, landed hard, all the breath knocked out of her. Then sat up gulping for air. She was feverish. It took her a moment to realize it had been a incredibly vivid dream. She was still lying on the hay bales; Rian was asleep next to her, undisturbed. The rain was falling noisily on the tin roof once more. The pig was snorting quietly down below and the gusting wind was causing a loose metal sheet to flap loudly above.

She stared into the darkness, unnerved. The dream was too intense, too real. Denis Malone was there. Denis had been in her classes for sure. He'd gone missing, she remembered that. One of the first to go from Spurlake, there had been 'Missing' posters pinned up on store walls all over town. She lay back, exhausted and tried to will herself to sleep. The building she recognized was the strange glass tower she'd seen as she passed by in the floodwaters. She was sure of it. She saw it again as the lightning flashed in her mind, the men inside with their bright flashlights, the cars stacked up by the flood. Why was it there? She closed her eyes. Did she really see it? Dreams like that were always a warning, but against what? Why had she dreamt of Denis, of all people? She'd never spoken to him, not once. And why wasn't he wearing any clothes?

Rian turned in his sleep and Genie stroked his arms. She was safe. Rian was here, he'd saved her. *But now what? Where are we gonna end up? Where can we go? How hard is it for kids to survive out here? Who can we trust?*

The last image she saw before sleep took her again was of Denis turning to run and save her. He looked hunted and scared. What on earth had happened to him? Was she meant to find out? Was that what the dream meant?

# 9

# *Marshall*

The sun streamed in from an uncanny clear sky. The yard was steaming outside in the heat and it was hard to believe there had been a deluge around the old farm. Marshall sat on a straw bale and contemplated the view before him. A pig, definitely not his pig – he had never owned a pig – was sound asleep where it had made a bed for itself. The pig was a handsome animal, somewhat muddy, but it had an elegant long snout and had been most likely well cared for back where it came from. There might or might not be a branding mark on its backside, hard to tell under the mud. There were two teenagers asleep at the top of the stack and he could see by the state of their feet, all bloodied under the layers of mud, that they'd been through quite a lot.

Marshall felt for his pipe and remembered he'd left it in the kitchen. He'd long ago given up smoking, but was unable to surrender the pipe itself. He looked back into the yard and beyond where the power line stood at an angle. The power was probably down right across the valley after the storm, the ground simply washed away from under the pylons in some places. The valley itself was underwater. Some farms would probably never recover, but then again, the water would find a way out. It had before, back in '77 when he was a kid. That's when they'd built the wall alongside the river. Built it to exactly one metre higher than the breach of '77 and here they were all over again with a wall crumbled before the force of nature.

Which brought him back to the kids and the stray pig. Had they brought the pig with them? The chances of a pig ending up here were so remote it was going to be an interesting story when he heard it.

He hadn't inspected the barn since he'd made the cider last fall. He generally took a tour of everything he owned after a storm. He had been lucky, no damage except to the barn roof. No problem to fix it. The boy would probably help him if he asked.

Who were they? How long had they been gone? He wondered if they were like the others.

Rian woke first. He saw the man sat on the straw bale looking up at them. He looked at Genie still asleep, curled up tight to him, her fingers tucked into his shirt.

He shook her a little and her eyes fluttered. 'Genie,' he whispered, immediately aware his voice sounded strange. 'Wake up.'

Genie sat up. Instantly awake, trying to reorient herself. She was in a barn. She wasn't in her bedroom. She was with Rian. It wasn't a dream.

Rian sort of acknowledged the man watching them. Tried to clear his throat.

'Sorry. We needed shelter.' He was surprised by the sound of his voice sounding and feeling scratchy. There was a lump growing in his throat too. Not a good sign.

Marshall pointed at the pig with his pipe. 'That yours?'

Rian and Genie looked down over the bales and there was the magnificent pig sprawled out as happy as could be, snoring.

Genie smiled. She looked at the man. 'Pig saved my life.'

Marshall nodded. 'Pig's a smart animal. I asked if it was yours?'

Genie shook her head. 'Got washed down the river with everything else, I guess.' She coughed. Her throat was tight and sore. 'We clung on together and he followed me here. It's huge. I can't believe it. Long walk too – for a pig.'

Marshall could judge a lot by what people said, or didn't say. The surprise in the girl's face was genuine.

82

And it was she who had saved the pig and that was more than most would do.

'It's a Tamworth sow. She's a grower, good sixty kilograms I'd say. Nice ruddy colour too. Someone would be proud to own such a pig.'

Genie looked down at the pig a moment and saw its feet shake. She felt quite attached to the beast.

'Where you from?' Marshall asked.

'Spurlake.' Rian had planned to lie but it just slipped out automatically.

Marshall nodded. Closest town.

'The Paramount Steakhouse on Peak is my favourite.'

Genie glanced at Rian, puzzled. She didn't know it.

'Hate to tell you, Mister, but they must of torn it down years ago. We never heard of it,' Rian confessed. Didn't want to upset the guy an' all.

Marshall stood up and smiled. 'I know that. Just testing. Breakfast?' He looked at the pig a moment. 'I'll leave out the bacon.'

Genie smiled. 'I should hope so. It's quite sensitive.' She tried to straighten her hair. She was a mess. 'We got anything for the pig?'

'Some apples, some cereal. They'll pretty much eat anything,' Marshall mused. He moved over to the side and pulled out a small bucket and filled it from a tap on the wall. 'I got a paddock I used to use for my horses. It can live there for now until we find its owner.' He brought the water over and left it a few feet away from the pig. 'Got to give them plenty of water. Pigs are like humans, they like to drink.'

Rian climbed down first and waited for Genie to join him. The pig opened an eye but didn't seem too bothered by the activity.

Genie slid down the ladder and landed on her feet too hard. She looked at the gash on her arm and realized it was sore. 'Ouch.'

'You're pretty cut up,' Marshall commented. He saw the bruises now that the light was on her face. 'What happened to your face, girl?' He narrowed his eyes at Rian as if reappraising him. 'Want to tell me how she got so cut and bruised, boy?'

'Not me, sir. That's why we're here, sir. On account of the bruises and . . .'

Genie walked up to the man. Let him see up close what kind of shape she was in. 'My mother.' She said nothing else.

Marshall nodded and turned. 'Close the lower half of the door as you leave so the pig can't get out. I'll send you back with some food for it in a while.'

Rian and Genie snatched a look at each other. No

choice but to trust him. Genie looked at the pig pretending to sleep. It was wary now, but she had a feeling it had no need to be. She hoped the man was OK. You could never really tell about people. Not right away. She caught her reflection in an old mottled mirror propped up on the wall and suddenly she remembered her nightmare. She literally stopped in her tracks and froze.

'What?' Rian asked. 'Genie? What's wrong?' He could see that she had turned ghostly white.

She had remembered something else that spooked her now.

'Denis Malone. He's dead. I remember now. They found him in Feather Creek last May. Buried him. Half the school went to the funeral.'

'You OK?' Rian asked. He sort of remembered something about the kid. Been missing for so long. Made the local paper when his body turned up.

'He was in my dream last night, but he wasn't dead.'

'Well, it *was* a dream.' Rian told her. 'You don't want to be dreaming of dead people.'

'I didn't dream of dead people,' Genie protested. 'He was as alive as you or me and just the same. I mean, he was still thirteen or whatever. Hadn't aged a bit. He told me to run. It was weird, Ri. He was naked, well almost. Had this big red scar on his shoulder, like he'd been hit by a bolt of lightning. It was a huge place filled with hundreds of computers. So hot, I woke up choking.'

Rian took her arm and squeezed. 'You were feverish after being in the water, Gen. That's all. Remember, I said you were hot when I arrived. Dreams are weird; you always remember stuff you just don't want to. Naked? Sure it wasn't one of *those* dreams?'

Genie frowned, attempted a weak smile. 'I promise you I have never once thought about Denis Malone, with or without clothes. It wasn't one of *those* dreams. It was a warning of some kind. I'm sure.' Nevertheless, Rian was probably right. Just because a dream was vivid, it didn't mean it was significant or anything.

She pointed towards Marshall, patiently waiting for them outside the barn. She took a deep breath and smiled at Rian. 'We're lucky to be alive, Ri. We really are.'

Then they were outside in the sunlight, blinking, astonished the bad weather could have vanished so completely. Marshall was still observing them closely. 'Where were you two headed?' he asked casually.

Rian squeezed Genie's hand to indicate he was going to answer this. 'We were staying on a friend's houseboat. By Coho Creek. I've been doing maintenance.' His voice was all over the place and sounded weird.

'Premier MacLean's old tub? Didn't know it was still habitable.'

'Huge tree hit it,' Genie said. 'Ripped the roof clean off. Scariest moment of my life.'

Marshall digested this information. 'So you were . . .'

'Hiding from my mother,' Genie jumped in. 'I'd like to stay hidden if you didn't mind, sir. If you were thinking of making a call.'

Marshall liked her courage. These kids were very close, he could see that.

'Phone and power are out. I'm not calling anyone. None of my business. I just like to make sure no one is doing anything against his or her will. I'm old-fashioned, but I'm not a man to stand in the way of young love. Been in love myself once or twice. Believe it or not.'

Rian smiled. Genie was still wary however. She wasn't used to trusting adults. He'd seemed pretty calm about them being in his barn. Some people might have just reached for their shotgun and run them off their land. She noted that he had a limp. They followed him down the track towards his house, both hoping he could be trusted.

# 10

# *Spurlake*

Spurlake was a disaster zone. Trees uprooted, blocking roads or crushing roofs, streets and houses flooded, cars up-ended, trucks overturned, some parked on top of houses. Six neighbourhood streets and the homes were completely flooded, all the way to the eaves, with families with river-front properties camping out on the roofs, scared to leave in case of looters. Everywhere people were yelling for a lost dog or cat. Spurlake wasn't a big town, but the sudden water and hurricane strength wind had devastated much of it, torn down the mall, ripped the roofs of two school buildings and the Veterans' Hall. People everywhere were stunned by the damage.

Mrs Tulane surveyed the debris from her driveway. She'd been lucky, the street was flooded but her home was on a small slope and the water had stopped short of her door. Mr Yates came wading through the water, back from a mission to find out what had happened. He had arrived by kayak this morning, the roads being impassable in places. He was pleased with himself for being so resourceful. He was still wearing slicks, but perspiring now the sun had come out.

'Any word of Rian?'

He waved to her as he approached. 'Sorry. Can't get any sense out of anyone. The police and rescue services are getting a "Missing" list together. Everyone in Gunny House perished. Lightning hit the home and it burned before the water hit. Sixty old folk sniffed out just like that. They say they think nearly two hundred drowned in Spurlake alone. Worst natural disaster for thirty years. Everyone is going to hate insurers. No one ever notices the "Act of God" clause on their policies until about now.'

'You're not helping, Jim. Did you check Rian's room like I asked?'

Jim Yates righted an upturned garden chair and sat on it facing her. He looked pretty serious suddenly. 'He's gone, Fern. Backpack, toothbrush gone. Accept it, the boy's gone.'

'But no note?'

'No note. Although I guess it could have blown out of the window. It was wide open and his bed's soaked. Face it, Fern. He went to rescue the Munby girl. I heard it from Officer Miller. Someone ripped the bars out of her window and drove off with her just before the storm hit. They could be anywhere.'

Fern Tulane thought about it a moment. She hadn't really thought Rian was that concerned about the girl, but clearly she had misread the signals. Stupid of her. She had to admire his determination, though. Ripped the bars out of the girl's window. The power of young love. Nothing like that had ever happened to her, she thought with bitterness.

'Look, I'll check with Officer Miller again,' Mr Yates was saying. 'But if Rian got her out of town before the storm, that has to be good, right?'

'But where would he take her? He doesn't have a car. Did you ask Tunis, next door? He plays basketball with him.'

'Yeah, I checked with them. They're worried too. Tunis didn't come home last night either and he hasn't called.' Mr Yates was just glad Rian had gone. Annoying little argumentative bastard.

'What about the boat?' Mrs Tulane remembered. 'His summer job, remember? He was doing up a boat.'

'Premier MacLean's old hunting boat? Yeah. Well. Yeah. If I was going to take a girl somewhere private – that's exactly where I'd go.'

Mrs Tulane looked at Mr Yates with fresh eyes. 'At least I'd know where to look, Jim.'

'I never . . . I . . .' he spluttered. 'Fern, you know I was only being hypothetical.'

'You are always hypothetical, Jim. Get the keys to the Range Rover. We're going down to the river. I want to get my boy back before he disappears with the rest of them.'

Mr Yates rose reluctantly. 'I don't think the roads are open, Fern.'

Fern turned her wheelchair towards the vehicle. 'That's why I own a four-by-four. Let's go. Before they move on.'

Officer Miller came up for air, sucked in as much as he could, then dived again. The water was cold, filthy, mixed with oil. No time to wait for help. There was someone trapped down there, still alive. He'd seen someone waving a flashlight from inside one of the flooded homes.

No amount of training prepared you for this kind of devastation. A whole row of homes underwater. You'd think everyone would have been evacuated, but experience told him that there was always someone, always one person who didn't leave, who wanted to stay to protect their property, even though if they'd thought about it for a minute they would have realized that the house was ruined the moment the water flooded the ground floor.

He entered via an upstairs window. Swam through two

91

rooms. Kicking a door open under water was tough. He braced himself against a far wall and kicked as hard as he could, his chest already bursting with the pressure.

The door gave way, a huge bubble of air escaped as water flooded into the room. A boy yelled at him angrily and began to panic as the cold water flowed in from the corridor. Miller managed to grab some air before the room filled completely. He snatched the boy and kicked out the window. The boy looked terrified now, gasping for the last air. He must have managed to stop the water flowing into his room somehow, but been trapped there ever since.

Miller wrapped a blanket around the boy's head in case the broken glass cut him and then he launched them both out of the window, swimming back up to the surface, now some two metres above the roofline.

He ripped the blanket off the struggling boy. They gasped for air. The boy looked around him, couldn't believe he'd been sat in a house under water all this time.

Miller put an arm around his chest and swam on his back to higher ground. He could hear shouts and cheering. There was still no sign of the rescue team he'd requested.

On higher, dry ground, he lay there in a heap, exhausted, as others took the bewildered boy off his hands.

Only then did he realize who he had rescued. Frickin'

Martin Pol. The thirteen-year-old juvenile he'd arrested two months ago for handling stolen property. The kid recognized him. Didn't say thanks. His tattooed father was stood there, took the boy off his hands. Didn't say thanks either. That's a police officer's lot. Saving criminals' lives. He smiled. Kind of ironic.

'Here,' someone said, offering him a drink of something. 'It's hot.'

Miller took it, drank it. He'd been on duty twenty-four hours now. At least the water had stopped rising. He lay back on the road. The sun came out. He felt like he could sleep now, never mind being soaked. Just needed to sleep.

'You'd better get out of those wet things,' a voice told him. 'Do you know where they're taking the bodies?'

Miller opened his eyes. The bodies. Hundreds of bodies. He'd saved one useless life. Some stupid hero he was.

'Last I heard they were being kept at the elementary school on Jackson Street.'

'Thanks, Officer. You did good.'

Miller sighed. He needed to go home, rest. He looked out across the vast expanse of water where at least a quarter of Spurlake was buried and for a brief moment wondered about that kid, Genie Magee. Had she survived?

He hoped so. Never been so shocked in his life in finding the heavily barred window on the ground outside and double locked jail door to her bedroom. What if there had been a fire? The mother's hostility to her daughter was another thing. What the hell was happening in Spurlake? Used to be such a good place to raise kids. What would it be like when the water receded? Would people even want to rebuild?

He stood up. Somewhere back up the hill was his own home. Dry, untouched. Safe. Time to go home.

# 11

## Faces

Marshall had an air of sadness about him. Seemed to carry it with him. Genie could sense it as they walked behind him towards his house. She looked around her at the battered trees and bushes and wondered how anyone could stand living so far out of town. There was no one around. No homes in the distance, nothing. It was a lonely farmhouse where no one would ever wander by. Had he chosen it because he was lonely, or because he wanted to be alone?

A dog came out of nowhere. Silent, but wagging its tail, excited to see people. It made straight for Genie and she hugged it hello. 'Hey, where did you come from, dog? Look Ri, it's a French dog. My cousin in Quebec has one just like it. Berger Picard. Isn't it beautiful? Look at its eyes, its ears. Oh, it's adorable!'

Rian saw how instantly happy she was, and smiled. Of course it *was* a pretty cute dog.

'How long have you had him?' Genie asked the farmer.

95

The dog was lying on its back so she could tickle his tummy. 'Not mine,' Marshall said. 'Moucher's my ex-wife's. She abandoned it.'

Genie could see that the farmer wasn't happy. If she had this dog she'd never be alone. Ever. Couldn't he see that? Bergers were the best friends anyone could have.

Marshall continued walking towards the house. Genie and Rian followed exchanging glances, the dog running ahead and back again, as if herding them.

The storm had done some damage to the surroundings here. A tree was uprooted very close to the house and the barn roof looked to have some gaps where the sheet metal had blown away. 'Lucky not to have that tree on the house,' Rian stated.

Marshall ignored him. Rian shot a look at Genie but she didn't seem to notice anything amiss. He trusted her instincts would warn them if something bad was going to happen.

He brought them in via the back door, leading into the kitchen. It was a large old-fashioned space with a huge range and a long wide pine table that could probably seat twelve people at least. Looked really old too.

Moucher went to his bowl, saw there was nothing and stamped on it, upturning it. Genie laughed because it was so expertly done, then felt sorry for it.

Marshall sat down at the head of the table and placed his hands flat on the pine surface. Genie noticed he was sweating a little and out of breath. The walk from the barn had been hard for him somehow. 'You OK?' Rian asked.

Marshall shook his head.

'Get me a glass of water, from the fridge. Can't trust tap water after that storm.'

Genie was at the sink and had come to the same conclusion. Brown water was cascading from the tap. 'Gross. Not nice.'

She went to the fridge. It didn't smell so good now the power was out and things were beginning to go off. She found three bottles of water still slightly chilled. Poured some for the dog and the farmer. She gave to the farmer first, then the dog, who quickly drank it, but was clearly disappointed it wasn't actual food. Genie had the beginnings of a major headache now herself. She was hungry, that's all.

Rian was looking around the kitchen. It looked uncared for. Now he looked more closely, the farmer looked pretty uncared for as well.

'Your wife left recently?'

Marshall took a pill out of a small tin box and popped it in his mouth, chasing it down with half the glass of cold water. He looked at Rian with a practised stare.

'Boy, I am going to tell you something that you need to remember as long as you live. Never,' he paused a moment to mop his brow. 'Never marry a woman you met in a bar.'

Genie almost laughed, but his serious expression told the story. Whoever she had been, she had gone and with it any happiness he thought he might have had.

Rian sat down. 'Duly noted, sir. Genie and I met at high school and I intend to be with her the rest of my life.'

Marshall looked at them both a while and slowly nodded. 'That what you want, girl?'

Genie frowned, snatching a look at the dog sitting looking quizzically at her. 'Well, I'm torn now. If Moucher doesn't ask me to marry him first.'

Rian laughed and Marshall smiled briefly. 'You can keep 'em both,' he told her. 'Like I told you, not my dog.'

Genie began to cough then and she could feel how sore her throat was getting.

Rian was looking at the kitchen range. Marshall saw him staring at it.

'I know what you're thinking, boy. Power's out. How we going to make breakfast? Well, so happens we got propane. There's eggs, there's bread in the biscuit tin, some beans in the larder and I think I got some mushrooms. Picked 'em before the storm. You want to get busy with that? I just need to sit a while. My heart . . .'

Genie looked at him more closely. He had seemed well when they had first met him, but now he looked quite pale and uncomfortable, as if he wasn't getting enough air.

One thing Rian liked to do was cook breakfast, and to cook for Genie was a double pleasure. He coughed and tried to swallow, wincing a little. His throat was getting worse. His hands felt clammy.

Marshall noticed that he was clearing his throat more than was necessary.

'Kids. I got some antibiotics in the bathroom cabinet, room next to my bedroom, across the hall. You're both going to need them – you especially, girl, that gash on your arm needs iodine on it. Brown bottle in the cabinet. Lot of nasty stuff in that river water. You're both going to be ill – I can see it in your eyes. You can both rest up here until you're ready to move on. I'm bad company most of the time, but I got the space. Bathroom shelf, next to the shaving cream. Pill packet marked Ampicillin. Understand?'

'Don't you need them?' Genie asked, her voice breaking up a little.

'I can always get more. You might have a problem with

that. Might have a problem with a lot of things in the near future. You'll need to be well.'

Genie went to get the pills. She was wondering how it was they had been so lucky to meet up with someone so generous. So uncritical. Meanwhile, back in Spurlake, they'd probably be going crazy that they were missing, but he didn't seem to care about that at all.

The hallway was almost as big as the kitchen. The staircase snaked up the centre of it to the next floor and clearly whoever had built this had wanted it to be very grand indeed. There was a huge framed photograph of Spurlake on the wall taken at least eighty years before. Empty streets and a mess of telephone wires everywhere. Must have been so strange to live back then. One thing caught her eye though. Munby Sawmill. There was a young man standing outside the building under the sign and holding on to a giant saw almost twice his own height. Her great grandfather maybe? There was a Roxy movie theatre nearby and she made out an ice-cream parlour. All vanished now. She remembered that her mother had told her that once the Munbys had money and influence in Spurlake. That too had vanished. Name was mud now.

She found Marshall's bedroom and entered. It smelled musty and damp. She did wonder why he slept on the ground floor, but then he did have that limp . . .

It was dark, so she pulled the curtains wide open to let in light, then turned and surveyed the room. An unmade double bed, pine cupboard and a canvas-backed chair with clothes piled on top. Several pairs of men's shoes kept in open boxes on the floor and women shoes gathering dust on a rack in rows. There was something curious about *his* shoes. She didn't immediately pick up what it was.

She turned to head for the bathroom when she spun on her heels and looked at his shoes again. They were all *brand new*, never been used by the look of them. Genie puzzled over that as she opened the creaking bathroom door.

The pills were exactly where he said they would be. A full packet. The label said: *Two a day, avoid milk when taking this medicine*. There was enough, she hoped, to treat both of them. She knew they were going to get sick, but if they could hit it fast, maybe it wouldn't be so bad.

She looked in the mirror and even though the light was dim she could see she looked a mess. She had no idea the bruises looked this bad. How Rian could like her at all she didn't know. Her heart sank. She looked like a crash victim. It was as she was dabbing iodine on the cuts on her arm with cotton wool that something else caught her eye. She looked into the mirror to one side, and saw faces. Young faces. She slowly turned and saw there were newspaper cuttings pasted on to the wall above the bath, all the way up to the ceiling. Every missing kid from Spurlake. Every pathetic plea for help. She stared at them and felt the hairs on her neck rising. She hadn't realized how many there were. Just one town. One small town, to have lost so many children. Was this why he had sent her to the bathroom? To see this? Why? She saw scissors lying on the floor, part of a dismembered newspaper in the waste bin.

What was going on here? Why did the farmer have these pictures on the wall?

Why was Julia, aged fifteen, on this wall? Why Miho? Come to think of it, how Miho? She was supposed to be in Japan. Since when was she missing? Why Randall? A huge obese kid of fourteen. Maybe he was being bullied for being fat, but why had the others gone? Were their lives in Spurlake so terrible? Hers was, but could it be so bad for so many others too? What did this farmer know? Did he make them disappear? Was this about to happen to Ri and her?

Genie was suddenly terrified. She put the stinging liquid down and had to pee, she was so scared. She lifted the toilet seat and quickly sat down. She couldn't help but stare at the pictures and count them. Thirty-four kids. Thirty-four children from her town had gone missing in just two years, not counting herself and Ri.

Was this bath where he killed them? Imagined she saw bloodstains. She stood up again. *Get us out of here. Out of this farm. What have we got ourselves into?*

She washed her hands in brown tap water. She realized she was shaking. She could hear Rian calling her now. He sounded real worried.

'Coming,' she answered, and stumbled out of the bathroom. She saw the man's shoes again and the wife's. A woman might leave a man, but would she leave her shoes? Had he killed her too? Was this man a serial killer? She was sweating now. She was dizzy and could barely walk in a straight line. She heard her name being called again, urgently this time.

He must have known she would see the newspaper cuttings. Was he taunting her? Clearly he meant to terrify her.

She made it into the kitchen, expecting to see Rian already disembowelled or his head cut off, but a completely different scene faced her.

'Help me,' Rian asked. He looked totally spooked as he stared at Marshall lying on the floor. 'He suddenly rocked back and fell. He's unconscious,

Genie, and his leg fell off.'

Genie looked at the man sprawled out on the floor, looked at Rian and his worried expression and then she felt her eyes fluttering and the floor was coming up to her. 'Genie!' Rian shouted as he dashed forward to catch her, place her on a chair.

She heard the dog barking in the distance. It was then she vividly saw Anwar's face again as he had looked down at her from her wall at home.

'*You're next*,' he'd said. '*You're next*.'

Rian had no idea what to do. He stood there and looked at the old farmer out cold on the floor with his false leg askew and then Genie collapsing. So weird. But then again he knew from the golf ball growing in his own throat that he was likely to be sick too. He knew he had to do something.

He woke Genie briefly and made her swallow one of the pills she had brought. He swallowed one himself, careful to read the label. It was definitely Ampicillin and he hoped it would fix things quickly. He dealt with Genie first, carrying her upstairs to a huge bed in the first room with adjoining bathroom. He could see this must have been Marshall's room at some time before he moved downstairs: his old clothes were still hanging in a cupboard. He made Genie drink bottled water and covered her with some blankets. Then he returned downstairs and made the farmer comfortable, straightened him out some, put a pillow under his head and covered him up too, rolling him on to a rug, because it was cold on the flagstone floor. He'd done enough caring for his mother to know the best thing to do was make people comfortable and be alert to changes. He still felt weird about the man's leg falling off.

It was almost an hour before he got around to actually making breakfast for himself and some coffee. He was hoping the smell of cooking would revive people, but only Moucher showed interest, so they ate together, face to face at the table. The dog seemed pretty used to eating at the table so he didn't question it.

'You want to come with us, Moucher?' Rian asked the dog. 'Don't exactly know where we're headed but you can come if you want.'

The dog cocked its head to one side as if contemplating a reply, then with a fast, deft paw movement stole the last of his toast and ran off to eat it under the table. Rian laughed, but instantly regretted it. His throat was raw and the pill had had no time to work its magic. He was sweaty now and knew that he had better find a place to lie down. He placed a mug of water by the old farmer, just far enough away so he wouldn't spill it and left him a note to call him if he needed help getting up.

He couldn't believe how shaky his legs were as he mounted the stairs. Shivering, he lay down on the bed beside Genie and pulled one of the blankets over him. As he fell asleep he thought he could hear the pig snorting outside the window. He wondered if Genie had given it anything. It would be hungry by now. He realized they had forgotten to shut the barn door. It would have to wait. Everything would have to wait. He touched Genie's hands and they were burning. Great. He'd done her no favours at all in saving her from her mother. Everything he had done had put her in greater danger. He felt guilty. Then he slept.

# 12

## Sick Daze

Marshall woke first. It was nearly dark. It took him some time to realize that he was lying on the floor in the kitchen. Took him a few more minutes to realize that his leg had become detached. He could hear Moucher scratching in his basket. He tried to make out the face of the clock on the range, but it was too far to focus. Judging by the light it was early evening. He'd somehow missed a whole day. The seizures were getting worse. He'd have to ask the doctor about that, but he knew that there was little chance of a cure. He remembered the kids suddenly. Where were they? Marshall turned and as his eyes adjusted to the dark, he could see that the boy had placed his leg beside him and a glass of water. Done the decent thing. Must have freaked him out to see a man's leg give way like that. He sighed. Bitch of a job to get the leg back on and get up off the floor, but he'd done it before, he'd be doing it again.

It took ten minutes to strap in and haul himself up. He tried the light switch, but the power was still out. Could be days or weeks before they fixed it, he guessed. He headed to the storeroom to find his flashlight. That's when he heard the familiar sound of a chopper flying overhead. Business as usual at the Fortress then. Moucher woke and stood up, stretching beside his basket. He'd be hungry.

'I'll attend to you in a minute, boy. Got to get a flashlight.'

Moucher was glad of the company and watched him moving slowly in the dark. A second chopper flew overhead, very low, the throb of its engines shaking the whole farmhouse. Marshall wondered why there was suddenly so much activity. What, he wondered, had gone wrong now?

Upstairs, Rian was vaguely aware of the house shaking, but didn't care. He couldn't move. He was in that place between sleep and hell when you're sick. His head and throat burned and he was sweating. A pill was placed on his tongue, water sloshed into his mouth and fingers gripped his nose to make him swallow. He couldn't fight it, somehow he swallowed. A soothing hand wiped his face a moment and a voice said something, but he didn't know what and he settled back again, into half-sleep.

Genie threw the flannel into the bucket and staggered back to the bathroom. She too was on fire and her chest hurt like hell, breathing was difficult. She swallowed another pill herself. Didn't know quite how she'd got here or why she was so sick, but Rian was with her and that's all that mattered. Rian had busted her out and she never had to see her mother again. That's all she wanted now. Never to have to see her again.

Marshall found the flashlight. Opened a can of dog food and a can of corned beef for himself. Didn't know which smelled the worst. Thirty minutes later wasn't even sure he'd eaten from the right can, but didn't care. The dog was happy, at least.

The kids weren't on the ground floor. He guessed they were sleeping upstairs. His son would probably come by in the morning to make sure he was OK. He usually came on a Thursday. He'd discuss the kids with him then. He wouldn't ordinarily interfere with runaways, but they'd run in the wrong direction as far as he was concerned and a big spider was out there to get them and these weren't the usual misfits. Someone was going to miss them. Even if they didn't think so. He had a strong feeling about that. Kids never thought anyone missed them; they were always so sure of not being loved or cared for, but in his experience parents learned a great deal from the ordeal and were always happy to see them returned. So many kids gone from Spurlake and he suspected, even if he couldn't prove it, exactly where they had gone, and why they weren't coming back. He took himself to bed. Wasn't tired, but it was dark, nothing could be done now till the morning.

Genie thought she heard birdsong. It was still dark, but a finger of light was visible on the horizon. She still had a lump in her throat but sometime in the night her fever had broken. She had woken and it seemed the antibiotics had started their work. She was going to get better, even if she did feel incredibly light-headed. There was a stale smell of damp in the room. Her stomach growled. How many days had passed since she'd eaten? She had no idea. The golf ball in her throat was uncomfortable and it was difficult to swallow, but she knew she was over the worst.

She discovered Rian was lying naked beside her under the blankets. He seemed to be on fire. The fever was burning him up and the sheets were soaking. She pulled the blankets up around him. He'd need it. It was so dumb. They were finally together and now they were both sick. Life truly sucked.

By the time there was enough light to see, she had had a cold washdown, gotten more pills down her own and Rian's throat and made them both swallow a lot of water.

Had to keep him hydrated. Rian was pretty sick, but she knew he'd be feeling better by the evening if he followed her pattern. 'Love you, Ri,' she'd whispered in his ears. He'd vaguely squeezed her hand, but he wasn't really there. He was still in the grip of this thing. She loved looking at him sleeping; he even frowned in his sleep. Cute.

Genie pulled on her clothes. They were dry now, but musty and stiff and it wasn't a good feeling against her skin. She had a rash on her chest, a reaction to the pills most likely. She had a memory of that happening before. All she needed. She made her way downstairs, her legs pretty damn shaky under her. The house was strangely silent.

In the kitchen, Moucher was asleep in his basket and clearly thought it was too early to be disturbed. Despite the time of year, the whole house felt chilled. The old flagstone floors were freezing underfoot and she had no idea of what had happened to her shoes. Of course, duh, stupid, she'd lost them in the river. She found a note from Rian on the table.

*Eat, keep taking the pills, Gen. I'm getting sick too.*
*Sorry, I'm supposed to be taking care of you. X Ri*

Poor Ri. She thought of him back upstairs shivering in the damp bed. Poor, beautiful Ri.

111

She boiled water on the propane range. At least she could have tea and oatmeal. The larder had a ton of oatmeal. She thought about home. Whether Reverend Schneider had moved in with her mother or she with him. Then she was thinking about why the old man lived in such a big old farmhouse so far from anywhere. No shops, no cars. Maybe that's what he liked. Genie wasn't sure she could live so isolated from other life.

She heard a door slam and a toilet flush. Someone else was awake.

Genie was still stirring the porridge when he came in wearing his red pyjamas, scratching his uncombed hair. She suddenly remembered the pictures of the missing kids in his bathroom, then a flash memory of this man lying on the ground with his leg missing and all the thoughts she'd had about him, and she froze. How could she have forgotten everything so quickly?

'Keep stirring, Genie, or it'll stick.'

She stirred. Whatever this man was, he wasn't so scary in red pyjamas, dressing gown and wearing an artificial leg. In fact, he looked pretty sick and emaciated. Genie turned back to the range. 'I made enough for ten people, I think. We got any milk? I guess not, huh?'

Marshall took a deep breath and rubbed his two-day beard. 'Deep freeze thawed out, but the milk will be fine. Lot of stuff to eat today by my reckoning. Everything goes off in three days and today's the day.' He looked at Genie carefully.

'You feeling better? I heard you guys groaning and coughing up there, sounded pretty bad.'

'Ri's not getting better yet. He's got a high temperature.'

'Well, keep him hydrated and let him sleep.'

Genie nodded, pouring out two bowls of oatmeal for them. 'Got any maple syrup?'

'By the flour jar.'

She went to get it. A photo dislodged from behind it and fluttered down to the floor. She quickly picked it up and saw it was a boy who looked much like Rian, but with longer hair. She looked at Marshall and he acknowledged her unasked question.

'My sister's kid, Dale. Went missing in Nelson about two years ago. Didn't get on with his father and was failing at school. Thought he'd come to me. That's what I wanted, but he's just one of many missing kids now.' He shrugged.

Genie took the oatmeal to the table as Marshall shuffled over to the deep freeze and took out a defrosted milk carton. He shook it and you could hear the ice hadn't completely melted yet. When opened, it came out like milk slushy, but at least it was milk. Tea and coffee was

113

going to be a whole lot better with it.

Marshall watched the girl spoon out the maple syrup into her oatmeal and then eat. He noticed her slim, elegant hands – artist's hands. Genie said nothing, just let him get his stuff together and they ate in silence.

'I'll make coffee,' Marshall said, rising from the table. 'Surprised you shook off the fever so quick.'

'Your pills helped. I recover quickly. Always have. Ri will take longer, I guess.'

Marshall was looking out of the window.

'Remind me to go looking for that pig. Probably hungry by now and I think we've got a lot of spoiled food it can eat.'

'I forgot about the pig.' She felt guilty. It would be starving. Then she turned to Marshall and asked the one thing that was on her mind. 'How did you lose the leg? Car crash?'

Marshall had the water boiled already and was pouring it over the ground coffee. He didn't answer right away. Genie thought she had upset him. She always asked direct questions, often embarrassed herself that way. Marshall found cups and gave them a wipe.

'I'm not sure you'd believe me if I told you.'

*Now* Genie was interested. The oatmeal was burning a hole in her stomach and she had to sit down suddenly, a sudden hot flush coming over her.

'You don't have to tell me.'

Marshall sighed. He brought the coffee cups to the table and set them down. 'No sugar. Use the syrup.'

The dog wandered over to the door to be let out and Genie stood up again, still dizzy. She let him out. 'Watch out for the pig,' she told him. 'It'll be hungry.' She took a deep breath, wincing at the pain in her chest. The air was surprisingly cold out there, the sun still lurking behind clouds. She turned to Marshall.

'So remote up here. How can you stand it?'

'I like the peace.'

'Drive me crazy, I think.'

'I used to live in town, but got tired of it. Discovered I liked the sound of the wind in the trees.'

Genie smiled. It was a good honest answer; she too loved the sound of fluttering leaves. She thought of Rian's mother. 'Ri's ma broke both her legs in a car crash. She makes Ri's life hell sometimes, but he looked after her well. Learned to cook and everything. I never met her, but she's got a boyfriend now who's pretty mean to Ri.'

'That why he left?'

She shook her head. 'Because of me. He saved me, but I'm not sure I'm worth saving. Nothing much goes right for me. Shit, I mean, a flash flood. Who was expecting that?'

'No one did. It was a freak event. You were lucky to survive. God might have a plan for you after all.'

Genie shook her head. 'Leave God out of it. It was God who got me all locked up in the first place and them all spitting and cursing at me.'

Marshall frowned.

'If I've got one prayer,' Genie added, 'it's for Reverend Bastard Schneider to have drowned and taken all his disciples with him. Far as I'm concerned, God is just an excuse to make people miserable all the time.'

Marshall was sympathetic to her anger. The girl looked hurt and suddenly quite frail. She'd been through a lot. He wasn't going to pry. She'd tell him or not, either way, it wasn't his business.

'I'm sorry I asked about your leg,' Genie told him. 'None of my business. I always ask stupid questions and get myself into trouble. One thing my mother got right about me. I always know how to make an embarrassing moment worse.'

'Actually, you probably do need to know,' Marshall attempted a reassuring smile. 'There's a lot you need to know, Genie. You might not believe me, but it has to be said. I'm hoping it might change your mind about what direction you and Rian take.'

'If you're going to tell me to go home, it won't work, I

can tell you that now. You've no idea of how crazy my mother is. She thinks I'm possessed. She believes I'm the devil's bride or something.' Genie could hardly even speak anymore. The sudden horror of home hit hard.

Marshall could see the distress on her face. Perhaps sometimes broken things couldn't be put back together.

The lump in Genie's throat was painful again. She wasn't as better as she thought.

'Why've you got all those cuttings pinned up in your bathroom? Why? Do you know where the kids are? Should I be afraid? I don't know what's happening any more. Life is stupid. Ri and me should be miles away from here by now.'

Marshall stirred some syrup into his coffee. He was trying to think of where to start. This girl had intelligent eyes, but would she believe anything he told her? He doubted it.

'It's complicated, but no, you don't have to be afraid of me, at least. Others, maybe.'

'But why the newspaper clippings of the missing kids? You got some upstairs too. I don't get it. It's weird. What's with those kids – did you know them? I need to know.'

'I began collecting the cuttings after my nephew, Dale, disappeared. Kind of puzzled me that no one was out there looking for them, y'know. Like they'd pray they'd

117

return in church, do the crying for the local paper, but secretly I suspected some folks were kind of glad these kids were out of their hair.'

Genie coughed, her chest sounded bubbly. She told herself to calm down, hear him out. It sounded exactly like her situation. She couldn't imagine her mother would ever care one way or the other.

'You kind of expect two or three kids to go a year. Disagreements, rows about drugs or unreasonable behaviour, any number of things can drive a wedge between parents and their kids. But it takes a lot to totally disappear. In other towns or cities, they go and they eventually call. Might be a month, maybe two, but they call collect, ask for money and turn up on the next Greyhound bus or whatever, looking a lot thinner. Everyone is just glad they got back safe.'

'You're dreaming if you think my ma would send me bus fare.'

'And that's what's odd about Spurlake. No one calls. No one comes home. OK, you'd expect some kids to be so angry about stuff they'll never call home, or at least one might end up arrested or something, somewhere, but no one *ever* hears from these kids again. Thirty-four now. Thirty-six with you and the boy. I started collecting the cuttings when I got home from my accident and I was living upstairs. Then I started getting these fits . . . I had a bad fall coming down the stairs last fall. I had to move downstairs permanently.'

He pointed to the wall and a photograph of himself by a chestnut horse looking younger, healthier, wearing shorts and with two healthy tanned legs. Genie looked at it more carefully. It was dated just four years earlier – but Marshall looked twenty years younger.

'How did you get so old so fast?' Instantly she put up a hand to apologize. 'Sorry, that sounded harsh.'

Marshall grimaced, unused to anyone being so blunt.

'I'm forty-five, Genie. Got a grown-up son of twenty-four. But you're right. I look sixty. Lot of things happened. Lot of things *still* happening to me. Nothing that can be fixed, I'm afraid.'

Genie swallowed with difficulty, her throat definitely sore again.

'I used to work at a place called the Fortress. You've probably seen their trucks in town. Fortransco Synetics is their real name. It's based in two buildings, pretty much equidistant from here. I believe you and the boy have already been close to the Synchro building during the flood when the riverbank collapsed. Topographically they are exactly level, if you understand that.'

Genie shook her head. 'Something to do with maps.'

119

'It's hard to grasp I think. Both are built at one hundred and sixty feet above sea level. Identical twenty storey buildings, but one is underground, buried under the mountain below the reservoir. There's thirty-five kilometres between them, but you could draw a straight line between the floors of each building and they'd line up. Their real purpose, secret.'

Genie sipped her hot coffee to numb her throat.

'There's a huge hydro-electric power station down the valley fed by the Spur river and a reservoir not far from here. The generators can produce 1,350 megawatts of power at peak. Fully operational it might use up to 10,000 gigawatt-hours of electricity in one year. Might mean nothing to you, but that's a lot of power and not one volt of it feeds into the national grid. That's secret two. There's pylons marching off into the distance but they connect to nothing. The whole power station was built just for the Fortress.'

'The Fortress is like military stuff?'

Marshall shook his head.

'Fortransco Synetics is a private, but military-funded, experimental site.'

'And you worked there?' Genie had vague memories of seeing a white Fortransco truck in Spurlake from time to time. Never thought much about it.

'I was a researcher. I was there from the beginning when it was something UTEC University was interested in. Just theory in the beginning, you understand. We got a little funding, attracted some attention and we tried a few experiments but we never really had powerful enough computers or enough electric power to make a difference. Then Fortransco came along and invested billions. Built fantastic new facilities – gave us everything we wanted. It changed everything, but they were always pushing for results. It's hard science, frontier stuff, and results don't come easy. We needed a breakthrough, or we knew they'd want to close us down.

'One day we tried for a big leap. We knew that unless we could prove it worked, the money would dry up and we'd all lose our jobs.

'We set up this huge test. Grabbed all the hydro power we could and it actually worked. For three crucial seconds, it actually worked . . . before it blew up and took my leg with it. Nearly took my mind too.'

Genie frowned. Tried to imagine what it would be like to have your leg blown off.

'I was pretty badly shook up for a few months. I was sent to a specialist burns hospital in Toronto. They taught me how to walk again. Never could fix the fits though. That's what I must have had last night. It's like I get an electric shock and my brain shuts down. They say it's epilepsy but I know it isn't. I got rewired that day and nothing has been right since. Hardly anyone recognized me when I returned. You're right. I look twenty years older.

'I was retired on full pension. I guess they didn't think I'd live so long.'

Genie didn't understand what this had to do with her or the missing kids.

'You look disappointed,' Marshall said.

'I don't get the connection. You lost your leg, but that's not unusual around Spurlake what with so many guys killing trees for a living.'

'Ah, you're a tree-hugger.'

'I respect trees. They're here for a reason. They help the planet breathe,' she replied defensively. Being Green in Spurlake wasn't an easy choice.

Marshall shrugged. 'Well we weren't killing trees, OK. We were experimenting with matter transfer. You know what that means?'

Genie shook her head still unimpressed.

'Teleportation. That mean anything to you?'

Genie blinked, then laughed. 'You mean, like *Star Trek*? Beaming up Scotty and stuff? No way.' She laughed again, not mocking, but caught by surprise. 'Really?

Teleportation? Isn't that just science fiction? I mean . . .'

Marshall took a swig of his coffee. 'I knew you wouldn't believe me. Sixty years ago the idea of everyone having a telephone in their pockets was science fiction. Our whole way of life is science fiction, if you look at it from the past.'

'And you invented teleportation?'

'No. I told you, I was a researcher. We were working on the Steeple project for NASA. They had this idea of setting up a base on the moon and once you had that, well you wouldn't need rockets to get up there anymore. It's easy to swallow a billion dollars on a project like that. It was cancelled in the mid-Nineties. I was seconded to another parallel project based here, but that too was cancelled in '98.

'I was taken on by Fortransco, who had development money and could get things done. My specialism is genetic holding patterns. DNA stability in photon transmission.'

Genie almost made sense of that. 'Like making sure your arms and legs come out in the right order.'

He smiled. 'I knew you were bright.'

'And they're still experimenting? They made it work yet? It would be cool to go anywhere you wanted without using a plane or car . . .'

'And that's why the money pours in to develop it.

Only it was hijacked by the military and some other investors. Think about it, Genie, you could ship a whole division of GIs to a trouble spot, catch the locals unawares and you'd stop a revolution or take out a dictator in no time at all. They'd never see you coming.'

Genie frowned. 'Sounded better when it was aiming for the moon. So, how does this connect to the kids on your bathroom wall?'

'It's connected. The people in charge now. They're new. Got a different agenda. They are searching for something else entirely.'

'What?'

'Eternal life.'

Genie laughed with surprise. It sounded like a sick joke. 'Eternal life? Who'd want to live forever? Why?'

'We were supposed to be developing teleportation. Matter transference. But, and this is theory only, you could take out the ageing genes. You could add new DNA strings, renew, replenish, rebuild. Every ten years you could completely renew yourself. Discard fat, old skin, thinning hair, renew your heart, lungs, liver. It's Pearson's Law.'

'Pearson?'

'Whatever your purpose in experimentation is, you will find three alternative uses for it and each one will be greater than your first idea. Pearson invented a chewing gum that never lost its flavour.'

'No such thing.'

'Of course there isn't. You'd never need to spit it out. The gum business would go under overnight. What he was really looking for was something to make gum disintegrate on the sidewalks in the rain. I knew him. He's just one of the many bums on Hastings now. Total breakdown. No one even cares. That's what happened at the Fortress and the missing kids are part of it.'

Genie knew what he was going to tell her. Knew everything suddenly. 'They're experimenting on these kids.'

Marshall nodded. 'I can't prove it. I don't even want to believe it, but somehow the kids know how to hook up with the Fortress and—'

'Rian thinks some kids are finding it on some chat forum. It's aimed at kids thinking about suicide. Y'know, promising money for participating in experiments. All you have to do is get to some place near here and they'll pick you up and pay you two thousand dollars.'

Marshall looked surprised. 'I hope you're kidding. I need to speak to my son about that. He'd be interested – he's been trying to find a link for a while now.'

'Promise any kid two thousand dollars for doing practically nothing, you're going to get plenty of volunteers,' Genie said with a shrug.

'Not you though?'

'I might be crazy, but experiments? No way. You really think all those kids on your bathroom wall were suicidal? Spurlake's a snake pit, but I don't believe it.'

'You and Rian made it thirty-six. That's how it grows. God knows how many more disappeared in the flood.'

Marshall searched his dressing gown pockets and took out his pipe. He stared at her for a while before speaking again.

'If they ended up at the Fortress, those kids are dead, for sure. I don't have any proof of course. Teleportation is an impossible quest. You can't keep it stable. It's possible there will never be enough computer memory to keep that much information stable for any length of time.'

Genie was thinking about a face on the wall. She was thinking about a boy in a glass building, a boy called Denis Malone. Was he a dream or was he real?

'Denis Malone,' she said suddenly. 'Is he on your wall?'

'I don't know. Perhaps.'

Genie left the table. Ran out of the room towards Marshall's bathroom. She had an urgent need to see all their faces. She arrived short of breath, her chest was tight as a drum and the porridge still burned in her stomach. She sat on the edge of the bath and stared at the wall in the gloom of the unlit bathroom.

Sixth picture. Denis looked just like he had in her dream. The room began to move, the pictures on the wall shook loose. Denis slid off his poster, other kids began to do the same. She was hallucinating, but she checked them all, the photographs were disappearing, one by one, they were going, sliding into the bath. Her eyes began to flutter, she felt light as a feather again, sensed she was falling.

Denis was kneeling beside her. She was back in the glass building, lying on the floor beside the computers. It was warm. Denis was smiling.

'You came back.'

'Denis?'

Other faces came into view. Some boys, a couple of girls, one she knew vaguely as Julia. They were almost naked or wearing odd one-piece body stockings. Something was wrong with their skin, some had arms and necks that were red or burned like they'd been over exposed at a tanning store, but they all looked happy to see her.

'Where am I? Who? What's going on?'

'It's the Fortress, Genie. You're in the Fortress.'

'But how?'

'You're next,' Denis told her. 'We've seen the list.'

A girl with red hair came forward and gave her a hand

127

to pull her up. Genie grasped it and although she felt an electric static shock, the hand passed through her own and she fell back.

'I don't get it?'

'We're here, Genie. We're alive. You'll be here soon. We know it.'

'No!' Genie protested. 'I'm not going there. I can't go there.'

Denis pressed a hand to Genie's shoulder. Her skin fizzed a little, even though she couldn't feel any substance.

'We're waiting for you, Genie. You can get us out. You're the one.'

'Get you out of what?'

'The Fortress,' several called out at once.

Genie shook her head.

'Denis, I don't understand? You haven't changed a bit. Do you stop growing here? What are they doing to you? How do you get here?'

There was a sharp electronic noise that hurt Genie's ears. A red light began to flash around her and abruptly they were gone.

Genie rubbed her sore head. She discovered she'd fallen in the bathroom. Woke to find Marshall was putting a plaster on her forehead.

'Cut your head on the bath. You're going to have a nasty bruise.'

She couldn't speak. She'd been inside the Fortress and the kids were alive! She glanced at the wall. The cuttings were all still there. She looked more closely at a Japanese girl. Miho Tanaka. She had been standing behind Denis, silently watching her. She'd been missing two years, like Denis. Several of the faces on the wall were familiar and none of them had aged. How was that possible?

'I was there,' Genie whispered. 'They're still alive, Marshall. I'm telling you. They're *all* still alive.'

'Best you lie down a while, girl. I got to feed that pig of yours.'

He walked her out of his bedroom and over to the old leather sofa in the lobby where she let him sit her down, swing her legs over. He put a cushion under her feet. 'You stay put for a while, OK? You're still sick and you need rest.'

And then he was gone.

Rian woke suddenly. There was someone in the room. He saw movement. A light was flickering, then came on bright. Somewhere a radio snapped on and music floated up from below. 'Genie?' he mumbled. He turned, realizing that the sheets he was lying on were damp. His throat was red raw, he felt twenty pounds lighter and he had a pit of despair in his stomach.

He saw the flicker of movement again and turned. He saw nothing but the window and the sunlight casting a shadow on the wooden floor.

He sat up. He blinked. There was a girl sat right across the room from him staring at him. It wasn't Genie. Then the girl was gone, vanished, didn't move a muscle, but vanished all the same. He decided he was delirious. He'd just seen a weird ginger-haired girl with wild green eyes and bushy eyebrows. He had to be going crazy. 'Genie?' he cried out again, but his voice was weak and he sensed no one could hear him.

He walked unsteadily on weak legs to the bathroom. The sun was pouring in through a small window. How many days had he missed? As he emptied his bladder, he was looking at the yellowing newspaper cuttings on the wall. He was startled to see the girl. Renée Cullins, from Cedarville. Colour of hair – ginger-red, particular markings: broad eyebrows, green eyes, small tattoo of a rose on back. Hadn't seen the tattoo, but the hair and those eyes were exactly her. This girl had been in the bedroom watching him. What the hell was going on? He shook his head. He was absolutely delusional.

He tested the water in the sink. It was surprisingly hot.

The power was back on. He took a shower and felt a million times better for it.

'Hey, not fair. I wanted a shower. Don't use all the hot water, OK?'

Genie was looking at him. She was smiling. She was real. Please God, he hoped she was real. She had a nasty bruise on her head and a small plaster on a cut.

'How do you feel?' she asked, stripping off to join him in the shower.

'You coming in here?' Rian asked nervously. He hadn't been expecting that.

Genie laughed. 'Yeah. You shy? You've been lying next to me naked and sweating like a pig for days – so I'm sure you can't be so shy, Rian Tulane.'

Rian got out of the shower. He wasn't ready for this. Nearly lost his balance too, his legs were made of rubber. Genie blew him a kiss and walked under the hot spray.

'Hell, I need this. I stink. I washed our clothes. Power came back on four hours ago. Nearly jumped out my skin when the radio came on.'

'You OK? What happened to your head?' Rian asked, quickly covering himself with her towel. She was acting so spookily normal. She really seemed happy. Just like the girl he'd fallen for so many months ago.

'Fell, knocked myself out.' She shampooed her hair.

131

'Lot of weird stuff to tell you, but I'm glad your fever's gone. You are better, right? There's oatmeal to heat up in the kitchen. Just add some milk. It's still OK.'

'Where's the old guy?' Rian asked.

'Gone to Cedarville to get provisions.'

'You trust him?'

'I guess. Hey, you stole my towel. Can you find me another? God, it's so good to be clean. You look like hell, by the way. Who's Renée?'

Rian nearly jumped out of his skin. 'Renée?'

'You were talking about her in your sleep.'

'I was not.'

'Sure you were. I came up an hour ago and you were going, "Oh Renée, Renée," like she was loving you up. Someone I should know?'

This was too much. 'I was not talking to anyone called Renée.'

'I didn't say you were talking, but she was . . .'

Genie had rinsed off the shampoo and was looking at Rian and what he was staring at. She turned to face the wall and the missing kids newspaper clippings.

'There's more of these downstairs in his bathroom. Thirty-four in all. Can you believe that? Every kid missing from Spurlake and Cedarville, right the way up to Lytton, not counting us.' She was looking at the seventh one along. Renée Cullins – aged fourteen when she'd gone missing last year. She looked back at Rian and he seemed utterly freaked. 'What? Was she here? Did you see her?'

Rian handed her a fresh towel from the cupboard as Genie turned off the shower. 'She was sitting in the room, watching me. I wasn't talking to her. I was asleep. I don't get it. How did she get here?'

Genie now knew for certain that the same thing had happened to both of them.

'Don't be spooked. They just want to talk, they're lonely, I think.'

Rian was looking for his clothes. He wasn't sure how to deal with this or just how normal Genie seemed to think it was.

'Are they . . . are they ghosts?'

Genie smiled. 'Uh-uh.' She leaned forward and kissed Rian on the shoulder. He put out a hand towards her, still nervous about the whole situation for some reason.

'They aren't ghosts. They're alive. They're alive just like me or you.'

'But why here?'

'Because they can, I guess. I fell and hit my head on the bath downstairs. See the bump on my head? They came to me when I was out. Denis first, came with a few friends. Then later when I was lying down. Denis thinks we can help them. I told Marshall about him. His picture is on the bathroom wall downstairs. Marshall says all the kids are dead. I told him they weren't, but he didn't believe me.'

Rian didn't understand either. He was annoyed he couldn't find his clothes. He discovered he was embarrassed to be naked with Genie and feeling dizzy and hungry too. Everything was just a little crazy now.

'I never knew you were so shy. It's kinda cute. Your clothes are in the dryer downstairs. Don't worry, no one is going to steal them.'

Rian felt his throat and tried to swallow. God, it hurt. Genie was so damn beautiful, so damn happy. He was being an idiot. He knew that. He was just freaked by everything, that was all. Wasn't well yet.

'You need food,' Genie told him. 'Oatmeal practically killed me when I ate it but it's kept me going all day.' She suddenly remembered something. 'Oh yeah, the pig's back. Ate a ton of stuff that wouldn't keep and she looks so happy on the lawn.'

Rian finally smiled. Genie couldn't be beat. She always knew how to make him feel good. He grabbed her and pulled her close. 'Love you, Gen.'

Genie pulled away a moment. 'That's what you told

134

Renée an hour ago. You sure it's me?'

Rian frowned. Then smiled again, realizing she was joking. 'Everything's too crazy for me. Way too crazy.'

Rian spread out a map of the Cascades Mountain region on the kitchen table, while Genie was sifting through a ton of clothes from goodwill bags she'd found under the stairs. Stuff that must have belonged to Marshall's ex-wife and his kid when he was younger.

'God, shoulder pads. This is like an Eighties' treasure trove.' She held up a sparkly sweater for Rian to see and he laughed.

Genie coughed and it hurt her chest. 'We both need to take another pill, I think. Marshall said we had to finish the course.'

Rian was studying the map. 'He said it was called the Fortress? You sure? It isn't on the map.'

'It's a nickname. Is there a reservoir? It has to be close to the hydro power station. He said it was huge.'

'There's nothing on this map. Not even the first place we washed up near. That glass building. I mean it was a big glass tower, right? They don't even have any road that leads to it.'

'You sure you're looking in the right place?'

Rian nodded. He checked the date on the map. 'It's

only a year old. They can't leave stuff off. I mean . . . can they?'

'Power's on. Google it. Google can see everything.'

Rian smiled. 'Genius. OK, where's his computer?'

They went looking for it. Tried every room, but couldn't locate it. There wasn't even a satellite dish outside, now they thought about it.

'You can't live out here without a connection, surely,' Rian was saying. But they both knew somehow that Marshall had, had deliberately cut himself off from the whole world. Perhaps the ex-wife had driven him over the edge.

An hour later they were standing upstairs when they heard a vehicle's wheels crunch on the gravel outside. Rian looked at Genie.

'Kill the light.'

She dashed for the switch.

They ran to the window, pulling the blind to one side. Marshall was slowly climbing out of his old Chevy truck, the dog excitedly running around his legs.

'We'd better go down,' Rian began, but halted, pulling Genie back.

Another SUV came in behind Marshall's. Rian recognized the driver and the four-by-four pick-up.

'It's a Spurlake cop. Bastard called the cops.' He turned to Genie. 'Grab stuff. We got to go.'

Genie ran for the bedroom.

'Don't forget the pills and sweaters.'

Genie grabbed as much as she could, frantically looking for a bag to stuff them into.

Rian watched the cop help Marshall in with his packages. Never seen a cop do that before, but . . . a cop's a cop and he'd want to take them back to town.

Genie was back, breathless. 'We can climb out by the back bedroom, get on to the garage roof and drop down.'

Rian was annoyed. He knew neither one of them was well enough to leave the farm. They needed another day at least to get over this infection and he still didn't know which way to go. Worse, he'd left the map down on the kitchen table.

'Come on,' Genie was whispering. 'We've got to go.'

They jumped down to the garage roof and from there down to the backyard. Genie caught her sweater on a nail and heard it rip. She swore. It was so dark and cold. There was a clear sky overhead filled with stars. The moon hadn't risen yet. There was no way they'd get far in this dense blackness.

'Damn, it's freezing, not supposed to be this cold

yet. We should have brought blankets,' Rian told her, grabbing her hand.

They ran for the trees. Genie was full of regret. Too late, she realized that she'd grown to like it here.

Marshall was making coffee. His son came back down the stairs with a piece of paper in his hands. He entered the kitchen, patted the dog and sat down.

'I guess they ran when they saw my uniform.'

'That was stupid. They're sick. They survived the flood, but it's going to be very chilly tonight. Temperatures plummeting. Weather's gone crazy. It's still August for God's sake, not supposed to be this cold yet at night. Damn it, son, I told you to wait behind till I spoke with them. They were bound to run when they saw your uniform.'

Miller sighed. 'You didn't tell them I was a cop? You get any names?'

'No, never got around to telling them. Didn't want to spook them. Girl's called Genie. Boy's Ri, or something. They're good kids. Not your usual runaways. She says he rescued her. Probably a romantic notion.'

Miller frowned. 'Genie? Well that's a turn up. I figured she'd drowned for sure.'

'You know her?'

138

'Not exactly, but she wasn't lying. She was rescued from hell. I've met her mother and that fool Reverend Schneider. That girl must have a real will to live because she was seriously abused, Dad. I can't prove anything, but there was something evil in her home and it sure wasn't her.'

'She mentioned this Reverend Schneider. Seems her mother is close to him.'

'He's got a lot of influence in town. Leads marches and vigils every time a kid goes missing. He's got half the town believing Satan's coming for their kids.'

Marshall looked at his son and sighed. 'Well she's really scared of him. You going to call it in, play dog-catcher?'

Miller shrugged. He was reluctant.

'Any idea where they're headed?'

Marshall pointed to the map on the kitchen table.

'Your guess is as good as mine. I tried to warn the girl off. They were a bit freaked out by the clippings in my bathroom. She knows one of the kids.'

'All of us know one of the kids. We've already been through this, Dad. The Chief went to the Fortress twice in the past year and saw nothing suspicious. The kids are going somewhere, sure, but not there. There's absolutely no evidence—'

'Son, Genie saw something at Synchro Research

plant. She claims she met one of the kids there. I know you don't believe in "phenomena" but she says she saw Denis Malone and I believe her.'

'Malone? Dad, listen to yourself. Malone is dead and buried. You know that. If she saw a ghost, well OK, let her believe it, but I know the Malone kid is dead.'

'Son, one day something will happen to make you see what's really going on. Someone is using these runaways, experimenting on them, and I'd hate it if those two kids were a part of that. Genie mentioned something about a chat forum? You know these things better than me. Something about a suicide help link and offering two grand to take part in experiments in BC.' He held up his hands. 'I'm not saying people at the Fortress are trying to attract loners and misfits, but . . .' He shrugged. 'Ask around. If one kid knows, others do.'

Miller nodded. 'I've heard stuff like that. We've got a cyber-crime officer in Hope I could talk to. She could try to trace that. There was rumour about an influenza research centre offering money. Never found it, but I had some parents insisting their kids had gone there. That's the Web for you. Everything's rumours and scams.'

'Follow it up. Has no one found any traces of these other kids?'

Miller shook his head. 'Not a one. And it won't get easier. Have you any idea how trashed Spurlake is right now? We had a major flood, Dad. There's two hundred dead, maybe more. Whole streets went underwater. As if the business climate wasn't bad enough for the town, now this. I just came to see you to make sure you're OK at least.'

'I'm fine. I just wish those kids hadn't run. As unhappy as they may have been at home, nothing is worse than what will happen to them at the Fortress.'

Miller grabbed his coffee. 'You don't even know they're headed there. And let's not argue about all that again. You said yourself that all that stuff you researched was never likely to happen in my lifetime.'

'You can't ignore that over thirty-four or more kids have gone missing from around Spurlake and there's the fact of the Fortress experimenting with transmission of matter. I think someone there has crossed a line. Someone should investigate. I just don't want those kids to wind up there, that's all.'

'I'm not arguing about the Fortress again. They pay their taxes, they've contributed a lot of money to help build shelters after this flood, they are good corporate citizens. I'll look for the kids, but if they're in the forest at night, they're lost, Dad. They won't get far. I've got to head back anyways. The bridge is out and it's a two-hour trip to get here now.'

'That's another thing. I told them the bridge was in the wrong place when they were building it.'

'Well you can tell them again when they start repairs. By the way, you know there's a pig out there? When did you start with pigs?'

Marshall grinned.

'Should be good for some quality bacon a few months from now.'

Miller picked up his hat. 'Flood took out more than a hundred and fifty homes in the town. We've got a makeshift camp up by Princeton Park and they're flying in tents and stuff. About five hundred people displaced and who knows how many missing. Your runaways were lucky, now I think about it. The part of Maple Street the girl lived on was torn apart. We've got mud and debris everywhere. The trailer parks by the river were just completely trashed. Flooded your favourite coffee shop too.'

'McBean's?' Marshall was quite disappointed. It was the oldest pastry shop in Spurlake. He'd eaten there as a boy when it was called Schram and Swelter's Continental Coffee Parlour.

'They're fixing it up as fast as they can. Many of the

historic buildings in town stand, but everything's knee high in mud. The new civic offices took a real beating. Floodwaters just sliced through them. Gonna take a while to get straight and the insurance people are claiming "Act of God" so no payouts. The Premier has allocated emergency funds to clear it up, but people are angry.'

'Same flood happened in '77,' Marshall remembered. 'That's why I told you to buy up on the ridge. Just because it hasn't flooded for thirty years, doesn't mean it won't. No one remembers anything, no one learns anything. I told the mayor, you need brick and stone at street level in Spurlake, not glass.'

'Well, thank God I listened to you, for once.' Miller grinned and drank his coffee quickly. 'Better check out the forest. If they're smart, they'll find a hollow and huddle up. You're right, going to be a cold one tonight. What the hell happened to our summer? Shortest ever.' He looked back at his dad and smiled. 'And no, I don't want another lecture on climate change. Take it easy, Dad. Look after yourself better, please.'

143

# 13

## Lost

The cough was getting worse. Genie could feel it building. Walking in a cold forest probably wasn't the best way to beat this thing. Rian wasn't doing well either, his fever had returned. They had been gone just an hour by her reckoning, but neither one of them could walk much further and they hadn't made much progress. It was really dark. Rian had sworn there was a track but they hadn't seen anything of it and he felt annoyed with himself for being so stupid. Genie was just disappointed about leaving the house without a plan. They were plain lost.

'We don't know where we're going, do we?'

Rian said nothing. He was shivering, regretting leaving the house, regretting a lot of things.

'We could go back,' Genie said. 'We could go back and—'

'We can't go back, Genie. We can't. They'd take you. I can go home. You . . .' He coughed. His chest sounded real bad.

Genie remained silent for a while. It was freezing and the forest seemed to have closed in on them. The weather seemed to have gone from summer to fall in one day.

'Besides,' Rian added a moment later, 'I've no idea which way we came from, let alone which way to go forward. I'm sorry, Gen, I just can't think.'

Genie took his hand. She had no words of comfort. They had gotten themselves into this mess.

'We have to go back. Get warm, Ri. We're still sick.'

'We can't, we . . .'

That's when they heard a dog barking. Rian felt his heart miss a beat. Police dog. He'd let Genie down. They would be found, be separated again. He'd done everything wrong, made Genie's life worse, not better. He felt like he was standing on the edge of a great canyon, about to fall to his death.

'We've got to move.'

'Where? I can't see anything but one tree ahead. You said there was a track but . . .'

'I lost the track. I'm sorry. I lost the track,' Rian mumbled.

'We could climb?'

'Dog will just sit and wait for the cop to arrive.'

'Then what?' Genie heard the desperation in her own voice.

The dog was suddenly on them. It jumped up on Genie. It seemed real pleased to see her. 'What? Hey boy?' Genie was thinking that this was one hell of a tame police dog. Weren't they supposed to bite you or pin you to the ground?

'Hey, it's Moucher,' she exclaimed, bending down and hugging it. 'You found us.'

Rian was puzzled.

'That you, Genie?' Marshall shouted from out of the darkness. He flipped on his flashlight, flooding the area with light. He stood some twenty metres away.

'You might also want to give me a hand getting back. Not easy walking for me out here. Next time you run off into the woods, take the firebreak. You're both headed for the ravine and it's a hundred-metre sudden drop hereabouts.'

Rian glanced at Genie. They could run but it would do them no good. Look stupid running from a man with a tin leg.

'My son, Max, has gone. He's a cop in Spurlake, visits every week.. Genie, got to tell you that your house was badly damaged in the flood. Seems you were very lucky Rian broke you out of there when he did.'

'Ri's sick, Marshall. I think he's got a chill.'

'Don't surprise me one bit. We got ourselves an

early frost on the way. Good for the apples, but little else. Come on. I've got a fire burning and there's a chicken in the oven that needs eating.'

'What about us?' Rian asked, sneezing violently.

'First you both got to get well. Let's get you out of this damn forest. You didn't happen to notice how cold it is out here? Don't they teach you city kids anything? Never leave home without a flashlight and a compass.'

They reluctantly followed him out of the forest. The track was apparently a hundred metres to their right. If they'd found it they'd have been a long way away by now or more likely dead at the bottom of the ravine. Fate makes plans for you and never consults.

'Moucher found you both with no trouble at all. Think he's fallen for you, Genie.'

'I was planning to kidnap him first chance I got,' Genie replied. 'Trade him for the pig.'

'That would be fair,' Marshall replied, chuckling to himself.

Marshall felt Rian's forehead as he drew alongside.

'You've got a fever, Rian. You can't just outrun sickness y'know. You have to give your body some time to build up strength.'

'Why are you helping us?' Genie asked, as they started towards the house.

'Because I don't want you to end up like all the other kids on my wall.'

'Your son think they ended up at the Fortress too?' Rian asked, his voice a croak now.

'My son thinks I'm crazy and I should mind my own business.'

Genie linked her arm through Marshall's to help him along (and steal some of his heat).

'We have to help them, Marshall,' she said.

'Who?'

'The kids. I know you don't believe me or understand, but they're alive. I just know they're alive.'

# 14

# Synchro

It had been three days since they'd returned to the house after their embarrassing episode in the forest. Three days of Ri coughing and being sick with a high fever. It was a mean virus. The antibiotics were taking their time to fix him. Marshall wanted him to see a doctor but Ri refused. He just had to sweat it out. Genie was pretty clear of it now. Whatever the pills didn't do for Ri, they had beaten it off in her.

She had found pens and a notebook and started sketching again. It comforted her to draw, although Moucher was a terrible fidget. She worked on getting Ri's frown just right as he slept too. She didn't know if she was any good, but it made her happy.

Marshall had been working on his truck for a couple of days as Genie nursed Rian and she'd kept him going with snacks. She'd been trying to get his house straight – cleaning stuff that hadn't been touched for years. He never said anything but at least there was light coming through the windows now and she'd put lots of linen and sheets out on the bushes for airing since he didn't possess a line. Just because you only had one leg it was no excuse to ignore dirt and fresh air.

They were drinking coffee in the afternoon. Marshall had been trying to explain the science behind the Fortress to Genie and she was having a hard time understanding.

Genie had fed the pig, who'd taken to coming around every day and rubbing up against the swing chair on the stoop to get her attention. She absently watched it eat slops as she drank the coffee.

'I don't get where the Swiss came in. I think I got lost there.'

Marshall tried again. 'There's a huge multi-billion dollar project they built over in Geneva called CERN where they built this Large Hadron Collider, a particle accelerator that is sort of looking for the source of the universe. It generated so much data, they had to build a new kind of data storage system that could cope with it. They call it the Grid. It's superfast, generates fantastic parallel processing power, using fibre optics to connect between centres. Some people from Switzerland joined the Fortress project about three years ago and they rebuilt it up from scratch using the Grid processing system. There's nearly a hundred thousand servers involved using dynamic switching to talk to each other; the energy they use is just unimaginable.

To get an idea, it's more than ten thousand times faster than the internet people use at home. And this is what they think will make it possible to process the data fast enough to digitize DNA and transmit it from one place to another without dropping an atom. Without the Grid they would be nowhere. And this is only the beginning, right? It can only get faster.'

Genie rolled her eyes. 'I think I got it. The bigger and faster it is, the more stuff they can get through it. You think they will make it work?'

'None of this would have been possible unless we knew how to map the human genome. Genome holds the code for all the hundreds of thousand differing proteins and billions of molecules a body needs. Something like six billion "bases" per person. That was my job, building the sequence and making sure it came out the same way it went in. That's the tough part of the science. One day, everyone will have their genome data on backup some place and if you lost an arm or leg or if a liver malfunctioned, we would be able to rebuild it using your own data. That's what everyone wants a piece of here. The real problem comes with who owns your DNA – who owns that arm or leg once it's built?'

Genie just shook her head. Like she was supposed to understand what the hell he was talking about.

Marshall stood up and walked over to his truck. He pointed to the linen and the sky.

'Wind's coming up. Get this packed away, Genie. Got an experiment I want to try. We can pick up my mail on the way.'

Genie put her mug down. She was surprised he wanted to go anywhere. She quickly grabbed the linen off the bushes and folded them. She was puzzled. What exactly was he going to do?

'We be gone long? I'll put some water by Ri's bed maybe.'

'Couple of hours at most.'

'Where we going?'

'You'll see.'

Ri was asleep when she went up. She mopped his brow, freshened his water and kissed his forehead. She whispered in his ear.

'Please get better soon, babe. I need you back.'

Marshall got into the truck and started her up. She purred into action and he looked happy for once. 'My Dad bought this truck new two hundred thousand Ks ago. Back in '68. They used to make stuff that lasted back then.'

Genie saw Moucher run after them, but stop dead at

the gate. She wished he could have come too.

'Hold on tight,' Marshall told her. 'Some of the pot-holes around here are brutal on your ass.'

They drove down several rough and ready forest roads, Genie hanging on to the strap real tight. He hadn't been kidding about the state of the roads. Genie lost track of how far it was but Marshall seemed to know the route pretty good. They stopped by the General Store at the crossroads and emptied his mailbox. Junk mail mostly.

'Going to be a dramatic sunset,' Marshall remarked as they started off again.

The sky was already glowing pink and they had a great view from the ridge. They bounced down another track – a huge modern building dominating the skyline ahead. Eventually Marshall parked his truck behind a boulder about one hundred metres from the glass tower, so they couldn't be seen easily. Below them they could see the fresh breach in the riverbank and where a bulldozer had pushed rocks and earth to fill it in again. The river had reverted back to its old course now and seemed almost placid.

'This is Synchro. I'm guessing you guys came in through that breach and the fast current took you all

153

south-east. There's acres of farmland underwater still. You were lucky the power went down, could have been electrocuted anytime.'

'I can't believe I walked so far. We've been driving for ages.'

'That's because the lower road got washed out. We had to take the long way. It's not as far as you think to my farm. The Synchro building is identical to the Fortress, except, like I said, the Fortress is underground thirty-five kilometres south of here.'

Synchro looked totally out of place in the fields, like someone stole a skyscraper from Vancouver when no one was looking. Marshall took out his field glasses and began scanning the building.

'The flood did a lot of damage,' Marshall was saying as he surveyed the scene below. 'Made one hell of a mess. You say you were in there?'

Genie squinted her eyes, looking down at the glass building. It had been pitch black when she had entered.

'It's bigger than I remembered,' she muttered. In truth she was no longer sure of anything.

'How did you get in?'

'I don't remember that.'

Marshall looked at her and frowned again.

'You *were* in there?'

Genie snatched a look at him and shrugged. 'I don't remember much now. Sorry. I just know I saw Denis in there.'

Marshall sighed.

'Can you remember how you got out? The security is real tight. I know there must have been confusion in the flooding.'

Genie's eyes fluttered as she tried to concentrate. Suddenly she was no longer so sure she had been in there, but she *knew* she had. She closed her eyes, her breathing slowed and she crossed her feet. 'There's two stairways. There's rows and rows of computer servers and there's . . .' she could see it more clearly now, 'a diagram. A huge diagram on a wall by the main stairs. Like a human body, a man, naked, with a triangle across him, like something out of history books.'

Marshall was watching her closely, the sweat on her brow and just above her lips – she was almost in a trance and he was fascinated. Her hands were suspended in mid-air. He wasn't sure what was happening to her, but he knew some part of her had somehow left the truck. 'I know that drawing. Da Vinci sketch,' he told her gently. 'You're on the mezzanine above the lobby. Turn to your left, Genie, there's some glass doors.'

Genie turned. She could see the doors and the glowing

155

red keypad beside it. 'It's locked.'

'Try twenty-seven-six-nine,' Marshall told her. 'Push the buttons on the pad. Twenty-seven-six-nine.'

Genie moved forward to the keypad and entered the numbers. The doors opened. She moved in. She was vaguely aware that she was now in the building and somehow simultaneously still in the truck. She didn't feel afraid. She felt like a ghost exploring a castle it once owned. It was almost exhilarating. 'I can see people working. There's men working on big computers, got hundreds of cables all over the floor.'

'They're servicing the mainframes. They get overheated.' Marshall kept his voice totally steady – guiding her, fascinated by her trance. 'What else can you see?'

'There's a glass corridor leading to . . .'

'The teleportation chamber. You're quite safe. No one can see you. Walk naturally.'

Genie walked, aware that she felt light and very, very warm. There were warning signs everywhere. *Authorized personnel only.*

Suddenly Denis was there. He opened the doors ahead of her and smiled. 'I told you you could make it.'

'Denis!' She felt a surge of optimism. 'You're all right.'

'Come with me.'

'Where are we going?'

156

'I'm going to take you to the Fortress. This is Synchro. It's the twin of the Fortress. Everything's identical.'

'I'm scared, Denis.'

'We're waiting for you.'

'I don't want to go there, Denis. I don't want to go.'

'You won't get hurt. We need you, Genie.'

'Why?'

'You can help us. You can help all of us.'

'How? I can't help anyone.'

She found herself in the teleportation chamber. It was a huge sterile space, completely white, with a concave raised platform. Sixteen round glass shapes with thousands of microscopic holes, like giant showerheads, protruded from the top and another sixteen were built into the smooth polished steel base.

'Here,' Denis was showing her. 'This is where they try to send people from the Fortress. You can see what happened to the last ones. They haven't cleaned it off yet.'

Genie was looking at shadows on the wall. You could just make out the human outlines. 'What happened?'

'Carbon blowback. Happens all the time. Either that or . . .'

Genie felt a rising fear. Denis wanted her to use this thing to get to the Fortress.

'No,' Genie shouted. 'I'm not going with you, Denis. I don't want to be . . .'

'Like me? You will be. Reverend Schneider is looking for you. He's collecting souls.'

'What? Collecting souls? Then you really are dead?'

'I'm not dead,' he insisted. 'I'm not. None of us are.' He stood on the platform looking upset and disappointed with her. 'You'd better go home then. Renée says Rian is sick.'

Genie felt a pang of jealousy. 'Why does she hang around Ri? I don't like it. Why does she just sit there and watch him?'

Denis looked puzzled. 'Don't you know? Renée's his sister.'

Genie was angry now. 'He doesn't have a sister.'

Denis smiled. 'He does now.'

Genie felt short of breath.

'I don't understand anything. How did I get here? What do you want from me?'

'Too late,' Denis told her suddenly, his expression changing to fear. 'He's here.'

He vanished. The lights flooded on in the room and she could hear voices approaching. There was absolutely nowhere to hide. She turned and there entering the chamber was her nemesis, Reverend Schneider. He stared at her in total surprise – he could see her! He dropped whatever he was carrying and swore.

Panic took hold of her. She slipped past him and sprinted back along the corridor, heart in mouth, frantically trying to remember the security code. Behind her he shouted, 'Stop her!' She reached the glass doors, but couldn't see the keypad to enter the code. Heavy footsteps behind her and then suddenly fat calloused hands around her neck.

'Got you,' said Reverend Schneider.

She suddenly heard screaming.

# 15

## Soul Fever

She woke – the screaming still in her ears. Marshall was holding her hands. She was bathed in sweat. Only slowly did Genie realize that they were still in the truck and it was *her* screaming. She sucked in air, desperate to breathe. It was dark. She had missed the sunset.

'It's all right, it's OK, you're safe now. You're safe.'

Genie shook. She could still see Reverend Schneider, feel his sweaty hands on her neck – and he had definitely seen her. She felt sick. She opened the door and spewed out on to the dirt. She heaved again, sweat pouring off her face as she clung on to the door and groaned.

Behind her Marshall had started the engine. 'Got to go,' he was saying.

Genie closed the door again, wiping her mouth on the back of her sleeve. She sat in silence, her legs curled up under her.

Marshall turned them around. Didn't switch his lights on till they were back on the road some two hundred metres away.

'I've seen some spooky stuff in my time, Genie, but you win the big prize.'

Genie snatched a glance at his face, lit by the light of the dashboard.

'I wasn't ever in there, was I?'

Marshall kept his eyes on the road.

'Not in a normal sense, no. But . . .'

'I'm a freak.'

'Gifted.'

'Freak.'

'Gifted, Genie. You were there. Got past the doors, went into the teleportation chamber. Heard your side of the conversation. Something really spooked you, something real bad. Hell, you can scream, girl.'

Genie allowed a little smile on her face. Yeah, scream. That's what she should have done the first time she ever saw Reverend Schneider. Scream and run.

'He saw me. He put his hands around my neck. He wanted to kill me.'

'Who?'

'Reverend Schneider.'

'Who?'

'The man who locked me up, Marshall. The one who told my mother I was possessed. He was there. He walked into the chamber and he could damn well see me. He's part of this. Somehow he's part of this.'

Marshall frowned. He didn't know how any reverend could be part of it, but he had no doubt she had entered the building. Whatever magic she possessed it was amazing. She had sent herself right into that building and walked the floors. What a gift to have. He'd heard that some First Nation shamans had it, but always considered it was a myth; and this girl just slipped right into it with no help or stimulants. Extraordinary.

'Why do you think Denis is always waiting for me?'

'Perhaps he thinks you can help him.'

'But why? And Renée, he says she's Ri's sister. He doesn't have a sister. Never had a sister. I don't get it. I don't get any of this. What the hell is carbon blowback?'

'Carbon what?'

'Carbon blowback. That's what Denis said it was. There's shadows on the wall in the teleport area. Human outlines. He said they hadn't cleaned them off yet.'

Marshall whistled, clearly astonished. 'Jeez, then that's exactly what they are, kid. They're closer to making this thing work than I thought. It's proof. Carbon blowback is what's left of the kids they're experimenting on. Shadows on the wall.'

Genie looked at him with a slow realization of the true horror of the place.

Marshall drove on in silence. Those guys in the Fortress had made a lot of progress. And it was as bad as he suspected. It was also criminal, insane.

He suddenly remembered Genie.

'There's a can of Coke in the cooler behind you. It won't be cold, but it might make your mouth taste better.'

Genie sat up and leaned over the seat to grab it. She desperately needed that Coke. Her stomach was twisted with pain and she still felt light-headed. She remembered suddenly that Marshall had given her numbers when she was in her dreamstate.

'How did you know the door code?'

'Twentieth July, '69. Date of the first moon landing. I wanted a date I could remember as emergency release when I was working there. By coincidence it was the twentieth of July in '08 that we had our first successful transmission. Transmitted a clock, before you ask, and it was the day I lost my leg, Genie. Something I'll never forget. It's an override number. One they can't change. I wrote the code, in case.' He offered her an awkward smile. God, if only he could go back in time and be standing some place else when it exploded. Go back and fix everything. No use living your life in regret they say, but regrets, he had a few . . .

'I think we might find a good use for your gift, girl.

God gives you a gift for a reason, in my book.'

Genie was thinking that God most likely gives someone a gift to spite them, but she kept that to herself. Ri was going to get a shock. He had a sister. Who was the guilty party? His mother, or his dad? Of course Denis could be lying, but why would he lie? She sighed. All her days she had just wished for a normal life, just like other people, but it always had to be impossible.

What if Ri liked his sister more than her? Family was always stronger than love ties, or so her mother said. But then again, her mother was crazy.

'Reverend Schneider,' Genie declared, rubbing her neck. 'He's the one behind all this. It's him you have to worry about. He's collecting souls.'

'Souls?'

'That's what Denis told me.'

Marshall had no idea what she was talking about. He drove on, mindful of the road, keeping one eye out for animals, the other in the mirror in case anyone was following.

Reverend Schneider stared at his hands for a moment. One second he had Genie Magee in his clutches, the next nothing. Granted he was tired, but he'd seen her, touched her. How was this possible? He turned to the technician who'd come with him to the teleport chamber.

'Did you see her?'

'Who?'

'The girl. She was running for the exit and screaming. You must have heard her, at least.'

The technician looked at him with raised eyebrows. 'Er, no. There's just you and me here, Reverend. You're tired – you said yourself you're exhausted.'

Reverend Schneider didn't want to argue the point and make himself out to be stupid, but he'd felt that girl's hot neck, heard her scream. He knew he'd seen her. How on earth had she got in? What did she know?

'You're right, must have been exhaustion. Not slept much since the flood.'

The technician nodded. 'You're not the first. Got a security guard here who complains about being taunted by some kid all the time. He's the only one who sees him. We've got a ghost maybe.' He smiled. 'If you believe in that kind of thing.'

Reverend Schneider regarded the young man with disdain.

'You don't attend my church do you? Might enlighten you a little, open your mind.'

The technician shrugged. 'I'm a scientist. I'll leave

ghosts and apparitions to you, Reverend. You said you had another volunteer?'

'He's on his way. Anwar – a Palestinian. He's an orphan. No one will miss him. A loner.'

'Aren't they all.'

# 16

# *The Boy is Gone*

'Ri?' Genie called up louder. 'Ri? We're home.'

She raced up the stairs to their room and burst into the bedroom. He was gone. The bed was empty, the sheets pulled back. The window was open to air the room.

Genie checked the bathroom. Nothing. Even his clothes were gone.

'Marshall? Ri's gone.'

Genie had a bad feeling about this. Ri wouldn't leave without her. She hadn't told him they were going out. She turned back to the room. The water glass was empty. At least he'd drunk something.

Marshall appeared at the bottom of the stairs. 'He's not down here. You think he went out for a walk?'

'I hope not. He's still not well.'

Genie ran back outside and called Ri's name. Then called it again. No response. She could hear the pig snort in the distance and decided to take a walk. *Where would Ri go? Why would he leave the house?* Sure, if he felt a little better he might want a walk, but . . . .

'Hi, pig. You happy?' She stroked the top of its head and ears and it seemed to enjoy it.

The pig was sat between two straw bales under a tree. It snorted when she stopped, probably wanting more. 'Hey, I'll scratch more if you can help me find Ri.'

She remembered the barn. Ri might have taken a walk there. Just for the exercise.

A sensor triggered the light as she approached the barn. The night was quiet except for a slight breeze tumbling through the branches of the trees. A quarter moon rising. She still hadn't quite adjusted to the eerie silence of the land. A town had a rhythm. She'd spent all those hours every day listening to the rhythm of the town as she lay trapped in her room. Out here, it was either light or dark. The trees swayed, waiting.

She entered the barn. Had no idea where the light switch was but waited in the doorway for her eyes to adjust.

'Ri?'

She saw a dim figure hunched over a hay bale. 'Ri?'

Genie ran forward. The figure moved. 'Genie?'

She caught him as he started to fall. Laid him down on the straw.

'What you doing out here in the barn?'

Rian looked into Genie's eyes. She could sense he was confused. 'Ri? What's going on, babe?'

'I thought you'd gone. I didn't . . .' She felt his brow. He was still feverish.

Ri fell asleep in her arms and she lay with him, keeping him warm. She had to get him back to the house somehow. Way too chilly out here. She looked around her in the dim light for something to help and finally she saw a wheelbarrow. All she had to do was get him in there and just wheel him home.

The pig had followed her. Stood in the doorway, sniffing.

'Found him. You were a big help, not.'

The pig wandered in and flopped down beside her on the concrete floor. Genie laughed. Didn't know what she had done in life to deserve the attentions of a pig but it was kinda cute somehow. Beside the pig was warm and at least whilst they were sat here it was sort of comfy.

Ri opened his eyes, realized his head was lying on Genie's shoulder. He was confused. 'Genie?'

'Right here.'

'Where are we?'

'Right back where we started. The barn.'

'Is that . . .'

'The pig, yeah. I think she needs a shower.'

Rian smiled. 'She likes you.'

'She likes anyone who feeds her. Trust me.'

'No, I think she considers you her friend.'

Genie smiled, gently pulling on the pig's velvet soft ears. It grunted in appreciation.

'Well, everyone needs a friend, Rian Tulane. Any idea why you're out here, instead of in bed where you belong?'

Ri shook his head. He had no idea at all.

'That girl come to you again today?'

'Renée?'

'That's the one.'

'She never says anything. Just stares at me.'

Genie wondered how he'd take it if she told him who she was. She decided against it for now. 'She's lonely, Ri. Be nice to her. You think you could get up now? We should get you back to the house. Marshall's making supper.'

'You left.'

'We're back. Come on. Pig, you get the straw now.' Genie stood up and gave a hand to Rian. 'Come on, pull you up.'

Rian allowed himself to be pulled up. 'I can walk. I got here.'

Genie nodded. 'Yeah. You did. Take my arm. You're leaning. You're not well yet.'

Ri took her arm and they hobbled out of the barn.

'Stars are out. Going to be a cold night again,' Genie commented. *Just like a country girl*, she thought. *I'm adapting*.

Rian stared up at the stars and halted a moment. 'We have to save those kids, Genie. I don't know how we do that, but we got to save them.'

Genie frowned. 'How?'

Rian didn't answer.

They walked back down the track towards the house, Genie puzzled by Rian's odd behaviour and worried he seemed to be getting sicker.

Rian was confused. Something had made him leave the house but he couldn't remember why now. Couldn't remember much of anything in fact.

Moucher was barking and raced towards them, frantically wagging his tail, happy to see them both. Genie realized with a sudden surge of pleasure that she was beginning to think of this place as home.

# 17

## *Renée*

Rian woke with a start, immediately cramping up. He rolled over, swore and tried to lift his toes, stretching the tendons to alleviate the pain. He rubbed his calves and could feel how stiff he was. God knows how long he'd been in bed. Rubbing helped some. He glanced over towards the open window and was happy to see how bright it was. Warm sun covered half his bed and he rolled over into it. He rested a moment, enjoying the feeling of heat on his back. The bed didn't smell good. He knew he'd been sweating up like crazy for days now, but other than feeling light-headed, he sensed it was finally over.

He wondered where Genie was, or Marshall. The house seemed quiet. He could hear the trees sashaying in the breeze and some birds arguing, a faint electrical hum in the background, probably the fridge downstairs.

He opened his eyes with a start. He realized he'd fallen asleep again. The sunlight had gone. It was still light though. He sat up. Looked around the room. He was alone. No red haired crazy girl staring at him. Perhaps that had all been an hallucination, part of the illness. He hoped so.

He heard laughter coming from outside somewhere. Immediately he recognized it was Genie. She sounded happy. He loved the way she laughed. There was a regular thumping noise and some swearing. He thought he recognized that sound but couldn't immediately place it.

'Time to shower,' he told the room. He realized that he had no idea what day it was, or the time, but he knew one thing for sure, he was hungry. That had to be a good sign, right?

It was when he was towelling off he noticed the post-it from Genie stuck on the mirror. *Gone to chop wood. Get better soon, this is supposed to be a boy's job!*

Rian smiled. Genie chopping wood. That's what that thumping sound had been. And the swearing. He grinned. Suddenly he heard his father's voice saying, 'Be good for her, toughen her up.' Yeah, exactly the kind of thing his father would have said. He wondered briefly where *he* was now, what he was doing. Wondered too why families had to be so messed up.

He turned. She was there. Sat on the empty bed staring at him. Rian quickly placed the towel around him, embarrassed, even if she wasn't real.

'Your clothes are on the chair,' she said, pointing.

Rian cautiously entered the bedroom and grabbed his clothes, hastily dressing with his back to her. He was flustered and not a little disappointed. He'd thought he was getting better. Now he was seeing things again. He felt spooked to hell.

'You don't look like your dad, y'know. He's taller. Of course he's older.'

Rian turned around to face her, pulling his sweater on, flicking his hair out of his eyes. 'You know my dad?'

'My father too.'

Rian stared at her, anger suddenly flaring. *Her* dad? What the . . . ? The stupid thing was, take away her red hair, the weird blue jacket she clung to, she really did look like a girl version of his dad.

Rian frowned. 'What did you say?'

Renée looked him straight in the eye. 'My dad too. He never told you about us, did he?'

Rian was staring angrily at her.

'Those business trips to Cedarville and the copper mine? He spent them at our house y'know. Used to pick me up from school and drive me to the Kawkawla Lake all the time. My mother was always saying he was going to leave your ma, going to keep his word. She knew he would, eventually.'

174

'You're my *sister*?'

'Renée Cullins. Half-sister. Born a year after you – also Scorpio.'

Rian, still angry, thought about it. How his father had the insurance business with his mother, but at least one week over every month he'd be down at the mine doing their accounts and other stuff. He'd been there with him once. It was a small outfit, a union buyout, and they kept it going even though the previous owners couldn't make a profit. He remembered trailer parks, a lake, and his dad's plans to buy an orchard that fell through. He sensed the girl was telling the truth. Why lie about something like that? He felt a sense of betrayal, a whole lot of sudden emotions. He'd had a sister all this time and never knew.

'My mother's called Alyssa. I've seen you many times, before I disappeared last year. Known about you a long time I guess. Seen you at school, then holding hands with Genie outside McBean's. You love her a lot, I can tell.'

Rian stared at her, plain astonished. He had a sister, a crazy red-haired girl, who seemed to know all about him. His father had another life, another family, kept secret all this time. His legs felt shaky.

'You don't have to say anything. You don't even have to like me. I just wanted you to know.'

'My dad is history now. Ma threw him out when he . . .'

Renée nodded. 'I know. He broke her legs. Ma came and got him, sobered him up at our place. She was furious. She won't even get in the car with him if he's been drinking.'

'He still living there?' Rian asked, despite himself.

Renée shrugged. He couldn't tell if she was sad or not.

'No idea. But I didn't leave because of him.'

Rian approached her. It was stupid to be angry at her. His damn irresponsible father. No wonder he never had any money. He closed his eyes a moment to bring his temper under control. This girl was just an apparition, he had to remember that. She had it doubly tough. Not dead, not alive, and she needed help. His help. Her brother's help.

'I'm sorry, Renée. I'm sorry I never knew you. Would have been cool to have a sister.'

Renée nodded. She knew it was a shock for him. He was taking it well considering. She looked at Rian with renewed hope.

'How did you end up like this anyway?' Rian asked. 'We're a long way from Cedarville.'

All of a sudden Renée looked angry. 'I was happy. I liked my life. It all changed when Reverend Schneider set up a church and—'

Rian was caught by surprise. 'Schneider?'

'Told my mother I was evil. She only gave his church all our money. Everything. She works for the church full time now. Worships him.'

Rian couldn't believe this. One man responsible for so much pain. 'How did you end up like this?'

'The great almighty reverend said he would drive me to the border. I was going to Portland, live with my cousin. Wanted me to have a chance, he said.' Renée sighed. 'Only he had other ideas and busy hands, about which I ain't going into. He tricked me good.'

Rian was sat right beside her now. 'Renée, I don't know what I can do for you. I'm your brother, I guess.' He was still adjusting to that idea. 'But I don't know what you are, exactly.' He placed his hands close to hers. They were almost touching now. There was a rush of static around their fingers. It was the weirdest feeling. 'I can almost feel you.'

'I can hear your heart beatin'.' She leaned in towards him and static seemed to rise up through all of Rian's body. Renée touched the side of Rian's head. 'I can see this.' There was a momentary flash of indigo all around Rian and he flinched as he got a small shock.

'What was that?'

'Your aura. We can see so much more than you.

177

Everything has an electrical field. Your aura was missing for a while, but it's back now. You're getting better.'

'You can see my aura? For real?' Rian was impressed.

Renée nodded, offering up a tight nervous smile. 'We can see a lot of stuff people can't see. Sometimes it's . . . um . . . sometimes you can tell people aren't well. It's like seeing a dark shadow.'

'An X-ray,' Rian suggested.

Renée nodded. 'Kind of.'

'Cool.'

'But we can't touch, we can't feel you and we can't feel the rain or the wind or smell anything – and I know it's stupid, but I miss feeling everything, Rian. We're just existing. I can't explain it. We've got all these cool things we can do, but I don't know what you smell like.'

Rian laughed looking back at the bed. 'Probably a good thing. These sheets are pretty skanky right now.' Then, because he could see she thought he was mocking her. 'I'm sorry. It must be totally scary for you. What does it feel like to be . . . well, like this, I guess?'

Renée shrugged. 'You never have to sleep. You're always on. It's pretty exhausting actually. I sometimes just go to the edge of the reservoir and sit there, watching the water. I sit calm and still as I can and pretend I'm sleeping and dreaming . . .'

Rian had no way of really understanding this. Never sleeping, never dreaming. She was right, it was scary. You'd never have a chance to repair yourself.

'But what if the power goes off. Does that scare you?'

Renée looked towards the window. 'Denis talks about that. How we'd all be able to sleep then. But, it never has. It never does. There would have to be a brown-out everywhere in Canada all at once, I think.'

'But where are you? How are you?' Rian asked. 'I don't understand exactly what has happened to you.'

Renée placed her hand in Rian's and Rian saw the hairs on his arm rise. It was like he was holding the wind by its tail.

'We're on thousands of servers. Ten, thirty, fifty thousand, maybe more. Once a bank of servers went down and I lost a foot a few weeks back. I was scared to go anywhere, couldn't walk. When they fixed it, my foot came back. I don't know how it works, Rian. I'm fifteen now. I don't know anything.' Her eyes lit up momentarily. 'Want to see something cool? Watch my hands.'

Rian stepped back a little, not sure what to expect. Renée put her hands together. 'Ask me something.'

Rian frowned. He could see she was concentrating. His head was blank though. 'What's the weather like in Spurlake right now?' Dumb question. Idiot.

Suddenly there was the Weather Channel on her palms and running up her bare arms. Showed the weather all over BC. 'Weather is easy. Storm over by Nelson see, look at my elbow. It's raining in Seattle.'

'It's always raining in Seattle.'

'Well I can access anything on Google. I'm a walking iPad. Facebook, Wikipedia, anything you want. I looked for you on Facebook. You and Genie are weird, only kids on earth not on it.'

Rian shrugged. 'Genie never wanted her mother to find her online, or Reverend Schneider. She thinks that's how they contact kids, get them to be their friends and then make them crazy.'

Renée nodded. She put her hands down, the images quickly faded.

'You got that right. That's exactly how they find them. Somehow they all find that two-thousand dollar deal for experiments and, oh yeah, no need to tell your folks. I mean, are we kids total suckers for that kind of thing, or what?

'Now we're inside the Fortress we're like – I don't know what. Denis discovered it. Whatever is online, we can access. No password can stop us. There's a lot of bad stuff out there, Rian. I just stopped looking after a while.'

She was staring at him again.

'Why don't you go to Portland, Renée? I mean. If you can materialize here at the farm, you can go anywhere, right? Mexico even. They wouldn't find you there.'

Renée shook her head. 'You know the percentage of brown-outs in Mexico? My head would be here, my feet stuck in Cabo St Lucas. They'd probably never get me back together again. There's maps. Y'know, grids. Electricity follows lines but you can get lost. Here's safe. This farmhouse is the middle. Electricity just flows right across everything, but when you're in it, you can't look right or left or straight on or . . . Cary Harrison is the only one who's tried to go outside the circle. He only just got back in one piece. You might meet him, he's bright, but he's not very sociable.'

Rian discovered he'd hit a raw nerve.

'I don't even know why I care,' Renée declared. 'I don't know why I'm here or why I'm alive or if I'm dead or just a ghost . . . I don't know anything, Rian.'

'We have to figure something out,' Rian told her, trying to sound positive, even if he didn't feel it. 'You're my sister, remember. We have to find a way to get you back.'

Renée shook her head. 'There's no back. The moment you enter the Fortress, you're dead, Rian. I'll never bleed, never have a headache and I'll never be real. Ever.

Whatever they promise, never listen to them. They don't know what they're doing.'

They heard footsteps on the stairs, Rian looked towards the door.

'Genie,' Renée said softly, then vanished.

Genie burst into the room. She looked flushed and excited and very pleased to see him up. 'Hey, you're dressed.'

'And you've been chopping wood.'

He picked off some wood chips and she fell into his arms.

'Hell, yeah. See my blisters?'

She pulled back to show him her wounds. 'Going to be sore. Can't believe how much sweat you generate, splitting logs.'

She hugged Rian and he held her tight, inhaling her scent.

Rian grinned. It was so good to feel her in his arms. Then immediately felt guilty. All these simple things Renée could never do. Must send you crazy to be like that.

Genie was looking at the sweat-stained bed. 'You smell great. Those sheets on the other hand . . .' She pulled away and stared at him. 'You're looking better.' She looked around the room. 'Was she here? Did she come?'

'Renée?'

'Yeah, she's been sitting here for days waiting for you to get better. Never seen anyone so worried.'

'You talked to her?' Rian was surprised. Last he remembered she was jealous.

'Well, she's your sister. Half, anyway. That's important, right. She had to tell you. I insisted.' Genie pulled a face. 'She's shy. Scared too.'

'I'd be scared if I was like that. I'm freaked, Genie. I mean – I have a sister and my Dad lied to me all those years. He had another family, for God's sake. I'm still freaked. But she does look a lot like Dad. She seems nice.'

'She *is* nice. She's lonely too. We've *both* got to help her.'

Rian took Genie's hand. 'But that's just it. How?'

'I don't know, Ri. Don't know why they think we can help. Did she tell you about Reverend Schneider? I couldn't believe it. He's involved somehow. It's him driving a wedge between families and their kids. I saw him. Marshall took me back to Synchro. I was actually in there speaking to Denis, don't ask me how, and then suddenly Schneider was there. He saw me. How weird is that? He put his fat hands around my neck. I screamed. Poor Marshall's still deaf.'

Rian was bewildered, so much information to take in. He kissed Genie's forehead. 'We're going to nail him. Nail him good.'

Genie nodded, smiling. 'Welcome back to the living, Rian Tulane. I missed you.'

She broke free and headed back to the door. 'Marshall's making meatballs. Grab those stinky sheets and bring them down, I have to cook the pasta.'

Rian smiled. He was hungry. Genie still loved him and they had an evil enemy to defeat. That's the way life should be.

He turned back to the bed and began to strip the sheets. His legs seemed to be made of sponge. It was as if Genie had switched him on when she came into the room and switched him off again when she left. That, he realized, was exactly what was happening to Renée.

Renée watched him leave the room with the sheets bundled under his arms. She could still feel the tingle from where he'd tried to touch her. Genie had been right. No use staring. She had to tell him and now she had. He seemed to take it pretty well. She was no longer alone, even if she was never going home.

184

# 18

# Orange Juice and Muffins

Of course, it is one thing to say you will help people. But where to start? Marshall hadn't met either Reneé or Denis, and he remained to be convinced they even existed or even could be 'helped'.

For Rian, getting himself and Genie well was the priority. Genie felt guilty about that, but sometimes even thinking about the impossible gave her a headache and she still had nightmares about seeing Reverend Schneider in Synchro. The truth was, they had no workable idea of how to free Renée or Denis or any of the other kids trapped in the Fortress. As Marshall explained, even if you could get into the Fortress and assemble all the different bits of their electronic files, and actually get out again undetected, they weren't exactly going to fit on any memory stick he knew of.

The weather seemed to return to normal as September progressed, with warm days and pleasant nights. The atmosphere in the farmhouse was almost impossibly cheerful and each night as they cooked supper they talked and argued about stuff, almost always ending up back where they started. But for Genie this was all new. She'd never lived in a place where her opinion was counted, or even listened to, and even if they pointed out she was wrong more than a few times, at least she'd been heard.

It was sheer bliss. No pressure, nothing evil happened at all. She concentrated on getting stronger, cooking, sketching, learning how to take care of the pig and the dog and collecting honey from the beehives in the orchards. She was scared to death the first time she did it, but Marshall suited her up and once she realized the bees couldn't sting her and, in fact, didn't seem to want to, collecting honey wasn't such an ordeal. Bees, she learned, were essential to pollinate the apple trees. All these simple things she discovered, things she'd never been allowed to do before, and she felt she was finally making sense of her life. OK, so pig care wasn't particularly high on her list of things she'd wanted to learn, but the pig had needs, wanted to be friends, and even though she was huge, she had, as far as she could tell, quite a sense of humour. It liked to hide and suddenly rush her when Genie came out with scraps. She liked to rub itself against Marshall's apple trees and try and catch the apples as they fell. Loved that game!

Marshall seemed happier too. He was content to let

them do as they wanted as long as they helped with chores and listened to some of the old jazz CDs he blasted out from his old hi-fi system. Dizzy Gillespie was a god in Marshall's house. Genie realized that she was even humming the tunes as she worked, stuff her grandmother might have boogied to. Now *that* was weird. She knew from overhearing a conversation with his son on the phone that he was reluctant to let them go. Not in a bad way. He told him that he'd never seen a girl take to country life so quickly as Genie and it was true. She *was* happy.

Rian was kind of enthusiastic, but not quite as captivated as Genie. For a start he'd always had some freedom. All right, he'd had to cook and clean for his mom, but he'd never had the restrictions Genie had, or the hatred that her mother had for her.

He had started to make the kind of recovery that boys always made. He was taking advantage of the good weather to build up his strength and learn some new skills. As he told Genie, they were on their own now and they'd have to earn a living. Anything Marshall could teach him was going to be useful. So he'd painted walls, learned how to fit a doorframe and door, dug new post holes for a fence Marshall was putting in. He wanted to try everything. Which is why he was on the barn roof with a clawhammer removing rusted tin whilst Marshall gave him instructions from the ground.

Genie was preparing fresh squeezed orange juice. They'd both be thirsty. It was one of those late summer hot days with the temperature hovering around 30°C. There wasn't any wind but Marshall had promised a thunderstorm. He could predict the weather by his leg. If his leg said rain, it was guaranteed. He didn't explain how, but Genie believed him, all evidence and a perfect blue sky to the contrary.

'You all right up there, boy?' Marshall was calling up. 'It's going to rain for sure, got to get that hole fixed. Can you see it?'

Rian was standing firmly on the barn roof, enjoying the experience. He had a metal sheet in his hands to replace over the rusted section. The roof was blazing hot and the soles of his borrowed shoes were sticky. He had a sudden whole new respect for roofers.

He ripped off the rusted corrugated sheet that practically disintegrated in his hands and tossed it off the roof. There was a gaping hole now down to the floor of the barn. One slip and he'd crash through it.

'Whole roof's rusted, Marshall.'

'Brush the area clean around the edges of the hole, then lay the new sheet with the top lip under the higher section, bottom lip overlapping the lower. Should fit snug. Use the watertight nails like I showed you.'

'Won't it slide off?'

'No. Make sure it's well caulked under at the top. Got to replace the whole roof soon anyway, been up there forty years I should think.'

Rian sweated in the heat, but followed the instructions to the letter.

Genie arrived below with the iced juice in a jug.

'He all right up there?' She hardly dare look. 'Is he safe?'

Marshall squeezed her shoulder. 'He's doing fine. Mighty hot though. He's going to need that juice when he gets down.'

He called up again. 'Check it's well wedged in, OK? Got to make it good and watertight.'

Rian signalled that he had it hand. 'I know. You forget I spent the summer fixing Maclean's barge.'

'If I recall, it sank without trace,' Marshall remarked with a sarcastic smile.

Rian laughed. He shifted his weight. He was getting roasted now. He was enjoying being out here in a different way to Genie. School had been back almost two weeks already. He'd worried about missing it at first, but realized now that he enjoyed working with his hands. Never thought he would. His mother had always wanted him to go to law school, but you'd never get a lawyer up on a roof fixing leaks, never get a suit stripping off the old plastic wood-effect cladding in the basement and taking it back to the original brick. Marshall wanted the basement for a music room, and Rian had enjoyed planning and working out how to do that.

He made sure everything lay down perfectly and he felt a small sense of accomplishment. Felt his feet burning from the heat too.

'I hope you got a good grip, Rian Tulane.'

Rian looked down at Genie staring up and he grinned. 'I'm cool. I'm done. Coming down.'

Genie turned her gaze away. She didn't want to look. One trip and he'd be squished.

Marshall saw what she was doing. 'Don't worry. He's a natural. He could teach a goat how to climb.'

'What you see up there?' Marshall asked as Rian paused to put all the tools in his pockets. 'Any clouds?'

'Nope. Not one. No way it's going to rain, Marshall.' He could see right across the forest and the power lines that straddled it. 'Which way is the Fortress?'

'Due south-east. Behind you. In winter, at night, you can see the light from it reflected on the snow caps,' Marshall told him.

'You must be right between the Synchro and the

190

Fortress buildings.' Rian was thinking about his previous conversation with Renée and how she said this farm was almost in the middle of the circle.

'Almost. It was kind of convenient when I worked there. Always had to be in one building or the other. Come on down, your girl has been squeezing oranges for you. Enjoy it now before she gets bored of you and starts watching the shopping channel.'

Genie turned and kicked Marshall on his false leg. 'That's not nice. Don't listen to him, Ri.'

'I'm not listening. He's a bitter man, Genie. Coming down. I think I earned my Spiderman wings.'

'For that you have to leap whole buildings,' Marshall retorted.

'Why didn't you leave here, Marshall?' Genie asked suddenly. 'I mean, when you had your accident? Why didn't you just go, live on the islands or someplace? Why did you stay in this old place so far from anybody?'

Rian was down on the ground safely. Genie took him a large mug of iced juice and he drank it all down, dribbling some as he tried to cool off.

'Ace,' was all he said as he held it out for more.

Marshall was thinking about his reply, staring up at the mountain.

'I could never quite see myself leaving the farm. See the mountain? We're higher up than Spurlake here, on a plateau. Cold in winter but we get the sun pretty much all day long and hot long summers. Important if you grow fruit trees. Farmer who started this place knew what he was doing ninety years ago. We've got water from our own reservoir. Soil's good. Besides, Genie, my son will want this place for himself one day. He loved growing up here. Had the horses then. But of course, he was young and Spurlake was where the action was, and the girls of course. It's natural he left. Max won't always be a cop. No one is ever particularly grateful or respectful. I think he's finding that out for himself. Also, being honest,' he scratched his head a moment, 'I guess I just could never quite believe I was off the project. I never quite understood that they didn't need me any more.'

Genie turned to go. That was the real answer. Heard it in his voice. And maybe the truth was that he was looking for a way back in. She had no idea why she thought that, but one thing she had learned in her life so far was that what people said and what they did were entirely different things.

'Hey, where you going?' Rian asked.

'Martha's on TV. Got to learn how to make chocolate muffins from scratch.'

Rian watched her go with amusement. Marshall called after her.

'You go girl. Muffins are the way to a man's heart.' He winked at Rian and Rian just shook his head. But it was true, thinking on it a moment. He could really appreciate some muffins right about now.

Rian watched her walk back towards the farmhouse and he felt real pride in her. She stopped to give him a little wave.

'Muffins in one hour,' she declared. 'I hope.'

He grinned, still couldn't believe she was all his.

Marshall walked towards the fence posts, stacked ready to go in the ground.

'We got work to do, Rian. And we still got to smoke the orchards so the wasps don't take hold there. They burrow into the apples, rot them out. They'll be ready to pick in about ten days. I sure hope you guys will still be here to help. Be a pity to let them go to waste.'

'Who picks 'em normally?'

'Max and his wife used to come up with some friends. We shared the profits. But they're busy this year, what with the flood and everything. A pity. Organic apples fetch a premium and it'll be a good crop this year.'

Rian nodded, looking back at the orchards. There were hundreds of trees. That would be a lot of hard work.

Marshall sure knew how to keep him busy.

Marshall looked up at the sky. Still a perfect blue. He frowned.

'I don't know where the rain is coming from, but it's coming. I know it. Leg's never been wrong.'

Genie left the chocolate muffins to cool. It was her first time baking and she acknowledged they could be a better shape, but they sure tasted all right and the smell was divine. She ventured outside, smelling smoke. She could see Rian and Marshall sending a really dense white cloud of smoke billowing up through the lower apple orchard. She worried about the bees a moment then realized that they were in the higher orchard. Country life was complicated. Everything was alive and you had to worry about just about every little thing.

'Come on Mouch, we're going for a walk.'

Mouch let out an excited yelp and immediately headed for the back field. Genie followed. Marshall had mentioned there were bald eagles flying up by the reservoir earlier and now she was determined to head for the ridge to get a closer look. His field glasses were really heavy around her neck and only moments away from the house she was regretting bringing them along.

She went behind the house, following the dog, and

crossed the hayfield, almost overwhelmed by the scent of wild mint that grew in clumps amid the hay. Moucher jumped and darted this way and that as he spotted rabbits. No matter how fast he ran, the rabbits ran faster, and he was exhausted just crossing the field, returning to her, panting hard.

'Foolish hound. I didn't bring water, Mouch. You'll have to wait till we get to the reservoir. It's a long walk, dog, pace yourself.'

On the other side of the field, she found a dry stream bed and followed it up the slope, stumbling over rocks from time to time where exposed lizards would be caught by surprise and scoot for cover. She was thinking that it must have taken a lot of effort and money to build a reservoir up on this ridge. The boulders everywhere were huge. Looking back for a moment she realized just how vulnerable Marshall's place was if any of them ever got loose.

The walk was tougher and hotter than she had expected, the route practically vertical in places. There would be waterfalls at these spots when it rained, she realized. Moucher led the way, finding paths where she saw none and they pressed on, the idea of a cool vast expanse of water for a swim more appealing by the second.

It took a full hour climbing, longer maybe. When she

finally got up there, breathless, her chest tight from the exertion and the thinner air, she felt very satisfied however, it was well worth the climb. She looked back at the farmhouse again, a tiny dot in the forest below her, the smoke still rising from the orchards. Mouch ran to the edge, desperate for water, plunging in. Genie splashed her face and arms and cupped her hands to drink, smiling as Mouch tried to lick the whole reservoir dry.

'Slow down, you'll get sick, dog.'

Genie wanted to strip off and skinny dip but was scared to. She knew this was Fortress territory and what if there were cameras? There were always cameras now. Probably nowhere safe on earth without a camera pointing to it by now. She decided to wait until she was sure it was private. She found a rock to lie on and just think a while. Above her bald eagles circled the tops of trees, swooping down and rising on the updrafts. A light warm breeze blew through the forest and Genie savoured the moment listening to the music of gently swaying branches. Moucher swam noisily behind her, not quite believing she hadn't leaped in with him or that she hadn't thrown him a stick to fetch.

Rian was helping keeping the bonfires going, heaping damp leaves on them to generate more smoke. The purpose wasn't to burn, but create as much smoke as possible in the orchard to drive the wasps out.

'You given any more thought to what Genie saw in Synchro?' Rian asked. 'She's still having nightmares about Reverend Schneider.'

Marshall was looking for the wasp hive in the crevices of the trees. He stood up and wiped his forehead, removing his hat a moment.

'It's that carbon blowback thing that gets me. I went to look at my notes last night. There's nothing on it and then I realized why. When we were experimenting we only used inanimate objects. The most daring thing we ever did was try to transmit a cup of coffee from one part of the lab to another.'

'It work?'

'It evaporated and the plastic mug melted. Not a huge success. One thing I do know, if they are testing on humans, then there'd be a huge carbon load.'

'If?' Rian queried. 'You don't believe her?'

Marshall looked at him and shrugged. 'I haven't met your friends, remember. I still don't quite believe that anyone who has been teleported and not survived, can then somehow reappear, like a ghost in my house and actually talk. Never mind make sense. You have to accept that we are made of flesh and blood, Rian. If that isn't transmitted and then reassembled, which is the exact purpose of teleportation, then what are you? More's the point, what are they? Where's their DNA now? Smeared on a wall in the transmission chamber? Renée and the others are just ghosts and as the servers start to die, so will they. It's harsh, but you have to know that.'

'But you accept Genie went into Synchro and saw people.'

'Astral travel is well documented. Shaman can do it moving through space and time. Genie's got a gift. I believe that. But I'm having a harder time accepting the others as being "alive" by any acceptable definition.'

'We should get Denis and Renée to talk to you.'

Marshall smiled. 'Well, put it this way, I'm prepared to suspend my disbelief. A good scientist must accept the challenge that one day everything he believes in could be wrong. Besides, there's something to this. You say that Renée told you she was maintained on at least ten thousand servers.'

'More, probably.'

'Well, it's true. That's what the Fortress project was designed to do. First you digitize the subject, store it on memory, then transmit. That was always the really hard bit, getting the DNA sequencing correct. Billions of calculations just to make an ear appear in the right place. Now imagine just how much storage and energy it takes to keep you intact after you've been turned into basic atomic particles. Every time you see one of those kids, it has to be draining an ocean of power on the system. You have no idea how much memory it must take to maintain the kids intact so you can just see them, let alone talk. That's why I'm a sceptic. It's been the holy grail at the Fortress since I can remember. You'd think they'd notice something like that was happening.'

Rian mused on that.

'I just don't understand how they think they can get away with it,' Marshall added. 'If they're using kids for real? It's abominable.'

'Why don't you confront them?'

Marshall looked at Rian through the smoke. 'They're dangerous people, Rian. Ruthless. There's billions of dollars tied up in this project. Somehow they've rationalized this. Maybe they tell themselves these kids don't matter, they're loners, drifters, no one will miss them. But confront them? First you need evidence. Evidence people would believe. That's harder. Remember the Fortress is one of the best kept secrets of the century. You try telling anyone about teleportation and before you know it there's a man with a white coat behind you ready to lock you up forever. They will do anything to keep it secret. Absolutely anything. Think on that.'

The reservoir was a huge manmade lake, kilometres long. It occupied a natural dip in the mountain and there were giant rock and earth walls built up to retain the water runoff from the slopes above. Genie realized she'd have to walk to the other side of the reservoir to get a good view down the valley where the Fortress was situated. The eagles were circling a distance away now and even from this distance looked huge. Any one of them, she realized, could swoop down and grab Mouch if they wanted.

'Keep your eyes on the sky, Mouch,' she warned him as they set off again. 'We'll swim together when we get to the other end.'

She was sweltering now, but feeling good about it. Fall weather wouldn't be far off and she wanted to enjoy all the hot days they got. Her skin was improving day by day out here, but she was still resentful that she'd been cheated out of a whole summer by her mother. It was unforgivable.

She finally got to the edge of the reservoir, the water held in place by deep giant boulders and a vast sloping concrete wall. She realized that whoever built it had only to seal off this narrow section and they had a natural lake, as the rest of the water was contained by the mountains on both sides. She felt like some pioneer, gazing down the steep valley for the first time – the green forest sweeping down far below her into the distance. A bird shrieked somewhere, alerting others to her presence.

She found a huge warm boulder to perch on, right on the edge, Mouch lying down in the shade below her at the waterline, panting loudly.

She trained her field glasses on the bald eagles and although it was hard to get used to observing them and getting the focus right for both eyes, it was amazing to watch them in flight. She felt she was right there and could see the updraught lifting their feathers. 'Wow, Mouch. These are amazing. You can see forever.'

She lost the birds for a moment as she was on maximum close-up and found she was looking at a bus stop.

'Huh?'

She steadied herself, lying on her stomach, and found the bus stop again. It was some distance away, far down the valley beside a narrow winding dirt track that snaked through the forest. No one even lived out here, so how could there be a bus stop? It made no sense. The birds swooped overhead, but she lost them and when she searched she found she was looking at the bus stop again and there appeared to be a kind of shelter there, and if she wasn't mistaken, a vending machine. Even more strange.

Then she saw there was someone, possibly a kid, hard to judge at this distance, walking along the road towards it. She could just make out he was wearing a backpack. Of course it could have been anyone just going trekking in the mountains. People did that all the time, nothing odd about that. But a bus stop in the middle of a forest? No way. Made no sense without a road. No bus was ever going to be up here in anyone's lifetime.

'This is so weird, Mouch.'

She forgot all about the eagles now. She watched as the boy reached the bus stop, put down his backpack and punched the vending machine. It must have dispensed a can because moments later he was sat on the ground drinking.

She lost him momentarily, couldn't find him again. 'Darn, can't get used to these . . .' she swore with frustration as she swayed on her elbows. 'Here he is.'

He was lying on his back now. Had to be exhausted after that climb. Who wouldn't be?

She saw sudden movement. A four-by-four came into view travelling at speed down a dusty track. She was too far away to hear anything, but it came to a sudden stop by the bus stop. Two men in what looked like space suits got out and went over to the kid. They picked him up. He didn't resist. Didn't do anything. They carried him to the four-by-four and carefully put him in the back, like they didn't want to wake him. Another guy went back for his backpack and slung that in the back too.

'Hey, that's not right.'

She focused on the four-by-four. She couldn't make out the writing on it, but she recognized the symbol. Fortransco. The Fortress!

'You see that, Mouch? They just abducted that kid. They weren't helping him. They stole him. Like they knew he was there and he'd be unconscious.'

The guy in the suit stopped suddenly and he was pointing in Genie's direction.

She swiftly put the field glasses down on the rock, dizzy from the concentration.

'Uh-oh, Mouch. Damn. I'm such a dumb ass.'

Stupid, stupid. Had a reflection on the glass given her away somehow? Turning too fast she lost grip and Genie slid headfirst down the boulder into the water.

She swallowed and choked and swore and swallowed more water again, feeling angry with herself as she struggled to get right side up. The water was deliciously warm however, and although she was fully dressed, she swam. Mouch leaped in as well, thinking it was a game, and paddled out to join her.

'I suppose you think this is funny, but we should

probably get out of here, dog.' He just swam, dead serious, concentrating on keeping his head above water.

For five blissful minutes they swam and savoured the crystal clear water. She knew she had to leave. They had definitely seen her but the water was so good and surely they wouldn't bother to come up this far.

Moucher noticed the sound first. His ears flattened and he abruptly turned and headed towards the shore in a panic.

'What?'

Genie tossed her hair and batted water out of her ears. Only then did she notice the water was vibrating all around her, literally forming droplets on the surface. The noise grew in intensity. Mouch was still frantically doggypaddling and the water was moving, definitely moving. She was beginning to move with it and began to swim towards the rock, the current gaining in strength.

Were they draining the reservoir? Did they know she was here? She swore. Why, oh why, had she brought the field glasses?

She was hardly making any headway at all and Mouch was coming back to her, unable to beat the current.

She grabbed him, flipped over on to her back with the dog on her chest and kicked as hard as she could to make it to the safety of the edge.

The noise intensified. Suddenly a huge helicopter swept in over the water, no more than ten metres above her, the downdraught pushing her under. It flew right overhead, engines roaring. She could see two men standing by an open door – they could have seen her. It slowed, hovered a moment, then dropped down over the other side out of sight.

She realized that the vibration and suction had stopped. She was safe again. Nevertheless she got out of the water quickly, Mouch shaking off the water beside her.

That was a Fortransco chopper and if they'd seen her, she was in real danger. How quickly could they get up here?

'We got to go now, dog.'

Mouch was with her one hundred per cent. His heart was still beating like a bird and he couldn't wait to leave.

Sopping wet, Genie collected the field glasses, regretting her afternoon had been ruined. She wanted to look over the edge, see exactly where the chopper went, but she realized that would be foolish. She had to get moving. This was Fortress territory and they'd be only too happy to snatch her for their experiments. How stupid she'd been to stay. She cursed herself for swimming and wasting time.

Mouch was gone already, heading back down the dry stream bed.

'You could have waited,' Genie shouted after him.

He stopped a moment, looked back at her, tail between his legs. He carried on. He was one scared dog and wasn't going to wait for anyone.

What had made the water vibrate? That was such a weird sensation watching a whole reservoir shake. She stripped off her top and shorts and began to wring them out. She thought again of the boy they'd grabbed and bundled into the vehicle. What must he be going through? Poor bastard. That's when she heard the distinct sound of an engine approaching. She bounded to the top of her boulder to snatch a look and her heart sank. A jeep was driving hell for leather towards the reservoir from the Fortress direction. They *had* seen her.

No time to dress. No way she could head down the way she'd come, there was no cover on the stream bed. Wet clothes bundled under her arm, she sprinted for the treeline.

The jeep was bouncing crazily along the forest road and would be here in two minutes flat. She had nowhere to hide. Could climb the trees, but there was no safety in sparse pine trees. They'd spot her in seconds.

She looked back, the jeep was just seconds away.

There was a small ridge ahead, a tree growing over the top of it, its roots exposed and a bunch of rabbit holes dug into the yellow earth. She jumped into the small recess, rolled in the earth, smearing dirt over her wet body, covering herself in pine needles. She covered every bit of her flesh she could in yellow mud and bits of the forest. She squirmed closer to the ground, pulled away at the edges of two rabbit holes, trying to make it bigger and provide more soil to cover her. She hid her clothes and field glasses in the hole, lay flat and said a prayer for invisibility.

Uniformed Fortress security guards got out of the jeep. Briefly glancing up she could see there were two of them, a man and a woman, and they had weapons. Genie closed her eyes, squished herself more firmly into the earth, covering her head with dust and soil.

She hoped Mouch had gone home. The last thing she needed was for him to come back and sniff her out.

She could hear them speaking, their voices carried far.

'Something was swimming in the reservoir for sure. Got paw prints on a rock here.'

'That doesn't explain how they saw a glint of light.'

'No, but I got still wet paw prints and could be a coyote.'

'Swimming? You ever see one swim?'

'It's hot. Yeah, coyotes can swim, Gerry. I've seen them do it.'

'OK, if you say so, but what caused the flash?'

'Maybe when the chopper came in from Synchro?'

'It was before that.'

Genie couldn't see, couldn't look, but she could hear one of them was moving her way. Grunting with the effort of climbing the slope.

'What you got?' the guard called from the water's edge.

'Trail. Someone was walking up here, got a partial shoe imprint on the clay down besides you. Unless you think coyotes wear shoes now.'

'Now you're getting sarcastic.'

Genie could hear the woman was getting closer to her. Hear her wheezing, smoker's lungs struggling in the thin air. Genie stopped breathing. Worse, she could feel something crawling over her head towards her bare back. Oh my God, a beetle? What was it? Were there scorpions up here? She *hated* things crawling over her.

'Anything up there?' The other guard was calling from further away.

'Can't see anything.'

'Footprint – could be old. Not much to disturb it up here.'

Genie was aware that someone was standing no more than one metre from her. Was she watching her? Waiting for her to move or breathe, or surrender? The bug had reached her back now and was crawling towards her ass. *Please* God, do not let it bite me! She stopped breathing entirely; she could feel each tiny footprint as it made its way down her spine.

'We're wasting our time,' the other guard was calling from below. 'There's no one around. Had to be animals.'

'You going to McBean's re-opening in Spurlake? It's a two-for-one deal on all pastries all day,' the security guard shouted down. She was practically standing over Genie now. She could probably reach out and touch her shoes. How could she not see her?

'Not unless you're buying,' the other guard called back. 'Never eat out. Can't afford it on these wages. Come on, let's get back. Shift change in thirty minutes anyways.'

The bug was circling on her back now – she wanted to scream, absolutely sure it was going to lay eggs or do something gross. The security guard moved away from Genie. Her feet crunched on twigs and gravel as she went back down the slope. Genie exhaled after thirty seconds more and drew new oxygen in, still not daring to look or move.

She heard the jeep start up but still she didn't move. Didn't move even when the jeep moved off, in case it was a trick. In case one of them was still there, waiting to catch her. The bug was suddenly moving south again. She had to move, she had to . . .

Genie rolled over and jerked to her feet, shaking the mud and bits of the forest off her. The jeep was gone for sure. She ran like some demented soul towards the reservoir and crashed in. 'Off, bug! Off, bug!' she yelled, rubbing herself all over. She stayed under the water for as long as possible to make sure nothing was still crawling on her.

She was walking out of the reservoir, shaking water out of her ears, when she heard the familiar whine of a chopper engine winding up again.

She raced for the forest hidey-hole again. She needed to retrieve her clothes and the field glasses.

Why, oh why, had she come up here? She flung herself back on to the forest floor. Instantly she saw a huge squashed ground beetle. She must have crushed it when she rolled over. At least it wasn't something poisonous. She felt foolish now, but feeling it crawling on her back had made her nearly wet herself and she could still feel its tiny feet on her skin, even though that was impossible. She shuddered.

The chopper rose up and flew out over the reservoir. Genie watched it go, saw guys looking out from an open door, as if they were searching for her.

·She most definitely had to get out of there. They weren't

going to give up. She scrabbled to get her clothes on, yellow mud smearing her all over again, pine needles sticking to her wet hair. This was one dangerous place.

Rian was resting on a bench in the backyard eating one of Genie's muffins when Mouch came back. He looked dirty and exhausted, his fur all matted with yellow mud and his paws bloody. Rian looked up expecting Genie to follow right after. Mouch wasn't happy and, desperately thirsty, annoyed his bowl was nearly dry.

Rian filled it up and checked his paws.

'Marshall?'

Marshall appeared moments later, mopping his brow. He frowned when he saw what condition Moucher was in.

'Where's Genie?'

'She say where she went?' Rian asked, worried now. He kept looking in the direction that Moucher had arrived in and expected to see an equally exhausted Genie return.

Marshall was looking at the dog more closely. 'His fur's all yellow. The soil up by the reservoir is like that. I was telling her about it earlier.'

Rian ran inside. Grabbed a water bottle and filled it. If he was going looking for Genie she'd probably need water.

211

Marshall was standing by the hay field when he came out. He pointed out where she'd tracked through it.

'She went across the field to the old stream. It's bone dry this time of year, Rian. Fastest way up there. That's Fortress territory up there. If they found her . . .'

Rian didn't need an explanation, he knew exactly what that meant. He began to run across the field.

Mouch collapsed in a heap by his bowl, unable to move a muscle more.

Marshall watched Rian go. He frowned. He realized that he was real fond of that girl and he sure as hell didn't want her in Fortress hands. He turned back towards the house. He had to hose Moucher down, treat his paws. Something must have really terrified him to make him leave Genie behind.

Rian was moving up the dry stream bed as fast as he could, amazed Genie had done this route. It was tough going, with lots of sharp edges. No wonder Mouch had come back sore. He looked up, saw a Fortress chopper circling over the mountain ridge in the distance. Curiously, it gave him hope. Perhaps they were looking for Genie. If so, it meant they didn't have her. He climbed faster, grazing his knees on a rock as he jumped from one to another.

Another chopper came roaring out of nowhere, seemed to be following the stream down the mountain. Rian threw himself down and crawled under a rock overhang. The chopper flew right overhead, he felt the downdraught as it banked right and headed towards Marshall's farm below.

Rian was scrambling up to continue where he heard a rockfall up ahead around the bend and someone swear.

'Genie?'

An apparition suddenly appeared above him. A yellow mud girl with streaks of blood running down her arm. She looked like a wild animal, the field glasses the only thing not covered in dirt. She stared at him, her breathing short, her adrenaline on overdrive.

Rian stared at her in shock, momentarily unable to move.

'Did Mouch get back all right?' Genie croaked. 'Please tell me he got back OK.'

'He's fine. He's back.' And then she was in his arms and they held each other tight. Genie filled with emotion, hardly able to breathe, biting on her lip so she wouldn't cry. It was so good to be safe in Ri's arms again. She let one stray thought escape about how awful she must look, crazily covered in yellow mud, but he just held her tight and said nothing at all, like he was the rock she'd been aiming for all along.

She drank the water bottle dry as they stumbled back down the stream bed towards the farm. Genie told him about the weird bus stop in the middle of nowhere and the boy who'd been snatched by Fortress people.

Rian let her talk, let her get it all out. He felt sorry for the kid they took, but he was more relieved that the Fortress security hadn't grabbed her too. The reservoir was off-limits from now on.

'Promise me you'll never wander off without me again?' Rian asked her as they reached the hayfield.

'It's a promise, Ri. An absolute promise.'

Moucher was waiting for her in the backyard, his back paws bandaged and his coat gleaming once again. He knew he'd let her down but he needed reassurance she still loved him. Genie let him lick her hand, about the only bit of her not covered in mud.

'Traitor,' Genie told him as she headed for the shower. But she was real glad he'd had the sense to run away. He would have given her away for sure had he stayed.

Thirty minutes later she met the boys in the kitchen and seemed to be totally back to normal, like nothing had ever happened. Rian was worried about her, but aside from a couple of scratches, some sunburn and sore feet, Genie looked to be in good shape. He was impressed by that. Genie was like the battery rabbit on TV, going on and on. He was more proud of her than ever. They sat around the table, ate her muffins and drank coffee as Marshall tried to explain just who owned what around his land.

He had spread a map out and they studied it as Genie tried to tame her hair, the reservoir seemed to have made it all static. Marshall had his old Led Zepplin CD playing in the background, trying to educate them as to 'good' music, as he called it.

'See here? It's the old pioneer trail used back in the 1880s. They pretty much turned over every hillside around here looking for gold. The track goes down here; you were up beside the reservoir, Genie.' He jabbed the map with his finger. 'The Fortress is down there, underground, built right under the old trail. Cost a damn fortune to keep it secret. Everyone had to sign non-disclosure forms and they had lawyers ten deep to make sure you kept your mouth shut.'

He looked at her over his specs, took her arm a moment and squeezed it.

'You sure you're OK? I nearly had a heart attack when I saw you come home. You looked so wild.'

Genie smiled and nodded. 'The guards were idiots. I

215

was scared, but the woman was practically standing on top of me and didn't see me. I kept thinking she must be able to hear my heart thumping, it was sooo loud. Didn't help there was a beetle crawling over my ass. I nearly had a heart attack, didn't know what it was or if it was going to bite.'

'Not sure I could have stood that, I hate bugs crawling on me. I'm not surprised she didn't see you, girl. You get an A-star for camouflage. Smart thinking.'

'I didn't know what else to do. Just roll in the dirt and lie still and close my eyes. An ostrich would do the same.'

'I think the fact that you don't see any ostriches around here proves that you were a tad smarter, girl.'

'Ha, ha,' Genie replied, but could see Marshall was being genuine.

'You didn't say why the water vibrated? It was so strange. You know how when it rains real hard and the water kind of bounces up? That's what the reservoir was doing – only it wasn't raining.'

Marshall frowned. 'Could be they were drawing down water if they needed more power or . . . I don't know.' He shrugged. 'I can't think of any reason why the water should vibrate like that. I'd like to have seen it. Could be a phenomenon of a transmission in progress or one of the power generators that's resonating slightly off-balance deep below. Who knows?'

He pointed out a huge lake area behind the Fortress mountain ridge. 'There's Hobb Lake further back in the mountains that supplies the main generators, but your reservoir will be mainly used to cool the building. It gets super hot down there. And I mean hot hot. The air gets super-heated in transmission and they have to extract it with huge fans, comes out with the force of jet exhaust. Seen birds flying over too close get cooked, it's so hot. Neither of you can go swimming again up there, it's far too dangerous, way too close to them. Y'hear me?'

'Not get me back up there,' Genie declared emphatically.

Rian was thinking about the kid Genie saw abducted. 'Spurlake kids have to be making contact with someone who's directing them here. The printout Tunis showed me had a toll-free number you could call and it talked about out how you had to be fit. If you're desperate you'd do it for the money, right?'

'It had to be the vending machine,' Genie said, thinking aloud. 'As soon as anyone selects a drink, it rings a bell some place and the Fortress people come running. The drinks have to be drugged. The guy passed out really fast.'

Marshall nodded, pointing. 'I really can't believe the Fortress would be that crazy. Cops would have to investigate it and they wouldn't want it to lead back to them.'

'But they're getting their "volunteers" from Spurlake and other places around here somehow. And don't forget Reverend Schneider. He's collecting souls,' Genie remarked.

Marshall looked at Genie and smiled. 'However mean you say this guy is, he didn't send you to the Fortress, Genie. He put bars on your window, remember, to *stop* you leaving. I just can't believe there's someone out there trying to seduce kids with money on behalf of the Fortress. It's diabolical, too immoral to contemplate.'

Rian and Genie exchanged glances. They had to find a way to convince him he was wrong.

Marshall was looking at the map again.

'If they started over here in Spurlake and headed south down the river, there's a rope bridge over it, look here, see where the river squeezes through the canyon gap. The cable engineers use it so they don't have to go all the way downriver.'

'So anyone could walk it if someone told them exactly where to go. Two thousand bucks would be a big incentive if you're desperate,' Rian said.

'It's a lot of money to most people,' Marshall replied. 'But where's your proof? I'd need to hear that from your friends. Just how did they get there and who did they

218

meet? Seriously, I'm open to being proved wrong, Rian.'

Genie wasn't listening any more. She'd felt funny ever since she'd got back to the farmhouse and now she could feel her eyes fluttering and she was suddenly falling down that valley, swooping like an eagle to the bus stop.

She opened her eyes. She was in Synchro again. Sitting on a chair. Somehow she was dripping wet. Everyone around her seemed tense and there was a rising electronic noise, like no other sound she had ever heard. She turned her head – men and some women were in a control room behind reinforced glass, all dressed in white and watching the transmission platform with a keen intensity. There was a digital countdown going on at the side of the room and Genie could feel the whole place vibrating slightly, as if all the electric power in the world was under her and coming to a crescendo. Something big was about to happen.

The digital countdown was suddenly triggered. Eight . . . six . . . two . . . suddenly there was a kid materializing right before her eyes on the platform. He was glowing slightly, his head shaved, and he looked frozen with fear. It had to be the boy who had only hours before arrived at the bus stop with his backpack. He opened his eyes. The sound around the room was deafening now at maximum power. The boy saw her. She could see his eyes dilate as he stared at her and then BANG! There was a huge flash and he vaporized, dense particles blown backwards against the wall. Genie had felt the heat, like that of an exploding sun. His shadow had been instantly carbonized on the curved back wall. She began to shake uncontrollably with horror. *This* was what carbon blowback looked like.

There was shouting all around her. She heard one voice in particular. A calm, almost mechanical female voice.

'DNA stability lasted three point two seconds.'

Then another voice, closer this time.

'OK. We're going with a second test at twenty-hundred hours. Get this mess cleaned up.'

Genie opened her eyes. She was lying on the grass, a deep pink sunset glowed overhead. Rian was watching her carefully with a worried expression. He took her hand and squeezed it.

'Welcome back.'

He handed her a glass of water and she drank it all, still needing more. All she could see was the boy exploding and couldn't get the vision out of her head.

'I just saw a boy vaporize,' she croaked. 'I was in Synchro again. He was transmitted from the Fortress.

He could *see* me, Rian. He stared at me and then just exploded.'

She closed her eyes, trying to breathe normally.

Rian pulled her close to him and wrapped his arms around her.

'You're all right now. It was just a vision. You're OK.'

Genie shook her head. It wasn't a vision. It *really* happened. She'd been there, felt the force of the explosion, seen the boy's eyes as they opened.

'You were gone for two hours. Marshall wanted to call a doctor.'

'He did? I was? But it was just a couple of minutes. I was there . . .'

'Shh,' Rian soothed. 'Try to put it out of your head.'

Genie knew that would be impossible.

'He materialized, he looked at me, Rian, and then just exploded. All I heard was this woman's voice call out, "DNA stability three point two seconds." Like they didn't care one bit a boy just exploded in front of them. What kind of people can do that, Ri? What kind of people?'

'Three point two seconds?' Marshall queried, suddenly interested, leaning forward in his chair.

Genie turned her head and saw he was perched on a lawnchair watching her. Mouch was lying beside him, fast asleep.

'Three point two seconds must be the longest they've ever achieved. That's amazing.'

'Amazing?' Genie protested. 'Amazing? Marshall, a boy was killed.'

'I know. And I'm sorry, Genie. I'm thinking like they do, that's all. Think about it. They are transmitting DNA from over thirty-five kilometres away from the Fortress to Synchro. For three point two seconds the boy was stable. You said yourself he saw you. That means he was conscious for three point two seconds. They will be writing that down as a success.'

'Success?' Rian protested. 'You heard her. The boy *exploded*.'

Marshall grabbed his cane and slowly stood up.

'Rian. Believe me, when I was working there we only used inanimate objects. Clocks, toys, dolls. We were aiming towards using laboratory mice, I admit that. After all, our goal was teleportation of humans. But there's different people there now with different values. They obviously think they can get away with this. I'm sorry about the boy, but I'm telling you, tonight they'll be popping champagne and calling that a success.'

He said nothing more and walked into the house. Genie and Rian stared after him, horrified.

'Help me up,' Genie told Rian. 'Take me for a walk. I need air.'

A roll of deep thunder sounded in the distance. Mouch ran for the house. Doom never sounded so close.

'It's going to rain. His leg was right after all,' Rian told her, surprised. 'You got wet once today already. I'm wondering if you caught a fever.'

Genie shook her head. What she had seen was no damn fever.

# 19

## A Dog's Life

It was much later, half an hour after supper. Just after the lightning storm and the downpour that followed that drenched everything. Rian was in the barn checking that his roof repairs had held. Genie was outside, watching her pig wallowing in a mudhole. She still hadn't cleared her head of the events that happened earlier. She wasn't sure she could keep her supper down, either.

'You really think Marshall will eat my pig?'

Rian came out of the barn to join her. He held her in his arms and they listened to the water dripping off the trees and the pig making little snorts as she dug herself in deeper.

'Pigs have a certain destiny, I guess.'

'She's free, why doesn't she go off into the forest and just live wild?'

'Because a certain person around here keeps feeding her scraps and talks to her and scratches her head and she ain't going to get that in the forest now, is she? Also there are bears in the forest. She ain't stupid. You sure you're OK?' Rian asked. 'You've been so calm since you got back and—'

They suddenly heard howling.

'Coyotes,' Rian declared. 'Another reason not to go into the forest.'

The pig had heard them too and stopped moving.

That's when they heard the tortured scream. Genie looked at Rian in alarm.

'Was that a person? Was that human?' Her heart practically stopped. She'd never heard such a horrible, agonizing noise.

Rian moved quickly. 'There's a flashlight on the wall in the barn. Grab it.'

Genie ran back into the barn as Rian looked for weapons. Coyotes would run off if confronted. He knew that, but he wanted a stout stick, just in case.

Genie re-emerged with the flashlight. 'Which way?'

The cry started up again, to the south of them, and Rian dashed off into the forest, Genie following. 'What are we going to do?' Genie asked, trying to control her breathing as they ran between trees.

'Scare them. Keep listening.'

Genie could only hear her beating heart and the sound of breaking twigs underfoot. Genie had this vision of some kid being hacked to pieces by coyotes. What the hell someone was doing out here puzzled her. This wasn't the way to anywhere. Then again she'd already seen one boy out in the forest that day – and look what happened to him!

Rian stopped momentarily and Genie drew level, trying to get her breath. Rian's face was red and his lungs felt tight. There were still scars from his illness.

'Listen.'

Nothing but the sound of water dripping off trees. Not even birds. Nothing.

Genie stared into the trees, looked behind her too to make sure they knew the way back. It was dark now and she was still a townie and slightly afraid of the forest at night.

The howl, when it came again, practically stopped their hearts.

'This way,' Genie declared. 'This way.'

She set off, ready for anything. No idea what to expect. She was becoming a wild creature. Who would have ever thought she could go feral, end up chasing coyotes? It made her feel astonishingly good about herself.

They pulled up at the edge of the forest. The ravine was before them, a vertical drop of some hundred metres. Thick power cables straddled it, suspended from giant metal towers. At the bottom of the ravine, a few kilometres further on, would be the dreaded Fortress.

Rian took Genie's arm. The coyotes were standing in a semi-circle by a rock outcrop over the ravine. They seemed spooked. They knew Rian and Genie were behind them but they didn't move. There was someone or something on the rock. It was hard to see anything clearly now but there was definitely something there.

'What do we do?' Genie whispered.

Rian wasn't sure. The animals were behaving strangely. They didn't like the position they were in and the leader of the pack was looking for a way out. Rian knew they didn't normally attack humans. They preferred small prey. This was altogether strange.

'This way,' Rian whispered. He moved away in a big circle. Genie followed. It would allow the coyotes to slip away without confrontation.

Genie turned back. Sure enough the leader of the pack led them away and they vanished into the undergrowth. She looked at Rian and was amazed he knew how to do that.

'Watched a lot of wildlife shows on TV when I was fourteen,' Rian informed her. 'One of my many secrets.'

Genie squeezed his hand with affection.

They moved back to the rock. There was no one there.

'Hey? What? Where are you? Hey, we're here to help,' Rian was shouting.

No one. Genie was up on the rock. There was no blood, no evidence anyone had been there.

'I don't get it,' Rian was saying.

'Someone screamed,' Genie was saying. 'We both heard it.'

'Sometimes a coyote can sound like a kid crying. I've heard it. Spooky, but they've got all kinds of different sounds and expressions. They have to so they can communicate with each other in the pack.'

'So what *did* we hear?' Genie asked.

Rian wasn't sure. Whatever it was had gone or jumped, and if it had jumped it was dead now.

Genie was shining the flashlight over the edge, convinced she'd seen something. Rian pulled her back. She let him. It was stupid to take risks like this. 'Come on. We're heading back.'

A low rumble of thunder echoed down the ravine. The late summer storm hadn't left the forest yet. Lightning momentarily flashed and travelled along the power lines, snapping violently on its way.

'Let's go. Dangerous place to be in a storm, Genie,' Rian told her.

Genie wasn't sure which way was home, but she

sensed it was north-west. She couldn't get her bearings. She switched off the flashlight because it was confusing her. 'You know the way?'

'This way, I think,' Rian was saying. Suddenly he tripped and fell hard.

'Ri!' Genie shouted and was down beside him in a flash. 'What the . . .'

It wasn't Rian. It was something else entirely. Warm and shaking with terror. Rian had tripped over it. Genie took out her flashlight again and shone it on the creature.

Rian sat up, brushing dirt off his face and then stared at the thing on ground.

Genie's heart thumped wildly. It was a dog, but seriously deformed. The head seemed about right but the back legs were fused together. How had it got here? Still alive. Barely. Clearly terrified, it stared at them both. Some time or another it had started life as a Labrador. But it was clearly half the size and just plain wrong. Its neck was bleeding, a coyote bite most likely. She couldn't believe it had made so much noise, but then again, she could – she felt like crying.

Genie suddenly knew exactly what it was. And where it had come from. 'They're using dogs, Ri. It's like with the kids, the Fortress is using dogs.'

Rian looked at her and the unlikely dog and instinctively knew it was true.

'But how did it get here?'

'Why didn't the coyotes eat it?' Genie wanted to know. 'There were enough of them.'

She tried to stroke and soothe it but it flinched, afraid of her.

'My guess is they were as scared of it as it is of them. The poor thing. I can't believe this. I can't believe it's here. I mean, it can't have crawled from the Fortress or the other place. This is like – utterly impossible.'

Genie agreed. She kinda wished the coyotes had eaten it. At least it would be out of its misery. 'We have to show it to Marshall.'

Rian nodded. He was a bit reluctant to pick the dog up. Clearly it couldn't walk; it had to drag itself along. Who knew how far it had come?

Genie tried to pick it up, but it was heavy. Rian took it over and slung it over his shoulders. The dog whimpered, but seemed to accept it. Genie couldn't look at its imploring eyes. Once this dog was complete, some kid's pet maybe, and now it had no idea what had happened to it.

'Hell, this is what is happening to the kids, right,' Rian stated, only now realizing the full horror of what the Fortress was doing. 'Renée is lucky this didn't happen to her.'

'Lucky? They lost *all* of her body, Ri. It's criminal. This is like, what's that old movie . . . I know I started it once and couldn't watch . . . *The Island of Dr Moreau*. He was turning animals into humans.'

'What was the point of that?'

'I never found out, but it was gross. Believe me.'

The thunder rolled closer. Lightning flashed.

'Rain's coming back,' Rian announced.

Marshall was incensed. He photographed the dog, took measurements and then, well out of sight of Genie, humanely put it down. He had pointed out to her that it couldn't live and every second it did it was in agony.

'It doesn't have an asshole. If it ate it would have nowhere to go.'

Genie turned deathly white. There wasn't going to be any magic to fix this.

Rian was sitting in the kitchen. More upset than he cared to admit to anyone. Seeing the dog in the harsh kitchen light had made him queasy. He just sat quietly, drinking some water, hoping his stomach would settle. Genie was sitting in silence at the end of the table, thinking.

Marshall came back in later and washed his hands. He didn't say anything for a while. He knew they'd want to ask questions. He wasn't sure he had the answers.

'What I'd like to know,' Marshall said at length, 'is how it ended up in the forest.'

'Couldn't have been there long. Few hours maybe,' Rian muttered.

'Much less. The coyotes would have smelled its fear, but it was interesting they didn't finish it off.'

'You think someone dumped it?'

Marshall wasn't sure. 'No road up there. Not even a track. Seems unlikely.'

'It couldn't fly there. No one shot it out of a cannon. Someone must have taken it there. It couldn't walk,' Genie said.

Marshall walked over to a map at the end of his kitchen wall. He was looking at it quite intently. 'Genie, you say you were at a rock outcrop by the ravine?'

'Yeah. You can see the power transmission cables, they're real close. We saw lightning travel along some. Crackled and snapped, looked angry. Never seen that before.'

Marshall was studying the map still lying on the table, looking at the distance between the Fortress and its partner, the Synchro building.

'There's a point just about five hundred metres from

that rock where the power cables swing over the forest. It's pretty low. They cleared a whole lot of trees to get it over the hump.'

'So?' Rian asked.

'Let's say you were there at around eight-thirty tonight. You didn't leave until the storm passed.'

'We went to the barn first,' Genie reminded him.

'You would have taken about fifteen or twenty minutes running in the forest to get to the ravine. If the dog had been there about an hour, it would mean he arrived in the middle of the storm. Lightning's always pretty fierce around here.'

'Then no one is going to go out in that,' Genie said. 'It was like a monsoon.'

'Exactly. No one did.'

Rian snorted. 'The dog got there on its own, with no back legs?'

Marshall turned to face them, his face filled with conjecture. 'It did. I wonder . . .'

'What?' Genie asked.

Marshall looked at the map again. 'You have to take me out there. Now. We originally installed ground receptors there and they'd still be there. In case of information drop out. They'd enable the Fortress to boost transmission. If the storm somehow activated them or reversed the flow . . .'

Genie looked at Rian and shrugged. They didn't have a clue about what he was muttering.

He was still thinking aloud. 'Lightning can carry up to a hundred and twenty million volts. Say it strikes during a transmission from the Fortress. They are transmitting photons using light waves, but what if, at the exact time they transmit, the line of transmission was struck with a hundred and twenty million volts? It could either just disintegrate or shed its load.'

Rian looked at Marshall. The man looked quite excited.

'Marshall, we're kids, were still at high school. Explain in English.'

'The purpose of the experiment is the jump from one place to another.'

'Like in *Heroes*. I used to watch it when I was younger. Hiro could stop time and go anywhere he wanted by just thinking about it,' Rian explained.

Marshall clearly hadn't ever seen *Heroes*. 'That would obviously be impossible. You can't just instantly be in another place, the G-force would kill you. Genie, you believed you had been inside the Synchro building, remember? You were, but not in the flesh. I absolutely believe that you have a special skill. But *no one* can

234

physically jump from one place to another, a distance away, unless their DNA is transformed into photonic light pulses and squeezed through an electron tube to a defined destination. That's the whole point of the Fortress experimentation. Teleportation is matter transference and because it is unstable, bodies don't hold together. At least, none have till now.'

Rian got it. 'So the dog's transmission was interrupted.'

'It was, and at least most of it materialized in the forest. It didn't disintegrate.'

'But it was deformed.'

Marshall was thinking about that too. 'What if the deformation takes places at some point between A and B? The integrity of the original dog remains intact but . . . It has to be the receptors.'

He was quite animated now, thinking about it.

'We know, thanks to Genie, they have managed to transmit a whole live animal or person to the end destination, but it's somewhere along the last stage that things fall apart. The sudden surge of power somehow enabled transmission to shed its load. It acted like a boost. Your dog materialized on the ground. It could only do that if the receptors are up and running and acting like an end destination. Diverting the load. It's exciting.'

'Exciting?' Rian queried.

'The transmission worked. That dog is proof that they can really do this now.'

'Except for the bit where they fused his legs together,' Rian pointed out.

Marshall sat down. 'Yes. Except for that. But perhaps the lightning storm had more to do with that.' Marshall grabbed the flashlight. 'Come on. Take me there. I need to see the exact place it happened.'

Rian looked at Genie. She shrugged. She was too spooked to move.

Rian left with Marshall and Moucher. Genie stayed in the kitchen, but in the quiet of the farmhouse she realized she felt scared to be alone. It creaked in the wind and she didn't like the thought of the dead dog left outside. She hoped Marshall had buried it.

She suddenly had to leave and ran out of the house into the open. Marshall and Rian had already disappeared, but she could see the flashlight bobbing in the trees as they walked ahead. She took off, praying she wouldn't trip on any tree roots in the dark. It was stupid, she was bound to fall or crack her head open, or something.

Thirty minutes later, Marshall sat on the big rock trying to get his breath back and massaging his leg stump. It had been hard for him to walk so far.

'You sure this is the place?'

'Yeah.' Rian splashed the light around. 'We found the dog right here. You can see where the ferns are crushed. The coyotes were totally spooked.'

Marshall nodded. 'OK. Turn around. Walk twenty paces west and stop.'

Rian did as he was told, aiming the flashlight just ahead of him.

'OK. Stop. Bend down, shine the light around. Can you see any instrumentation in the ground, maybe some cables?'

Rian was looking at the forest floor. It was pretty dense, the plants had long taken over.

'No, nothing . . . wait . . .' He put the flashlight down and pulled at some ferns. The unmistakable light of a flashing red diode was blinking at him.

Marshall was beside him in a second. He whistled in surprise. 'Shine the flashlight on it.'

Moucher suddenly dashed off into the trees.

'Moucher? Don't disappear,' Marshall called after him.

Rian pulled up more ferns and exposed a stainless steel encasement and a strange-looking object with the Fortransco logo half obscured by mud.

'We installed these receptors around here about five years ago for another project. They didn't work. Like I said, they were supposed to boost the signal and prevent data dropout. Didn't do squat. They must have forgotten about them. There's several out here in various arrangements. I can't believe they're still powered up. They tried everything to make it work.'

'And now it has,' Genie remarked.

Rian started and swung the flashlight over in her direction. It found her by a tree, Moucher all over her like he hadn't seen her in weeks.

'I got lonely,' Genie confessed.

Marshall hardly registered her presence; he was so absorbed by the working receptor.

'It worked, well, to a point. No, I think it's stunning actually. Never thought I'd live to see it happen. Not in my lifetime. It's amazing. I think you're right, Rian. The storm must have triggered the receptors. It was just one of those happy accidents. Everything coming together at a certain point in time. Remarkable.'

'I don't think the dog would agree it's remarkable,' Genie mumbled, 'or happy. Imagine if they had got hold of Moucher here and transmitted *him*?'

Rian shook water droplets out of his face. Thunder rumbled in the distance.

'We should head back,' he stood up. 'It's going to rain again.'

Genie hung back. She didn't like the enthusiasm in Marshall's voice.

'You going to tell them about it?' Genie asked as they moved off.

Marshall could tell there was an air of disappointment in her voice.

'Genie, I'm a scientist. I'm just excited, that's all.'

'But you think it's possible it might work – one day?' Rian asked.

Marshall shrugged. 'Yeah. Clearly sooner than I thought.'

'But why's it so important? The experiment went wrong, didn't it?' Rian led them back the way they came. Genie followed closely now, Marshall behind them.

'You heard of Einstein, Rian?'

'Of course.'

'What about Tesla?'

'Tesla's an electric roadster. Pretty cool. Not seen one around here though.'

Marshall sighed, he'd forgotten about that. 'Well, the car is named after a pretty important inventor called Nikola Tesla who invented alternative current – all modern industry owes a debt to him. What about Crick and Watson, who jointly discovered the DNA molecule? What they're doing at the Fortress is as important as anything those scientists ever achieved. Science is ninety per cent experiment and ten per cent sheer chance. If the Fortress went public with this they'd get the Nobel Prize for sure.'

'But they won't. They can't,' Genie said, her voice flat and distant. 'They can't say anything to anyone. They're running an illegal experiment using humans and live dogs. They're criminals, Marshall. You know that. They still need to be shut down.'

There was an awkward silence for a while. Just the swish of their legs brushing through bracken audible.

'You're right, Genie. You're right. I'm just amazed by it all, got carried away by the science.'

Genie suddenly felt Rian's hand in hers. He squeezed it hard. Comforting as it was, she had a terrible foreboding now. Something very bad was going to happen.

'Promise me you won't tell them about the dog, Marshall. Please don't tell them.'

Genie wanted to cry. Had no real idea why, but she'd heard Marshall come alive for a brief moment and even though he'd lost a leg, been badly affected by the experiment, he was still as much in love with it as he had always been.

Dr Frankenstein apparently loved the monster.

# 20

## *Men with Guns*

An hour later, the rain and lightning came back more fiercely than before. Genie couldn't remember a summer like it. She'd experienced floods, heatwaves one day, freezing cold nights the next, and now these intense storms with freezing rain that fell like hard sticks hitting the ground with such force it flooded everything in just minutes. It just seemed to dump on the house all at once, arriving with a sudden wind rush that blew through the forest with astonishing ferocity.

Marshall had been in the barn when it arrived, trying to close the doors. He was trapped there now, as water literally gushed past the buildings, taking anything not nailed down with it. Genie fretted about him. This wasn't a secret he could keep. Instinctively she knew he'd called the Fortress, or at least someone he knew who worked there. It was too much to resist. He'd want to reconnect with scientists he'd worked with. They'd be really interested too. She and Rian had made a big discovery. She wondered if that kind of thing had ever happened

241

before? Some unfortunate kid, or bits of them, left dying on the forest floor. But then again, it would need the lightning to strike just so and she guessed it was a one-time thing. Marshall had tried to hide his excitement and she could see that he didn't want to bury the dog. It was pioneer science. It was something to be poked and prodded and sliced up – research, don't you know.

Rian had found a box of old shoes in the back room upstairs and was trying them on. It worried him he didn't have decent footwear. The blisters on his feet told that story well enough.

'You OK down there?' Ri shouted out over the rain drumming on the roof. 'I think I got two good pairs. They don't match exactly but . . .'

Genie smiled to herself. Rian would look ridiculous, but at least he might be more comfortable.

She turned, her eyes attracted to a flickering light behind her. Denis was suddenly standing there. He looked terrible. He seemed to have aged ten years. Genie's heart skipped a beat.

'Denis? God, what happened to you?'

'Genie.' His voice seemed strained as well. 'You've got to get out of here. They're coming. They've got guns.'

Genie closed her eyes and cursed. She knew this would happen.

Denis seemed to be fading right before her eyes. He looked sick. How was that even possible for digital boy?

'Something is going wrong. They are shutting servers down. We're losing kids. Something has changed. You have to go *now*! They're coming. They know about the dog. We heard them. They don't want witnesses. You have to *go*!'

Genie felt a heart rush, looked up the stairs and called Rian. 'Ri?'

Rian appeared, Renée in tow. Obviously she had delivered the same message.

'Go now,' Renée urged them. 'Please. You've no idea what—'

There was a sudden power cut, plunging them all into darkness. Denis and Renée instantly vanished.

Abruptly the rain stopped. The last sputter of lightning flickered outside, revealing Genie at the bottom of the stairs. Thunder rolled overhead, shaking the whole house.

Rian sat down and put on the shoes he had found. 'Damn. I knew that dog was bad news.'

'We go?' Genie asked, unsure.

'Damn right, we go. You were right. You heard them. Marshall must have told someone, I guess he couldn't keep it secret. We have to get out of here, Genie. Now.'

Genie knew it and was dreading it. She swore under her breath. Why, oh why, had they gone into the forest? Why did they have to find the dog?

'We need stuff,' she declared. 'We're a long way from anywhere.'

'No time,' Rian answered, starting down the stairs. 'Where's Marshall?'

'The barn.'

'Grab water, some food. I'll get a blanket and a couple of sweaters. Wait by the door.'

Genie ran into the kitchen, colliding with a chair. 'Damn.' She rubbed her shins, her eyes watering with the pain.

Moucher whined. He was sitting in his basket. He'd taken to it the moment the first crack of thunder had shook the house and lay there, quaking with fear.

'It's OK, Mouch, it's just me. Power's out.'

She groped her way to the larder and grabbed water, a plastic bag, cookies. She looked for the flashlight, but couldn't find it. Always the way, you need a flashlight to find a flashlight.

'Genie!' Ri was calling.

Genie spun around. Time to leave. She made her way back towards the door.

Rian was waiting. Door open, rain dripping off the porch. 'You got shoes on? It's going to be muddy.'

Genie whispered, 'Yes,' and moved outside. It seemed wrong to leave without saying goodbye to Marshall. She felt something brush by her legs. 'Eew, what . . . ?'

The dog barked once.

'No. No. You can't come, Mouch. You can't come.'

Rian was already walking away. 'Genie, come on. Ignore the dog. He knows where he lives.'

Genie ran to catch up. It was pitch black. No stars. No moon. The dog close at heel, happy to be with her. Perhaps feeling guilty he'd abandoned her before.

'Which way?' she asked.

'The track up the hill. We get up high and then wait in the cave.'

'There's a cave?' Genie asked, looking at him with surprise.

'There's a huge rock with a hollow. I found it a few days ago. Was going to surprise you with a picnic there on Monday.'

'You were? How many other secrets you got, Rian Tulane?'

Rian took her hand and squeezed it. 'Remember I asked you to make a cake?'

'The one I put in the freezer 'cause you said you weren't hungry.'

'And you sulked for about three hours.'

*That* she remembered.

'That was for Monday. Been building up to it.'

'But why?'

'Anniversary, Genie Magee. And I thought you were the romantic one.'

'But we didn't kiss until . . .'

'We met. We talked outside the ice rink exactly twelve months ago on Monday.'

Genie shook her head. Unbelievable. He was right. She was supposed to be the romantic one. 'We should have run away then. First day. I should have grabbed your hand and made you run.'

Rian took her hand again and held it firmly. He kinda wished they had run. Might have avoided all this. Would have been living in Florida or some place by now.

Moucher suddenly stopped beside Genie and let out a whimper. Genie turned her head to see what he was staring at.

'Ri, look.'

They were already above the farmhouse. In the distance they could see three distinct pairs of car headlights making their way towards the farm. Engine noise was only just audible. No one, but no one, came out here for anything. It had to be the men from the Fortress. It would be a struggle. The road would be mush and mud after all that rain.

'Renée was right,' Rian muttered.

Genie was suddenly thinking of Denis. How ill and pale he looked. Like part of him was missing.

'Keep moving,' Rian told her, moving off. 'We got to put some space between us.'

Genie followed. She needed no telling. The dog seemed to know where they were headed and moved on ahead. She wondered how they'd feed him or how they'd feed themselves. It was a distance to the next town. Two days walking in these conditions at least and all they had were cookies.

'I hope Marshall knows what he's doing,' Rian remarked.

Genie stopped a moment, a stone in her shoe. She looked back down the slope. The car headlights were getting closer. She reflected on the fact that there always seemed to be someone to be scared of. Always.

They reached the cedar forest just as the cars arrived. Even from up on the hill they could hear car doors slam and voices calling out. Genie felt relieved they had gotten away. If they started out after them, they had a good headstart and they were fit and young and the Fortress men wouldn't be. She drew comfort from that.

Rian moved right, scrabbling between rocks. Up above them the cloud cover was clearing, stars could be glimpsed in places. 'Come on. Not far now,' Rian whispered. 'Say nothing. Voices carry at night.'

Genie nodded briefly. She wanted to see this cave. She was still slightly annoyed he'd kept it secret, even if it was for their anniversary.

By the time they reached the rock, the cloud cover had gone entirely. The night was filled with brilliant stars and below them they could see the farmhouse reflected in the car headlights. Hear angry shouting too.

Genie looked into the dark cave and smiled. Rian had carried two old canvas chairs up here and made what looked like a picnic table. He hadn't been joking.

'Cute,' Genie whispered, her hot breath on his neck as she kissed him.

A sudden shot rang out below them. Another. A car exploded. Another shot was fired and then they saw the first flicker of flames from the barn. They had torched the barn.

'Damn,' Rian mumbled, instinctively wanting to run and help.

Genie grabbed his arm, held him back. She began

to shake. She imagined all kinds of things. All scenarios had Marshall lying there dead. 'You think they'll come looking for us?'

Rian held her tight. Didn't know any more than she did but he kissed the top of her head. He was worried about something more immediate now. 'The forest could burn.'

Genie had thought about that too. But the rain would have soaked everything earlier. Nevertheless, it was still late summer and it had been dry before today. It depended on how wet the forest floor was, she guessed. She wondered where her pig was. She prayed she'd run away but feared not; the pig liked to sleep in the barn.

'We safe here?' Genie whispered.

'For now. We wait and watch. All we can do. Wait and watch.'

The barn burned quickly, roaring and popping with all kinds of things exploding and showering the yard with sparks. Luckily the wind had dropped completely. Trees behind the barn burst into flame, but by chance Marshall had clear cut the old growth beyond that just a week before. The fire wouldn't cross that empty space.

By a small miracle the forest didn't catch, even though sparks flew high into the sky. Hot cinders and ash climbed vertically and drifted over towards the farmhouse rather than the forest. It was sheer chance everything was soaking wet.

The barn burned intensely for about forty minutes. Genie had a vision of Marshall lying shot dead or burned alive – she tried to shut it out of her head.

'What do you think they're doing down there?' Genie asked after a while.

'Looking at everything. His notebooks, whatever. Digging up the dog.'

'I don't think he buried it. He just said he was going to bury it to please me.'

Genie knelt down and rubbed Moucher's head. She wondered again if Marshall was dead. She realized that she really cared about that. He'd been the first adult ever to be nice to her. She said a little prayer for him and hoped it was enough.

Around four a.m. they heard a car door slam. Then more. The cars turned around. They watched two cars leave.

'Should we go down?' Genie queried.

Rian shook his head, barely awake, his head felt so heavy.

'Uh-uh. We don't know they all left.'

'Marshall might need—' Genie began, but Rian held her back.

'He'd be the first to say be cautious. We'll wait till first light. Not long now.'

Genie felt guilty. What if Marshall needed help? Rian was only trying to protect her but . . . She stared at the ground. Sandy and dry, it would be OK to sleep here for an hour and she had Ri and Mouch to keep her warm.

'You think there are any snakes?'

'Moucher here is a snake dog. Aren't you, Mouch? Anything comes close to us, pounce. Got it?'

Genie smiled as the dog seemed to nod at him. 'He looks very serious.'

'He'd better be. Got you to protect now, Genie.'

He took Genie's hands and pulled her arms around his neck. 'I think we're safe. But we're staying put to make sure. All right? I know you want to go down there. But I think Marshall's dead. We can't help him now.'

Genie bit on her lip. She wasn't convinced. Not till she'd seen him with her own eyes. She felt Rian lean in to kiss her. She felt his lips and his hands holding her tight and she began to float. A huge shiny wall of glass was suddenly wrapped around them both and they were utterly, completely safe.

They didn't witness the shooting star streak across the indigo sky.

# 21

## Devastation

Moucher woke Genie. He sat up straight and whimpered like he was scared. Genie sat up instantly awake. It was daybreak, the sun had not yet risen. Rian was still asleep beside her, his head resting on a rock. She turned and suddenly saw what Moucher was staring at.

The white-tailed deer was beautiful. It didn't seem afraid of them at all and grazed on a lush patch of grass. Genie stared at its antlers and as the light grew in intensity she could see some scarring too from fights. She reached out to Moucher and held his collar. She didn't want him to do anything rash. Moucher looked at her as if to say, 'Are you crazy, have you seen the size of that thing?' but at least he stopped shaking.

The deer moved off back down towards the forest.

By the time Rian woke, the deer had vanished and Moucher was sniffing the ground around them, impatient to get home.

'Ow, my neck.'

Genie smiled. 'My shoulders. Can't believe how

hard sand is to sleep on.'

She brushed sand off Rian's back and he got up and ran to the bushes. Genie had already done the squat, deathly scared that a snake would find her whilst she was so vulnerable. She was looking at the cave when she noticed graffiti. *G & Ri Forever*. She felt suddenly very warm inside. *G & Ri Forever*. Exactly. She decided not to say anything about it – just commit it to memory. She wondered when he'd written that. She would have written it in the sky in reply if she could, in giant letters for the world to see.

Moucher came up to her and barked once. He wanted his breakfast.

'Cookie?' She dug the last cookies out of the bag for him and he snapped them up.

Rian was looking down at the farmhouse below. Smoke was still rising from the burned-out barn, a wooden skeleton all that was left. The sun was slowly rising now.

'You think it's safe to go down now?' Genie asked.

Rian wasn't sure. 'Maybe.'

Genie stood up, brushing sand off her jeans.

'I hope they left some food.'

Rian looked at her and shook his head.

'All you can think about is breakfast?'

253

'I'm trying not to think about the trouble we're in, Ri. Or what happened to Marshall.'

Rian looked back down at the farmhouse. 'Anyone who can use live, lonely kids and dogs for experiments, knowing they're going to die, wouldn't hesitate to kill someone who knew about it.'

'You realize that means us,' Genie said.

'And that means us. We go down, get stuff and get the hell out, Gen. It was good being here, but we've got no business being here now.'

Genie shivered. She'd grown used to this place, even happy – and she couldn't remember when she'd ever been happy.

They set off down the slope towards the farmhouse. Moucher racing ahead, glad to be going home. Her heart went out to the dog. He was going to have a shock when he got there.

The farmhouse was silent. The burned-out shell of a Fortransco Ford Edge SUV stood outside the house. It had taken several surrounding trees and bushes with it but hadn't caused major damage. There was no sign of Marshall. Moucher was barking and if that didn't get anyone's attention, nothing would. Genie looked at Ri and he signalled that they should go by the back way. Genie nodded.

They looked in through Marshall's ground-floor bedroom window. It was a mess. Someone had trashed it. Rian listened for trouble at the back door left ajar but all he could hear was the sound of the fridge. The power was back on, at least.

They didn't go in. Rian didn't feel it was safe. He signalled to Genie to go around to the front.

They emerged by the overgrown blackberry bushes at the side of the house.

Moucher spotted them and ran up, wagging his tail. He had no idea what was going on. Genie could see a lot more trees had perished behind the barn than she'd originally thought but weirdly one tree stood untouched and green, whilst those all around it were crispy black.

'Where's Marshall?' Genie asked him and Moucher immediately dashed off towards the barn.

They followed, cautiously, hoping there was no one in the house watching.

The barn frame was a charred ember, still smoking. The remains of an old tractor all that had survived inside. The smell of cinders and ash was strong. Moucher was barking again. Genie recognized that his tone had changed; it wasn't a happy bark.

'I don't think I want to look,' Genie said, wincing.

255

Rian said nothing, but rounded the corner and checked his steps.

Marshall was lying on the ground, his prosthetic leg detached and partially burned where he'd fallen. Beside him lay his shotgun, the stock blackened and blistered. The paint on his truck was scorched, but the truck itself had survived intact and Rian could see that Marshall had been trying to save it; an empty fire extinguisher lay on the ground. Marshall must have been overwhelmed by the fumes or the heat. Certainly his face was red and looked sore. His jacket was badly singed. Rian knelt over him and felt his pulse. He was still alive! Moucher was pawing him, trying to wake him.

'He needs to get to the hospital now.'

'We should phone his son. The cop.'

'We have to help him, Genie. Go to the house, get some water.'

'What you going to do?'

'See if the truck still works. He has to get to hospital today. We can't wait for people to come.'

Genie ran off, Moucher following.

'Be careful, we don't know if anyone's still inside,' Rian shouted after her.

Genie was strongly aware of that. She nervously approached the farmhouse, heart beating wildly. Marshall hadn't looked very alive to her, but they had to try and save him. Worse, the closest hospital was in Spurlake, the very last place she ever wanted to go back to.

The door swung open. Bravely she let Moucher enter first. He found no surprises. Not unless you counted the wrecked furniture.

Genie walked in, stepping over broken glass. The kitchen had been turned over, but the fridge was still on, the water inside would be safe in the sealed bottles. She quickly emptied some chow for Moucher into his bowl and then ran out again clutching a bottle of water.

Rian somehow got liquid down Marshall's throat, Genie holding his head up. She noticed the burns on his hands and how his nostrils were swollen. The fire had burned his nose hairs and that had to hurt!

'I'll get the truck started,' Rian said. 'Go back to the house. Get rugs, a pillow, bandages, there's some in the bathroom. Also some ice and grab us something to eat. It's a long drive.'

'We have to go to Spurlake?'

'The next hospital would be Abbotsford and that's too risky. Sorry, Genie, but we've got no choice.'

Genie knew that, but had to ask. She had a real fear of going back. She set off again. Rian was suddenly so self-assured and in control. It helped calm her.

257

All the pictures of the missing kids were gone from the
bathroom. The medicine cabinet was emptied, all the
pills and potions lying in the bath, most spilled. Genie
plucked the bandages out and then some painkillers, in
case Marshall woke up.

Back in the kitchen she swiftly made some fried egg
sandwiches. It was about the only thing she could think
of that was fast and wasn't spoiled. Keep them going, she
figured. She needed ice and knew there had been some
cubes in a bag in the deep freeze.

She ran to the back, Moucher at her heels again.

'We're going back to Spurlake, Mouch. Got to get to
the hospital. You're coming too.'

Moucher looked at her expectantly as she opened the
freezer. Genie looked inside. Her scream was probably
heard all the way down in Vancouver.

When Rian arrived, out of breath and wild eyed, Genie
was still shaking. He was carrying a tyre rod, ready for
anything. Genie was packing the sandwiches. She had ice
and dog biscuits ready to go. He could see she was trying
to be 'normal'.

'What?' Rian asked. 'I heard you scream.'

Genie just pointed towards the freezer. She still

couldn't speak.

Rian went over to the deep freeze. The remains of the dog they had found were in there. The dog's head had been severed. Beside it lay the carcass. Gross. Just lying there on top of the frozen meat and vegetables.

'Did you call his son?'

'No. Sorry. I was freaked.'

Rian slammed the lid down. That he understood.

He went to the phone on the wall. Miller's number was first on the list.

'What do I tell him?'

'Tell him Marshall's still alive first,' Genie remarked. 'Then tell him about the men who burned the barn. I'm going to brush my teeth and get rugs.'

Rian stared after her. One moment she's acting totally spooked then utterly normal. He dialled. He didn't want to be calling a cop, but they had no choice. It went straight to voicemail. Rian sighed with relief. He could say everything now without fear of interrogation.

Upstairs, Genie hesitated. Why couldn't she and Ri just keep going? She knew they had to help Marshall. You don't really have a choice about that kind of thing. Karma and all that stuff. You had to do what's right, but go back to Spurlake? Face her mother and Reverend Schneider all over again? She didn't know if she could do that.

She saw the shadow on the wall move as she left the bedroom. She jumped.

It was barely a shadow, just a finger of light.

'Denis?'

It was Denis, she was sure of it, but he was barely there. He had no voice, just his eyes followed her.

'We're taking Marshall to Spurlake hospital,' she told him. 'I'm sorry I haven't helped you, Denis. I guess I haven't helped anyone.'

Denis shook his head. Genie thought she saw him say goodbye. Denis soon would be no more, she knew that. It must take a huge effort to even come to here. She felt hot tears forming. Denis had been so sure she could help him.

'Got to go,' Rian was shouting from downstairs. 'Genie?'

'Coming.' She moved towards the stairs and glanced back at the wall. Denis had gone. As she walked down the stairs she resolved that this could not end here. She had to do something to help the missing kids – stop the Fortress experiments, expose it somehow.

They rolled Marshall on to a rug, heaved him on to Rian's shoulders and then finally tipped him into the back of the truck. He was heavy, even if he did only have one leg.

Genie was scared to hurt him further. She wrapped rugs around him, wedged him up against a hay bale to stop him rolling.

'The cop wasn't answering. I left him a message to come to the hospital. You got ice in the bag? Wondering if you should put some on his burns.'

Genie looked back at Marshall lying there in the back and thought she remembered something from first aid classes at school. 'I'll cool the burns first, then put the plastic bag over his stump, cover the worst of it anyway. You can't put anything there that might stick to the flesh. You sure you can drive this thing?'

'I drove it back from the store on Monday,' Rian confessed. 'Marshall was too tired to drive. You slept in, remember?'

Genie blinked. She remembered he'd got up real early and gone to get stuff for the roof. Well, at least he'd had some practice.

'When we come back you have to teach me. All right?'

Rian looked at her a moment, then smiled. 'Deal.'

'Get going,' Genie told him. 'I'll close the gates after you.'

Moucher was last up and settled in beside Marshall. Rian got the truck started and lurched off. Genie watched, impressed he didn't hit anything as he drove forward. He stopped to wait for her to close the gates.

'Wait,' Genie shouted, as she put the chain on. She suddenly ran into the forest.

'Genie? What the . . . ?'

Genie wasn't listening. She crashed through the undergrowth and found what she glimpsed only briefly. The pig was sat there, covered in ash, singed for sure, but alive and eating wild mushrooms, as far as she could tell. She hugged it. The pig snorted but didn't resist.

'Hope you find lots to eat in the forest, pig. I am so happy you're still alive.'

The pig made no comment, just continued eating, stopping for just a second to look at Genie, perhaps in recognition, she hoped so. Genie felt her spirits lift. The pig was still alive.

She ran back to the truck, her face covered in ash.

'She's OK,' she declared as she climbed in the back with Marshall. 'Get going. Pig seems unhurt. She must have been pretty near the fire though.'

Rian set off again, shaking his head. Loving someone who cared so much about people and pigs gave him a good feeling, even if it did drive him mad from time to time.

'Where are the sandwiches?' he shouted through the open window.

'On the floor, pass me one,' she shouted back.

Rian found them, passed one out for her and ate his as he drove. They were still slightly warm. Tasted pretty good.

Genie winced as she saw Mashall's burns. She pulled back the rug and started to soak the gauze bandage with ice. She knew you couldn't put the ice directly on the skin as it would burn it still further. The wounds were red raw. She loosely wrapped the damp bandage on the worst affected areas to keep the air off it. She looked at Moucher watching her; he looked distressed.

'Don't worry, Mouch, I'm not hurting him, I promise.'

She tried not to think about where they were going. She was dreading going back to Spurlake. She wondered how they'd ever get out of there again.

The track was bumpy and amazingly had mostly dried out from the rain the night before. The sun had risen above the treeline now. Rian concentrated hard. The truck was easy enough to drive, but he wasn't looking forward to being on the highway. He hoped they wouldn't be stopped. With no licence and an unconscious guy in the back, it would take a lot of explaining.

# 22

## *Working in Mysterious Ways*

Reverend Schneider was sat in a pool of sunshine under the oak tree on the luscious green lawn outside his Church of the Free Spirit. It was his favourite place in the mornings and a good location to write sermons. Alyssa Cullins was arranging flowers in the church, as was her custom on a Wednesday, and he kept note of the time as he had a baptism at noon. The church was thriving and that was his message this week. Life has its own rewards if you know how to recognize them.

A man in a dark suit loomed into view, casting shade over his writing table. Reverend Schneider looked up and inwardly groaned. It was the overbearing security chief from the Fortress. They shared a mutual loathing for each other. He had a habit of arriving unannounced.

'There's a cop asking questions about your little volunteer scheme.'

Schneider frowned. He didn't like these kind of unannounced visits. 'Good morning to you too. What kind of questions?'

'Seems some kids are passing around an offer to pay two thousand dollars for experiments in BC, no questions asked, no need to alert your parents either. There's a toll-free number.'

'You call it?' Schneider asked, laying his pen down, surprised that he was so well informed.

'Disconnected.'

'You want volunteers, you have to have the tools to find them.'

'This is your set up? A little sick, ain't it? Even for you.'

'It's non-traceable. They only stay up for a week at a time and the toll number dies after ten days. It's based in Eastern Europe. They specialize in this kind of thing. Don't worry, it's carefully targeted. Like I said, untraceable IP address. The cops can look all they like, but it all ends up in Moscow or some place and they aren't the type of people to cooperate, if you know what I mean.'

'I don't like it. Fortransco doesn't like it. *Particularly* if it ends up in Moscow. Finish it.'

'You're the people who can't find test subjects. I'm merely doing my part.'

'You were just supposed to look for orphans, as I recall.'

'And disaffected teens who wouldn't be missed. Spurlake is full of 'em. Their parents come here to pray for understanding. I should know.'

'Spurlake is a cess pit now. Take months to get it straight.' He looked around him at the elegant newly built glass church and its fancy tower, as well as the Mercedes Benz parked in the first parking bay.

'You've done well out of Fortransco, Schneider.'

'I only take what I deserve.'

'Seems you live well on our generosity.'

'It's an investment in the wellbeing of the town, as the sign says: *Fortransco, Building Better Communities for All*.'

'All I'm saying is, we've had a security problem.' He lay a piece of paper on the table. 'We want these two. Matter of urgency.'

Schneider looked at the names. He wasn't at all surprised to see Genie Magee's name there. Didn't know the other, but he supposed it was the boy who'd broken her out. It'd be a pleasure to teach him a lesson he'd never forget.

'Find them. You understand? I don't want any prying eyes or cops looking under rocks. No more toll-free numbers. We're getting too many "volunteers" from this location. Your profile is too loud. You understand me? Praying for the missing is a nice picture in the local paper, but cool it, Schneider. No rocking the boat. Find these two and you're done.'

He walked away without another word, his black suit and shiny shoes worn like a badge of authority. Schneider watched him get into a muddy Chevy Volt and silently drive away.

'Everything all right, Reverend?'

He looked up at Alyssa and smiled. 'You ever hear from your daughter, Renée? She's been gone an awful long time. I was hoping she'd found it within her heart to at least send you a letter to say how she is.'

Alyssa Cullins tugged at the white pearl necklace she always wore around her neck, her lips tight. 'I ain't holding my breath, Reverend. She was wayward from the day she was born and I suspect you're right, she's most likely on the street or worse. You can't make a bad heart pure and I only pray she doesn't make others suffer as much as she made me.'

Reverend Schneider picked up his pen again.

'Nevertheless, I wish those who are so quick to leave us would set our hearts at rest. It grieves me that so many children have run rather than come to us for help.'

'She's a wicked girl. Wickedness finds its own punishment, Reverend.'

'I regret to say that I believe you are correct in that matter, Alyssa. It's a harsh world.'

267

# 23

## *Reunion*

Spurlake seemed uncannily normal, considering. Sure there was damage, but people were shopping again and Rian drove by McBean's coffee shop – *Celebrate our re-opening with us* – where people sat outside drinking lattés, even though there were piles of debris in the road still to be collected. They had expected more visible signs of devastation. Perhaps it was the late-afternoon sunshine that made things better than they were.

Spurlake Community Hospital was still a mess from the floods, however. Mud was piled up on the walls of the east wing and several temporary buildings had sprung up in the car park.

The ER unit had taken Marshall off their hands and spirited him up to the burns ward. They didn't like the fact that he'd been unconscious for hours already.

Rian had filled out forms, given phone numbers and played it as cool as he could. They'd wanted him to wait for the cops, but he made a genuine excuse – he needed to park his vehicle which was blocking the entrance – and then got the hell out of there. No way he was waiting for the police. Frankly he was just surprised they weren't waiting for them, considering it was a cop's dad and all.

Genie waited with Moucher in the truck. Her heart leaped when she saw Rian heading back, walking with a calm determination. He was just one metre away when a cop car pulled up and Officer Miller got out.

'You Rian Tulane?'

Genie slipped down in her seat, but Moucher barked excitedly, jumped over her and bounced clear out of the open window. He ran right up to the cop, wagging his tail in desperation, so happy to see the man.

Rian saw the cop bend down to greet Moucher and knew there was no escape.

'I guess I owe you a great deal,' Miller said, fending Moucher off.

Rian said nothing.

'I got your message. They just called me. Dad's on a drip and he's pretty confused, but he's going to be all right. Thanks.' He turned to look at the truck.

'Thanks to you too.' Genie popped her head up. It was dumb to hide.

'I'm glad he made it,' Genie told him.

'I need to know what happened. You want to talk?'

'We in trouble?'

'Down, Mouch. Sit.' He looked at Rian in the eye.

'If you mean, do you need to talk to your mother, who's been worried sick about you, I'd advise it. Genie's mother is staying with Reverend Schneider, which is not a place I'd recommend you or she visit. So you're still responsible for her, Rian. You understand? You broke her out. She's your responsibility.'

Rian understood. The cop was giving him a long rope to play with.

Miller looked at them both and could see that they looked tired and scared. 'Take the truck to Jonah's Diner. Order what you like. I'll be there in twenty minutes. Can I trust you both to do that? Get Moucher something as well.'

Genie exchanged glances with Rian, both unsure about this.

'Jonah's, OK?' Miller reasserted. 'I'm going to check on my dad.'

'We'll be there,' Rian said, making a decision.

Miller took off, walking towards the hospital entrance. He didn't look back. Clearly he believed that they would do as he said.

Genie watched Rian get in and Moucher jumped up beside her.

'He's got Marshall's eyes,' Genie remarked.

270

Rian looked at Genie and shrugged. 'I guess we go to Jonah's.'

Genie sighed. Ninety per cent of her wanted Rian to get them out of town, drive till it ran out of gas and they were miles away from Spurlake, but that ten per cent would make them do what the cop said. He hadn't seemed mean or angry. If he were anything like Marshall, he would be fair. They'd find out soon enough.

Genie waited until they were back on the road before talking again. Her head was full of 'what if's and 'what to do's.

'You going to call your mother?'

Rian had to think about that. He knew he was supposed to call or go see her, apologize for running out or whatever, but . . . he glanced across at Genie's pensive face and knew that his heart was full. Genie was his responsibility now and she came first, before mothers or anything. The cop had said as much.

'Later,' he replied. Jonah's Diner was one block away.

'Moucher needs walking,' Genie said. 'Order me fish and chips. I heard it's good.'

'You've never eaten here?'

'Never allowed. You forget I've been held prisoner all my life, Ri. I've never eaten anywhere out, anytime.'

Rian felt a hot flush of anger. The way she had been raised and treated. He was going to make it all up to her one day. Somehow.

'Order a burger for Mouch too, with extra gravy. He deserves it,' Genie added.

Miller was sat at his father's side. He was on drips and painkillers. They'd covered his exposed skin with soothing creams and bandages and his father was awake. He looked rough and his front teeth were broken. They had beaten him good. His upper torso was bruised to hell. Someone was going to pay for this.

'The kids?'

'Sent them to Jonah's to eat.'

'Don't do anything to them, Max. They're good kids.'

'I know. They got you here, remember.'

'Fortress might know about them too.'

'Dad, just calm down. I'll take care of them, OK? You want to tell me what happened? The message said that the barn was torched and men with guns came.'

Marshall seemed to go in and out of consciousness. He opened his eyes again.

'We found proof in the forest, Max. They're using kids and dogs for testing.'

'Who beat you?'

'Fortress security chief. I shot and wounded one of the guys. He tried to kill me. They were looking for the transmission sample. The dog. It was in the freezer. I . . .'

Marshall went under again. Miller put a hand on his father's arm.

'I'll be back later. Rest.'

He got up to go. Was his old man ranting and raving again? Or was this something real? Why would the security chief beat him up? Didn't make any sense. His dad was getting a pension from Fortransco. Certainly there hadn't been any report of a shooting. He glanced back at his father, couldn't believe he looked so old. The Fortress had used him up and spat him out.

He looked at his watch. He hoped the kids were still there. He was counting on them being hungry and the boy being too scared to go home. He stopped at the nurses' station on the way out, made sure they knew it was his dad they were dealing with. He wanted him to get the best care.

273

# 24

# *Jonah's*

'Aren't you Genie Magee?'

Genie looked up, surprised to hear her name called. The girl with frizzy dark hair seemed to look genuinely surprised to see her. 'It is you!' she added with obvious relief. 'My God, you're alive. Rian Tulane too. I love the clothes, so retro, genius.'

Genie blinked. 'Mandy?' They went to some classes together and Mandy was always full of gossip. She had the attention of a gnat for learning but was big on sports, she remembered. 'I didn't recognize you. What happened to your hair? And I swear you used to wear glasses.'

Mandy looked embarrassed and flicked her hair in front of her face. 'Nooo, don't look. I went blonde and my dad went absolutely crazy and forced me to dye it back and I think I killed it. I may have to shave it all off and top myself it looks sooo bad. My God!' She was looking more closely at Genie. 'You're so brown and your skin looks great. You look so different. We all thought you were dead. You too, Rian. I mean, so many people are missing since the flood and your house was wrecked, Genie. I just can't believe you're alive.' She turned to Rian. 'Your ma has been going insane, seen her wheeling around town putting up posters everywhere. I can see now why no one recognized you though. Don't look a bit like the kid on the poster.'

Rian had no idea as to what she was talking about and couldn't remember the last time his mother had taken a photo of him. He looked at this well-toned, broad-shouldered girl and couldn't seem to remember her at all. He was annoyed she'd spotted them. It was kind of inevitable, it being such a small town.

Genie smiled at Mandy. 'How's school?'

Mandy shook her head. 'Well, we're having classes in the gym. The east wing is full of homeless people now and there's people with broken legs in just about every class and no one is really doing anything serious. You're missing nothing. You coming back now?'

Genie shook her head. 'Uh-uh. Done with school.'

Mandy looked kind of surprised. 'Really?' She couldn't imagine what a person could do if they didn't finish high school. 'I can't wait to tell the girls you're alive. I mean, we heard all kinds of stuff. I didn't believe it, but hey, at least I can rule out abducted by aliens.'

She laughed at her own joke and Genie smiled.

'Where you going? What are you gonna do?' Mandy asked, a look of genuine concern on her face now. 'I can't wait till Grad. I'm heading to Victoria.'

It was Genie's turn to be surprised.

'Of course, you don't know. I won a gold medal at the BC Summer Games and I'm representing BC in the Aaron Baddeley International Championships at Lion Lake in November. I'm going semi-pro as soon as I can. Already got sponsors lined up and everything.'

Genie looked at Mandy with amazement. She'd known this girl for three years already and never once knew she played golf, let alone was good at it.

'Wow.'

Mandy nodded excitedly. 'I won a Nissan Leaf in the Alberta tournament last month. Can't even learn to drive it until my birthday, but I was like stunned for days when it arrived.'

'Double wow. I'm jealous.'

'And you?' Mandy asked.

'I'm going to raise pigs. Already got my first sow. She's huge, with the softest ears you ever saw.'

'Pigs?' Mandy whispered, clearly taken aback. 'Like farming? Dirt and stuff?'

'That's where we've been,' Rian intervened. 'Studying animal husbandry. It's a big career now, lots of opportunities.'

Mandy was now definitely thinking that Genie had been abducted by aliens after all.

'Pigs?' she repeated, not quite able to remove horror and disbelief in her voice.

Rian enjoyed watching her face. It wasn't even a lie. Mandy began to back away like they had some kind of virus.

'Really cool to see you guys. I'm so glad you're alive.'

Genie nodded. 'Me too.' She gave Mandy a little wave as she scooted back to her table and the safety of her parents.

Genie glanced at Rian and rolled her eyes. It would take like twenty whole minutes for the whole town to know she was alive and going to raise pigs. She realized that she didn't care. Rian was the only person she cared about and he was right here. Her foot stroked his legs under the table and he smiled at her.

'Just remembered I need to go to the bathroom. Don't run off with anyone. Even if she does have an electric car, fa-na.'

Rian grinned. 'Not even for a Leaf.' He looked back towards the door. 'I hope Miller comes soon, they're going to bring the check any minute now.'

'He will,' Genie reassured him.

She headed off towards the restroom, her tummy

bloated. She hadn't eaten so much ever and she was definitely experiencing a sugar-high or something.

She heard a hiss as she walked by a table and there was one of Reverend Schneider's disciples eating her dinner with her spotty child. She glared at Genie and Genie immediately remembered her, the petite poisonous pale face with tight thin lips viciously spitting and name-calling from behind the barred doors. It shook her momentarily and all her terrors instantly came flooding back. She stumbled and fell against the woman's table, upsetting a glass of orange juice over her. The woman shrieked. Genie backed off, stunned. This was why she could never return to Spurlake. The whole town was full of poison that could appear around any corner her whole life. She rushed into the restroom and rested her head against the wall a moment, feeling dizzy and not a little sick. She remembered the woman *exactly* now. Her expression of hate as she prayed on her bony knees and tried to grab her and pinch her flesh when she handed food through the bars. She instinctively rubbed the scar on her arm that would be there forever now to remind her of their cruelty.

Genie suddenly turned around and went back out of the restroom and returned to the woman's table. She was trying to mop up the juice and her kid was whining. She looked frightened when Genie suddenly reappeared.

Genie leaned in towards her, whispering. 'I'm out. I'm free, and remember this, Satan and I know where you live, Mrs Garvey.' Then turned on her heels and headed back to the restroom. She didn't know why she'd done it, but it made her feel a *whole* lot better.

There was a Missing Child poster behind the toilet door. Rian's face peered out of it – and Mandy wasn't kidding, he had to be about twelve in this picture. She wondered why his mother didn't have any recent photos. She guessed there weren't any 'Missing' posters for herself behind any toilet doors.

When she returned, the evil woman was gone and Miller, the cop, was sitting with Rian. They both glanced up as she sat down.

'Dessert?' Miller asked her. 'Blueberry pie is pretty good here.'

'Eaten enough for a week,' Genie answered, rubbing her tummy. 'How's Marshall?'

She noticed the fresh scars on Miller's knuckles and how his neck was bulking out. He needed to watch his weight, like most other cops in Spurlake. Altogether too much blueberry pie, in her opinion.

'Marshall was conscious for a while. Real grateful you got him here. Me too. He would have died without you guys taking responsibility. I really appreciate what you did.' He was feeling awkward. 'He seems pretty fond of you both.'

Genie said nothing. She noticed Rian seemed edgy, but then again it was kind of natural in the company of a cop. They didn't know what he would do to them and he had every right to force Rian to go back home.

'He's going to be all right?' Rian asked.

Miller shrugged. 'He won't be heading back to the farm for a while, that's for sure. He'll fret about the apple crop, 'bout the only thing that brings in any money for him.'

'Barns gone,' Rian pointed out. 'Nowhere to store the apples, I guess.'

'If they get picked, Pickards might take 'em. They've got refrigeration.'

Genie looked at Rian, a question on her face. He picked up on that quickly.

'Who's gonna pick them?' Rian asked.

Miller looked at them both and you could see he was making a big decision.

'You know I'm supposed to turn you in, right? I'm guessing, Rian, driving without a valid licence? You don't have to admit anything. You can go home, of course. Your mother is pretty frantic to have you back. Posters all over town. But then again, there's so many missing or dead now and people have to face up to the fact that the flood took a whole lot of people with it.' He looked at Genie and sighed. 'You've got no one. Your home is gone and your mother claims you aren't even her daughter.'

Genie felt her heart lurch a moment.

'She said what?'

'She was mad at you. But then again, she and Reverend Schneider . . .'

'Don't even mention his name,' Genie snapped. 'He's utterly evil.'

Miller put his hand over hers.

'He is and you aren't. That's the one thing I am sure about. Dad is a good judge of character. You have a choice, Genie. You can go into foster care. You're still only fifteen. And back to school, of course.'

'Yeah right, foster care,' Genie remarked with sarcasm, withdrawing her hand from the table. 'That's so gonna work out. Anyway I'm finished with school. At least in Spurlake.'

'Or we can come to a deal,' Miller suggested. He leaned back in his seat to allow the waitress to bring his pie and coffee. He looked up at the waitress when she arrived and smiled. 'Bring the check, Shannon. Put the kids' on mine.'

The waitress looked surprised but nodded, moving away without comment.

'You and Rian go back to the farm. I want you to straighten it out. Record all the damage. I'll mail you the insurance forms. You know where to collect the mail? The mailboxes by the crossroads?'

Rian nodded. 'Marshall went twice a week to collect mail there.'

'Good. If you can find the digital camera Dad keeps in the back room, all the better. Take pictures. Fill in the forms and send them back to me. I'll include the postage with the letter and you can just mail it back at the crossroads. The barn can be rebuilt. Marshall is a great believer in insurance. You guys pick the crop and keep the place running until my dad is better.' He looked at them both, gauging their reaction.

'It's not just the apples, you understand, that's just Dad's pocket money. You just can't leave a place like that empty and I can't get out there as often as I like with the bridge down.'

'What about the Fortress? They just came in and torched the place. The whole forest could have gone with it. You going after them?' Genie asked.

Miller said nothing for a moment and took a taste of his pie. He shrugged.

'They will deny everything.'

'One of their vehicles is burned-out there,' Rian pointed out.

'They will either claim it was stolen or it will be gone already. Fortransco is well protected in this town. They're powerful and secretive. I don't have their influence.' He shrugged. 'Sorry. Just trying to be honest.'

Genie and Rian exchanged glances again. They didn't need to say anything. Going back to the farm was exactly what they wanted to do, but she was scared the people at the Fortress would come back. She guessed this was the catch. There was always a catch.

'We'd be happy to go back,' Rian said, after a moment. 'We can pick the crop and fix the farm up, but we've got no money, not even for gas.'

Miller held up his hands.

'That's taken care of. The real stuff is this, Rian. I am happy for you two to go back. I know you guys are in love. Got married at nineteen myself. I understand why Genie would want to go back, but what about you? Your mother says you're bright; you've got a future. You can go back home, go back to school, no harm done, you understand? You have to think hard about this.'

'And Genie?' Rian queried. 'You think I want her to go into foster care? You think I can walk away from her?

She's—' Rian was about to explode and Miller weighed in quickly to diffuse.

'She can go back to the farm. She'll be safe there. You visit on weekends. I'm just trying to say that there is a sensible option and a—'

'He's right, Ri,' Genie intervened. 'He's not being mean. You could go home. I'm cursed, remember? I ain't going into care, but wherever I am, I'll still love you and be part of you and—'

Rian slammed his hand down on the table. Heads turned across the restaurant.

'No. I made a promise. I look after Genie. I don't care about school or my mother or anything. I'm never leaving her. We're going to the farm.'

Miller said nothing. Just ate his pie and stirred some sugar into his coffee as conversation resumed around the diner.

'Well,' he declared after a moment, smiling at Genie, 'he seemed to pass that test, OK, eh? Looks like we have a deal.' He looked at Rian directly. 'And you have to do one thing, Rian. Go see your mother. What you say to her is your business, but she's been going frantic for news of you. At the very least she deserves that you see her. You understand?'

Rian understood. He'd rather be facing giant rats

than the wrath of his mother, but it had to be done. He owed her that.

'And you,' Miller informed Genie, 'I know I'm not supposed to say this, but stay clear of Reverend Schneider. Don't go near him, or your mother. I really don't think they have your best interests at heart.'

'He'll know I'm here. Mrs Garvey was here. She's one of his disciples.' Genie pulled up her sleeve. 'See this scar? She twisted the skin off my arm. Her friend, Mrs Meyer, branded me with this.' She showed him the Celtic cross scar on her other arm.

Miller looked away. There was nothing he could say to comfort her. Certainly not tell her that Mr Garvey was a big-time lawyer who effectively kept the police off Reverend Schneider's back. How could he tell these kids how little power and influence he really had in this crazy town?

'What do you know about some scheme to give kids two thousand bucks for participating in some fool experiment? You think some kids believe that?'

Rian looked at Genie and she nodded, it was OK to talk.

'Your dad said that you didn't believe that the Fortress was responsible for all the kids going missing from Spurlake.'

Miller sighed. 'It's not about me believing anything, it's about getting proof. You have proof?'

Rian wasn't sure they had. 'Speak to Tunis Lehman. He showed me a printout. It comes with a toll-free number so they can give you directions.'

'The deputy-principal's adopted son?'

Rian nodded.

Miller shook his head. 'He's listed as missing. The flood . . .'

Rian felt his heart skip a beat. Tunis, his friend, was dead. But maybe he wasn't missing. Maybe he'd gone to find his girl in Vancouver. He didn't have to be missing at all. He was with the blonde girl he met online.

'His truck washed up in the river along with a few others,' Miller added.

Genie squeezed Rian's hand. She knew how that had to hurt.

'You guys were so lucky to survive. That flash flood came out of nowhere, caught a lot of people by surprise. You OK?' He was looking at Rian.

'Tunis was his best friend,' Genie said to him. 'Helped break me out of the house.'

Miller suddenly made the connection. 'Red truck, black kid. I got the description, didn't make the link. Poor guy. I'm so sorry, Rian.'

286

Rian shook his head, didn't want to talk about it. 'We found a dog in the forest near the farm. Its legs were fused together. Your dad believes it was part of a transmission from the Fortress that went wrong.'

'There was a storm last night,' Genie interjected.

'We brought the dog back and he got real excited. Made us show him where it came from and . . . We think he called someone at Fortransco,' Rian told him. 'Next thing we knew three Fortress cars turned up, there was shooting and they torched the barn. We ran. We found your dad by the burned-out barn at first light.'

Miller digested this, frowning. 'Dad said he shot at someone. I've got no reports of any gunshot injuries though. A dog isn't any kind of proof, but I can see that my dad might think it would be.'

'And we've been talking to some of the missing kids from Spurlake,' Genie said softly. 'I don't think you're ready to hear it though.'

Miller looked at her with a puzzled expression. They were exactly the same words his father used to say, *'I don't think you're ready to hear this, Max.'*

'I'm trying to keep an open mind. I really am.'

'Renée Cullins,' Rian said. 'Turns out she's my half-sister. She says Reverend Schneider drove her there, tricked her. Genie saw him at Synchro. He's definitely involved.'

Miller twiddled a spoon on the table, not sure what to make of this information.

'Denis Malone,' Genie added. 'He still looks thirteen, not grown a centimetre in two years.'

Miller looked away a moment. Second time Denis Malone's name had come up recently.

'Kid's dead, guys. I was at his funeral.'

'Cary Harrison,' Rian told him. 'Said he went to Reverend Schneider for advice and wound up at the Fortress. He doesn't even remember how.'

That got Miller's attention. 'Harrison? His dad still roams the mountains looking for his body every weekend. You were talking to these kids? You know where they are?'

Genie was wishing they hadn't mentioned this.

'They're in the Fortress. They aren't like us any more. They've been—'

Miller signalled them to keep quiet. A man and woman walked by and he said good evening to them. They took the booth at the end of the restaurant. He waited a moment before talking again.

'I know what you were going to say. It's something my father was working on, right?'

Genie nodded. 'You could look for them, but you'd never find them. I don't think we could give you proof like "evidence", it's not like that. More like a magic trick. Makes no sense until they show you how it's done. Even then you can't really understand it.'

The check arrived and he picked it up. 'I want you guys back on the road the moment he's spoken to his mom. We clear on this?' He took some folded banknotes out of his pocket and discreetly slid them over to Rian. 'Buy clothes and food, stuff for Moucher, whatever you need. But don't do it in this town. Gas up at Ferryman's by Cedarville. Ferry's OK. You can trust him. All right?'

They nodded.

'Don't use the phone at the farm. If there's an emergency, go to the next farm or to the general store by the mailboxes. Y'know, in case anyone's listening. Do nothing stupid. Don't go near the Fortress or Synchro, don't be part of that madness. Understood?'

'Understood,' Rian and Genie repeated.

'I'll be up there in about ten days. Get the apples in, or at least as many as you can, and store them in the back of the house in the cold store. It's a windowless room behind the stairs. There's a brick floor and concrete walls in there to keep the room cool. Should be boxes and tissue paper in there as well. Keep them separated with the paper between each layer and keep yourselves to yourselves. There are powerful people around here who think they can do pretty much as they please.'

Genie knew that already.

'Thanks,' she said.

'You can say thanks when it all works out. And kids . . .' he looked at them both very keenly. 'This is all between us. As far as anyone knows I asked you to go back to your folks and that's what you agreed to do.' He checked his watch. 'It'll be dark in three hours. Don't leave town till then. End of story. Now go.'

Miller watched them leave. He stayed in his seat a while thinking about what he'd just done, how much trouble he could get into and the rights and wrongs of it all.

# 25

# *Mrs Tulane Awaits*

Rian pulled up beside a white clapboard home, its roof covered in blue plastic. He reverse parked into a space between two cars. They both heard the clunk.

'Oops,' Genie said, trying to see what they'd hit.

Rian pulled a face, embarrassed.

He got out to take a look as Genie surveyed the storm damage in the street. Trees were torn down, roofs ripped open, garages demolished and smashed vehicles abandoned. Someone was going to get rich fixing them up.

Rian opened the door, climbed back in and tossed the bent licence plate behind his seat. 'There's a damn wheelbarrow full of metal junk left here. Have to get that fixed back on tomorrow first thing. Don't need to give the cops a reason to stop us.'

'That's all? You could put the one from the front on the back maybe?'

'Uh-uh, doesn't have one. At least it didn't damage the tail lights. You OK? You look spooked.'

'No. I'm fine.' She was looking at the old-fashioned

wreck of a house they were parked in front of. 'You live here?' It didn't seem right somehow, smaller than she remembered. Not that she'd ever been inside.

Rian shook his head. 'I didn't want to park outside mine. She'd only fret I'm driving without a licence and . . . y'know.'

She understood.

Genie could see that Ri was reluctant to go. They sat there in silence for several minutes, only Moucher making a fuss, wanting to go outside.

She knew that seeing his mother wasn't the only problem – he didn't know what to do with her.

Rian sighed and stroked the dog a moment, trying to find the words he needed.

'It's OK,' Genie whispered. 'I'll take the dog for a walk. You go see her. You should do it alone. She will have missed you, Ri. She loves you, remember.'

'It's not the going in, it's the leaving,' he said finally. 'She's going to be double mad at me. You don't know what she's like.'

Genie looked away. She was thinking that if she were ever a mother herself she would make it her business that no kid of hers would be afraid of her. She hoped it would be a promise she could keep.

'Take the dog for a walk. Don't go further than

this block and don't lose sight of the truck, OK? I'll be as fast as I can.'

Genie put a hand out to his and squeezed it. 'Take as long as you like, Ri. Mouch and me will be here.'

Rian took a deep breath and opened the door. He looked back at Genie and she gave him an encouraging smile, even though she feared the worst for him and wondered if he'd really come back. She grabbed the dog and realized that she hated losing sight of Ri, even for a minute.

'Let's go for a walk, Mouch.'

The dog was out of the truck in a flash and Genie followed. It was twilight now. She didn't think anyone would recognize her. She stayed close to the houses and let Moucher sniff around to his heart's content. Half of her wished Rian had taken her with him, the other half was glad he hadn't. Either way she wasn't going to be happy until he returned.

Rian stared through the window at his mother working on business accounts in her office. She looked well and there was no sign of Mr Yates. For that he was grateful. He stirred himself and went to the front door. It was open. No one locked their front doors in Spurlake until they went to bed. It was one of the things most people boasted about, how safe the town was compared to the big city.

Rian had wondered for hours as to what to say, but when it came to it, he said what he always said. 'Ma. I'm home.'

'Rian? RIAN!'

His mother rolled out of her office, confusion and surprise on her face. Rian entered and she rolled the wheelchair up to him in the hallway and stopped short. She didn't put her arms out to him and he didn't put his arms out to her. That kind of stuff had ended years before. Rian could see his mother was crying and struggling to say something but was fighting with herself somehow.

'I saw the posters today,' Rian told her. 'I'm sorry. You must have worried.'

His mother still couldn't talk.

'The flood, caught us by surprise. Nearly drowned. Got lucky I guess. I . . . we . . . were ill for weeks. Picked up something in the water. A farmer looked after us but there wasn't any power or even a phone.'

His mother took out a handkerchief and blew her nose. 'The things I wanted to say to you . . .' she began. 'You just left. You just went off with that girl . . .'

Rian could see the anger rising, the familiar face of his mother.

'Genie. She's called Genie. She nursed me, Ma. Wouldn't

be here now if she hadn't got me through it.'

'You wouldn't have left this house if it wasn't for her.'

'I did. I had to. There's things you have to do and I had to free her.'

Mrs Tulane looked up at the ceiling, as if looking for inspiration. 'And where is she now?'

Rian felt his gut twisting. He hated this.

'She's waiting for me. Outside.'

'Too ashamed to show her to me?'

'Too scared. Look, Ma . . .'

'Don't "Look, Ma" me. I had people searching for you. I have looked at,' she shuddered, 'many dead bodies, Rian Tulane. I cared enough about you to look for you. Prayed for you. Did you think about me even once? Did you ever think about your responsibilities to me? Or school? Or that you are a minor and have no right to—'

'Ma, don't start. I came to see you. Tell you I'm OK. Make sure you're OK but I'm not coming back. I'm with Genie now.'

His mother blinked. Clearly she hadn't expected this.

'What do you mean you aren't coming back? You – you're just a kid; you're not *with* anyone. Understand? You have an obligation to finish school. You're an A-grade student, Rian Tulane. You're going to throw that all away on a Munby girl? A girl possessed by God knows

295

what? What has she done to you? Are you so bewitched by that little bitch you don't know what a laughing stock you've become?'

Rian began to edge towards the door. This was the part he'd been dreading.

'She's the best thing that ever happened to me. She loves me. I love her, Ma, and you can shout and scream and hate me, but I made a choice.'

'A choice? You call that a choice? She pregnant already? You think life will be great when you are on minimum wage and trying to raise barefoot Munby brats?'

Rian stared at her, disliking the way her mouth twisted with hate when she was angry. He had reached the door, making a decision to bring something she wouldn't like to the conversation.

'Dad ever tell you about my sister, Ma? Or did he keep Renée secret from you too?'

His mother was caught off-guard. Rian could see from her face that she knew about Renée. He briefly wondered what other family secrets there were.

'Renée was a nice kid, Ma. Dead now. Seems no one quite loved her enough. Well I'm not going to let that happen to Genie. We have each other and we will find a way to survive. She's mine and I'm taking care of her.'

'How did you find out about Renée?'

'Not important, Ma. Look, I'm leaving. You can stop looking for me. I'm fine and I can take care of myself. You take care now. OK?'

His mother suddenly realized that he was leaving again.

'Rian. No. Don't go. I need you here. Rian. I'm sorry. I was angry, I—'

'Got to go. Be well, Ma. I hope Mr Yates is good to you.'

Rian walked out and closed the door behind him. He realized that he wished he'd run upstairs and grabbed some clothes and sneakers but he was out now and it was too embarrassing to go back.

Mrs Tulane stared at the front door, tears streaming down her face. She'd made a complete mess of that somehow and he'd gone again. She felt a wrenching pain in her heart. She'd lost her son. Really truly lost her son. And to a dreaded Munby girl. It was a tragedy. He couldn't see it and she couldn't stop it.

'You want me to go after him?'

Mrs Tulane looked at Mr Yates hiding in the shadow of the dining room doorway and she shook her head. She turned her wheelchair around and headed back to her office without another word.

'I'll make some peppermint tea,' Mr Yates called after her.

'Genie?'

Rian was running towards the truck. It was dark now and he was still shaking from his encounter with his mother. He didn't know what he had really expected. He was the one who had run off, he was the guilty party, and she had every right to be mad at him. He knew that. It was just . . .

'Genie?'

He came to a halt three metres from the truck. The cabin was empty. There was no response to his call. Not even Moucher barked. 'Genie? Come on out, this isn't funny.'

She still didn't answer. A Mercedes sedan went by, the headlights briefly touching Rian as he stared around him at the houses and the open ground opposite. It was unlike Genie to play games. He began to feel very worried.

'Genie?' He heard the desperation in his voice. Perhaps she'd gone? He knew she was worried that he'd stay with his mother and she'd be left out in the cold. Genie was full of doubts and perhaps she'd just feared the worst and taken off. But didn't she know he'd made a promise? Surely she knew he kept his promises.

'Genie?' he called, louder this time.

He thought he got a response. Whimpering. It came from the empty lot across the road. He ran to the clearing.

'Genie? Moucher?' He'd disturb the neighbours shouting but didn't care. 'Genie?'

The whimpering got louder. He went deeper into the long grass, working back towards the ground opposite his house. He stopped and listened again.

'Moucher?'

A pizza delivery car went by, its headlights sweeping across the grass revealing the emptiness and the abandoned truck he used to play in when he was a child. He thought he saw something, but couldn't be sure.

'Genie? Mouch?'

The whimpering got louder. He wished he had a flashlight. 'Mouch? Where are you?' He moved further into the grass towards the mound where he'd once pretended to be King Kong. Moucher made a noise and he turned to his right.

Moucher was lying prostrate in the grass, clearly in pain and injured. He was all sticky from bleeding and couldn't seem to move at all. Of Genie there was no sign at all, but one thing was certain, she hadn't run away. Someone had taken her.

Rian gathered the shaking dog in his arms. There

was something in his mouth. Rian was wary of harming him further; a dog's liable to bite if you hurt it, friend or not.

'What happened to you, Mouch? Where's my Genie?'

Rian carried him over towards his house. It was the only choice he had. The porch light was on and he could see movement inside.

His heart was beating fast with rising anger. Genie and Mouch must have been waiting for him across the road from his house. What if she too was lying somewhere unconscious, injured or worse? He didn't want to think about worse.

The front door opened. His mother was there, saying goodbye to Mr Yates.

Rian stepped into the light and his mother screamed.

'Rian!'

Rian staggered by her, the dog beginning to slip from his arms.

'Genie's gone. Moucher's been attacked. Genie's been taken, Ma. She's been taken.'

Mr Yates and his mother stared at him. He was covered in blood from the dog and the animal looked in terrible shape. It was a shock. Mrs Tulane closed her eyes a moment trying to regain her composure. This was no time for petty arguments, rights and wrongs.

'Get the dog on to the kitchen table. Rian, the flashlight by the fridge. You'd better be sure your girl isn't out there before you assume anything.'

Rian ran with the dog to the kitchen. He could see now in the light that Mouch had a huge gash in his head that had to be really painful. No wonder he'd bled so much. His fur was soaked in blood.

His mother rolled in behind him. 'This your dog?'

'Genie's. The farmer gave it to Genie.'

'Someone beat that dog with a stick,' his mother was saying. 'Get my sewing kit, rubbing alcohol and a sleeping pill, all in my office. You know where.'

'Not going to call a vet?' Mr Yates asked.

'This dog will die if we don't stitch him now. He'll bleed out. Rian, get back out there. Make sure your girl isn't lying out there too. Jim, turn me around.'

The dog needed help now. She approached the table and saw that it was shaking with fear and pain. She knew all too well that she had to save the dog if she was ever to get her son back on her side.

Rian was frantic. He should be out there looking for Genie, but in his heart he knew she had gone. Some evil person had taken her. Moucher was lucky; he was in good hands. His ma used to breed terriers before the accident, she knew all about dogs and how to fix them.

301

He returned with the stuff and placed it beside the dog. 'I'm going out to find her.' Mrs Tulane grabbed his arm.

'Be careful, Rian. Remember this: what you feel about this girl right now, I feel about you.'

Rian blinked, momentarily confused. He broke free and ran for the back door. All he could think about was Genie and didn't need any weird stuff from his mother.

He was in the long grass, sweeping it with the flashlight. He'd played a hundred games in this place when he was a kid, knew every square metre of it. If they'd hidden Genie anywhere, he could find her.

'Genie?' he called, not expecting an answer.

He ran to the drainage channel, then the mound. From here he could shine the flashlight pretty much everywhere. Genie was nowhere to be seen. He was wasting his time. He should be out on the road looking for her. Where, he didn't know, but he knew he was losing precious time here. She was long gone. He just hoped that Moucher had given whoever it was a lot of trouble.

He checked the area by the fence where he'd nearly broken his arm once, checked too the clearing which was often used for burning stuff when no one was looking. Nothing. This was useless. She could be miles away by now.

He ran back to the house, sick with worry.

'Ma?'

Moucher was splayed out on the kitchen table, his legs twitching as Mr Yates held him down whilst his mother finished off the stitching. The dog was flinching, making growling noises, but under sedation allowing it to happen. She had shaved the area where she was sewing and it was one hell of a gash.

His mother acknowledged his arrival and pointed to a bloodied gold Celtic cross with a broken chain. 'It was in his mouth.'

Rian picked it up and realized instantly whose it was. The initials on the back confirmed it. Reverend Schneider.

'Schneider. Reverend Schneider took her.'

Mr Yates looked at Rian, taking an interest for the first time.

'That's quite an accusation, Rian.'

'I know him. He's the one who locked up Genie in her house. He's the vilest man on the planet, Ma. He took Genie. He's involved in all this, the Fortress, everything.'

Mr Yates wasn't impressed. 'Why would he do that? Why is he interested in your girlfriend? Doesn't make sense to me. It could be anyone's cross. Anyone's.'

Rian just looked at Mr Yates and then at his mother. 'And you wonder why I left.'

Rian put out a hand to Moucher and touched his paw. The dog barely responded under the effect of her sleeping pill.

'I'm going to find her, Mouch. I'll get her back for you.'

Rian turned to leave but Mr Yates blocked his way.

'I don't care for your manners, Rian Tulane. I don't care for the way you have abused your mother and disrespected her. I understand this girl may mean something to you, but you are not going out covered in blood. Just how far do you think you'll get?'

Rian looked down at his shirt and hands and realized that Mr Yates was right. He looked back at his mother who was cutting the fine thread she'd sewn up the dog with.

'I'm sorry, Ma. I'm sorry.'

His mother looked across at him and nodded. 'The dog will be sore and we're going to have to stop him scratching it open again, but he'll live. I'm going to give him the other half of the sedative. OK?'

'I didn't mean for everything to turn out like this,' Rian told her, 'but you have no idea what is going on out there

304

and what Reverend Schneider is doing. I didn't mean to disrespect you. I can't think about anything except Genie right now. I have to find her. I *have* to try to save her.'

Mrs Tulane turned around in her chair and fixed her eyes on him.

'You'll be saving that girl all your life, Rian. There's something about a Munby girl that brings out chaos and pain in the world and I am desperately sorry you have fallen for her. I really am, but you have and you have to do what you have to do. Whatever comes, if you find her, keep her safe' – she bit her lip as she said this – 'bring her here so you both have a chance at a better life. Understand? I am not rejecting you. Find her and then come home.'

She looked back at the dog twitching on the table.

'Your dog will be waiting for you.'

Rian made towards her, as if he was going to hug her, but she backed up in her wheelchair, putting up her hands. Rian suddenly remembered he was covered in blood. 'I'm sorry, Ma. I wasn't thinking.'

'Shower and change. Mr Yates is right. If anyone sees you like this they'll think the worst. Get going.'

Rian turned and fled. His head filled with emotions. His mother had forgiven him. He didn't know why, but she had. He raced upstairs to his bedroom. She was probably right; he had to get cleaned up. If he got stopped for any reason and they saw the blood, the cops would have him cuffed in seconds, never mind that the truck had no plates and he didn't even have a driver's licence.

## 26

# *The Good Man of Spurlake*

'It's a shame your dog is dead, Genie. Could have used it at the Fortress, we have been making some useful experiments with dogs.' He checked her reaction in the rear-view mirror. 'But then you know that. You seem to know a lot of things about us. Never heard that curiosity killed the cat? Of course, if you'd stayed in your room, you'd be a lot better off than you are now.'

Genie was quietly seething with anger. She was glad Moucher was dead; at least Reverend Schneider couldn't do anything worse to him now. She was sat in the back of Schneider's Mercedes, feet and wrists bound tight. She hadn't seen him coming. One moment she'd been waiting for Rian to come out of his mother's house, next moment a sack had been pulled over her head and he'd kicked her legs away from her and she'd fallen hard on the ground.

She'd heard Reverend Schneider swear when Mouch took a bite out of him, then the dog's final howl as he struck back.

'Doesn't bother me you don't talk, Genie. I know what

you are going to say anyway. But you know what? No one is going to listen to you. Especially a girl who everyone knows is possessed by evil. Your bad luck, I guess, to run into Mrs Garvey. You think she wouldn't call me?' He chuckled, slowing down for a T-junction. He turned off the highway and Genie briefly saw a road sign announcing Klaklacum First Nation Reserve. They were definitely headed for the Fortress.

'I did a bit of research on the Munby family,' Reverend Schneider said suddenly. 'Hundred years ago the Munbys owned this valley. Actually, Alfred Munby discovered the gold back in 1888. He had a lot of run-ins with the First Nation natives who naturally considered this their territory. They say your great grandmother was Stó:lō, one of the Siska Native band, a real beauty. It caused quite a scandal. Some claim the town was cursed because of old man Munby. He owned the mill, the general store, the dairy, the gold mine, everything. Lived until he was ninety. Left everything to his daughter, your grandmother.

'But she was crazy. She gave all the money away and built herself a shack by the railroad. She hated her father. No one knew why. She built your high school. You didn't know that, did you? Naturally, they changed its name when she killed your father. Of course you don't know about that either. Happened when you were less than a year old. They called it an accident, gun went off by mistake, but I tend to think there's no accidents with a Munby. Your mother's sister, your Aunt May, met with an unfortunate end when she was fifteen, just like you will. Odd coincidence, don't you think?'

Genie blinked. Her mother had a sister? Her father had been shot by her grandmother? She knew none of this. Her mother had never once mentioned anything, ever. How could you never mention you had a sister? She suddenly thought of Renée, half-sister to Rian. No one had mentioned her either. What was going on in Spurlake? Why did this town have to have so many secrets?

Genie's eyes began to flutter. She began to feel dizzy, her head was swimming and she could feel she was going under, couldn't stop it, she was floating away . . .

She was flying. She was a bird on the wing, proud of her fine brown feathers. There were two men standing on top of a building, talking. She circled around trying to get her bearing. It was a tall building in the middle of nowhere. She looked at the forest beyond and understood that this was the Synchro building and there was a helicopter parked on the roof in a large painted circle. Reverend Schneider was listening to a small man with white hair in a shiny suit. She couldn't understand what they were saying, but whatever was discussed was sealed by a handshake. They both looked up at her as she flew close and she quickly dived away to avoid their gaze. She wasn't certain, but it was as if they knew she was there. She hadn't liked the expression on their faces.

She flew on, swooping down past all those glass windows and as she turned again she saw young faces pressed against the glass. Renée was staring at her, Denis stood beside her and Cary Harrison too. They were pointing at something on the ground. She turned again to look behind her. Reverend Schneider was opening the trunk of his Mercedes.

She was trying to comprehend how he could be on the roof and simultaneously on the ground, when the banging on the glass got her attention again. Genie didn't understand what it was they wanted. They kept pointing. She looked back at Reverend Schneider again and suddenly understood. He had a rifle in his hands, trying to find the range. She tried to fly away, flapped her wings, beat as hard as she could, but as she heard the blast of the gunshot, she knew he'd found her heart.

She plummeted to earth. Landed hard, felt the air knocked out of her lungs. Three rats were running crazily in a circle in the dust beside her. So this is how it ends, she was thinking, as Reverend Schneider's black shiny shoes appeared by her head. This is how I die.

'You're back?' Reverend Schneider remarked as he saw her eyes flicker in his mirror. 'I hope you enjoyed your sleep, Genie. We need you alert. Lots to do once we get there.'

Genie's throat was dry, she could barely speak, she was in pain. She couldn't bring herself to look at those hooded eyes staring at her. She could still feel herself twitching in her death throes on the ground. She'd been a bird, he'd shot and killed her. How weird was that?

'You're next, Genie. One more volunteer for science. You should be proud. You're a pioneer. One of the few who will make it possible for the many.'

*You're next*, Genie noted. Kind of heard that before. Was this fate then? Is that what her dream was? The thing you couldn't escape. No matter what, she was going to end up in the Fortress.

'It was you I saw in the Synchro building, wasn't it?' he asked, studying her in the mirror again. 'I don't know how you got in there, or how you got out, but you must know, we can't overlook a thing like that.'

'How many?' Genie croaked. 'How many kids have you killed?'

'It's God's work, Genie. Transforming pathetic lonely kids into souls. I know you know them. Little Denis Malone and that red-headed girl, Renée. You think we can't tell where they are at any time? Of course, we found a way to stop that. Can't have our little souls escaping now, can we, scaring the nation. All stored safely now, can't harm anyone. And your boyfriend Rian will be right behind you. He'll have to follow. If he loves you at all, he'll follow.'

The worst of it was that Schneider was right. The moment he found out who had abducted her, he'd follow.

'And my soul?'

'You, Genie Magee are going straight to hell, where, incidentally, you belong. This is the end of the line for the Munbys. The absolute end of the line. As your friend Satan says, "Abandon hope all who deign to enter my kingdom".'

Reverend Schneider's phone began to ring. He checked the number of who was calling and sighed. He pulled over and got out of the vehicle to take the call.

Outside he seemed to be arguing with someone, pacing up and down beside the car.

Genie frantically began to look for a way to escape but the doors were locked. She couldn't move her arms or feet. She knew once he got her into the Fortress it would all be over for her.

He got back into the car and swore, glancing back at her a moment. He looked annoyed about something.

'Got to pick someone up on the way. Don't get up any hopes, Genie Magee. You know where you're going. Makes no odds if it's an hour later, you'll get there and you'll be out of my hair forever.'

# 27

# *Pay the Ferryman*

The Ferryman gas station five Ks outside Cedarville was run down, a last outpost before Highway 1 that clung to life with a grim determination, with a flickering neon Coke sign in the window that always said *Happy Holidays*. It was the kind of place where old tractors came to be fixed but mysteriously always lay dead in the field out back, along with the old yellow school buses, gutted vehicles and abandoned pick-up trucks. Optimistically they stood ready in case a part was ever needed. The gas was overpriced and most people passed on by to fill up elsewhere if they could.

Rian knew this place well. He used to ride out here on his bike in summer, always trying to improve his time. He'd buy an apple, maybe have a milkshake in the half-assed drug store tacked on to the side of the building. Then he'd ride home, uphill all the way. Best time: one hour and twenty minutes.

It was eleven at night. He was exhausted, eyes red-rimmed. He filled up with gas and knew in his heavy heart that he'd set out too late. There was no way he could intercept Reverend Schneider or gain access to the Fortress. He'd let Genie down. At least Moucher had tried to bite the man, done some damage. But Reverend Schneider had her and could pretty much do what he liked with her.

Rian felt empty and powerless. He did not want to admit that he was never going to see that girl ever again. He didn't know how to stop the man, didn't have a plan to rescue his girl. They didn't train you for this kind of stuff in school. Equally he knew that if he didn't go, didn't at least give chase, Genie would never ever forgive him, and that was why he was filling up under the dim naked light of the gas station with the bugs swirling around his head.

'Rian Tulane, ain't it?' the old man asked. Rian looked up, surprised anyone would recognize him or know his name. Then again the old man must have been there since they built the place in 1950, or whenever. Maybe longer. He stared at him and the jacket and scarf he was wearing. It was a warm, windless, stuffy kind of night. The man looked liked he'd been fixing something, his hands were covered in oil and his broken nails looked sore and infected.

'That's Marshall Miller's vehicle you got there.'

Rian nodded. 'Marshall's in hospital. His son asked me to run his truck back to the farm.'

The old man didn't look convinced. 'Max said that?'

Rian nodded. 'You can check. Someone burned down the barn, left Marshall for dead.'

The old man's huge hairy eyebrows raised up.

'Burned the barn? You don't say. Bad business. Marshall's one of the good guys. I am very sorry to hear that. How is he?'

'In hospital. He's got burns and breathing problems, but he's conscious. Officer Miller's been to see him.'

'How old are you, boy?'

Rian shrugged. 'Old enough.'

'You been coming out here few years now. Always on your bike. People reckon I don't see 'em but I do. Shame about your sister. She was a good kid.'

'You knew Renée?'

The old man smiled, exposing extraordinarily white unnatural teeth. 'Like peas in the pod you two. Only she's ginger. You got the same nose.'

Rian was staggered. Everyone knew he had a sister except him. Spurlake was like a . . . he didn't know what it was like, but he knew he didn't like it.

'Your father did my accounts. You seen him lately, by the by?'

Rian shook his head. He couldn't get his head around the idea that Renée looked like him. No way.

'Last place on the road and first place the cops look. Every missing kid comes by here. Never buy anything sensible. I tell them, stock up with water, take beef jerky, but they buy chocolate and Coke. They leave and no one ever hears from them ever again.'

There was an awkward pause. The old man looked at him with penetrating eyes.

'You're not planning to disappear, are you, kid?'

'I already did.' He spotted a calendar on the wall. No nudes in this garage. It was pictures of Reverend Schneider and his flock on his wall with his disciples. He couldn't believe that this old man was one of Reverend Schneider's flock. Didn't seem the type.

'You seen Reverend Schneider today?' Rian asked casually.

The old man spat on to the floor. The sound of it nearly made Rian retch. 'You don't want to be messing with him. He's the devil himself, that one. He keeps giving me calendars. God knows why people don't see through him.'

Rian frowned.

'But he was here?'

'Filled up about thirty minutes ago.'

Rian's heart began to rush.

'Was he alone?'

The old man narrowed his eyes, scrutinizing Rian more carefully. He wasn't sure if he could trust this kid. His father was OK, but . . .

'Smoked windows, can't see shit, but he wasn't alone. Had a girl in there, sat in the back.'

He pointed to the CCTV screen on the wall. Rian turned to see Marshall's truck parked by the pump, the swarm of bugs around the light. The image was unusually clear and in colour. 'Had new camera fitted. Can see everything now. Got robbed, insurance company fitted it. You'd be surprised what people do in their cars, kid. Some of it ain't polite either.'

'Can I see the picture?' Rian asked, his heart pumping harder still.

'If you're chasing him, or her, you'll lose. He's thirty minutes up on you on his way to the Fortress. It's what I told the cops. If kids go that way, they ain't coming back. Ever. No one listens to me.'

Rian ran out of the booth to the truck. He called back to the old man who was watching him carefully now. 'Call Officer Miller. Tell him you saw me, tell him there's a girl in the back of Reverend Schneider's car. Her name's Genie Magee. Tell him.'

The old man watched Rian drive off, noticing that the vehicle had no licence plate. The cops would stop him for sure if they saw that. His hand hovered over the phone, but then he noticed the time. 11.15 p.m. Time to close up. Wouldn't be anyone else passing this way tonight.

Rian drove off at high speed. The Fortress was at least half an hour's drive away. No way he'd catch up now. Didn't rightly know what he'd do if he did. Had no plan. Just knew he wasn't giving up on Genie. Never giving up on her.

'Genie,' he said to the night. 'I swear I'll kill him. I swear I will kill him, if it is the last thing I do.'

# 28

# The Fortress

Genie was already in the prep room. They'd shaved off all of her hair, made her shower, then almost freeze-dried her and forced her to put on some one-piece underwear that felt like a second skin. It was clammy to touch. A female technician with fierce nasal hairs had then examined her, probing everywhere to make sure she was 'fit'. Then someone else had painted the outer extremities of her body with a kind of silver liquid. Painstakingly applying it to her head, arms, legs and the undersoles of her feet.

She didn't protest. Didn't do anything to resist. She knew it was pointless and these were her last moments of life – at least as flesh and blood. She was extraordinarily calm. She had no idea why, but she felt as if this had always been her destiny. To be chewed up and spat out. The last month had been the very best of her life, even counting being ill. She had been loved and had loved in return, and it was as if Rian was with her every moment. She only had to think of him and he was holding her hot hand, their fingers entwined and making sure she was OK. Moucher had loved her, Marshall had been kind, even the darn pig saving her life was special. Everything had been perfect, every day. Warm sunshine. A safe place. Without all that she'd be hysterical right now, but she knew that when she was gone Rian would always have a space for her in his heart. She'd exist there, just like the kids in the Fortress who were still here, somewhere, forever stored in the system, ready to be alive at any time . . .

There was an annoying electrical buzz coming from a screen in the prep room and it soon became apparent that there was a fault on the transmission platform. They heard the system suddenly power down and Genie heard everyone moan with irritation. She didn't have to be told she'd have to wait. She knew from Marshall's explanation that they couldn't transmit unless the Fortress and Synchro were in complete harmony.

'You have to drink this,' the technician was telling her, clearly irritated that there was going to be at least an hour's delay to transmission.

'What is it?'

'It's just juice, but you have to irrigate your body.'

Genie looked at the fluid and she knew without any doubt that it wasn't 'just juice'. It might as well be poison because as soon as the system was up and running they were going to kill her.

As soon as the woman turned away Genie poured the juice down a heating duct. Hopefully none of the cameras or technicians witnessed this. She imagined the pink goo sliding down towards some really important electrical equipment – any moment everything would explode. Sadly though, nothing happened.

'Hello? I seriously need to pee. I don't know what you put in that stuff but . . .'

The woman looked at her with impatience.

'You're prepped and ready,' she snapped.

'But I have to go. Come on, the system's down, I heard it, you heard it. I really have to go.'

The woman sighed. She was clearly reluctant to help, but equally she knew it would be a while before everything was up and running again.

'We will have to process and prep you all over again. It's—'

'Seriously, I am going to have to pee right here, right now, unless you let me go.'

The technician swore under her breath, but she could tell from the way Genie was hopping from one leg to the other that she was serious, and an accident was not what she needed on her sterile transmission platform right now.

'Follow me. Don't touch anything.'

As she turned Genie smiled. Anything to be annoying and occupy her time. She followed the woman to the heavily reinforced doors and watched her flip her finger over the button. It flashed up her name: Ulrich, Helen. Then it turned green. The doors opened on to a brightly lit corridor.

'Follow me. I have to check there's no one inside the bathroom first, we don't want you contaminated.'

Genie waited in the corridor, hopping from leg to leg and doing her best impression of someone desperate. There was a noticeboard on the wall nearby with all kinds of information. Sign up here for the softball team, vacation swap in La Paz, and a photo of a chubby man with severe black-framed glasses and a ruddy complexion, like he'd drunk too many whiskeys: *Employee of the Month – Mr Jim Yates, Assistant Finance Director, Fortransco Synetics Development.*

Jim Yates? The same Jim Yates who was practically living in Rian's home and dating his mother? The man Ri detested more than anything in the whole world? Did Ri know he worked in the Fortress? Did his mother? Was this possible, or was it just a man with the same name? No, couldn't be. Spurlake was a small town, couldn't be two of them.

'You can go in,' the technician told her. 'When you finish, strip off and step into the ion shower. It will snap on the moment you enter. You understand? Pee then shower. Got it?'

Genie looked at her with loathing. What did she think she was, five years old? Couldn't work out that you pee first. She entered the bathroom and the door shut behind her and was locked. As if she was going to escape from this place. They were at least a hundred metres underground.

She sat on the toilet. Her brain was racing. Mr Yates worked in the Fortress. If he knew Rian, he knew about her. How many others were working here and living in Spurlake? They would all know what's going on. They would know kids were being sacrificed in the name of science. They would all know these kids were dying right here. How could they look their neighbours in the face? How could Mr Yates lie to Rian's mother? This was a terrible secret. If people knew, they'd riot, for sure. Wouldn't they? Or that was it. They *did* know and didn't care as long as it wasn't *their* kid that disappeared. Reverend Schneider turns up and prays for your kid's reappearance to keep it all respectable, but they weren't coming back. People like Mr Yates and this ice queen technician woman, Helen Ulrich, would be standing next to you in Safeway and you wouldn't know she was judge, jury and executioner. Probably fried your kid the night before.

'Hurry up,' the executioner called out, the impatience clear in her voice.

Genie peed then flushed. 'What's the hurry? Nothing's going to happen yet.'

She caught sight of herself in the mirror. She looked awful. Why did they have to shave her head? She had pointy ears. Where had they come from? What did Ri ever see in her? At least he'd never see her look like this. What he was doing right now? Was he looking for her? Or had his mother locked him in? She briefly thought about him coming to rescue her, but how utterly impossible that was. How would he get in past the guards and then find her a hundred metres underground, let alone get her out? Impossible. Poor Ri. Poor perfect Ri. She'd never see him again.

She entered the ion shower and it clicked on. You couldn't tell if anything was happening as it made no noise and you couldn't see anything, but you could feel it inside your body as it bombarded you with ions. It wasn't so bad though. Felt like a tornado passing through her body. *Memo to self: when in heaven or hell find out what the heck an ion is.* Weird.

325

The door opened and the shower shut down.

'We got to prep you now. System will be back up in forty-five minutes.'

Genie stared at the impression of the woman's silver Celtic cross hiding under her T-shirt. Ulrich, Helen was another of Reverend Schneider's flock, another believer doing the devil's work for him.

'You going to paint me again?'

'Don't worry. This will be all over soon.'

Genie nodded. Yes, exactly, she realized. It would be all over very soon.

Rian had to slow, bringing the truck to a stop by the barrier. He was at least five hundred metres from the Fortress and yet they had the road blocked with big concrete slabs either side of a gated barrier, so you couldn't go around. Worse, there was a tunnel ahead. Marshall hadn't been kidding: this place was buried under a mountain.

The barrier was unmanned, but there were CCTV cameras mounted on the gates so they would know he was there.

He didn't know what to do. He knew Genie was in there, but this was no bedroom with a few bars to keep her in. This was the Fortress and further in they had watchtowers and armed security. They meant to keep people out.

Rian sighed and reluctantly turned the truck around. He'd have to go back to the junction and find the narrow track to Marshall's farm, the way the Fortress people had come when they came to burn it.

He felt sick and alone, stupidly hungry and was finding it hard to stay awake. The windows were down; he pushed the fan to maximum. There was no air con. He flipped on the radio. Razorlight were singing, '*I can't stop this feeling I've got.*' Perfect timing. This was the night of his shame, the night he didn't save Genie Magee.

Rian suddenly jammed on the brakes, skidding to a halt on a bend by a stream. He was being a wuss. Genie was in the Fortress. She would be waiting for him to get her out. That was *his* job. Any moment they would be trying to teleport her and he was just driving away. He had to try to save her. Had to.

He pulled the truck over on to the verge and switched off the engine. He left the keys under the visor. Marshall would want his truck back and this was, he knew, a one-way journey if things went wrong.

He leaped out of the cabin and ran down the slope to the stream. The water flowed from the upper slopes and passed alongside the Fortress. He could follow the stream. It was dark; he hoped the cameras wouldn't be able to see him and the cold waters of the stream gave him direct access.

The first barrier was the razor-wire strung across the water at the roadblock. Fortunately the water was deeper here and he managed to submerge enough to crawl under it. The water was icy and tasted odd, but that didn't matter. He had to keep moving. Every moment was precious.

The stream veered left and for a while he thought he was making a big mistake as it took him away from everything. Maybe he had to go back, get into the tunnel and hope he could get through before they could get to him. He walked on despondent, aware that Genie could be dead already; time for action was precious.

Two armed uniformed security men popped up from under a drain cover. They approached the truck cautiously from either side, guns at the ready. As one gave a signal they both swarmed the cab. The window was left open, nothing to smash. It was empty.

One of them got on to his cell and called it in, suspicious there was no licence plate. No ID in the cubbyhole either. The other was looking all around him with night vision goggles. He saw nothing. He signalled to the other guard to fall back as he ducked underneath the truck a moment, withdrawing two small devices from his pocket.

This could be innocent, a breakdown, but highly unlikely. One thing was sure, there was nowhere for the driver to go. Either the driver had been collected by someone or he was still around – and if he was still around they wanted to know exactly where.

They vanished back down the hole in the road and pulled the drain cover back over their heads.

Reverend Schneider was exhausted. He was waiting in the transmission observation room. It was two a.m. He was drifting in and out of sleep, irritated beyond belief. The system was still down and perhaps this illustrated exactly why they weren't making progress. All they made were promises and yet glitch after glitch. He'd done his bit. God only knew he'd done his bit in providing the 'volunteers'. The least they could do was get the science right. No one ever seemed to realize just how big this project could be. The commercial potential of eternal life and instant transportation was absolutely extraordinary. Billions would be made, billions upon billions, and in that scheme of things, what was the sacrifice of a few miserable kids? Nothing. Absolutely zilch.

They wanted this meddlesome girl gone. She had been nothing but trouble from the beginning. At least it wasn't a waste. At least she would be contributing something to the advancement of science. There was still the matter of the boy. Security said they had it in hand. There was a suspect vehicle outside the Fortress barrier. They were seeking the driver. It was all so predictable. He'd followed just as he'd surmized. What on earth the boy saw in this girl, he had no idea. But Reverend Schneider had fulfilled his side of the bargain. Reverend Schneider always delivered.

Rian began to climb up a small waterfall, the water forcefully splashing down over him, his feet and hands struggling to grip on the moss-covered rocks. He reached for a tree growing out from one side of it and swung up to a ledge and from there pushed up. It being dark didn't help and he was scared to death to look down. At any moment he could slip and crash to the rocks below. He heaved himself over the ledge at the top and finally stood, amazed he got up there at all. He found himself looking at a lagoon.

He swam forward through the water, noticing it was distinctly warmer now. Gradually the stream grew more shallow again and he had to walk towards bright lights ahead. The other side of the tunnel was suddenly right there in front of him, the Fortress surrounded by parked cars and trucks. He realized that the Fortress had been built in between two rock formations. A perfect hiding place. He knew from Marshall that only the admin block was on top, the real business was underground. He could see guards leaning up against a wall, smoking and talking. Could they see him standing in the stream? He had to take that risk. There was a tower bristling with cameras. At any moment he could be seen. That was the chance he had to take as he searched for a way in.

All the trees were dead around him. He'd hoped for cover, but he was exposed and had to crawl on his belly in the water towards the building. As he got closer he could see where a large pipe was emptying steaming fluid into the stream. It stank like acid. He had no idea what it was doing to him or his skin but he tried to make sure he didn't swallow or get it in his eyes.

He lay in the stream, watching a moment. There had to be a way in. A siren suddenly sounded and the security guys moved inside. Something was about to happen. Was he too late? Had Genie been transmitted already?

A hand shook Reverend Schneider awake. It was 3.05 a.m. 'Ten minutes, Reverend. They've started the countdown.

331

Can I get you a drink? Tea? Coffee?'

Reverend Schneider wiped sleep from his eyes.

'We're ready?'

'Yes sir. They're bringing both systems up to speed right now. The test subject is ideal. She's prepped and ready.'

'She sign the release form?'

'Signed. Most willing volunteer we ever had, I think.'

'She's deceptive. Devious actually. Sometimes I'm frightened people will judge us too harshly for what we do in the name of science, then someone comes along like this girl and I realize we are doing a service. She makes a contribution to knowledge; society is saved from another troubled soul. God's work is harsh and difficult, but eventually humanity gains.'

Reverend Schneider stood up and stretched, suddenly realizing that he was alone. He stared at the transmission platform the other side of the glass. It was just as it should be. He'd be the only one to witness the death of Genie Magee and, since her mother wasn't ever going to have another child, end of the Munby line. He was alert and ready. From behind the one-way glass he could see Genie standing on the transmission platform. A countdown going on behind him. He found he was smiling and quickly assumed a more serious pose in case anyone was looking. In ten minutes she would be gone. Just ten little minutes.

A door opened nearby, about three metres above the waterline. A woman in a protective suit was taking a smoke break. Rian quietly made his way to the opening. The women had her back to him, busy talking to someone on her cell.

Rian jumped up and ran for it. Even though the opening was high above him, he found some pipes to grip on to and hauled himself up, wishing his hands weren't so slippery. Clinging on, he listened to her conversation.

'No, I'm taking Tyler to a basketball match in Pitt Meadows and I've got to have my truck serviced.'

The woman still had her back to him, flicking her ash outside behind her.

'T minus eight,' came a voice over a tannoy.

'Damn. Better get out of here. See you when the shift ends, Bob.'

The woman reached for the door handle to bring it in. Rian grabbed her hand and tugged hard. She let out a shriek and fell hard into the stream below.

He was in. He closed the door behind him. He'd have two minutes at the most before she raised the alarm. Rian had no idea where to go or what to do, but at least he was doing something.

'T minus seven minutes.'

Rian tried a door. Locked. Found three more, all opened by a security keycard. All he had succeeded in doing was getting into a corridor. Useless.

He was trapped. Any minute now the woman would be back with security.

He felt something crunch underfoot. He looked down. It was the woman's keycard. She'd dropped it when he'd pulled her out.

'T minus six minutes.'

He picked it up, swiped the first door and entered.

The lights came on automatically.

He was in an enormous storeroom. Backpacks, shoes, assorted objects, a teddy bear. Each pack shrink-wrapped and identified. Fifth one across: *Denis Malone, age thirteen, Spurlake*. Second shelf: *Kayla Williams, age fifteen, Cedarville*.

He couldn't believe they kept all this stuff. Why? Why keep it? Looking along the line he realized that there were way more bags and shoes here than the thirty-four missing kids he knew about.

This was worse than useless; he was in a dead-end. This wasn't helping him, wasn't helping Genie. He was wasting time.

'T minus four minutes.'

Rian went back to the door and opened it, carefully, hoping there wasn't anyone outside in the corridor. Empty. He stepped out. There were two other doors. One had to lead into the Fortress proper. He swiped number two. As soon as he opened it he knew he'd made a mistake. The air pressure was intense and all the air was being sucked out of the corridor. He'd opened the access door to the air-conditioning shaft. There were thousands of servers in this building that needed cooling. He tried to shut the door, but instead it flipped open completely with a loud bang and Rian was sucked in.

He began falling down the shaft; the air was super-hot, he thought he was on fire. He was headed straight down to the bottom of the Fortress – his only thought was that he'd be dead before Genie.

'T minus two minutes.'

Rian suddenly discovered he was suspended in mid-air. He'd stopped falling. An uprush of incredibly thick superheated air was forcing him back up the shaft. It was impossible to breathe. Rian was rising fast now. He vaguely remembered something Marshall said about birds getting cooked as they flew over the Fortress. He hit a wall as the air changed direction and the last of the oxygen was knocked out of his lungs. He was gasping, sucking in poisonous, acrid, boiling hot air and felt he was going to explode.

Suddenly he was sailing unsupported through the night air and dropped like a stone into a cooling pool just above the Fortress building. He plunged down into a thick noxious liquid and instinctively he kept his eyes and mouth shut tight. He quickly found his way to the surface again and, gasping, struck out for the edge.

He realized with utter despair that he'd completely failed to save Genie.

*Eight seconds.*

Genie stood barefoot on the platform. It was warm underfoot, whereas it had been cold before and she wondered if pouring that juice down the vent had been a good idea, or not. The countdown was relentless, although it seemed to go in slow motion, like crashing. The technicians were all wearing protective suits and sat behind reinforced glass in a large booth overlooking her. *She* should be the one wearing protective gear. She regarded them all carefully. Six people to watch her die. Any one of them could have been her neighbour in Spurlake. Maybe they told themselves that they weren't killing kids. That had to be it. No one really died if they were left on some server. That would help them believe they were doing science and not just playing God.

What if she just exploded? At least that would be inconvenient and they'd have to scrape her off the walls. If I'm going to die, God, at least make it horrible and messy, like that boy before, make it so gross they feel sick. It's the least you can do.

*Five seconds.*

What kind of people knowingly experimented with kids, who would die each time they flipped that switch? How did they live with themselves? Maybe they didn't sleep well; maybe they fooled themselves and told each other they were creating 'souls', just like Reverend Schneider. She wondered where the Reverend was and why he wasn't there gloating. And that was when she started smiling.

*Three seconds.*

Soon she would be with friends. Denis and Renée, nervous Julia, silent Cary, all the people she'd met at the farm. Her eyes began to flutter, she felt herself changing, getting lighter. She opened her eyes, it seemed to her, but it was surely impossible, she was disintegrating, her flesh turning to millions of grains of sand, all just flying away.

*Two seconds.*

Please God, let me be with friends and not in limbo or trapped in a machine. Please send Reverend Schneider to a special hell when he dies. At least promise me that. It's all I ask.

*One second.*

The noise was suddenly terrific. The technicians were frantically trying to stop the transmission, arguing amongst themselves, pointing to smoke rising around her and then, as if by magic, there was total silence and everything around her completely disappeared. She was nothing, nowhere and utterly free.

*I have vanished*, was her last thought.

Reverend Schneider stared at the transmission platform. Slowly a little smile crept across his face. He knew. He didn't need telling.

'We lost her,' one of the technicians called out over the intercom. 'They've got a fire down in the transmission room and it occurred at the critical moment.'

'This is getting to be a habit,' he complained loudly, faking his anger well. 'I can't believe you people, I bring you willing volunteers and you mess up every time. It's an utter disgrace. She was a perfect specimen. A fire did you say?'

No one wanted to look at him. This was transmission eighty-six. Thirty-ninth human volunteer and it was as if there had been no progress at all. She didn't even come through for a millisecond. It was a total failure.

A senior scientist explained. 'There was a glitch. Synchro dropped the signal in the last second. She left the Fortress but . . .'

'You sure she's gone?' Reverend Schneider queried.

'One hundred per cent disassembly of all DNA took place at 3.16 a.m, Reverend. She was totally deconstructed, we had the power drop out, all data was lost. I'm sorry. Truly sorry, sir.'

Reverend Schneider shook his head and did his best to look downcast.

'We didn't even save her soul.'

Reverend Schneider walked out of the observation area without another word. Genie Magee was gone forever. Amen to that. In the elevator he realized he no longer felt tired. In fact breakfast, that's what he needed. A good hearty breakfast. Someone had to celebrate the departure of Genie Magee.

Inside the Fortress, alarms were sounding, red flashing lights screamed for attention on every wall. Space-suited fire suppression teams were running in panic in every direction. There was shouting and confusion everywhere.

Rian crawled out of the pool and ran into the forest. He

made his way back down towards the stream. He knew he had to wash urgently, whatever he was covered in was disgusting and made his eyes itch and skin crawl.

The clear water felt good. He found a deep mountain pool upstream from the buildings and washed himself, drank and rinsed out his mouth and ears, trying to clear out whatever poison he'd swallowed. He tried not to think about his failure. He had to get out of here, back to his truck undiscovered. They'd know someone was out here. The woman would have alerted them.

He followed the downstream path, nervous it would go past the Fortress again, but there was little choice. At the point where he'd climbed into the Fortress he saw the woman was still lying there where she had fallen. She hadn't raised the alarm. Had he injured her? Now he felt guilt rising. Nervously, he approached her lifeless form. She was lying awkwardly in the water. Surely she must have drowned.

Rian crept close. She was lying on her back in the water, still breathing. She was unconscious but alive. Rian moved away. Someone would soon realize she was missing and go looking for her. He had to keep himself safe. He felt guilty for leaving her there, but then again, had she ever felt any remorse for the kids who'd died?

Going back down the waterfall was twice as hard as

climbing up. He couldn't find a grip and slid the last six metres, jarring his legs in the rocky stream bed. He had to press on, grit his teeth, ignore the pain and crawl through the contaminated water. Twenty minutes later he made it back to the truck.

Cautious now, dripping wet, he was lying on the grass just below the road surface by the truck and saw a tiny flashing red diode under the driver's side of the vehicle. That most definitely hadn't been there before. He'd had a visitor. Sheer luck he'd seen the blinking light.

Clearly someone wanted to track him. Damn. It was his fault for leaving the truck out in the open. He hadn't even tried to hide it. Just wasn't thinking straight at all. He looked down the road. There didn't seem to be anyone moving or watching and he figured even if there was a CCTV camera out here it couldn't pick out much in this light. He slithered towards the truck, rolled underneath, now saw there were two tiny trackers secreted under there. He prised them off and pocketed them. He'd stop a distance away and leave them on another vehicle. Perhaps find a quiet spot and check everywhere to see if there were any others. He rolled back out, jumped into the cab, grabbed the key and got out of there before anyone could stop him.

Only now did he notice the colour of his hands and face. He was blue. His skin was *blue*. No wonder all the trees and plant life were dying around here. What was in that water?

He felt ashamed and guilty. He was driving away from the Fortress without Genie. He'd achieved absolutely nothing. Now she was gone forever. What the heck did he think he could have done anyway? In the movies they always find a way to save the girl. Always.

He drove away, totally numb.

By five a.m. Rian was back at the farm at last, utterly exhausted, filled with despair. The house was still a mess; he couldn't think about that now or much care. He stumbled into the kitchen, managed to grab a glass of water and then staggered up the stairs to bed. He just flopped across it and buried his head into the pillows. Everything smelled of Genie. She was everywhere around him and nowhere at all. He felt tears welling. He felt so guilty, so utterly useless.

'Genie!' he cried out. 'Genie.'

And then somehow he fell asleep, unconscious to the world.

## 29

# *Alone*

He woke at first light. It was uncannily still. No wind, no birds chirping, no sound at all. He rolled off the bed and headed towards the bathroom. Then he remembered that Genie would be gone by now. How was he ever going to get used to that? One thing was certain, he wasn't going to forget or forgive. Somehow he had to find a way to destroy Reverend Schneider and his evil influence in Spurlake. He wouldn't be able to do it on his own, he'd need to persuade others and prove the reverend's part in all the missing kids. He had no idea how he was going to do that, but he was resolved to try.

He showered. Astonished at the blue stains on his hands and face. It wasn't coming off either. His neck was sore, red raw from the burns in the ventilator shaft. Proof he'd tried something, even if it was a failure. No consolation for Genie though. She'd never know he tried, always know he failed though.

Downstairs he made tea – surveying the mess in the kitchen. The Quaker chairs overturned and smashed, broken cups and plates everywhere; they'd trashed the place. He decided that this was a good place to start. He'd made a promise to fix Marshall's home up and he'd keep his word. Anything to try and stop thinking about Genie. The only problem being that everything made him think about her.

He had electricity, water, a stock of food; he ruled out eating the frozen stuff as it would have defrosted and refrozen at least once, but there was enough dried food to live on for weeks if he had to. He did wonder if the Fortress people would come looking for him. He'd put the trackers on to a truck heading to Alberta. With luck they'd follow that for a while. He was hoping that now they had Genie, perhaps they'd leave him alone. He'd listen out for strangers arriving though. He had to be ready to run at a moment's notice.

At eleven Rian took a break in the morning sunshine. He enjoyed the heat of the sun on his face and the sound of the trees creaking in the smallest of breezes. His heart was heavy and he tried to tell himself that Genie wouldn't want him to fall apart, but falling apart was exactly what he felt like doing.

He moved some stuff from a chair on the stoop and a scruffy notebook fell to the floor. He picked it up, immediately recognizing Genie's handwriting on the cover. It was filled with sketches of the farm and Moucher. Wonderful sketches he had never known she'd done. They were so lifelike he couldn't believe she hadn't shown them to him. He felt a little cheated. There were pages of him sleeping when he was sick; she must have sat with him for hours and he'd never known that either. There was a sketch of Denis and Renée and Marshall with the pig and Marshall adjusting his leg. He was stunned they were so accurate, the light and shade and expressions on faces were so damn real. Never once had she mentioned these or talked about them and now he felt sick. To think someone with so much talent was gone forever. His Genie was an artist – a brilliant artist – and she was dead for some stupid crazy experiment that wasn't ever going to work or be good for anyone. A loose page fell to the ground with her writing on it. He snatched it up, he hardly dared read it.

Genie Tulane-Magee at 20

Mrs and Mrs Tulane-Magee will be happy to invite you over for Thanksgiving supper at our perfect, safe, beautiful studio in Kits. Come and see Rian's latest designs for eco-living. Your home can save the planet too!

Meet Alexandro our perfect son who is destined for great things – I just know it.

*Come and buy my latest illustrations or see them in Alexandro's Potty Adventure, my latest book for kids. (Note to self: Must improve my skills in drawing hands and feet. Why are toes so hard to do?)*

*Meet all my new friends and play with our latest puppy . . .*

Rian stared at Genie's sketch of himself with the puppy and choked up. She'd even named the kid they would now never have; there was even a tiny illustration of a little boy sitting on a flying potty. Rian realized his eyes were wet and a splash landed on the paper, smudging the ink. He quickly shut the notebook, clutched it to his chest, sinking to his knees and silently sobbed. He'd never known she'd planned so much, never even asked, and now she'd never have any future at all. He was unable to stop the flow of tears, his throat felt constricted and he was feeling nauseous. He wanted to throw something, smash something. His heart felt like a lump of lead. Everything was ruined – her life, his.

'Genie,' he said softly, sending her name out on the breeze. 'I love you Genie, I'll always love you.'

\* \* \*

He stayed on his knees for an hour, unable to do anything. The notebook seemed to have paralyzed him. Why did she keep it secret? He so wanted that house, that child, that future. It had been snatched away from him by an evil, evil man.

He had no idea how he forced himself to do it, but he had to continue bringing the house back to life. Genie's notebook was stashed in a safe place now in the basement. Just knowing it existed gave him strength, he refused to be overwhelmed by despair. She wouldn't want that. He'd figure out how to get revenge later. Definitely figure something out.

Sometime later he had the kitchen functioning again and he'd straightened out the bottom rooms so Marshall could settle in without a problem. The broken chairs and debris were stacked outside and he realized some of it would make good firewood. Might come in handy at the next power outage.

He ate a bowl of cereal with half-frozen milk and watched the pig happily scoffing the spoiled food. He'd never really taken to the pig the way Genie had, but now, he kind of understood what she meant. You had to care about everything, then maybe someone would care about you.

'You miss her?' he asked the pig. The animal grunted,

ignoring him, munching on cabbage and briefly glaring at him as if to say he was interrupting her concentration. It was the way of pigs.

348

# 30

# The Awakening

Genie opened her eyes. Water dripped on to her face from a tree, she felt it trickle down her neck. She felt pain in her lower back and moved, realizing that she was lying uncomfortably on a rock. Rock!

Rock? Pain? Did this mean she was alive? She was real?

She closed her eyes suddenly, really scared that she was only partly formed. She had awful, horrid memories of the howling dog with the back legs fused together. This meant that she had definitely been transmitted. She remembered the actual moment she began to fade. It was almost like watching a sandcastle disintegrate under the force of a high wind, grains of sand flying off and disappearing into thin air. She opened one eye and sneaked a look at her legs. *She definitely had legs.* Two of them. And they looked normal, like her legs should, kinda skinny and still scuffed from her ordeal up to the reservoir. She could feel the warmth of the sun on her face and arms, but exactly where was she? She opened both eyes now and sat up. Everything seemed to be in working order except she had a tight knot in her stomach, like she was travel sick.

She looked around her. She was in the forest and she realized that she wasn't alone either. Other kids were grouped around her in a semi-circle, all asleep in various foetal positions, lying on grass or ferns. She realized the whole clearing was filled with lush green ferns and bright red fireweed. Above her head power lines softly hummed.

She wondered if she could stand, nervous her legs wouldn't work. She stood, and with immense relief they took her weight. She had a sudden wild thought: *Am I still Genie Magee?* They may have transmitted her body, but had her memory come with it? Was her heart in the right place? Her kidneys? What about her blood, lungs, all the little bits that were right now making her feel dizzy? She realized she was shaking with anxiety. Her nostrils told her that her nose was working. Sweet pine and decaying vegetation. She took a deep breath and filled her lungs. As she did so she noticed her left arm. The moles had gone. All her moles had gone. She had three, like a little triangle on her left arm. Rian had always rubbed them for luck. It was just a little thing, but what else was missing? It made her more nervous. Annoyingly, the scar, the Celtic cross, was still vividly prominent on her other arm.

She moved toward the other bodies. Scared of what she might discover. Were they still alive? Or were they . . . ? Many were almost naked, some wore the one-piece underwear she was wearing.

She shook the first boy awake. He turned and stared at her, fear in his eyes, then slowly he began to smile as he recognized her.

'Jesus, Genie. What they do to your hair?'

'Denis?' Genie realized that he looked different in real life. Even smaller. She liked the green socks though.

Denis smiled and tentatively unfurled his body, embarrassed that his underwear had holes in it, but much more curious about whether his arms and legs actually worked. 'I'm real. I'm frickin' real,' he told her with pleasure and astonishment.

'And almost naked. You might want to do something about your underwear.' Genie moved on to the next kid.

Denis laughed and just the sound of it made him happy. He stood up, testing his body, feeling everything. It was so weird for him to touch and feel again.

Genie was shaking the next kid awake. Cary Harrison, she remembered. He'd been so quiet and scared when she'd met him at the house. She looked across the forest and wondered, why here? Why now? The whole area looked very familiar to her. Was this where she'd found the howling dog? She moved cautiously to the edge and looked down across the ravine and the huge hundred-metre drop. The Fortress was somewhere down there, beyond range. Weirdly, this was *exactly* where the dog had materialized. Maybe Marshall had been right. Something was making this happen. Couldn't be a coincidence.

She leaned up against a rock and looked back at other kids stirring. She hoped it wasn't a dream. It would be cruel if this was just a dream.

'Genie?'

Genie turned and sat upon a rock and smiled at Renée, who stood up and stretched, wobbling on her feet a little.

'My God, you're so tall,' Genie remarked. 'At least they left your hair on. Look what they did to me.'

Renée was feeling her body, testing it, just like Denis had done. She coughed, then spat blood, which unnerved her some.

'Can't believe this! I'm real. I'm solid.' She looked at Denis and the others and then without warning began to cry.

Genie rushed over to comfort her, giving her a big hug.

'Open your mouth. You're bleeding.'

Genie looked into Renée's mouth, checked teeth, tongue, everything was exactly where it was supposed to be. 'Maybe you bit your cheek.'

Renée spat again but it was clear this time. She looked relieved and hugged Genie back.

'We're all alive, we're alive, Genie,' Renée said quietly, totally amazed.

'It worked, I don't know how it worked, but it worked,' Genie told her.

Denis was frowning, moving around and helping the other kids get up. He looked back at Genie.

'Nine of us.'

Genie broke away from Renée. She looked at Denis, still so small. She wondered if he would ever grow normally. She didn't recognize one boy who stirred and looked so frightened to be in the forest.

Julia, the blonde girl, was last to awake and was staring at her stomach, totally unaware of her near nakedness. 'My scars. All my scars have gone.'

'My hair,' a girl Genie didn't recognize was saying. 'I was blonde. My shoulder?'

Denis knelt beside her. She seemed distressed.

'Does it hurt, Danielle?'

'No. That's just it. I can use it again. I had an accident. Couldn't move it.'

Genie watched each one of them re-familiarize themselves with their bodies. It was the weirdest thing to watch. Every single one of them checking their ears and noses were in the right places. Two more were crying with relief and happiness. The silent boy was looking at his stomach and legs with total wonder.

'What's wrong?' Renée asked him. 'You OK? What's your name?'

'Randall.'

Renée looked at Denis and exchanged looks of surprise.

'Randall, the blimp? You ain't Randall. Randall was like – huge.'

Randall looked at Denis and began to cry.

'Oh my God, it *is* Randall,' Julia trilled. 'What did they do to you? You were like the fattest kid in our year.'

Renée looked at Genie and shrugged.

'Well, that's one diet that finally works. You should send them a letter of thanks, Randall. Can't believe you were that obese kid.'

Genie realized she'd have to take charge.

'We have to go. We can't let them find us. We have to stick together and that means not being mean to each other. I think we've all been through enough. I have no idea how this worked or why, but we're here and we have to make sure we stay alive now.'

'But where are we?' Julia whined.

'I know exactly where we are,' Genie said, smiling. She helped the girl up off the ground. 'And I know where we can go.'

'But how did this happen?' Cary asked. 'I mean, one minute we were like nowhere and now we're here and we're alive?'

'It was Genie. She came for us. I told you she would,' Denis declared.

'I didn't do anything. They just put me on the platform and pressed a button.'

But Denis was looking at her curiously. He stepped forward and stroked the silver paint on her arms.

'And this?'

'They painted me. I don't know why.' She smiled. 'They gave me juice too, but I poured it down the heating duct. I think that's what started the fire.'

Denis and Renée looked at her with surprise.

'I remember that gloop,' Renée told her. 'Disgusting. It's filled with stuff so they can see you.'

'Nanobots,' Denis told her. 'I heard them talking about them. They make us swallow them and they can track all our organs if they go astray. Or something like that. It stays active for about two days. Lucky you didn't drink it, they'd know exactly where you are now.'

'But where are the others?' Julia asked. 'Is this it? Just us? Is that Miho? Miho, is that you?'

Miho uncurled, then abruptly became aware she was practically naked and curled up again, embarrassed and afraid.

'It's OK,' Julia was telling her. 'We're alive, we're alive. Come on, get up.'

Denis ran behind a tree to take a leak.

'Ow, pine cones.'

Genie smiled. They were all barefoot except for Denis in his socks. It was going to be hell walking back to the farm.

'Plumbing works,' Denis shouted back. Some of the girls smirked but you could tell they were relieved to know.

'Come on, we have to go. I don't want them to find us. Hell, I don't even want them to look for us,' Genie told them. 'They might think I'm dead. After all, I didn't arrive in Synchro and they don't know about you guys.'

'Then why are you crossing your fingers?' Renée remarked. She turned to the others. 'Genie's right. We have to leave.'

'There's a farmhouse near here. There's some old clothes we can have and we can get something to drink.'

Denis returned from the tree.

'You think there's any more of us?'

Cary was looking at where people were standing and the pattern of how they had arrived. Genie remembered he was the smart one.

'We arrived in a semi-circle. Look where you are. It's a pattern.' He looked up and saw the huge power cables strung above the trees. 'I don't know how, but we're here and if anyone else came and they were outside the—'

'Don't say anything bad,' Julia begged him. 'I don't want to see anything bad.'

'I remembered something,' Genie remarked, but didn't explain. She had a flash of being inside a swirl of electrons, being able to see everything, like the secret of the universe – every atom and nothing, all at the same time. She suddenly thought of all those pictures on the walls of Marshall's bathrooms. How many kids were missing? Why only the nine of them in the circle? Marshall would know.

'Come on. It's not far. Watch out for pine cones and thorny things. I don't know what they are but they stick right in your foot and they're hard to get out. Oh yeah, and coyotes.'

'Coyotes!' Julia protested.

'You're too skinny to interest them,' Denis told her.

'And you're too short,' Julia shot back.

Genie ignored them and walked ahead. She was thinking about Rian. Would he be there? And then she remembered Mr Yates, employee of the month. How were they going to handle him?

'Hey,' Denis shouted. 'Another one.' He walked cautiously off the track towards a heap half hidden by ferns.

Genie turned to see all them follow Denis and she turned back to join them.

Miho was puking before she even got there and Denis was pushing them back. 'Back up, don't look. Don't look.'

'Who?' Genie was asking, but stopped when she saw Denis' face.

He shook his head. 'It's a what. Seriously, don't look, Genie.'

Renée had the stomach to look. She stared. 'It's inside out – it's gross.'

'There might be more.' Genie didn't want to think about it, didn't want to see them. If they weren't normal, she didn't want to know. The deformed dog had been enough for her.

Something was shining in the undergrowth. She

approached it cautiously. Once it had been white, but now, covered in sticky stuff from the trees, it looked like a plastic road cone. It was half a metre wide, with the familiar Fortransco logo. It was warm to touch and vibrated slightly. She looked back suddenly. Now she studied the ground more carefully she could see they formed a large semi-circle, just as Cary had observed. Some probably buried under plant life as the forest grew around them. Marshall's receptors. It was no accident they had appeared here. Something had triggered them. The last storm brought them back to life, exactly as Marshall said.

Cary was at her side and he saw them too, his face deathly white.

'These things must be here for a reason,' Cary said. 'I can feel my heart pumping. It's a weird sensation. You?'

Genie nodded. 'You will have to get used to lots of things you used to feel, I guess. You going to be sick?'

Cary was trying to be tough, but he was increasingly feeling nauseous.

'What if there are more kids here and they haven't woken yet?' Renée asked.

'I think it's just us,' Genie told her. 'I can't tell you how I know. Everyone outside the semi-circle will be too damaged to put back together.'

Cary was sensing that too. Someone actually transmitted inside out. He couldn't bear to think about it, way too gross to handle. He turned away, taking deep breaths to stay calm.

'We have to stay together, stay alive and we have to expose them,' Genie told everyone as they started back down the track again. 'We have to take Reverend Schneider and the whole Fortress down.'

Denis was suddenly beside her, white as a sheet.

'Genie? My parents think I'm dead, don't they?'

Genie nodded. A lot of parents were going to get one hell of a shock when these kids came home.

'You were buried. I wonder what's in your coffin?'

'Am I dead?' Julia asked, wiping her mouth. 'I bet they think I'm dead.'

Genie turned to look at her.

'I don't know. But right now you're alive, girl, and I suggest you start enjoying it.' She smiled. 'I can't wait to see Reverend Schneider's face when we all march into his damn church and bear witness against him. He is going to be so sick. He's going to prison. They all are.'

Everyone assented. That's *exactly* what they wanted to happen.

Cary was frowning and stopped dead suddenly, causing others to bunch up.

Denis heard the commotion behind him and he turned to see Cary staring at a bird in a tree.

'It's a bird, Cary. You never seen a bird?'

Cary shook his head.

'In a tree? No. Never. I'm supposed to be nearsighted. I wear glasses.'

'Well you ain't wearing them now.'

'I know. I can see perfectly.'

Genie and Denis exchanged glances. Well that wasn't so bad, was it?

Renée was walking at the rear and thinking about that. 'Did they ask you about your eyes back at the Fortress?'

'They tested me for days. I had to answer hundreds of questions and they gave me special glasses.'

'Me too, I mean questions,' Miho piped up.

'And me,' Randall told them.

They all looked at Randall again with wonder. He was less than half the size he had been. Each one of them had been altered in some way.

Genie understood. It was exactly what Marshall had explained to her and why Reverend Schneider was interested.

'That's what they want. In the future you'll be able to get anything fixed, anything at all. No one will have any imperfections,' she informed them. 'They can change your DNA, stop ageing, make arms work again, give people back their eyes, fix obesity. It's about regeneration. Eternal life.'

Denis' eyes widened. 'Stop people growing?'

Genie shook her head. 'You got older, but your body didn't, Denis. You'll start growing again now, I promise.'

Denis wasn't convinced.

'I hope so. I frickin' well hope so.'

Renée was examining her hair.

'I swear my hair has changed. This just isn't my hair.'

Genie agreed.

'It was red. I remember it was red. We've all changed a bit.'

'What about inside?' Cary asked, clearly nervous about this now. 'I mean they made lots of mistakes before. How do we know it's all been done right?'

Genie continued walking, she didn't want to think about that. There was a way to go yet. What else had they changed? Would any of them ever be truly normal again? She looked at her arm. Why the moles? What could they do with a few moles?

# 31

# Ghosts in the Forest

Rian was clearing up in front of the farmhouse, satisfied that things were beginning to get back to normal. He wanted to keep as busy as he could to avoid thinking. Thinking about Genie only made him ill. He stood on a rock by the burned-out shell of the barn and surveyed the orchards. The apples would need harvesting soon or they'd ripen on the tree and just rot. But there were so many apples he knew he couldn't pick them in time.

Miller had been right. The Fortress had come back for the burned-out SUV and taken it away. He hoped they were finished with the farm now and wouldn't return.

He missed Moucher, he missed everything. It just wasn't the same without Genie there, catching one of her brilliant smiles. He only had to look at her and he was instantly happy and then he remembered that he'd never see her smile again. He didn't even have a photo. Nothing left of her but her sketchbook he'd found and the memory of those brilliant blue eyes.

The pig suddenly started. With the corner of his eyes he caught sight of it running into the forest and was amazed to see something so big set off so fast, without warning. He wondered what had spooked it and listened for approaching vehicles, but heard nothing.

It was curiously hazy now that the sun was high in the sky. He heard the familiar sound of thunder in the distance. The air carried the expectation of change. Clouds were scudding overhead. He was getting to know this place well enough now to know there would be a downpour in about two hours.

'Wow, you've been busy, Rian Tulane.'

Rian spun around and slipped on the rock, falling flat on his ass.

He heard familiar laughter and to his astonishment Genie stepped out from the forest, the pig beside her as she stroked its ears. Her head was shaved and she was wearing the weirdest white one-piece underwear. The sun was reflected off her silver skin and dazzled him. For a moment there Rian had the strongest impression he was looking at an angel.

'Cat got your tongue?'

Rian realized he was too scared to ask anything. She'd been in the Fortress. She was glowing. They had turned her into something else. She was going to be like Denis or Renée and he couldn't bear it.

'Genie?'

Genie came closer. 'You look disappointed.'

Rian struggled to speak and get up off the ground. He was elated, nauseous, scared – hell, *terrified*, all at once. Genie stood right above him and put out a hand.

'You going to get up or lie around in the dirt all day?'

He made to grab her hand, knowing it was a wasted effort. When she grabbed his hand there was an immediate electric shock that coursed through his entire body, but she held firm and she pulled him towards her. She laughed at his astonishment. He stared. Her teeth looked beautiful, she *was* beautiful, and somehow her hair being shaved made no difference at all.

Genie felt hot tears flowing down her cheeks as she watched the wild range of emotions on Rian's face.

'You're real. You're real. You are REAL!' he shouted.

He grabbed her, crushed her to him, nearly squeezing all the breath out of her. She inhaled. He smelled beautifully of sweat, he was hot and was perfectly, absolutely Rian.

'I never—' Rian tried to say.

'Shh,' Genie whispered. 'Hush.' She felt his hands pressing against her, felt his fingers experimenting with her stubbly head. She realized that Rian was crying, his tears flowed down her neck. She understood that this was the most perfect moment in her life. She never wanted it to end.

Rian pulled away a second, didn't care that his eyes were wet.

'I never want us to be apart again. Not even a second. I love you, Genie. I truly love you.'

Genie closed her eyes and rested her nose on his forehead.

'Even looking like this?'

Rian pulled away again to look at her. He sensed her nervousness.

'It looks cool.'

She nodded and began to smile. Cool was good.

Rian kissed her and their lips tasted of salt. Genie sighed. Then she frowned as she felt the heat on his neck and saw the colour of his skin.

'How did you get so blue? Rian? And your neck is burned.'

'Accident. It doesn't matter.'

'It matters. I leave you alone for just a few hours and you turn blue!'

'I've got a million questions,' Rian began, but Genie put a finger on his lips.

'I've got another surprise for you.'

Rian suddenly looked worried.

'Your leg's not going to fall off, is it?'

Genie laughed. 'No.'

She took a deep breath. A simple thing like breathing was suddenly a miracle. She'd never underestimate *that* again.

'I remembered we'd agreed to pick the apples. So I brought some friends.'

Rian frowned. He had no idea what she was talking about. Genie turned and signalled back to the unseen eyes in the forest. Denis was first out. He wore the rotting underwear and tatty green socks with pride. Rian stared with complete astonishment as eight perfectly formed and very pale kids walked out of the forest.

'Denis? Renée?' He didn't recognize the others immediately and noticed some were wearing underwear and some were almost naked. But they were alive and real, just like Genie. He turned to look at Genie.

'You do this?'

He recognized Miho, the girl who'd disappeared right after graduation. She'd supposedly been kidnapped by her father and taken back to Japan. It had made the national newspapers. How many other lies had he swallowed about why kids were missing in Spurlake? He looked back at Genie for some kind of explanation.

367

'We ended up in the same place as the howling dog. Can you believe that? Marshall was right, there's something special about that area.'

Renée stood looking at Rian, pursing her lips. 'You think you could stop pawing each other for a moment and get us something to wear?'

Rian laughed and stood up, wiping his eyes. He approached Renée and attempted to give her a hug. She resisted.

'Not without clothes on, even if you are my half-brother.'

'Come on,' Genie told them. 'There's a goodwill bag under the stairs and I'm sure we can find stuff in there for all of us.'

Rian regarded them all with awe and wonder.

'I am just plain astonished. Come on. Anyone hungry? We have cereal, almost defrosted milk and er . . . noodles.'

'Are they wheat-free?' Julia asked. 'I'm on a wheat free diet.'

Genie looked at her and frowned. 'Julia, get real. You just spent over a year inside a computer. No diets here. This is the country.'

Denis was looking at Rian curiously.

'How come you're blue?'

'Went swimming,' Rian said, suddenly embarrassed.

Genie shepherded them all into the house. She wanted to know why he was blue too, but she'd get it out of Ri, later.

'I want to call my folks,' Julia declared as she adjusted the shorts and T-shirt she had found. She looked funny wearing khaki tied with string, but kinda cute, even if she was impossibly skinny.

Denis, dressed in cut-off jeans and a shirt five times too big for him, looked at Genie and shook his head. Renée was thinking the same. Most of them were too scared to call home. Some remembered why they had left in the first place.

'No calls,' Genie told her. 'Julia, they probably think you're dead by now. Denis was already buried, for God's sake. Who knows what they put in his coffin. We can't just call your folks. They'll think it's a hoax. We have to plan this. Got to take Reverend Schneider and the Fortress by surprise. Right, Denis?'

Denis agreed. 'We're out. But they'll be looking for us once they realize we're gone. We got to stay hidden till we can plan something.'

'Genie's right,' Rian told them. 'You can't just call home. Besides, the Fortress might be listening. I'm beginning to think they control everything around here.

369

Ever wonder how come the *Spurlake News* never says anything about the Fortress? Like it doesn't exist. Did any of you know about it before they grabbed you?'

Most kids shook their heads.

'You're not kidding. I've got bad news for you, Ri,' Genie said. 'You aren't going to like it.'

'What?' Rian was thinking the worst now. 'You're OK, right? I mean, no missing bits? I was looking at Renée and I swear she used to have red hair.'

'She did. But we're all fine, some small changes, but no big deal. But listen, Ri, you, of all people, can't phone home.'

Rian was confused. 'Why?'

'Mr Yates. That's why. There's a picture of him at the Fortress. Employee of the Month, no less.'

'No way,' he scoffed. 'Can't be him. He works in town. He's an accountant. You're mistaken. I mean, I hate him, but it can't be him.'

'Red face, chubby, got a big neck, black-framed glasses, stupid moustache,' Genie described. She could see instantly from his face that it was his Mr Yates.

Rian looked at her, astonishment giving way to anger.

'Mr Yates works for *them*? That bastard's known about this all this time? My mother's boyfriend?'

'I'm sorry. But he's not the only one. You ever think

370

about that? The people who work at the Fortress live in Spurlake. They know us. They know exactly what's happening. They know all the troublemakers, the awkward squad, the loners – and I bet a lot of them go to Reverend Schneider's Church. The woman who prepped me at Fortress was wearing a Celtic cross. He handed me over to her like they were old friends. Hell, I bet our school principal sends them a regular list of people she wants to get rid of. She has evil eyes.'

Renée pushed her empty bowl of cereal away.

'They know *all* our secrets. My mother is devoted to that church. Denis' folks too. I swear we got to do something, Rian. We got to make sure people know.'

Cary was thinking. 'But if they all work at the Fortress, who can we trust?'

That was exactly what Rian was thinking. All those rows he'd had with Mr Yates, about how he'd sworn teleportation and science fiction was bunk, and all this time he was working for the Fortress. Cary was right. Who could they trust in Spurlake? They would have to let people know outside. But then again, it was so fantastic, who the hell would believe them?

Julia put her spoon down; she'd hardly eaten anything. She was sulking.

'I still don't see why I can't call home. I mean, I've been

gone over a year. They have to have forgiven me by now.'

Genie looked at this petite girl and wondered what she did that was so bad she fell into the hands of Reverend Schneider. She didn't look to be the sort who'd do anything wrong.

Denis looked at her and shook his head.

'Remember why you left, Julia. It's been two years and I can still remember exactly why I ran.'

'They were beating you. They never did anything bad to me. Nothing.'

Cary stood up. 'Julia, you weighed sixty-five pounds or something when you came to the Fortress. You hadn't eaten any food in like a month. I was there, remember? Reverend Schneider told you what? He could cure you? Make you whole again?'

Julia blushed. Reverend Schneider had said exactly that. Told her she'd never be hungry ever again. He hadn't lied actually. She looked at Cary.

'Well at least I didn't try to run my father over.'

'It was an accident.'

'That's not what your father said.'

Genie slammed her hand down on the table.

'We've all got reasons to be here. Think about the kids who didn't make it. We're alive. We made it. We have to tell people what's going on. We need to stick together and watch each other's backs. We don't call anyone right now. We have to keep the element of surprise. We only have two or three people we can trust back in Spurlake. OK? No calls and we don't return until we're ready. If anyone knew we were here they'd grab us back so fast you wouldn't have time to blink. Understand?'

It took a while to get everyone to agree. That, and Rian disconnecting and dismantling the phone. Temptation is a hungry animal.

Genie was making sure everyone had a place to sleep. For most of them it was a completely new experience and they'd have to learn how all over again. They'd been sleepless from the moment they had been teleported and for Denis that meant a long time awake. Genie was happy that they'd kept the food down, so far. She had only been in the system a few hours, she'd had it easy. The others were all experiencing problems with simple things, bumping into stuff mostly. Getting distance right was a biggie and even climbing stairs had to be relearned. Suddenly having a mouth full of spit was awkward, feeling the blood in your veins disconcerting, somehow gross. It was so weird. Feeling your teeth with your tongue or being warm or cold were new experiences all over again.

She found Miho crying in the bathroom, sitting in the corner with some face cream on her nose.

'Miho?'

'I'm scared. I don't know what I'm feeling. I feel sick and my teeth hurt and my hands feel like lead and I'm scared about going home. I don't think I've got a home any more.'

'How did you end up in the Fortress? I remember you. You painted all those fantastic murals at school. I heard you won a scholarship to Emily Carr. You already graduated, right?'

Miho rubbed the cream into her face, hot tears rolling down her cheeks.

'My mother is seriously ill. My father wanted me to go to Japan to study. I mean . . . I don't even speak Japanese. He said I couldn't go to art college. He was very angry. I went to see Reverend Schneider and . . .' she sobbed, trying to take in a breath. 'He said he'd talk to my father. He said he'd put me somewhere safe where he couldn't get me.'

Genie hugged her, let her cry on her shoulder. She figured that Reverend Schneider was going to come up in all their stories. They had to find a way to fix him, just had to.

Rian came back upstairs with blankets from the

storeroom. He handed some over to Randall, who'd hardly said anything yet. He was utterly bewildered by being back in real life and seemed the worst affected by memory loss.

'Smells of dog but they'll keep you warm,' Rian told him. Suddenly Rian remembered something. 'Hey, Genie?'

'What?' she called from the bathroom.

'I forgot to tell you. Moucher's still alive. My ma stitched him up. He lost a lot of blood, but he'll be fine.'

Genie appeared at the bathroom door with red eyes. She was wiping away tears.

'No way. Schneider hit him so hard I swear he was dead.'

'He was in bad shape, but she sewed up the wound and I think he'll heal.'

Genie felt a surge of hope. Mouch was alive. It lifted her spirits. She took Randall by the arm and led him to a pile of cushions in a corner.

'You're sleeping here, Randy. You OK?'

Randall nodded. He seemed confused.

'Genie? I know I heard it before, but what's a dog?'

Genie looked at him with confusion. 'Dog?'

Rian had also noticed his disorientation. 'He's tired.'

'You know what a cat is?' Genie asked him.

'I had a cat when I was a kid. Can't remember its name though.'

'Can you remember where you lived?'

'Seven-five-six Mulberry. You don't forget where you live.'

'Then you'll remember what a dog is tomorrow.'

She helped him lie down. Randall was strange. Maybe he'd always been strange.

She met Rian on the landing, a question unasked about Randall on his lips. Genie shrugged. She didn't know any more than he did. Perhaps the kid would feel better in the morning. It must be weird to be downsized like that.

Downstairs, they drank tea and held hands. The two of them together at last.

'You know what worries me most, Ri?'

'What.'

'It worked. The Fortress don't know it worked. They don't know we're alive, but when they do, this thing is going to be worth billions to someone. We're just nine kids who want revenge on Reverend Schneider, but someone has a fortune invested in this idea and they won't want us telling anyone about it.'

Rian understood.

'We'd have to get us all to Spurlake, hope Officer Miller

will protect us and then get out fast.'

Genie nodded. 'We just proved teleportation works. We're going to be valuable. The Fortress will want us back real bad. We're like returning astronauts or something. Y'know, those guys who went to the moon, like forty-odd years ago.'

'They'll want to study you all,' Rian agreed. 'That so sucks. You're right, I don't know why I didn't think of that.'

'They'd cut us up like lab rats or something. Don't tell the others. But we have to keep it secret until we're ready.'

Renée appeared in the doorway suddenly, wearing one of Marshall's sweaters. 'Your pig is making noises outside. I can't sleep.'

'Probably needs water,' Rian told her. 'I'll get the bucket.'

Rian left to deal with the pig and Genie looked at Renée and smiled.

'I heard what you said, Genie. We got to be smart. We have to protect ourselves. You're right, we're like the first people on Mars. We could be celebrities.'

'They'd never let us get that far, Renée. If they let the world know we exist then they will have to account for all the other missing kids. Either way, they won't

377

ever want to admit to the world they were using live kids in experiments.'

'I guess you're right.' She looked disappointed. 'And tomorrow?'

'You'll see. We need to build up strength. Everyone's muscles are so weak right now. Get some sleep. OK?'

'You look cute with a shaved head, y'know. You going to grow it long again?'

'I'll just be happy if it grows. I want to be normal.'

Renée laughed. 'Yeah, right, normal, whatever. That's so going to happen. Night.'

It was four a.m., still dark outside. As far as Genie could make out, everyone was asleep, although most were restless, having shallow dreams. Genie was stood in the bathroom, resting her head against the mirror as she let cold water flow over her hands. She had no idea how long she had been there but it had been a while. She'd hugged Rian until he'd fallen asleep in her arms and then lain there, totally awake. She, more than most, realized what a miracle it was that she was alive and able to see Rian again, let alone hold him, feel his hot flesh against her, something so simple and utterly precious. Amazing also to be able to stand here and feel cold water trickling over her hands. But did she deserve it? She had doubts.

Someone entered the bathroom behind her and closed the door.

'You too?' Renée asked.

Genie didn't move. 'I never realized how much I like water flowing over my hands. Never knew how important it was to simply breathe, Renée.'

'Can't sleep. Can't get used to being solid. Feels so heavy. I never knew how you could feel how heavy you are. It just feels so weird.' Renée came forward and sat on the toilet. She totally understood why Genie was acting strange.

Genie shut off the tap and dried her hands, moving towards the door to give Renée privacy.

'I used to dream about snow,' Renée whispered. 'I had the same thing going over in my head for over a year. Kept looking up and seeing snow and imagining it melting on my eyelids. Just that, thinking about snow and knowing I'd never feel anything, ever again.'

Genie understood. She'd only been trapped in the Fortress for moments, but it was enough. She was again standing on the transmission platform, watching her own body disintegrating, like so many grains of sand in the wind. It was a terrifying but fascinating impression that would stay with her for always.

'I'm worried, Genie,' Renée finally confessed. 'I'm

worried about what's inside us. If everything is going to work inside. I mean, what if it suddenly goes wrong. How do we know this is going to last? What if I start falling apart? I saw what happened with other kids.'

'We're OK,' Genie reassured her. 'I'm pretty sure we're OK.'

'How do you know?'

''Cause we can walk and talk and see. It's all in the right place, Renée. If it wasn't, nothing would work, nothing would work at all . . . and it does.'

Renée wasn't mollified. 'Of course you could be more worried than you're letting on, else you wouldn't be standing in the bathroom for half an hour wondering if your hands are going to wash away.'

'It's not like when you were in the Fortress, Renée. You're out now. They can't switch you off. We're real. We're OK. I know it.'

Renée didn't say anything. She finished her business and flushed, quickly washed her hands.

'Come on, let's try to sleep. Still time before it's light,' Genie whispered, opening the door.

'I'm not sure I know how any more.'

Genie took Renée's hand.

'You have to find a happy place and curl up there.'

'That what you do?'

'Yeah. Sometimes it's hard to find, but that's where I go. No one can find me there.'

Renée was looking at Rian sleeping. 'He's so lucky he's got you. I got to get myself someone like him.'

Genie smiled and gave Renée a hug. 'You will. I know you will.'

Genie moved away and crawled back on to the bed and lay beside Rian. Barely awake, he turned over, pulled her close. She listened to his heartbeat and wrapped an arm tight around him. She realized that she was scared of the future. She wished that they could slip away and disappear, just the two of them. She wanted him all to herself, forever.

Renée paused a moment to stare at them. Yes, she wanted a boy just like him. A boy who would hold her tight, every night, and care desperately about her. But from out of town and a little taller and definitely not blue. Preferably someone who had never heard of Spurlake.

'Go to bed, Renée,' Genie told her from the darkness.

'Going.'

# 32

# *Mosquito Attack*

Genie had worked out a work schedule. Each one of them needed to build up their strength, their arms and leg muscles in particular, and find a way of being 'normal' again. There was a lot of bickering. Between them all they came up with ten crazy ideas a day, but nothing exactly workable. No one could quite decide what to do next, except they were all agreed they needed to get revenge. They pretty much accepted Genie's argument that they had to stay secret – that if the Fortress knew about them they'd come running with guns and grab them back. They knew that. Didn't want to accept it, but it was a reality. Renée had pretty much got everyone in line, making them think they were all precious escaped animals and the zoo would be pretty keen to get them back if they knew where they were. But of course, they would have to make contact with their families soon. Couldn't stay out in the boonies forever.

It was late morning on the third day. Cary came to find Genie and Rian in the back room, where they were sorting out suitable boxes and baskets to collect the apples. He looked pretty serious and dramatically dropped the phone on to a sack.

Genie and Rian stared at it with surprise. It was supposed to be in pieces.

'Someone made a call,' Cary said.

Genie was incensed. 'You're kidding me. Who? After all we said.'

Cary looked at Genie and shrugged. 'It had to be someone smart enough to know how to put this back together. I found it under the sink. I was clearing the blockage and—'

Genie hit the wall in anger. 'We're so screwed. They'll be monitoring calls. The Fortress listens to everything.' She was feeling crushed. She'd felt so safe here.

'Who? And how much did they give away?' Rian asked.

'I feel sick,' Genie stated, flopping down on to a box, feeling intense despair. 'We have to call the group together. We have to find out what they said.'

'I would suspect Julia, she's desperate to call home – but no way would she be able to put the phone back together,' Rian said.

Miho appeared at the doorway suddenly. She looked guilty and nervous.

'It was me. I made the call. I'm sorry.'

'Miho!' Genie exploded. 'How could you? You put us all at risk.'

She looked down at the floor. 'I know, I know, but I wanted to hear my mother's voice. Just wanted to hear her.'

Cary kicked a box across the room. 'What did you tell her, Miho?'

'I just told her I was coming home.'

'That's it? That's all?'

'Nothing about the farm?'

'You don't understand. She's sick. She has cancer. I didn't want to wait,' Miho said, tears in her eyes. 'She's in hospital. I just wanted to know if she was still alive.'

'The Spurlake Hospital?'

Miho shook her head. 'Abbotsford. There's a clinic there.'

'You sure you absolutely didn't say anything about the farm? What exactly did you tell her, Miho?'

Miho looked away. 'I told her I was alive, that I loved her and I was coming home . . . soon.'

'What did she say? Where does she think you are or what you've been doing?' Rian asked.

'She thought I was in Kobe in Japan. She thinks my father kidnapped me. He went back there two years ago. They don't talk any more.'

Genie felt for Miho. Another messed-up family.

Cary was thinking. 'Maybe it's all right. Maybe because she called Abbotsford it might not have alerted them?'

Rian shook his head. 'You don't get it. Marshall's in hospital, the Fortress put him there, they know there's no one here. The phone gets used and immediately they'll be interested.'

Genie put aside her anger and went to embrace Miho. 'I'm sorry you called and I'm sorry about your mother. I just hope and pray it hasn't started something.'

Cary picked up the phone and took the batteries out of it. 'I'm keeping these.'

Rian nodded. He was about to do the same.

'I'm sorry,' Miho repeated.

'I'm just sorry we don't have a real plan yet,' Rian said.

'We need to talk to Officer Miller,' Genie said firmly. 'We need protection.'

'A cop?' Cary queried. He looked at Rian for support. 'I don't think we should. I don't think there's anyone we can trust in Spurlake.'

Genie went back to stacking the boxes. 'He's all right. I mean it. We can't do this alone, Cary. If we ever want a normal life again, we have to trust *someone*. Now more than ever.'

Rian looked at Miho. 'We won't tell the others about your call. It will only make them fret.'

Miho nodded, mouthing 'thank you', then turned and left the room, her face impassive.

It was later that afternoon when the screaming started.

Randall was sorting the picked apples into the boxes. Rian had organized everyone, two to a tree. One to pick and one to catch and place in a sack so they wouldn't bruise or spoil. It was a warm day and at Genie's insistence they all slapped on a ton of sunscreen she'd found in the bathroom and they wore the paper hats Miho had made for them all. Genie was well tanned already, but the others' skin was so unused to sunlight they could so easily burn. It was hard work and although the apples were sweet and tasted good and they'd eaten three or four (in Randall's case ten) they'd pretty much had it with apples until next year already.

Julia was the first to scream. She literally fell to the ground clutching her head, hands clamped over her ears. Cary slumped to the ground soon after and then one by one they fell, yelling with pain. Rian couldn't hear anything but their screaming. When Genie began to

386

scream too he knew he had to do something. But what? At first he thought it was the apples. They'd all eaten them, but then why wasn't he screaming or lying in a foetal position on the grass?

'What is it? Genie? Tell me?'

But all of them were in excruciating pain, rocking from side to side, their eyes full of terror. Genie looked at him with imploring eyes, expecting him to do *something*, but what?

Randall suddenly started running and ran smack into the brick wall at the end of the orchard, as if he'd forgotten he was made of flesh and bone again.

Rian cradled Genie in his arms. 'Talk to me? What's going on?'

'Mosquitoes,' Genie gasped. 'Thousands of them. Mosquitoes. Can't you hear them?'

Rian couldn't hear a thing and there were certainly no mosquitoes anywhere to be seen. He looked up into the sky for inspiration and then he saw them. Two slow-flying helicopters flying in formation some distance north of the farm. Was it coming from them?

'Genie? Look. Choppers. I think . . .'

Genie was looking, dizzy and nauseous now. She understood what she was seeing and, she, like Rian, guessed this was the source of their 'noise'. 'Get us inside, Ri. Don't let them see us.'

Rian didn't need telling. He was running for the wheelbarrow. He tipped out the apples and ran from figure to figure loading up the kids. He could get two on it at once. He raced them towards the farmhouse, literally tipping them out there before going back for the others. He made four trips, Genie staggering home on her own. He could see the choppers more closely now as they made their way towards them, the Fortransco logo visible on the sides.

Rian had just recovered an unconscious Randall and slammed the front door when the two choppers directly flew low over the house, shaking the whole building, making the windows rattle. He'd made it just in time.

Minutes later, Denis uncurled his limbs and looked around him, astonished to find himself in the kitchen. 'Jesus,' he mumbled. 'I thought I was back in the Fortress. I thought they'd got me.' He stood up uncertainly. He looked deathly pale. Suddenly he ran for the door, managing to wrench it open, and was violently sick.

Rian winced – it sounded real bad. One thing was sure, it wasn't the apples.

Cary was trying to revive Danielle. He was feeling

pretty shaky himself but Danielle wasn't moving at all.

'Rian?' he called.

Rian was there quickly, feeling for Danielle's pulse. He looked up at Cary in alarm. 'Shit, I think she's dead.'

Genie staggered over to check for herself. She pressed her head to Danielle's chest and listened.

'I can hear a heartbeat.'

Cary looked at Rian and they clearly disagreed with Genie. This girl was gone, the mosquito attack must have affected her worse than the others somehow.

'Get her up, put her on Marshall's bed,' Genie told them. 'She might just be taking longer to recover, that's all.' Genie wasn't even convinced of this herself.

The others said nothing. They'd had a big scare.

'Why do you think she's so messed up?' Denis asked as he helped carry her through the house.

No one answered, each knew it could have so easily been them.

They left Danielle to sleep. There was little else to do for her. Denis discussed electric shock but short of sticking her fingers in the wall socket and killing her for sure, Rian didn't think it was a great idea.

'Let her be. We'll check on her later. Let's have a break to recover, then finish the job we started – and everyone, keep an eye on the sky. We don't want to go through that again.'

Half an hour later they were almost back to normal, shaken definitely and worried about what had happened. Rian had made everyone iced tea and they sat around the kitchen table trying to make sense of it all.

Renée had described it as a mosquito attack as well. They all heard the same thing, thousands of the bugs buzzing in their head and the pain was so intense you just lost control of your mind and body. She knew what it meant though. 'They know we escaped. Don't they? Those bastards are hunting us.'

'How do they know?' Julia asked, looking at Renée for an answer.

Rian looked at Genie and she pulled a face. They knew exactly why. Miho's phone call. It was just as they had feared. Cary said nothing, couldn't even look at her. It would be their secret.

Denis pulled a face. 'Maybe it's because we're not there. They can't control us, but they can try to blow our brains out.'

'Well, they know exactly what to do,' Cary told them. 'They can jam our brains with that mosquito signal. We wouldn't be able to do anything; we don't know how to stop it. We could be anywhere and they just need to turn it on and we'd fall to the floor. That's why Rian couldn't hear it, it's just aimed at our frequencies.'

Randall shook his head. He could still hear an echo in his ears. 'It works. I'm still dizzy.'

'You're dizzy because you ran straight into a wall,' Rian reminded him.

Denis laughed but Randall wasn't amused.

'Look, they don't know exactly where you guys are,' Rian added. 'That's why they had to broadcast it from the choppers. Right?'

Cary nodded. 'And that's the good news. But the bad news is . . .'

'We can't go home,' Renée chipped in. 'If we did, they will know exactly where to find us.'

Denis kicked a chair in frustration. 'Then we have to get them before they get us.'

'How?' Julia whined. 'We're just kids.'

'We need to speak to Miller,' Rian told them. 'He's the only guy I trust.'

'Who's he?' Denis asked, not sure he was ever prepared to trust anyone.

'Marshall's son. He doesn't believe that teleportation is possible, but he's going to get a big surprise,' Rian replied. 'I should go down the track to the next farm. Maybe I can call him from there. He knows about

Reverend Schneider and he's been making enquiries. He just wants evidence, that's all. You guys are all the proof he needs.'

'So why hasn't he shut them down already?' Denis asked.

'He needed proof, I told you, and because, as we've discovered, it seems they employ half the town,' Rian told him. 'They've got a lot of power and he's just one cop.'

'If we want to do anything, we'll need him on our side,' Genie told them. 'We can't just throw rocks at the Fortress. We have to plan something, something that will get people to realize what we've all been through.'

'Just turning up. Won't that do it? People think we're dead. At least, they think Denis is dead,' Julia pointed out.

'And all they have to do is turn on that mosquito thing and we drop like flies. Literally,' Cary pointed out. 'If we do anything, it has to be a surprise and then we have to get the hell away.'

'And how do we do that? How do you make your mom move house just because we say so?' Randall asked.

'Because if you don't, Randall, you're dead meat. We're guinea pigs, we're worth millions to them,' Cary repeated.

Miho said absolutely nothing. She knew she'd

caused this with her phone call, that was the guilt she'd have to bear.

They all heard the scream. Randall spilled his tea, Rian jerked his chair back in shock. Everyone at the table missed a heartbeat.

'I'll go,' Genie said getting up. 'It's Danielle.'

No one else moved, as if they had been nailed to the floor. That had been a powerful, terrified scream.

Cary watched Genie go. 'Well, I guess she's not dead after all.'

Renée shuddered, pouring some more iced tea for herself. 'Not funny, Cary. If we call the cops, they'll be listening. One thing I did learn at the Fortress – they listen and read everything. They've got ways of finding out anything anyone says about them. I'm not being paranoid. They use some word-pattern recognition software, just like Homeland Security. It listens for keywords. I don't think you can even call from the next farm, Rian. It's too close.'

Genie was tired of all this arguing. They should call Miller and have done with it. She headed to Marshall's bedroom, scared to death of what state Danielle might be in. That had been one frightened scream.

Danielle wasn't lying on the bed. The pillows were covered in blood, bright scarlet blood. Genie heard her throwing up in the bathroom and ran to join her.

Danielle was wiping blood from her face. She glanced at Genie as she entered the bathroom.

'Can't stop the bleeding.'

Genie knew how to deal with this.

'Stand in the bath, put your back to the wall and put your head back, right back and pinch the top of your nose.'

Danielle turned to face her, blood was still streaming from her nose.

'Now, Danielle. We have to stop the bleeding.'

Danielle climbed into the bath and did as she was told as Genie soaked a flannel with cold water.

'Head back, lean back against the wall so you don't fall, OK?'

Danielle followed the instructions. She put her head back and pinched the top of her nose. Genie got in beside her and slapped the wet flannel on her neck and held it there.

'Will this stop it?' Danielle asked, fear in her voice.

'Yes. Don't move, don't talk.' Genie wiped blood from her mouth. 'This is one hell of a nose bleed. You get them a lot?'

'Not since my brother beat me one time.'

'I mean, aside from that?'

394

Danielle shook her head.

'The mosquito thing must have started it. Affects you more than the others maybe.'

Denis poked his head around the door. Did a double take when he saw how much blood there was.

'Jeez, guys. Gross.'

'Get me some ice, Denis. Now. Go fetch,' Genie told him.

Denis vanished.

'Ice?' Danielle queried.

'Got to keep your neck cold.'

Danielle was feeling faint, could feel her legs giving way.

'Stay up,' Genie told her. 'We have to stop the bleeding.'

'I'm scared, Genie. They know we're out, don't they? They're going to come looking for us.'

'We'll be just fine, Danielle. We'll expose them and they won't be able to touch us. Ever.'

Denis was back with six ice cubes and handed them to Genie. She wrapped the flannel around them and put them back on Danielle's neck. It was so cold all thought of fainting vanished.

'She looks so pale. Need to get her out in the fresh air,' Denis suggested.

'In a minute. Get Ri. We'll get her out on to

the stoop. It's shady there.'

Denis wandered off again.

'I'll be fine,' Danielle protested. 'We have apples to pick.'

'You're not picking anything, girl. You need to rest.'

Rian came at last, saw all the blood everywhere and grimaced. 'All this from a nose bleed?'

Genie signalled for him to say nothing more.

'Help me get her outside. She'll be fine in a few minutes.'

Rian looked at Genie again and shrugged. Danielle sure as hell didn't look fine.

'It's beginning to slow down,' Genie told Danielle. 'Five minutes and we can get you outside.'

'I'm scared, Genie. I don't even want to go home. I'm waiting for something to go wrong. I'm bleeding today, but tomorrow? What else? How do we know we're OK? We've been teleported, for God's sake. How do we know we aren't going to die or get sick or get cancer or—?'

Genie squeezed her arm. 'We don't, Danielle. But right now, everything works. I'm thinking if it works now, it'll work tomorrow. OK? One day at a time.'

Danielle said nothing. She wasn't convinced. Not convinced at all.

\* \* \*

They got her out to Marshall's favourite chair eventually, made her lie there with her head back to make sure the bleeding didn't return. Everyone was still debating what to do, still spooked by the mosquito effect. They were all gathered on the stoop in the shade, reluctant to start picking again.

'You want to know why no one ever tells you about the Fortress?' Cary was saying. ''Cause if they hear or read anything critical at all, they will turn up at your door a day later and you'll lose your job.'

'How do you know this?' Rian asked, removing Danielle's bloodied shoes from her feet. He noticed Danielle's ankles were swollen but said nothing.

'Because I know what happened to my father, Ri. I found a way back home. I thought if I explained what had happened to me everything would be all right. I was stupid, y'know. Found that web link looking for volunteers for some experiment. I just wanted the two thousand dollars. I mean, how dumb was I? No one is ever going to give kids two thousand dollars cash for taking part in a drug trial, or whatever they pretended it was. We're just kids. We never read the small print. We just see two thousand dollars and think, hell that's easy. Only take a week and I'll be made. I was just as stupid as all the others before me.

'I was going to reveal myself, but things didn't look right. My dad had made some noise. He'd hacked my computer and discovered about the money and the toll-free number and was making a fuss. He's a math teacher, he knows computers, he can hack anything. He asked awkward questions. I was there. I could see what was happening.'

All the kids were paying attention now.

'My ma has a bad heart. I realized that if she saw me, and then realized I wasn't real, wasn't flesh and blood . . . she'd probably have an attack. It was bad enough she missed me so much. I never knew that. I had no idea how much they missed me.'

'So what happened?' Denis asked.

'The people from the Fortress came around and the next thing you know he lost his job. He was just ruined. In one day. My mother got seriously ill. I saw it all happen and I knew right then that if I *did* show myself, it would finish them. Better they think I might be dead. I know Renée was always telling us that we were alive as long as we could see and move around, but I didn't really go along with that. If you can't touch, or feel things or . . .' His voice faltered. 'If we want to expose them, we have to do it big. We have to do it quick. If they know we're coming, they'll grab us so fast, we'll be disappeared, and our families along with us. They're truly evil. They'll do anything to keep it secret.'

No one said anything for a while. There was a strong sense of gloom now.

'If we can't use the phone, why don't we send an email to the cop?' Denis suggested finally. 'They can't read every single email.'

'They can identify the computer it comes from – and that's exactly what we don't want them to do,' Cary pointed out.

'No use anyway, there isn't any computer,' Genie told Denis. 'Marshall doesn't have one.'

'Yeah, he has,' Denis replied, puzzled.

Rian looked at him, frowning. 'No, he hasn't.'

'I've seen it. When I was here before. The small room off the kitchen.'

Genie shook her head. 'That's the pantry. Just boxes and cans in there.'

Denis went back inside the house to the kitchen to prove them wrong and several followed him.

Genie exchanged glances with Rian and they shrugged. They had no idea what Denis was doing. They followed the others inside.

Denis walked across the kitchen, straight into the pantry. And stopped. He turned around and came back to the door. He saw all their faces looking at him. 'I just remembered I can't walk through walls any more.'

'Tell me about it,' Randall agreed, rubbing the side of his head.

'But there's nothing in there, Denis,' Rian told him from the doorway. 'Genie and me looked everywhere for a computer.'

Denis turned around again. 'Come here. I'll prove it to you.'

Rian sighed and joined him. 'If it's there, it's got to be well hidden.'

Denis was standing by a stack of boxes in the pantry with his eyes closed trying to remember what he'd seen before. 'Help me with these boxes.'

Rian and Denis heaved and the boxes came away pretty easily – there was virtually nothing in them. They both saw the door was barely visible, cut with the grain of the wood so you really had to be looking for it. Clearly it wasn't meant to be found. Rian pushed on it. It was surprisingly heavy. It squeaked on rusty hinges. A neon light flickered on inside.

Denis entered first, closely followed by Rian.

'Wow.'

Rian was looking at a room only two metres wide, but

the full length of the house. A good fifteen metres long. It was filled with electronic and scientific equipment. A fully fitted lab. Dusty broken computer bits sat on a table along with some of the receptors they had found in the forest, some still to be assembled. From the amount of dust it looked like Marshall hadn't been in here in a very long time. Certainly he hadn't used a computer – it had been deliberately smashed to bits.

Denis turned to him and frowned. 'I guess he didn't want to use his PC.'

'I can't believe it,' Genie said, entering the room with the rest of the gang. 'This is like so cool. A secret room. He never said anything.'

'Neat, huh? You'd never know it was here, unless you measured the house on the outside and compared it to the inside,' Rian said.

'Point is, can we use any of this stuff?' Denis asked, looking around.

Cary entered. You could see his instant disappointment when he saw the smashed computer parts.

'This place hasn't been used in years,' Denis protested.

Cary picked up electronic equipment, bits of a cell phone, some cables. 'I can't work with this.' He looked at Rian. 'Sorry. I guess he didn't want them listening to him either.'

'You'll have to go down the track to the nearest phone,' Genie told Rian.

'Guys, we have apples to pick. Got to finish the job, OK?' Renée was calling.

They all groaned, but they trooped out back to the kitchen to join her.

Cary hung back a moment and looked at Rian.

'How far is this phone?'

'About ten Ks. By the mail drop.'

'We'd better work out what we're going to tell him. He's probably not going to believe anything you say. I wouldn't. Keep it real short too.'

Genie had an idea. 'Leave him a message, Ri. Tell him this: *Moucher is harvesting. Needs a new basket.*'

Rian understood and smiled. Yeah, that would work.

An hour later Rian found Cary standing in the shade of the house, cooling his temple against the stone wall. He'd stopped picking for a while. Rian had brought him some water to make sure he was OK. He silently took the bottle from him and drank. Cary's left eye was swollen and he had a slight nervous tic.

'Go in, cool down. You've done enough today.'

Cary rubbed his face. 'Can't seem to adjust to my new eyes. I can see perfectly, but I've got such a blinding headache. They're flickering.'

'Flickering?'

'Y'know, like when you stare at a computer screen for too long. Always had problems with my eyes. I once played *Assassin's Creed: Brotherhood* for about ten hours straight, then discovered I was practically blind for a day. Couldn't lift my head I was so nauseous.'

Rian sat down on his haunches. He needed a break himself. 'What was it like – y'know, being inside the system, being part of it?'

'Like being a Borg,' Cary answered with a wry smile. 'Only worse. Whoever wrote the code was pretty smart though.'

Rian glanced over his shoulder. 'That was Marshall. This is his farm.'

Cary was surprised. 'Well, he did a good job. You know that computer data is just made up of ones and zeros, right?'

Rian nodded.

'Ones and zeros aren't conscious of each other. Can't be, right? Computers aren't sentient. But he wrote this code called Vallhund.

'Vallhund?'

'Vallhund makes everything associated with your DNA go hunting, to keep it all together. It tracks every bit of information about your individual DNA make-up on every server constantly. It herds. Keeps you whole. That's why we still existed. That's how Renée and Denis were able to come here and you could see them. The code kept them in one piece pretty much all the time, unless a server went down. Fanatical about it, checking every bit of data a million times a second.'

Rian realized that Cary understood how all this stuff worked.

'You worked it out?'

Cary smiled. 'Yeah. I was looking for flaws. I figured that if I was intact, then there had to be a way to transmit me out of there again for real. I wanted to know what they were doing wrong.'

'Did you find out?'

Cary shrugged. 'No. Sheer dumb luck that I came out with Genie. I don't know what she did, but she brought us out somehow. When you're inside, everything is infinite and yet you feel like you are in the smallest box in the universe and can't breathe. I can't explain it. Eleven months and six days, Rian. Doesn't feel more than eleven seconds right now, but I never ever want to go back in.'

'Got to make sure everyone has water,' Rian told him. 'Take it easy. All right? You're free now.'

Cary watched Rian go. Why didn't he feel free? Why

did he feel he was still inside that box? He took long deep breaths of clean mountain air and closed his eyes. His heart beat loud in his ears, blood was pumping around his body. Rian didn't know what a miracle it was to be able to feel that. Had no idea at all.

They had already stripped one side of the orchard of all the best apples and were already on to the other side. They had a good system going now, sorting good from bad, small from large and layering them in the boxes, separating each layer with blue tissue paper to stop possible contamination. The boxes were stacking up under the shade of the old oak tree in the corner, ready to be moved to the cool room at the back of the house. It was exhausting work for weak muscles. Julia complained a lot, but was an expert picker, so they put up with it.

Danielle appeared just as they had all decided they were exhausted and needed a break. They were laid out flat in the long grass drinking water and groaning as unused muscles and aching necks throbbed.

'Hey, I thought you guys were picking apples.'

Everyone protested and some pelted apples at her. She just laughed.

'You feeling better?' Genie asked.

Danielle nodded. 'Yeah. Sorry about what I said earlier.

I was just panicking. I sure hope those bloodsucking choppers don't come back though.'

'Got to find you something different to wear,' Genie said, looking at Danielle's bloodied T-shirt.

Danielle looked down and shrugged. 'Nothing white I think.' She smiled. 'In case.'

'We're going to get our own back soon,' Denis told her. 'We're going to go back to Spurlake and make such a lot of noise when we do, they won't be able to touch us ever again.'

'I want to see Reverend Schneider's face when we suddenly challenge him,' Julia said. 'I hope he squirms. I hope they throw things at him. I hate him.'

'We'd need TV and newspapers,' Cary said, as he returned with an empty basket, ready for work again. 'They'd have to come. It's the only way we'd be safe. Us coming back from the dead all at once would be a real big thing. But until then, we have to stay well hidden.'

Danielle sat down beside Denis and munched on an apple. Her colour had returned at last.

Ri signalled to Genie that he was going. He got up slowly and strolled towards the barn. Genie followed.

They hugged beside Marshall's truck a moment. Rian held her tight, reluctant to leave her behind.

'You think this is a good idea?' Genie asked.

'I'm just going to leave him the message on his cell. Not talk to him or anything. I'll come right back.'

'Pick up some milk. Get two four-litre jugs, OK? Oh, and some bread.'

'Can I kiss you now or are you going to—'

Genie kissed him long and hard, then broke off suddenly. 'Go. It's getting late. Come right back. Avoid any Fortress people. Don't attract attention.'

Ri nodded. He opened the truck door. 'Love you.'

'Of course you do. Come right back, Rian. I just don't want any surprises.'

'Better clean up the blood,' he told her. 'You'll need bleach.'

Genie nodded. It was next on her list of things to do.

She watched Rian go until he disappeared from sight completely. The pig wandered over and let her scratch her ears.

'No one is going to make you disappear, pig. No one.'

Genie woke at first light. She thought she heard a noise, the drone of a car maybe. Her arms ached from all that apple picking. She'd been on edge all night, worried about the message they'd sent to Miller. Would he understand it? Or dismiss it? He wouldn't be able to call back and might think it was a prank or something.

She rose, careful not to wake Rian. He looked so peaceful lying on the bed and didn't seem to have a care in the world. She definitely heard a car again. She quickly dressed and hurried on out of the bedroom and down the stairs. What if it was the Fortress? Would they have time to get out?

Outside, the sound of a car struggling up the miles of dusty track was confirmed. She ran down the track to the big rock some twenty metres from the gate. Climbing up, she could get a good view from there. It would give her time to warn the others if it was trouble coming.

It was going to be a sunny morning. There were a few pink clouds but they'd soon disappear. They were heading for the normal kind of weather they got in the fall, long sunny days and chilly nights. No more rain for a while, at least.

It was a four-by-four. She had a good feeling about it. It would have to stop by the gate. Rian had insisted on closing it, it would give them a fraction more time to get ready for trouble. Renée had found cowbells to hang on it. No way now to open it without making a racket.

'You think it's him?'

Genie started. Rian was standing just below her, still in his shorts.

'I hope so.'

'Me too.'

Rian reached out and squeezed her foot, all he could reach. 'I'll go back, get them all up. In case.'

'Get the water boiling. He likes coffee. They'll all want oatmeal.'

Rian smiled at her. 'Scream very loudly if it's trouble and run like hell. OK? I'll find you.'

Genie smiled at him. 'Very loudly.'

Rian ran off back towards the farmhouse. She watched him go. She loved watching him. How many times since she'd come back had she just wanted the two of them to run away together, hide from all this forever. But she couldn't do that. She had to look out for the others and Rian would never leave them. And that was just another reason to love him. He understood.

The four-by-four stopped by the gates. Genie watched nervously as the driver got out.

She suddenly jumped down and ran towards the gates as the cowbells clanged, a broad smile appearing on her face.

'I hope the heck you're real,' Miller said as he tied the gate back to the post. ''Cause someone here will be disappointed if you ain't.'

'I was thinking the same about you,' Genie replied.

That's when she saw a little head pop up beside the empty driver's seat. A little shaved head with many stitches that squeaked with pure joy when he saw her.

'Moucher?' Genie yelled, her heart leaping. 'Mouch?'

She tore around to the passenger door and flung it open. Moucher just launched himself into space and landed on her. They fell down on to the track together, laughing and squealing, Moucher practically wetting himself with happiness.

'Eew,' Genie laughed, rolling in the dirt.

'Well that's my good deed for the day and it ain't even seven a.m. yet,' Miller remarked. 'You going to tell me what happened to your hair?'

'Calm down, Mouch. Calm down,' Genie said, doing her best to stop him licking her to death.

'Took me a while to make sense of the message on my cell but I got it in the end,' Miller was saying. 'Mouch, back off now, back off.'

Genie struggled back up on to her feet, trying to brush the dirt off her clothes.

'Get in, we can drive up to the house. Need to keep in earshot of the radio.'

Genie climbed in, picking up Moucher, who sat on her lap, proud as anything to be back with her and on his way home.

Genie was inspecting his head. 'Oh, cute, little bit of fur growing already.'

'He'll be fine. Lucky dog. Luckier than you, I guess. I had to go see Rian's mother about an insurance claim and there he was. Wasn't about to be left behind either. Howled until I took him. Schneider do that to your head?'

'Some woman called Helen Ulrich, she works at the Fortress. Lives in Spurlake, no doubt.'

Miller frowned. Ulrich. He knew the family. Had no idea one of them worked at the Fortress. How many other Spurlake people worked there? He was beginning to believe it was one heck of a lot.

'I'm getting used to it. Don't spend that much time in the shower any more and no more knots to get out of my darn hair,' Genie smiled, looking at Miller properly for the first time. 'Thanks for coming, I really appreciate it. Ri's got coffee on the stove. I know you like your coffee.'

Miller nodded. 'I'm just happy to find you alive. Never expected that.'

'No one did. Got more surprises for you at the house. How's Marshall?'

'He's recovering now. Slow, but he's over the shock, at least. He'll be tickled pink to find out you're alive. You may not know this, but he's really taken with you and Rian.'

411

'Take a look in the cool room when you get inside.'

Miller was looking at the orchard as he slowed. There was a distinct absence of apples on those trees.

'You picked the whole crop? You've been busy. Just the two of you? Impossible. There's like hundreds of trees.'

'We had some help,' Genie replied with a little smile.

'Dad's recovery will be a whole lot faster when he finds out about this. Shock might kill him mind. Never picked the whole crop before. In the old days pickers would go from farm to farm to pick the apples in season. Can't find people like that these days.'

'We need a big truck and cold storage,' Genie told him. 'Today, if you can arrange it.'

'I can fix that with one phone call. But who is "we"?'

'You're going to have a heart attack when you meet them, believe me.'

Miller looked at her as he slowed to a stop by the house and put the brake on. 'Now I'm nervous.'

Moucher barked, struggling to get out. He was finally home.

412

# 33

## *Strategy*

Miller couldn't help staring at the kids. Denis Malone had been dead and buried, for God's sake. Reverend Schneider had shed tears for the boy at his graveside. Yet here Denis was – and still the tiny kid he had been two years before. He'd not grown one centimetre. Miller thought he'd like to hear the scientific explanation for that! He'd wanted proof, well here it was. All he had to do was believe it. His dad hadn't lied, hadn't made it up – the Fortress had made a breakthrough, teleportation was apparently real. He drank his coffee and watched all these kids eating their breakfast in his father's house and marvelled at it all. They all looked so well. He didn't want to think what they had been through, but just looking at them, it was like they were at summer camp and this was just a perfectly normal day.

The other sceptical side of his brain was telling him that these kids had been hiding some place all this time, but seeing Denis Malone and the size of him, seeing that Japanese girl, Miho, and realizing that she hadn't

413

been kidnapped, as he had been told, was mind-blowing. All the fantastic stories people had spun about why and where these kids were – and here they were, some, like Randall, changed beyond recognition, but alive and well. Each one would testify that Reverend Schneider was actively gathering up misfit kids and surrendering them to the Fortress for transmatter experiments... it was sick. It had to be true. Their stories were identical. They were all completely convinced this had happened to them.

'You do realize we have been subjected to slave labour conditions,' Julia piped up, trying to get Miller's attention. 'I mean, who picks these apples normally? And I couldn't call home. It's like a prison camp here. There's laws against this, y'know.'

'Shut up, Julia,' Renée told her. 'We're lucky to have a safe place to hide and you know it.'

'Maybe you would prefer to be back in the Fortress, Julia?' Denis asked. 'He's come to help us. After that mosquito attack, you know we can't do this alone.'

'Mosquito attack?' Miller asked, looking at Genie.

'I'll explain later,' Genie told him.

Miller scratched his head. 'You realize that people in town are going to say this is mass hysteria or something. They're going to deny you were ever in the Fortress.'

Rian and Genie weren't sure Miller was persuaded either.

'We're here, we're alive and we can describe everything that happened to us. We can identify people. If it comes to a trial, we could point out everyone who works there,' Renée told him. 'We all can.'

Miller shook his head. 'It wouldn't get that far. You've no idea what you're up against. You'll never convince anyone that you were teleported. It's science fiction. Best you can do is claim they kept you against your will all this time and questions will have to be answered about that. Abduction and kidnap are serious charges. But about the other . . . it would have to be demonstrated – and they aren't going to do that now, are they?' He was looking at Rian. 'Any particular reason your skin is blue, Rian?'

'It's a long story,' Rian answered. He didn't want to have to explain his failure to save Genie that night.

It was Renée who thought of a way to prove the Fortress was guilty.

'Take him out to the forest, guys. Show him.'

Genie understood immediately. 'Why not? Come on. You got a camera in the truck?'

Miller nodded. 'What are you going to show me?'

'Something to change your mind.' Genie stood up,

setting her coffee mug down with a bang on the table. 'Moucher!'

Moucher led the way, with Miller, Rian and Genie following as they headed off into the woods, towards the ravine, the site of their great return.

'Dad talked about what was possible,' Miller was explaining as they made their way through the trees. 'When he first arrived at the hospital and raved about some dog, I just thought he'd gone over the edge, y'know. I know you were afraid of Reverend Schneider, and you were dead right to be, but you have to understand my point of view. Even though I grew up with all my father's crazy ideas about teleportation, I never believed it. It's too fantastic. I'm a cop. I have to have evidence before I believe anything. I'm trained to be a sceptic. Can't help it.'

Neither Genie nor Rian said anything. They just concentrated on making their way towards the rocky outcrop by the ravine. Hoping that what they wanted to show him would still be there, not been eaten by wild animals.

Moucher stayed close to Genie. He was at home in the forest and happy.

They had been walking for twenty minutes or so now. Genie sensed Miller was getting anxious. 'It's near.

416

You should brace yourself.'

'Brace myself?' Miller asked.

'It's evidence,' Genie said. 'You're not going to like this. You too, Ri. You don't have to look. It's totally gross. Here.'

Moucher hung back. Unsure, a low growl in his throat as he sniffed the putrid air. Genie didn't want to look, but Miller had to be persuaded. Had to.

Miller stepped around Genie, not at all sure as to what he was going to see. He stopped in his tracks. The decomposing body was a shock. The fact that it was also inside out, just lying there, the organs rotting, made him feel instantly sick. He felt dizzy. The shape of a human form were plain enough, the inner organs still distinguishable, but decaying and mushy.

'There's another, over here,' Rian pointed out, quietly fighting nausea. He looked away, took some quick breaths to regain his composure.

'Half of one, further around,' Genie added. 'They must have bled out instantly. They wouldn't have known about it, right?'

Miller couldn't say anything, had to grip a tree to stand up. He was as pale as a ghost now. He'd seen dead bodies. Many more since the flood, of course. He'd seen kids murdered, old women beaten, seen a man with an axe stuck in his head, many terrible things, but this, whatever this was . . . was just horrible, horrible.

Rian had to take the digital images eventually. Miller's hands shook too much.

Genie patiently explained about the receptors Marshall had installed but forgotten, the lightning storm, and the arrival of the half-dog (even now his frozen head lay in the freezer) and how all the kids had been stored on the system. She explained about how she'd been abducted by Reverend Schneider from right outside Rian's house, and about Mr Yates, Employee of the Month, and how he must have known all about what really went on in the Fortress. And she talked about how she had thought that she too would die, but how there had been a fire, and then suddenly arriving here, in the semi-circle with Julia, Renée and others. She explained how some of the ones that didn't make it probably wouldn't have ever made it, being half formed, or inside out or like the half-dog, kinda melted together. She explained everything until there was nothing left to say.

The hardest thing for Miller was knowing that his father had been part of this until his accident. He always claimed he used inanimate objects, but if he hadn't had the accident, would he be working there, knowing they used kids for experiments? He hoped not. God knows how many times his father had tried to tell him what the Fortress was up to. He'd just blocked it out. He'd stopped listening to his father and that had been his big mistake.

Not only had his father figured what the Fortress was doing, but it seemed half of Spurlake knew. How could they not know? Spurlake's own kids lured to the Fortress and Reverend Schneider's sickening Church of the Free Spirits and community prayers for the missing. What an idiot he was, trying to keep order in a town living on a lie and endlessly searching for kids that were apparently utterly expendable. He felt sick at heart.

'Is that all of them?' he asked at length.

Genie shrugged. 'We didn't go looking for more.'

Rian handed back the camera. He didn't want to look at any of the photos he'd taken.

'You realize I can't just walk away from this. I have to call it in.'

'Cary says the Fortress monitors all our calls, yours too. They know exactly what everyone is doing and where and why,' Genie told him.

Miller looked at Genie, and saw it was the plain truth. That was when he realized that they had to bring in outsiders. Only Vancouver's RCMP IHIT (Integrated Homicide Investigation Team) could handle something as big as this. They had the resources and manpower to do it and none, as far as Miller knew, would be beholden to the Fortress. He'd send them the images Rian took. It would be at the very least a major investigation. This was real evidence – tying it to Schneider or the secretive Fortress scientists would be difficult.

'This is Fortransco property around here,' Miller said, realizing where they were standing. 'Those bodies are going to be an embarrassment for them at least.'

Rian led them out of the forest towards Marshall's boundary line. Each silent, each filled with their own thoughts and fears; Miller overwhelmed by new doubts and fears. He was beginning to realize the enormity of this crime.

Moucher had to be carried for the last part of the journey, but Genie didn't mind. He was a tired dog who loved her and she'd always, always, wanted a dog that loved her. Never knew how much till now.

'You're right,' Miller told them as they approached the house. 'You can't tell anyone you guys are back. We have to keep it secret for as long as possible. You're all in danger. I can see that now.'

Rian and Genie passed little smiles to each other. *Finally* they were sure he was on their side.

# 34

## Pick of the Crop

Miller touched his father on the shoulder and was happy to see him wake and look alert again.

'You look good, Dad.'

'Be better when they let me out of here.'

'Tomorrow. Got something to cheer you up meanwhile. I suggest you come to the window.'

'What?' Marshall frowned. 'You got Schneider on a skewer down there? That I'll look at.'

Max laughed. 'Better.'

Marshall flung off his blanket, revealing he wasn't wearing his prosthetic leg. 'You'll have to help me.'

Max was only too happy to oblige. He scooped his father up out of the bed and set his foot down on the floor. Marshall put an arm around his son's shoulders to get support and together they moved towards the window.

'Check out the car park.'

Marshall stood at the window and looked down. His eyes fixed on a huge refrigerated truck, with a trailer behind it, loaded up with crates of boxed apples.

'What?'

Max grinned and gave a signal. Nine heads popped up from behind his truck behind it and began cheering.

'Rian. Who are the other kids? My God? Did they pick my whole crop? Where's Genie? I don't recognize her.'

'The one with Moucher. They shaved her head.'

Marshall felt incredibly touched. They had done him a good turn and he felt quite emotional. He waved, not sure they could see him.

'They picked everything. Pickard's are taking them. There's a big demand for organic apples now. Couldn't get it all in one truck. Got a good price too.'

'They did all that? I don't believe it.' He watched them pile into his truck. 'Who shaved her head?'

'Get back into bed. I'll fill you in. There's going to be quite a showdown tonight.'

Marshall watched his truck being driven away. He was still feeling stunned. He had never managed to get his whole crop picked before. Those kids were amazing, but where they hell had they come from? At least two looked familiar.

Max was watching his reaction.

'Don't worry, I've got Carl watching out for them. About the only cop I trust in this town any more.'

'Carl's a good guy,' Marshall agreed, then frowned, puzzled. 'Who are the other kids?'

'I'll tell you, but I'm afraid the surprise might finish you off for good. Remember all those cuttings you kept on the bathroom wall?'

Marshall blanched. 'No! You're kidding. Genie said she was talking to some of them, but I thought she was hallucinating. It's impossible.'

He could feel his heart rate racing as he considered the possibility.

Miller smiled. 'I had a very hard time believing it too. Now get back into bed. I'll tell all I know.'

Marshall hopped back to his bed. This story he wanted to hear.

# 35

# Showdown at Seven

> *The Church of the Free Spirits welcomes you:*
> *Witness Night – Tuesday 7 p.m.*
> *Families and pets welcome – followed by*
> *Organic Coffee and Home-Made Cakes 9 p.m.*

They watched Reverend Schneider's Mercedes being towed away by RCMP forensics. The Vancouver-based investigators were waiting in their cars as people arrived for the Tuesday service, discreetly taking photos. Among them many strangers to the church, invited by Miller. Parents of children known to be missing in Spurlake. Some were about to get a big surprise.

Genie was worried. So many people were involved with the Fortress in Spurlake. Once the kids revealed they were back, they were immediately vulnerable. Anything could happen, including disbelief. How could they prove that they were used as lab rats? How could they prove they were held prisoner on computer servers? Even ones as powerful as theirs. Who on earth would believe that?

Most likely they'd laugh, it was so incredible. It was reluctantly agreed by all, that they would go home to Spurlake, say as little as possible to friends and try to get their folks to leave town. Leaving Spurlake was all they could think about and Miller tended to agree. They had all suffered enough.

He'd called all the big city newspapers and TV news people. It was a good story, kids claiming to have been abducted by a major corporation. Most promised to come. This would be the protection they needed. Genie was concerned the choppers would fly over and they'd play the mosquito trick. But with journalists watching, it wouldn't look so good if they all ended rolling on the ground screaming. First they had to confront Reverend Schneider at the Church of the Free Spirits. Then disappear again, real fast.

They gathered at the grand glass and steel structure on Fir Street that could accommodate five hundred souls. The Fortress had been very generous to its major conspirator.

Genie watched Denis Malone's parents walk by into the building. They looked anxious. Denis' little sister would be taller than him now – that would be embarrassing for Denis; he was very touchy about his height.

She watched Julia's parents arrive too. They were rich.

Genie never did find out why Julia had run away from them – they looked pretty normal. Of course, they were already members of Reverend Schneider's flock. Had they joined before or after Julia had disappeared? She'd forgotten to ask. Perhaps they didn't even want little Julia back. Everyone in Spurlake thought her own mother was a good person and yet she had imprisoned her own daughter behind bars and screamed abuse at her for weeks on end. Genie wondered just how many other horrible secrets there were in her hometown.

Miho had already departed. Miller hadn't wanted her to go anywhere outside of his protection but Miho couldn't be stopped. She was desperate to see her sick mother. Miller had made a friend of his drive her to Abbotsford and warned her to approach the hospital with extreme caution. He'd also given her a hundred bucks to get to Vancouver and an address of a safe place to stay. On no account, he'd told her, should she come back to Spurlake or call anyone there.

Rian took Genie's hand. He was pointing to a wheelchair being lowered from the back of a Range Rover.

'My mother.'

Genie watched a well-dressed woman getting into her wheelchair being pushed by a red-faced man who'd eaten way too many pies. She knew that face.

'Mr Yates.'

'Yeah.'

Genie looked at the car clock. 6.50 p.m.

'It's going to be full. What's gonna happen, Ri?'

'Reverend Schneider'll go to jail for many years,' Rian declared. 'They'll close the Fortress down and Spurlake can get back to being a normal town where the kids don't disappear all the time.'

Genie squeezed his hand. She wasn't so confident. There were a lot of jobs at stake; people tended to vote with their wallets.

'I wish I could believe that. I think Reverend Schneider will claim the kids all coming back is a miracle and he'll be bigger than ever. Hell, it will even look like a miracle. I don't think this is gonna work, Ri.'

'I hope you're wrong, Gen. I really hope you're wrong.'

Miller walked over to his vehicle and looked in on them both. Genie smiled at him. He'd been so good to them. She didn't want him to be disappointed if all this backfired.

'You look sad, Genie. You should be happy. This is the night you get your revenge.'

Rian glanced at Genie and then back at Miller.

'She's afraid he'll claim it's a miracle.'

Miller hadn't really thought about that, but he could

see that would make sense. He looked at his watch. He wondered where the press and TV crews were. He'd made the calls personally and they had seemed real keen to come. Surely they'd want to be here for this. It would be the scoop of the decade. Why weren't the newspapers here? They'd promised. He was getting worried now. Perhaps he should call it all off. Had the Fortress leaned on them? Maybe they thought it was hoax call? He dismissed that notion – some maybe might think that, but not all would stay away.

'Keep the faith, kids. Focus on parents getting their kids back. They're going to be angry once they understand. It's hard explaining miracles to angry parents. They'll realize that Reverend Schneider only pretended to care about the missing kids. The whole town trusted him and he lied to them all. Even if your folks never came to his church, he's betrayed you all. That's what counts here. No one needs to be afraid of him any more.'

He looked at his watch again. 'The RCMPs will be raiding the Fortress right about now. This time they know what to look for thanks to you guys. Come on. Let's go. It's showtime.'

Genie leaned in and kissed Rian. She was scared to death of what might happen next. She knew Rian was too.

They should be miles away and still running rather than facing all this. Being grown up about this stuff really sucked. Rian hugged her back.

'Come on. We can do this.'

'And then we run?'

Rian smiled but didn't say anything.

'Hey, there's Renée,' Genie shouted getting out of the car. 'She looks so cool. What you wearing, girl?'

'Charity glam. Same as you. Can't believe what was left in the flood donation pile. Miu Miu, girlfriend. How could they not want this?'

Genie grinned. 'Not many size zeros in this town, that's why. This is the most electric-blue outfit I ever saw. People are going to see you coming all right.'

Renée laughed, really happy to be looking good again. They hugged. Renée looking around.

'Did my mother come?'

Genie shrugged. 'We don't know what she looks like.'

'She'll be here. She worships the Reverend. Bet she takes his side.'

'Remember you're with us, no matter what,' Rian called out to her.

Renée smiled, but Genie could see the sadness in her eyes. She was the least happy to be back and the most scared to meet her mother.

A senior RCMP officer approached Miller to talk with him and Genie, Renée and Rian went into the church alone.

The reporter from *The Straight* slowed to a stop by the roadblock. Private security guards, not RCMP, were manning the block on the Highway 1 turn-off to Spurlake.

'What's going on?' she asked a uniformed guard, checking the clock readout on her dash. She was supposed to be there for seven and it was already five minutes to.

'Accident ahead. The police are dealing with it, they're short-handed so we're helping out. Might be a while until they clear it.'

The reporter couldn't see any flashing lights or activity ahead.

'Isn't there another way in?'

'Only road. Best park over there with the others. We have to keep the way clear for emergency vehicles.'

The reporter saw a CTV truck and another journalist she knew from *The Province* standing at the side of the road. She backed up and drove over to where they were talking. They waved in acknowledgment as she parked.

'What's going on?' she asked, getting out of her vehicle.

The CTV reporter was putting on her coat; it was chilly waiting around.

'They say there's been a volatile chemical spill up ahead. Haven't got verification though and there's no signal on my cell. Yours?'

The reporter checked her phone and shook her head. 'Uh-uh.'

'You think this abduction thing is for real at the church?'

'Cop who called said it was. We're all being bottled up here. Don't you think that's kind of convenient, keeping all the media out?'

'Don't even try to walk it. These guys pulled their guns on Steven. They're sticking to the chemical spill story, but I'm not sure I buy it. I can't smell anything and we've seen no fire department trucks coming in. This small town couldn't cope with a spill on their own.'

The reporter tended to agree and went back to her car to get her fleece. She noted that the security guards all sported Fortransco Synetics logos. Coincidence or conspiracy? Wasn't this the company the cop was going to expose? Something wasn't right here.

The service was in full swing. Reverend Schneider leading his flock in witnessing. It was important to witness God's work in this world and he called up his flock to account for themselves and their ways.

Reverend Schneider was dressed in purple flowing robes with a swatch of white cloth across his shoulders. He looked like a medieval high-priest. He was looking triumphant. A full house meant a good night's takings.

Genie looked around with growing nervousness. Where were the TV cameras? Surely they should be in here, waiting for something to happen. She began to fret. They had counted on them being there. The Vancouver cops had come but they kind of had to. Where were the journalists? It was starting to go wrong.

'And who now will say their proofs?' Reverend Schneider began. 'Who will speak and bear witness to the special kindness of the Lord?'

There was that moment of tension when no one wants to go first. A woman looked as though she would get up and speak but Denis Malone stepped into the aisle.

'I'm Denis Malone. You abducted me, took me to the Fortress and made me disappear. I am your witness. You kidnapped me, Reverend Schneider.'

A woman screamed, a man stood up, clearly shaken. 'Denis? Denis? Is it really you?'

'You're not a member of this congregation . . .' Reverend Schneider began, trying to shut this down quickly, clearly amazed to see Denis in the flesh.

Denis' father stepped out into the aisle and ran towards his son.

Genie saw Denis' mother faint. His sister was staring at him with absolute astonishment. So far, so good.

'What trick is this?' Reverend Schneider began again.

'I can bear witness too,' Julia called out, standing up and walking into the aisle. 'I'm Julia Wasserman. You said you would help me learn to eat again. You took me into the Fortress and they made me disappear.'

'Julia?' a woman yelled. A man and woman were frantically struggling to get past people to the aisle. 'Julia?' Tears streaming down the woman's face. Genie felt a lump in her throat. Saw Julia break down into sobs as her parents reached her.

Sweat was appearing on Reverend Schneider's upper lip and his eyes nervously swivelled around the congregation. Rian noticed some people getting up to leave, Fortress employees who sensed trouble, he guessed.

Danielle's father was speechless, his face a mess of tears when he saw his Danielle stand, ready to say her piece. He just leaped up from his seat, grabbed her, embraced her and led her out of the church without a word.

Reverend Schneider looked distinctly uncomfortable

now. 'This must be some kind of miracle,' he began to mutter, trying to regain control. 'Jeff Wasserman, you have prayed for your daughter's safe return and now here—'

No one was listening as another person stood up.

'I bear witness against you, Reverend Schneider,' Renée began. 'You stole my body, you stole my life. You're a criminal. God knows what a real monster you are.'

Renée suddenly noticed her mother in the choir stalls, angrily glaring at her. Obviously she had chosen sides.

Outside the church, Miller and other cops were busy interviewing people who left, taking them to one side and checking their IDs. Still no TV or press people. Surely the Fortress couldn't keep everyone away, could they? Just how much influence did they have? He should have called news organizations south of the border, in Seattle maybe. If they didn't come, how could he protect these kids?

Inside the church, Cary was standing up.

'I'm Cary Harrison and I accuse you, Reverend Schneider, of abducting me.'

Cary's mother cried out. His father just stared at Cary with bewildered astonishment.

'I know the Fortress got you fired, Dad. I'm sorry. But I'm back now. We can make them pay.'

Cary made no attempt to move, but someone took his hand and led him towards his father. Cary turned his head and saw it was Renée.

Miller appeared at the door and Genie caught his eye. She had spotted a large overweight man lumbering towards the door. Clearly Mr Yates wanted no part of this. She stepped out in front of him.

'Going somewhere, Employee of the Month?'

He looked at her, uncomprehending. Miller intervened. 'Mr Yates, some people would like a word with you, sir.'

Mr Yates looked at Miller and beyond to the flashing blue lights of the assembled RCMP and realized he had problems. A plain-clothes man from IHIT flashed his badge at him.

'You are Mr Jim Yates, Assistant Finance Director of Fortransco Development, commonly known as the Fortress?'

Mr Yates nodded, too surprised to lie.

'This way, sir.'

That was when he saw Rian standing nearby. His face turned to thunder. 'You little squirt, I might have known you were part of this.'

Rian watched him go. He felt a little happier. He could see his mother glaring at him from her wheelchair and knew that she didn't share his sense of relief. She'd be thinking that there was no one to look after her now. Immediately he felt guilty about that. Suddenly he heard Genie's voice, cutting through the hubbub. There was an audible murmur as the Reverend's disciples all noticed her walk down the aisle.

'Reverend Schneider, I bear witness against you. I'm Genie Magee.'

A sudden spate of whispering swept through the assembly. Genie heard one word repeated like a wave from aisle to aisle: 'Possessed'.

Reverend Schneider was astonished to see her. He had seen her die. He began to stutter. 'You are c-con . . . confused . . .'

Genie felt her anger rising. 'You smashed my dog's head open, abducted me.' She pointed to a woman who was trying to avoid her gaze. 'You handed me over to this woman. Yes, you, Helen Ulrich – no need to hide your face – stripped me, shaved my head and made me disappear. We're alive. You didn't expect witnesses, did you? No kid is safe in this town from you people.'

She paused for breath. All around her the flock were agitated, standing, trying to leave. Denis' parents were examining their son, trying to make sense of why he'd never grown a centimetre in nearly two whole years.

A huge woman bore down on Randall, screaming his

name. He looked scared and pleased at the same time as she crushed him in her arms.

'Randall, Randall, Randall . . . you got so thin . . .'

Miller entered the church with two IHIT investigators and indicated Reverend Schneider.

Reverend Schneider was frantically trying to get through to someone on his phone. Genie thought for a moment that it might be the devil and he was trying to renegotiate his contract.

'Reverend Schneider, you're under arrest,' Miller said.

'You believe the rantings of a stupid, spiteful girl?' Schneider shouted, red with anger.

Miller took his phone from him, read him his rights and put the cuffs on him.

One of the officers turned to the congregation. 'No one leaves. We have a list of names of people we'd like to talk to.'

Genie glimpsed her mother at the back of the church, staring with intense hatred at her. There was no homecoming due her, for sure. Nothing had changed.

Someone touched Genie's arm. Denis, his mother and sister beside him.

'I'm going home.' He hugged Genie. 'None of this would have happened without you, Genie. Thanks.'

Genie hugged Denis back. 'Thank you.'

'For what?' Denis looked confused.

'For showing me the way.'

'You'll visit?'

Genie nodded. 'You must make them leave town, Denis,' she reminded him. 'None of us can stay until we know we're safe.'

Denis' father put his hand out to her.

'For he who is lost, shall be found,' he said.

Genie watched them leave, slightly bemused, jealous of how tight that family was. She called after him. 'Don't forget to tell them about the mosquitos, Denis.'

'So you're Genie,' a voice announced behind her.

Genie looked behind and saw Rian's mother in her wheelchair.

She looked at Genie with sadness in her eyes.

'Rian thinks a lot of you.'

'He's my hero,' Genie replied.

'And you're intending to take him away from me.'

Genie blinked at the distinct hostility in the voice.

'I . . .' She thought suddenly of Mr Yates. 'You knew Mr Yates worked at the Fortress, didn't you? You must have known what he was doing. All those children disappearing and you said nothing?'

Rian's mother narrowed her eyes.

'You'll ruin his life. You Munbys are all alike. You ruin everything you touch.'

'You could have told Rian the truth. You could have protected him,' Genie told her.

'He'd have been safe if it wasn't for you,' his mother answered bitterly.

Rian was suddenly at her side.

'We've got to go. The police want to talk to us.'

His mother grabbed his arm with desperation.

'Don't go, Rian. Don't let this girl ruin your life. Don't you understand she's—'

'She's what, Ma? Abused? Possessed? Evil? She's the best thing in my whole life.' Rian signalled Renée who pushed through the crowd to join them.

'Is your mother here, Renée?'

Renée shook her head. 'She ran off. Some things never change.'

'We're leaving. You have to come with us. They need to talk to all of us.'

'Renée?' Mrs Tulane enquired. 'This is Renée?'

Renée turned and looked down at Mrs Tulane.

'Hello, Mrs Tulane.'

Rian was pulling Genie and Renée away. He didn't want a scene.

'If you ever see my dad again,' Renée was saying,

'tell him that I'm going to look after *my* family. We're sticking together.'

Rian led his two girls away and Mrs Tulane stared after them, angry and frustrated.

Outside, Genie got the satisfaction of seeing Reverend Schneider being bundled into a squad car. Women were screaming around the car, some for him, some against. It was hard to tell which.

'Ri?'

'Yeah?'

'I feel nauseous.' Genie ran to the fence and dry-heaved. Way too much emotion. She took deep breaths. Why did she feel so nervous? Hadn't it gone to plan? Something was definitely wrong. Where were those promised newspaper people? They needed the protection of the media. Without them being on the news, the Fortress could pick them off, one by one.

Julia's mother was suddenly beside her.

'Are you all right, dear?'

Genie nodded, wiping her mouth.

'I wanted to thank you for bringing Julia home to us. She told us what you did and how you looked after her. I don't know what she's been through exactly, but I just wanted to say thanks.'

Genie blushed. She hadn't done anything as far as she was concerned, but she smiled and accepted the remarks.

'Don't let her disappear again,' Genie told her. 'She loves you very much.'

Tears welled in Julia's mother's eyes.

Genie surveyed the confusion outside the church. Police questioning people. Everyone was bewildered, and some folks were staring at her with hostility, as if it were all her fault.

Miller rescued her and escorted her to his car, where Renée and Rian waited.

'Better?' Rian asked.

Genie shrugged. She wasn't sure.

'What's going to happen to us? Where are the journalists, Miller? Where's the TV people? I can't believe no one's interested, I mean this is an event, right?'

Miller was tense. 'I just learned that Fortransco set up a roadblock to prevent the press getting here. Someone leaked what we were doing, Genie. I'm sorry.' He got behind the wheel and locked the doors as a precaution.

Genie instantly realized they were in trouble. Not even the local press turned up. The Fortress had outsmarted them. Homicide were taking it seriously. But without the media asking awkward questions she knew Fortransco

441

would get away with everything. She swore. This should have been the biggest story of the year.

'Taking you to meet some people who've flown in from Vancouver,' Miller said. 'It includes the Deputy Commissioner of the Pacific Region and Commanding Officer of E Division. That's like as high as it gets in the police. He's got questions. My dad is already talking with his people.'

'No TV reporters got through at all?' Rian asked, confused.

'No. I'm sorry, OK. I should have thought of that. I can't even get through to them on the phone any more, the signal's jammed.'

Genie sighed. She had feared this. She realized that Miller was more upset than she was. 'Maybe they aren't here because it isn't a good story if we aren't dead. Dead teens are a news story. Stabbed teens, teens with gunshot wounds. But we're tanned and alive, claiming to be abducted by the most respected man in Spurlake, stored on a server in a place that doesn't actually exist on the map and teleported to the middle of a forest? Crazy talk. We're probably lucky we aren't on some tacky daytime TV show with people who think they're Martians.'

'You've suddenly became all cynical, Miss Magee,' Miller said, snatching a look at her. He could tell she was

442

really upset, and probably a little scared now.

Renée and Genie exchanged glances.

'Perhaps with the Vancouver police involved we'll get some protection,' Renée suggested, but you could tell from her voice that she didn't really believe that.

'What happens now?' Genie asked.

'Marshall wants to talk to you about something,' Miller answered mysteriously.

Rian squeezed her hand and tried to reassure her.

'We did good in there. People were shocked. Those parents will guard those kids now. I'm sure. It's up to them now to persuade their families to leave town.'

Genie nodded, looking out of the window as Spurlake passed by. 'God, I need something to drink. Can we stop at the store on the way? I have an urgent need for Coke and chocolate.'

Renée laughed, putting an arm around Genie and hugging her. 'God, chocolate. When did I last eat chocolate? Put me down for that.'

# 36

# *Guiding Light*

Two days later Genie threw up for real and there was blood in the bathroom sink. Marshall was out of hospital now and recuperating at Miller's home. He'd immediately dragged her to see his doctor. The doc did X-rays and tested her blood and urine. Said they'd found nothing wrong, but she was concerned about her blood pressure. She'd talked to her and asked if there was any tension in her life. Genie smiled at that. Even though the doc had given her a clean bill of health she knew Marshall was still worried about her. He drove back from the hospital in a thoughtful mood.

'You have to hand it to those guys in the Fortress. They may not know what the hell they're doing, but the fact that you've still got your nose in the right place is still pretty damn impressive.'

Genie looked at him and frowned.

'You do know they're evil, right?'

'I'm not defending them. But you're here and your X-rays show that everything is pretty much where it's supposed to be. OK, your blood pressure is a bit high, but that may have been the case before you were teleported. It takes a lot of skill to programme human DNA in such a way it can reform in the right order. I mean, I wrote a lot of those programmes, but it was theory, all theory. I never had a chance to make it work.'

Genie thought about what he said.

'If you were still working there, would you have tried to send me through the system? Be honest now.'

Marshall shook his head. It was a question he'd been asking himself.

'The most I was prepared to do was mice. We bred mice to do that. But I never got to send 'em. If we couldn't send a damn clock, we weren't going to be able to transmit a living mouse. You have no idea how complex the DNA structure of a mouse is. And keep its heart beating.'

'But you wouldn't have sent kids?'

Marshall thought about it.

'If we had sent mice and they had lived, we would have worked our way up to larger animals. At some point we would be where they are now and be looking for human volunteers.'

Genie said nothing. Marshall snatched a look at her.

'I'm trying to be honest, Genie. I'm a scientist. But to answer you, no, I'd never be part of anything that was illegal, dishonest and frankly criminal. None of those kids knew what they were getting into. That means they weren't volunteers and what they did to them was murder. That's not how you do science. Sure you take risks, but first demonstrate you can do mice. Prove the theory, then do the practice.'

Genie understood. Marshall was one of the good guys; but only just.

'I'm concerned with you throwing up. You aren't . . . ?'

'I'm not bulimic, if that's what you're thinking.'

'Then what?'

'I get all churned up. You have no idea how churned up I get. I worry about everybody. I've always been like this. About Rian, about me, about you, Moucher – hell, I can't sleep nights because I'm worried about the pig, for Christ sakes. I mean, she's all alone back at the farm, who's going to feed her? I wake up worrying if I have clean underwear to wear. I throw up when I get churned up. That's all.'

Marshall smiled. He understood this. Anxiety churned him up too.

'That pig's fine. They love to forage. That's why God gave her such a huge snout, help her find stuff to eat.'

Genie smiled. Weirdly enough, Marshall's explanation made her feel better. She could cross the pig off her list at last.

'You should keep a worry diary,' Marshall suggested.

'A what?'

'Y'know. Every time you throw up, keep a record of why or what came up. You're a guinea pig, one of the first people to ever teleport. Scientists would expect you to monitor your health and that includes your mental health. Keep a note on changes. Just in case.'

'In case of what?'

'In case. That's all. In case.'

'There's not something new I have to worry about is there?'

'No. But put it this way, when I lost my leg and my DNA got screwed, the doctors made me start a diary and it helped. Every time I had one of my fits, I wrote it down, and that's how I knew not to worry about them. I discovered they come in regular cycles, I can survive them, and I can get through it because I know what it is. No surprises.'

Genie nodded. She was still cross with him, but it was a logical idea. Particularly if something *did* start to go wrong.

'I've been thinking,' Marshall mused. 'It was a default error that made you guys reanimate in the forest. We saw the old receptors we planted years ago functioning again. Most likely triggered by the storm. The area you materialized in is exactly halfway and turns out there's a powerful natural magnetic manifestation there. It's most likely that that has been interfering with the transmission programme. There was a power surge at the Fortress and fire at the very moment you transmitted. I spoke with one of the technicians who would take a risk and speak to me. That surge of power, the magnetic field and the receptors combined meant that all that digital DNA that had been sitting waiting to be delivered was just dumped, all at once, right there in the forest.' He turned to look at her. 'Like a lot of emails that suddenly get delivered all at once, y'understand?'

That last bit Genie understood.

They were slowing. They were at Miller's home at last.

'What do you think is going to happen to me, Marshall?'

'Now? Or in the future?'

'In the future.'

Marshall parked and shut the engine off. He didn't answer right away, but he didn't get out of the cab either.

'I read something about your grandmother whilst I was in hospital. Hell of a woman. Born in 1929. Inherited millions when old man Munby finally died. She never married but had a lover, or two. She gave birth to twins at the age of forty. Your mother and her sister, May. Not very socially acceptable back then, but she didn't care.

'Grandma Munby began a great civic works programme. She built the hospital I was in, lots of things. Spurlake has a lot to be grateful for, except they aren't. They took her name off all the buildings when she had that altercation with your father.'

'This is all in a book?'

'Yep. Seems your father was a lawyer and liked the drink too much. Your grandma went to see him about that, to get him to treat your mother better and somehow he ended up dead. Foolishly he also kept loaded shotguns mounted all the way up the stairs. Your grandma claimed self-defence and got off on account of it. But of course no one took her side. Least of all your mother.'

'Sounds familiar.'

'But your Grandma Munby was a remarkable woman. She built herself a log cabin above the railway line overlooking the river. I remember it because it was like a postcard of a classic English garden, you know with hollyhocks three metres high and roses everywhere. That and the old Caboose she told fortunes in.'

'I remember that Caboose.' She closed her eyes, saw all the wind chimes that surrounded it and the dreamcatchers suspended from the roof.

'Respectable people shunned her, but if you ever had a problem or were concerned about your future, that's

449

where you went. My first wife used to go see her all the time when we were first married. She had trouble conceiving. She really liked the old woman, even if she was pretty eccentric.'

Genie had a sudden vision of herself an old grey-haired woman surrounded by flowers, telling fortunes. It wasn't quite the future she craved.

'The thing is, she spent much of her life helping people. I think you will too. You already have. You saved me. You saved those kids.'

'I don't want to tell fortunes.'

Marshall smiled. 'No, but I want you to use your gift. Your grandma passed it on to you. Find a way to use it.'

'You really think what I have is a gift?'

'I do. Some people get handed a gift of numbers or supermodel looks. The way I see it, it's a gift from God. Use it well.'

'What's Rian's special gift?'

'Loving you. It's going to be a constant challenge. Now, get out of my cab and go make me some fresh coffee.' He looked up at the sky a moment. 'Rain's coming. Going to be another storm, I think.'

Genie smiled, opening the door. She turned back momentarily.

'That book still in the hospital library?'

'Yeah. *Munbytown*. That's what Spurlake was called when it first got started.'

Genie nodded. She jumped down. Somehow, despite the tragic tale of her grandma's life, she felt a lot better about being a Munby girl now.

Moucher met her at the door with his usual enthusiasm, wagging his tail. He was recovering quickly now and although he wasn't as bouncy as before, he was making every effort and hardly ever left Genie's side, watching her every move. She went to the kitchen and made Marshall his coffee.

Genie was staying in the basement and felt safe there. Rian was reluctantly living at his own home. Miller had insisted and she understood. Everyone had their futures to think about and things to forgive and forget. As yet there had been no mosquito attack but all of them were ready for it. The Fortress would do something. They wouldn't just forget about them. Genie was sure of that.

Miller had even talked to her about re-starting high school. Genie wasn't convinced, even though she'd be able to join Ri there. Her mother wouldn't have her back home, besides there wasn't exactly a family home to go to anymore thanks to the flood. Genie had only one wish: to live with Rian forever; but every day she could see that slipping away. Mothers had a lot of pull and then again there was the law. She would have to be fostered.

It was the same for Renée. She'd been taken back to her mother's home. She had no choice in the matter. It was the law.

The interrogations with the homicide detectives had been pointless. They were trained to investigate dead bodies, not live ones, and they simply refused to believe in teleportation. Miller had been right. They actually did call it mass hysteria. Of course, they couldn't account for why the kids had been missing all this time or where they had been. Miller had flown back to the farm with the investigators and shown them remains of the two others that were transmitted, but failed to materialize. They wouldn't even admit they were human. It seemed to Genie that no one wanted to believe them and, in fact, they were out to disprove everything that had happened.

Worse, with no TV news or newspaper coverage, it was a non-story. The local Spurlake paper, which hadn't even bothered turning up to Reverend Schneider's shaming, now claimed it as a 'miracle'. It was all going very wrong, just as she had feared. The Pope was sending investigators from Rome, for God's sake. They had interviewed Randall and his mother and of course Randall couldn't seem to remember anything except picking apples. Alien abduction, his mother told the local paper, and they had done 'experiments' on her poor boy. '*Look how thin he has become.*'

Genie kinda knew the truth wasn't going to come out. Ever. Not now.

Rian had already called to say that they let Mr Yates go and he was back living with his mother. It was hell in his house already. They drove him to high school every morning to make sure he went and they wanted him fitted with an electronic tag so they could track him twenty-four/seven.

Marshall's testimony had been ignored since he was receiving a disability pension from the Fortress; his word was 'tainted'. No one believed anything. Not even Denis Malone. His doctor had put him on growth hormones. They said he suffered from dwarfism and that was ridiculous. They wanted him to go back to Grade Eight with kids two years younger than him now. It was ridiculous. No one had any interest in the truth at all.

Marshall's cell rang and he went outside to get better reception.

Genie left the hot coffee in the cafetière for Marshall to pour and went downstairs, Moucher clattering down the steps with her. She was happy that the doctor had given the all clear – and the worry diary thing seemed like a good idea. She began to hunt for a notebook to start it. She could hear Marshall shouting outside. Stress wasn't good for him. She wondered what had happened.

Moments later she registered the landline ringing upstairs. Heard Marshall's heavy footsteps as he went to answer it. He shouted down the stairs.

'Genie? There's a phone call for you. Sounds urgent, girl.'

Genie looked up the steep basement stairs. 'Coming.'

Genie gave Mouch a quick hug and went upstairs to join Marshall. She took the phone from him and put it to her ear. 'Me.'

'GET OUT NOW! RUN! They're rounding us up. Get away now!' Denis yelled. She could hear shouting in the background.

The phone suddenly went dead in Genie's hands. She began to shake.

Beside her, Marshall had switched on the TV with a very concerned look on his face. Genie stared at the TV news and realized what she was looking at.

'Oh my God. They let him out?'

Marshall nodded. 'Just happened. Insufficient evidence. Reverend Schneider is out, girl, and he'll be looking for you. My son just called, everything's unravelling fast.'

Genie looked at Marshall. All her doubts were coming true.

'What shall I do?'

Marshall frowned. He looked crushed.

'I wanted you to come back with me to the farm. I had plans to adopt you. But—'

'You did?' Genie's heart was beating like a bird now. Reverend Schneider's being out free and Denis' news was devastating, but not unexpected.

'I know you think you're too old to be adopted, but legally you're still a minor and I feel I owe you a lot, Genie.'

'But . . .' She felt stunned. It was the nicest thing someone had ever said. 'Adopt?'

'But now, with him out and the way things have gone. I've got to admit, I don't think you're safe, even living with me.'

'What do you mean?'

'I was hoping that things would be different. I was hoping that you could settle down, live a normal life. But that's not going to happen.'

'Something else has happened, hasn't it?'

Marshall nodded. He was getting out his wallet.

455

'The Fortress has procured a court order. My son thinks they are getting ready to round up all you kids who survived. They have powerful backing, Genie. There's big money behind this now. They will want to experiment further.'

'They can't do that. The parents won't stand for it. No.'

'They've started. They got a girl called Danielle already and some kid called Randall and they're trying to get back Julia Wasserman. They have the best lawyers. They're claiming you're an experimental group and they own your DNA.'

'No way.'

She was feeling distinctly shaky. They'd lost. The Fortress had won. If they were sent back to the Fortress, anything could happen to them. Marshall took out his wallet and offered her money.

'There's four hundred dollars here. You earned it. The apple people paid me well. Find Rian and get out of town.'

'But go where?'

'My farm isn't safe now. You'll have to head south or extreme north. Your choice. But you have to go, now.'

Genie curiously felt quite settled suddenly. All feelings of nausea had gone. This was what she'd been worried about. Now at least the way was clear. But would Rian want to come?

'Think you can drive my truck?'

'Already have.' She smiled guiltily.

Marshall had suspected as much, smiled briefly.

'Pack. They won't come for you yet.'

'What will you tell Miller?'

'The truth. He's not happy anyway. Everything he believed in is being turned inside out. I think he might quit the force. He's getting quite a lot of pressure from the sheriff's office for bringing all this trouble to Spurlake.'

Genie went forward and hugged Marshall.

'I'll miss you.'

Marshall nodded, touched. He stroked the fuzz on top of her head.

'Get packing. Take my cell. I'll get another. No one knows that number but my son, I've barely ever used it.' He had another thought. 'You have to make a detour. There's something else you're going to need.'

Moucher appeared at the top of the stairs and barked. Genie looked at the dog and back at Marshall. 'Can Mouch come too?'

Marshall looked at her with surprise.

'You don't have enough problems?'

He could see from Genie's face that that was the wrong answer.

'He likes chicken-flavoured biscuits best and make sure you give him bones to clean his teeth and don't overfeed him.'

Genie grinned. She turned to the dog.

'We're heading south, Mouch. Pack your bags.' She glanced at the phone. 'I have to call Renée.'

She drove over to Rian's house, proud she could handle this old truck on her own without Rian telling her she was doing it wrong. Like all boys, he believed he could drive better than a girl, as if either of them ever had any lessons or anything. She parked two houses over, so his mother and Mr Yates couldn't see the vehicle. This time she looked around carefully in case Reverend Schneider was hiding anywhere. She'd already resolved that if she saw him she'd run him over and just keep on driving. Only way to deal with evil. She heard the rumble of thunder. The sky was darkening. It would rain soon, for sure.

She dialled Ri's number, hoping he was back from classes already. Marshall had warned her that his cell would be bugged, so she had to keep it short.

'Hey.'

'Hey yourself.'

'Two things,' Genie told him. 'One: Reverend Schneider has been released.'

'You can't be serious. Really?'

'Two: Wildcard.'

'Wildcard?'

Genie waited for the penny to drop.

'It's your choice. Now or never, Ri.'

Rian suddenly remembered their last conversation and the agreed code word for trouble. If anything went bad, they had to have a bag packed and ready. His eyes went to his closet. It had been the first thing he'd done when he came home.

'How long?'

'Right here, right now.'

Rian swore. His mother and Mr Yates were downstairs. No way he could get past them with a packed bag. He looked at the window. This would the second time he'd escaped this way. This time he'd have to jump off at the back of the house else they'd see him.

'Two minutes,' he told her.

Genie disconnected and started the engine. She looked at Mouch and smiled. 'You think you'll like Mexico, Mouch?'

Mouch had already decided that he'd like anywhere Genie went. He was easy.

Less than a minute later Rian's bag was tossed under the tarp at the back and he jumped into the cab.

'You're driving?'

'Shut the door, Rian Tulane, and strap in.'

Rian nodded. Genie was running this escape plan. She didn't immediately drive off though. She looked at him with narrowed eyes, a question on her lips.

'Last chance to change your mind. Stay, finish school, be normal, live in Spurlake, go to college, become someone . . . I told you, Ri. I never want to hold you back. I love you too much to stop you getting an education.'

Rian smiled, giving Mouch a hug as he stared at Genie.

'Drive. We're leaving. You call, I go. I told you, Genie Magee. We're not ever going to be separated again. Anyway, I hate being at school without you.'

Genie smiled and let in the clutch. She drove off smoothly, as if she'd always driven.

'Marshall says they're rounding us all up. The Fortress has won. Miller might give up being a cop. Some serious stuff going down.'

Genie crossed Main Street and pulled up outside the Shopper's Mart. Renée dashed out of the store, carrying her overnight bag and some groceries. She tipped her stuff in the back and swung into the cab, slamming the door after her.

She smiled at them as Genie let out the clutch again and Moucher noisily greeted her.

'Lucky I was in town. Had a sucky interview at the Dairy Queen – like I so crave working there. Don't take any of the main streets. Just back roads, Genie. There's Fortress trucks everywhere. Take the bike path by the old railroad.'

'Bike path?'

'It's wide enough and we can get off at the track behind it after the shooting range. I know it's slow, but I don't want us stopped.'

Genie did as she suggested, pulling off the road and bumping across the park to the bike path beyond. It was just wide enough. As Marshall predicted, it started to rain. The windshield wipers creaked to life and smeared the windshield.

'Shoot, I can't see anything. If there's anyone on a bike they are going to regret it big time,' Genie said, trying to get the windshield washer to squirt.

'You hear? They got Julia Wasserman,' Renée said. 'I called everyone. Her mother is hysterical. They grabbed her on her way to school. Mrs Wasserman said they've hired a lawyer to get her back. I think they got Danielle too. Did you know she tried to kill herself? They grabbed her at the hospital.'

'Kill herself? That makes no sense,' Genie protested.

'Denis told me she was depressed. Couldn't handle being home again or something.'

Genie felt bad for her.

'Reverend Schneider is out too,' Rian told her. 'I tried to call Cary just now but he isn't answering his phone.'

Renée stared at him amazed. 'Schneider is out?' She looked at Genie for confirmation.

'No wonder you said it was urgent. Jeez. I knew that something was up when us coming back didn't even make the news – nothing, zilch. We were dead the moment we walked into that church.' She looked at Genie again. 'The turn-off comes up soon, keep it slow. The track's gonna be muddy in this rain but it'll be safer.'

Genie found the opening and drove up on to the ridge. It was a popular place to walk in summer with views across the whole of Spurlake. The rain started to fall harder with a strong wind behind it and she began to worry they'd get bogged down on the muddy track.

Rian looked out at his town spread out below them now. He knew with absolute certainty he'd never be back. No matter what.

'You bring a map?' Genie asked Renée.

Renée nodded, pulling one out of her jacket pocket. 'It only goes as far as the border. How are we going to get across? I haven't got a passport. You? They're really hot on documents these days and they sure aren't going to let us drive over.'

Genie smiled. 'Ever been fishing?' she asked them both.

'On the river a few times,' Renée answered.

'Tried for salmon once,' Rian admitted.

'Did you know Reverend Schneider owns a yacht? It's waiting for us in Vancouver some place.'

Rian looked at her and then began to smile. 'We're stealing his yacht?'

Genie pulled a face. 'We're borrowing it. Miller discovered he owned it when he was investigating him. Keys were hanging up in the church. Marshall made me take them.'

Renée laughed with astonishment. 'We are going to sail a yacht to where?'

'Mexico. Hell, further. Who cares? That's the plan.'

Rian frowned. It sounded cool, but . . . 'You ever sail a yacht before?'

Genie laughed and looked at him a moment. 'You're a boy – anyway, it's a motor cruiser. You'll figure it out. I'm counting on you, Rian Tulane. How hard can it be? Turn on the engine and point south.'

Rian shook his head. 'Turn on the engine and point.' He laughed. 'Well, that's my sailing education dealt with. What next?'

'Keeping us safe,' Renée told him. 'A boy's job never ends, y'know, eh. Lots of responsibilities.'

Genie was smiling to herself as they drove on. Night was falling. Fewer cops on the roads further south, she hoped. Vancouver was one hundred and eighty kilometres once they reached Hope. First stop Ferryman's, to gas up. She'd let Rian drive from there. Didn't want to bruise his ego too much. She felt guilty they weren't helping the others but Denis had been right. Run. They had to run to fight another day.

Mouch shifted to get comfortable on Rian's lap. Rian bent down and talked to the dog.

'Apparently, Mouch, I always wanted to go to Mexico.'

Mouch licked his face. Genie and Renée laughed. They were breaking free of Spurlake and it felt good.

# 37

## Hell's Gate

The gusting wind must have brought it down. A huge old oak tree lay across the track just before it joined the main highway and Rian swore. They didn't have time for this. They'd barely done two Ks in the mud and rain, taking this old farm track out of town.

The thickening mud had slowed them to a crawl and then this incredible wind blew up, throwing leaves and small branches at them as they bumped down the uneven surface. It just seemed every time they ever tried to leave Spurlake the weather gods did everything they could to prevent it, or kill them – either way, they were stalled and pretty soon Reverend Schneider would be giving chase.

Genie pulled up short of the tree and angrily banged her hands on the wheel. 'Can we pull it off?'

Rian checked the back of the truck and sighed. He could have sworn he'd seen rope there earlier. He looked behind the seat; there were some old bungee cords, maybe they'd do, but they weren't strong, not for an old oak.

Genie didn't wait. She backed up to a gap in the

fence and made a three-point turn.

'We can't go back that way,' Renée protested. 'There ain't a single turn-off before town.'

'I'm not going back. I'm going to try and back it up a bit, least ways so we can get past. No way we're going to lift it.'

Rian didn't think it such a good idea, a branch could get underneath and lift the rear wheels off the . . .

Genie slowly reversed towards the tree, looking back out of the window, her head getting soaked as the rain fell even harder.

'Move, you bastard!' Genie yelled. The tree didn't seem to give an inch. They could hear the tyres spinning trying to find grip.

'It ain't gonna . . .' Rian started. Suddenly the tyres found grip and the tree moved half a metre. Genie shouted something and then repeated the whole process. The tree moved some more.

'Get out, Renée. Check we can get through.'

Renée grabbed the flashlight and bounced out of the truck to the muddy ground. She squelched towards the tree surveying the situation, wiping rain from her eyes. She turned back towards the truck. 'Turn her around again, Genie. We can squeeze through.'

Rian leaped out of the truck to help Renée.

Genie looked at Moucher, who was clearly frowning and doubting she knew what she was doing. 'See? We can move trees. You didn't think we could, but we did.'

Moucher barked a couple of times to show enthusiasm, but you could tell he was still unsure. He didn't like the weather much either.

Genie made another three-point turn in the tight space. It turned out to be five turns to get it all way around – but who was counting? – and brought the truck to face the tree, the headlights picking out Renée and Rian lifting huge branches out of the way. She grinned like a maniac. Nothing was going to stop them this time. They were going to drive down to Vancouver, find Reverend Schneider's yacht and sail away. Nothing was going to stop them at all.

Rian was waving like a crazy loon suddenly. Fast-approaching vehicles with bright headlights could be glimpsed through the trees.

'Kill the lights. Kill the lights,' Rian was yelling and she quickly switched them off. Seconds later, two fast-moving Fortress vehicles flashed by. They had a momentary glimpse of men in the back seats armed with shotguns poking out of open windows. Genie knew for sure that they were out looking for them. Either way, it meant that there were Fortress people ahead of them on the road up ahead – and this was the only road out of Spurlake to Highway 1.

Rian jumped back in, Renée staying put to hold back some branches as Genie inched the truck by the fallen tree.

'They looked mean. Shotguns? They want to kill us now?' Rian asked. He shook the rain out of his hair.

Genie nodded. 'I don't think they want us to get out of Spurlake alive, Ri.'

Renée jumped in, soaked to the skin.

'Get on the road, travel about half a K to the stone quarry and take the track behind it. I used to ride my bike there. It comes up the other side of the bridge. If the Fortress is waiting for us, they'll be at Hell's Gate motel. We'll come out a hundred metres behind it.'

Genie just drove, thankful that Renée knew her way.

Rian wiped the water from his face and placed a cold hand on Genie's shoulder. 'You did good back there.'

Genie said nothing. They'd got nowhere and now armed Fortress people were ahead of them. She didn't want to let Ri know she was scared.

# 38

## The Change

The wind was sheer; a brief squall of hailstones beat against their heads and collected around their sodden feet. They were gathered on the rooftop of the Fortress, watching the huge helicopter swaying in the wind as it attempted to land. It was the type of chopper presidents used, no expense spared. Everyone stared, clutching their collars to the necks or holding a cardigan over their heads in useless attempts to stay dry. Each staff member on the roof filled with uncertainties and not a little fear. An hour earlier the three leading executives had been fired, other jobs were certain to go. Someone had been appointed to clear things up, make cuts, get the Fortress back on track and they all knew it would be someone ruthless, someone who wouldn't care about their mortgages or debts, someone who'd fire them at a drop of the hat. The bigger the helicopter, the more cuts he'd make.

For a moment it looked as though the wind would flip the aircraft and abort the landing, but at last it set down with a thump and the rotors began to wind down – the engine whine was deafening.

Now the moment of dread came. Who would it be? Finance people in the city called the tune now. Whoever emerged from that chopper, it wasn't going to be Santa Claus.

Reverend Schneider pulled his jacket closer. He was soaked through. He'd been summoned to this roof-top humiliation. He wasn't even an employee of Fortransco but they had insisted he be here to greet the new CEO, whoever it might be. The previous administration had been lax, everyone knew that, they had managed to snatch defeat from the jaws of victory. Genie Magee was on the run. They had only managed to recapture three of the successful transmissions and now they had lawyers involved. They certainly weren't going to be able to keep Fortress activity secret any more.

'I don't like the look of this,' Mr Yates muttered at Schneider's elbow.

Schneider turned and frowned. He'd never liked Yates. Everywhere in Spurlake and around he was faced with people who lacked vision or guts. Of course, they urgently needed to know how and why the transmission had worked, why the instrumentation recorded it as a failure when in fact it had been a fantastic success. Teleportation was a proven process now. But why had it suddenly worked? Why had there been no trace of Genie Magee in the system, almost as if she had never been there? They had to recapture her. He had to convince the new CEO that she was the key, the number one priority. Security people had reassured him that they'd have her in hand by nightfall, but here it was, nearly ten, and no one knew where she was. She was the missing link, he was sure of it. He'd be the first to confess that he'd been happy to know she was dead, and when she'd burst into his Church with the others, confronted him, no one had been more surprised than himself. To see her alive, along with all the others he'd been so certain were dead, had filled him with dread at first, then astonishment and finally exhilaration. If ever there was a proof of miracles, this was it. Genie Magee had to be found, he was certain she was the key.

A gasp went up from the assembled group. 'Oh my God, it's Strindberg.'

There was a uniform feeling of dread. Carson Strindberg. He had the reputation of being ruthless, a man with a huge ego. Been with Fortransco from the beginning as an investor. He'd made several fortunes in IT and had always kept his eye on Fortransco.

'We're in bigger trouble than I thought,' Mr Yates said,

wiping the rain from the end of his nose.

Reverend Schneider watched a small man with silver hair and a very expensive suit step down from the helicopter. Immediately people ran forward with umbrellas ready (nervous of the still-turning rotors overhead). They weren't going to let a drop of water land on the new CEO. (No one noticed the kid trailing behind him with a backpack in his hands.)

Strindberg didn't even look at the assembled staff dripping with the water and headed straight to the door, giving instructions to one of the minions who listened carefully.

As Strindberg disappeared, the minion turned to the disbelieving staff.

'Mr Strindberg will see you all in the blue room in fifteen minutes. Be sure to bring your IDs.'

Reverend Schneider looked at the faces around him and knew what they were thinking. Strindberg would be firing people tonight. The last company he took over, he fired half the workforce on the first day.

Wet soggy Fortress employees headed for the door with heavy hearts.

# 39

## Ferryman's Pie

Genie felt the phone vibrate in her jeans and she dug it out, looked to see who was texting. Caller ID said it was Miller. She looked at Renée and raised her eyebrows. 'Should I open it? Can they trace a text?'

Renée shrugged. 'Might be important.'

Rian was dozing; Moucher sprawled across his feet. Genie wanted to ask him if she should open it but knew he needed his sleep. They had paused on the track behind the quarry because of the rain. They just couldn't see further than four metres ahead. The track was navigable, running right along the edge of the river, but this rain was falling so hard she was scared of ending up in the water.

'I'm going to open it.'

'What does it say?' Renée asked impatiently.

She handed the phone over to Renée and gunned the motor. To hell with the rain, they *had* to move on now. There was a deeply worried frown on her forehead as Renée read the message out aloud.

GET OFF THE ROAD NOW! ROADBLOCKS. 10,000 DOLLAR

REWARD ON YOUR HEADS. DITCH THIS PHONE. TRUST NO ONE. DON'T LOOK BACK. MOUCH.

Renée looked at Genie and pulled a face. 'We sure it's from him?'

Genie nodded. 'Mouch is our signal. He wants us to just dump the truck? I mean, won't make it any easier getting us to Vancouver if we're walking. It's like two hundred Ks from here.'

Rian, suddenly awake, grabbed the phone from Renée and read the text. He rubbed his face and began to assess the situation.

'When we rejoin the road there's the Ferryman gas station just before the Cedarville turn-off.'

'I know it,' Renée interjected.

'I was heading there anyway,' Genie pointed out.

'If there's no cops waiting for us there,' Rian continued, 'head in and go around the back.'

Genie looked at him, glad he was awake again. 'But . . . ?'

Rian rubbed his face again, fighting off exhaustion. 'If they're doing roadblocks, it'll be at the Highway 1 junction five clicks down the road after Hell's Gate motel. It's the only place where anyone would have a choice of directions. When we join the road, keep the lights off and roll down the hill quietly. I know the guy there.

He's all right.' Rian switched off the phone, snapped off the back and removed the Sim card, then wound the window down and tossed them both into the river. Genie and Renée exchanged glances but Miller had said ditch the phone. It was truly ditched now.

Genie drove keeping a keen eye on the edge, the lights barely penetrating the rain. They were suddenly at the track's end. She instantly killed the lights.

'Can you see anything? Can you see the hotel?'

Renée and Rian stared into the blackness but could see nothing.

'Good, that means they can't see us,' Rian stated. 'Let's go. Keep the lights off for as long as you can. Can you see the road, Genie?'

Genie eased out on to the road. Everything was black. The road, the side of it and to her right, the river. Without headlights and in this rain it all looked pretty much the same.

'Stick to the middle,' Renée advised. 'Anyone on the road will have lights on and we'll see 'em coming.'

Genie did just that. Anyone else would be crazy to be out on the road in this weather. She could make out red lights on the huge power cables running alongside the river. That was a good sign, meant the rain was easing.

'You think they'd take any of this in consideration

when I take my driving test?' she joked.

Renée laughed. 'Yeah sure, when they let you out of jail to take it.'

She felt more confident now, the rain was lifting, a silver moon was briefly glimpsed before clouds swallowed it up again.

'There's a narrow canyon here some place, road and river real tight together. Keep your speed down, Gen,' Rian advised. 'Steep drop to the water and the river will be wild in this rain and wind.'

Genie kept it steady. Mouch had one paw on her lap and he seemed happy and she was sure he'd be real sensitive to any danger.

Renée recognized the old gas station as they approached it. The lights picking out the pumps and old-fashioned Husky sign. 'Hey, I really do know this place. My trailer's just over there some place.' She pointed beyond the river and the flatlands on the other side. 'Old guy here, always got something to say. He's lonely, I guess.'

'How do you know we can trust him, Ri?' Genie asked as she rolled the truck silently down the hill.

'He hates Schneider.'

Genie nodded. 'Good enough for me. Renée, check the map. We need a place to go.'

Renée shook her head. 'There's no place. Just the trailer

park and the river. This is the only way south.'

'Ten thousand dollar reward. That's a bummer,' Genie said. 'Didn't say whether dead or alive though.'

'Alive,' Rian told her. 'Believe me, they want you guys alive.'

Genie drove the truck on to the forecourt and with Rian pointing found the narrow alley that led behind it. She parked it beside a gutted yellow schoolbus and switched off the engine. Moucher looked up at her expectantly.

'Let Mouch out.' She turned to Rian. 'Now what?'

Rian opened his door and Moucher bounced out and dashed for a pee. 'We go see the old man. Maybe he knows an old trail or something. Either way, we have to get out of here.'

They all piled out of the truck, dragging their knapsacks with them. The garage wasn't well lit and garbage was strewn in plastic bags floating in puddles. 'He should know better than this, the bears love hunting through garbage,' Renée said. She hated an untidy back yard.

'Hello?' Rian called. 'Hello?'

Genie was listening to the rain loudly running off the metal roof into various barrels and buckets. She looked back at the abandoned vehicles in the field illuminated by a lone weak floodlight. Gutted trucks, buses, cars, pick-ups, earth-diggers. It looked like a vehicle graveyard.

'Hello?' Rian was shouting again.

'We should go around the front,' Renée said. 'He's got a bell to get his attention. Used to come here and buy sherbet and liquorice. Ma wouldn't let me have any. Cedarville store didn't sell it.'

Genie took Renée's hand and pulled her away from the back door. 'I used to dream about sherbet. Only had it like twice, maybe. My ma always promised some and of course I never had any pocket money. Parents are weird. I'd probably gag now if I had to eat it.'

They moved around to the front of the gas station. A cop car drove by at speed, sending up a huge spray of water. They pressed themselves into the shadows as it sailed by. No one said anything.

Moucher found him. Asleep under an awning by the carwash machine. He was sitting in a plastic chair, some dribble down his chin.

'I guess there isn't much business around here at night,' Renée whispered. Rian jumped up and down on the rubber wire on the forecourt that would ring the bell. Had to do it a few times to get it to work.

The old guy opened his eyes. Moucher barked once. He looked at the three of them for a moment, getting his bearings.

'If you've come to buy liquor, I ain't selling to minors,

478

no matter how much money you got.'

Rian moved further out into the light. 'Hi.'

The old man recognized him, then looked at Renée. 'See you found your sister.' He looked at Genie. 'This the girl you was chasing? What happened to your hair, kid?'

Genie shrugged. 'Had a close shave.'

The old man half smiled. 'A comedian.' He looked at Renée more closely as he stood up, standing with a slight stoop. 'You used to have red hair. Still looking for sherbet?'

Renée smiled, looking back at Genie. 'Told you. I think I ate a lot of sherbet.'

Genie smiled.

The old man was looking for their vehicle. 'I thought I didn't hear a vehicle arrive? You walk here? You ain't wet, so I guess not.'

Rian shook his head. 'It's out back. Still driving Marshall's truck.'

The old man suddenly understood. He indicated the door and began moving towards it. 'Better get inside then. Lot of people looking for you guys.'

'We know,' Renée told him, following him through the doorway.

'Fortress been going crazy. I listen to the squawks on the radio. Got a tow truck business to run, y'know.

Lot of chatter about ten grand per head on offer.'

Rian and Genie exchanged glances. Two heads standing right here. Twenty grand would make a lot of difference to this man. Couldn't do much business out here.

The interior was surprisingly neat and organized. Rian hadn't remembered that.

'Not sleeping well lately. Decided to clean up. Got a ton of garbage out back. You'd be surprised what you find when you tidy up. Got road maps going all the way back to '58, before they built Coquillah highway even.'

'We saw the garbage bags,' Genie said. 'You know about the roadblocks?'

'You must have missed the one coming out of Spurlake. They got them set up tight at Highway 1 junction too. Your truck ain't worth anything to you.'

Renée suddenly flopped down in a heap, letting escape a wail. It was quite unlike her. Moucher came forward and began to paw her, placing his head on her knees to comfort her.

Rian and Genie exchanged glances. Sure things were bad, but they were still free.

'You want my help, right?' the old man said. 'Name's Ferry. God knows what curse I was born under to have a mother with a sense of humour. Ferry Mann. You try going through life being called Ferry.'

'Can you help us?' Rian asked. 'We know about the reward. If you're thinking of trying to collect we'd appreciate a headstart.'

Ferry just smiled and pointed at the drinks chiller. 'Help yourself to a Coke and grab some chips. Go to the back room and wait. I'm going to shut down. No more business tonight, I reckon.' He pushed open the door and headed on out to the gas pumps.

Genie pulled out three cold cans of Coke from the fridge and handed one to Renée. She grabbed it, placed it on her neck to calm herself down.

Heavy rain fell from the heavens again, drumming heavily on the asphalt roof.

'Great. We're going to have to walk and it's pouring,' Renée protested.

'You sure we can trust him?' Genie whispered to Rian.

Rian nodded. He opened his can and drank. Judging people was difficult, but he believed Ferry was an honourable guy.

Ferry came back in. Flipped a switch and the outside disappeared. The neon sign in the window clicked off and crackled as it cooled. Ferry wiped rain off his hat and tossed it on to the counter.

'You guys are going to have to take the river. It's the only choice you got.'

Genie shuddered. The last time she and Ri and had been on the river they nearly drowned – it was how they got into this mess in the first place.

'No way around the roadblock?' Rian asked.

'Sure, but you don't look like the mountaineer types, and then there's snakes.'

'Snakes?' Renée asked, looking up from the floor.

'Sleeping snakes. They get pretty annoyed when people tread on them.'

'The river then,' Genie agreed. It would be faster than the mountain. No way there could be a flash flood again, could there?

Ferry smiled and stole one of her chips. 'Follow me.'

They followed him into his residence part of the gas station. It was like something out of some Fifties movie. Even the sofa was still covered in clear plastic. Rian was impressed by the promotion images of the '62 Studebaker Golden Hawk. Made in Canada, it boasted. The Jag poster from '67 for the E Type Roadster was amazing too. It was just like a museum.

'Got meatloaf and mash – enough for a few mouthfuls each,' Ferry said.

'Meatloaf?' Renée asked. She seemed OK now, a little bit spooked, but with them, at least.

Moucher sat at Genie's feet and did his very

best to looked starved.

'So happens I have dog food – always someone who forgets to buy stuff for the dog. Keep dog biscuits by the kitty litter next to the postcard stand if you want to get it.'

'Postcards? You have postcards?' Genie asked. 'Of Spurlake? You're kidding, right?'

Ferry laughed at her amazement. 'Well, put it this way, I sell more dog biscuits than postcards. Go get. I'll warm up the meatloaf.'

They sat down to eat fifteen minutes later. Moucher had finished his in ten seconds flat. Renée was reading a magazine that was at least thirty years old.

'I love this. It's like a time machine. You never throw anything out, huh?'

'Now you're wrong there, girl. Got ten sacks of garbage floating out there to prove it.'

'Well I love it. Makes me feel like I'm in the Fonz's house or something.'

'You kids know about the Fonz?' Ferry seemed surprised.

'Hello. Daytime TV. *Happy Days* is like on forever.'

Ferry smiled. He was enjoying having company, even if the clock was ticking. He looked at the wall map.

'You're going to have some problems. The river isn't exactly friendly for some of the ways. At least you're

483

passed Hell's Gate. You wouldn't like that in this weather. People pay good money for white rafting around here. I got some Army surplus rafts. At least one should be serviceable.'

'Raft?' Rian asked. He had an image of logs lashed together on open seas.

'The army use them when a normal boat won't get through. Can float in just inches of water and they're light and fast.'

'And you don't think they'll be watching the river?' Renée asked him.

Ferry shrugged. 'It's night. You'll get quite a ways down before dawn. My advice is sleep during the day and travel at night.'

Rian nodded. Made sense.

'How long will it take? I mean, do we just go with the current?' Genie asked. She had strong memories of the current and clinging on for dear life with the pig.

'Got paddles. You can get all the way downstream in about three days I reckon. Used to run the rivers myself when I was younger. Faster if you risk daylight as well. Further you go the deeper it gets and the current's swift, especially after all this rain. After Hope it spreads out and gets real lazy though and you got to keep to the deep channel. Understood? You could do it quickly if you knew the currents and didn't spill. I only got one life jacket. If you don't mind me suggesting it, put it on the dog. It's small.'

'Thanks,' Genie told him, then, putting up her hand like she was in school. 'But can I ask why? You know about the reward. Ten grand is a lot to . . .'

Ferry swallowed the last of his meatloaf and looked at her a moment, considering his reply.

'I see a lot of kids. From Cedarville, like Renée here, and Rian. You all find this place at some point in your lives and then forget it. It's like some kind of ritual. It's a long way out of town, risky to go any further. Place you turn back. Seen a lot of kids stop by, head down the reservation road and you know they ain't ever coming back.'

'The road to the Fortress.'

'Exactly.'

'We came back,' Renée pointed out.

'You're the first. Bet you're the last,' he said. 'They want you guys real bad and that means you've got something they need. What that might be, I don't know, but if I can do anything to stop them from having it . . . I will.' He smiled, revealing a silver front tooth.

Genie was finally satisfied he was on their side.

* * *

The moon was high now; it shone brightly as the rain began to tail off at last. Ferry took them down to the river at the end of his property and pulled out two heavy-duty rubber rafts from a semi-derelict boathouse. One had the base torn; the other looked ragged, but was in good shape otherwise and inflated. He tipped the rainwater out of it.

'It's tough.' He hit it hard and it didn't even dent. 'Four metres long. Can take you guys easy. It's got eight air chambers and there's thigh straps as well as hand straps. You'll need 'em. There's a hard shell, so it can withstand rocks and anything else that's out there. But steer clear of logs, got that? They can rip these things to pieces. I use to rent them out for river runners and fishermen until the recession bit.

'Won't save you from anyone firing at you, but you keep your head down and hold on to these grab handles right here. The three, hell, I mean four of you,' he noted Moucher at his feet, 'can survive the rapids easy from here. Category two at the most. Hell's Gate would be six tonight and I wouldn't fancy your chances. They're supposed to be self-bailing, but don't count on it. Make sure the dog is secure, he might panic, and here,' he handed over two pairs of old socks and a bailer, 'put socks on the dog. His claws could go through the base. Don't let him take them off.'

Genie laughed. Moucher in socks, it was funny. Mouch wasn't keen but as long as it was Genie doing it he was almost OK with it. They didn't smell too good but hey . . . what could they do?

'If you can't see your way, use the paddles to check for deeper water. There's a number of places where you'll be exposed, but beyond the bend here it gets deeper. The tricky bit is when this stretch of water joins the Fraser, OK? Can get real busy and there's undercurrents. You think you can do this?'

Rian nodded. 'We don't have a choice. Thanks, Ferry. Will you call Marshall in a couple of days and tell him where his truck is?'

Ferry nodded. 'I'll give it a service. That way I make a buck or two out of it. It looks pretty beat. At least you put the licence plate back on.'

'Survived a fire. Drives good though.'

'Noted. 'Bout thirty clicks downstream, there's Bear Island in the middle of the river. Betty Juniper runs a lodge there.' He took out a letter from his back pocket, looked greasy and worn, even in moonlight. He put it in a thin plastic sandwich bag and sealed it. 'Meant to post her this but keep forgetting. She'll feed you. Tell her to bill me.'

'We'll pay our way,' Rian told him.

'Just saying, she's a friend. All right, son? Friends are hard to find in this world.'

'Bear Island?' Renée queried. 'Like bears? They live there?'

'I guess they used to. Good place to catch salmon in spring.'

'Around here, everywhere is a good place to catch salmon in spring,' Rian said. He got into the raft and took Moucher from Genie's arms.

'We'll give her the letter,' Genie told Ferry, taking it from him and slipping it in her back pocket. 'Let's go. Sooner we're gone, safer we'll be.'

'Don't take risks,' he said as they climbed in and cast off.

'*Don't take risks*, he says,' Renée muttered as she climbed in, 'and he sends us to an island full of bears!'

Moucher barked, unnerved by the experience, but they were on the water and moving – dim moonlight showing the way.

They looked back but Ferry had already disappeared. They were on their own now.

Genie said a little prayer. A whole lot of river lay ahead of them. How long before the Fortress realized they had evaded the roadblocks and came after them? She prayed for luck and invisibility.

'I sure hope we're doing the right thing,' Renée said, squinting ahead into the darkness.

Genie gave Mouch a hug to reassure him it was going to be fine, but he shook; he'd just found out he hated being on water.

'We're leaving Spurlake, Mouch. No one will ever be mean to us again.'

'I don't want to worry you,' Rian said quietly, 'but this river is running a lot faster than he said it would.'

They could all feel the raft picking up speed, the river was beginning to toss them up and down, as they got to mid-stream.

'What's that noise ahead?' Renée was asking. 'Sounds like a waterfall?'

'There's no waterfalls on this river,' Rian declared, desperately trying to remember if that was true or not.

They were going faster all the time now and it began to feel suddenly very dangerous.

'I don't think this is a good idea, guys,' Genie said, clinging on to Mouch.

Rian looked back at her and sensed she was right. 'Hang on, hang on real tight.'

'Not good. Not good at all,' Genie said, gripping the handle.

Moucher began to howl. He sensed they were doomed.

489

Cary walked out of Pizza World on Pioneer Street holding the warm box steady, his stomach growling, hungrily anticipating the hot pepperoni with double cheese. His mom had made a snap decision to eat pizza as they were driving back from seeing the lawyer.

He suddenly realized he wasn't alone. The guy wore a dark suit, no coat, wet black shoes. Looked like he'd been waiting for him. Cary glanced behind him and realized another guy was standing there too, to stop him from running. He must have been in Pizza World all that time and he'd not noticed. Cary's mother was waiting for him in the car just four metres away.

'What?' Cary asked, but he instinctively knew why they were here.

'We spent all day looking for you, Cary. Seems you might be hiding from us.'

'Mom?' Cary yelled, but a truck went by and drowned out his words.

Another guy appeared from nowhere and grabbed the pizza from him and pulled him towards a waiting SUV.

'Mom!' Cary yelled again, realizing he had only seconds to raise the alarm.

Another suit was running towards Cary's mother's car. His mother was just beginning to realize something was happening and was opening her door.

Cary felt a prick on his neck. They had injected him with something.

'Mom,' he yelled again, but knew he was losing consciousness.

'She can't help you, Cary, we own you now,' someone was saying as they bundled him into the back of their vehicle.

'Harrison secure,' another voice said into a cell.

Last thing Cary saw was a sign saying: *We deliver twenty-four/seven.* The Fortress had possession of him again. And then he felt nothing, absolutely nothing at all.

# Acknowledgments

For Roxy, who was my inspiration and guiding hand.

With thanks to Freya, Victor and George Olden who gave excellent advice and to Lionel and Catherine, who provided the ideal mountain view to write in – not to mention the guard dog Moucher. Appreciation must go to the City of Vancouver, BC, for being so welcoming, it constantly inspires my writing.

And of course much credit goes to Beverley, who believed in the project from the very beginning and Carine 'Kit' Thomas for keeping my feet firmly on the ground.

# The story continues in
# THE HUNTING

The river picked up speed suddenly. They were once again in deeper water, steeper slopes on either side and the water was incredibly choppy.

'We getting faster?' Renée whispered; her voice betraying her anxiety.

'Hold on,' Rian called. 'Ship your paddle, Genie. Damn, I can't see anything, but we're . . .' He nearly lost his paddle and the raft spun all the way around as it collided with some rocks mid-stream.

Not seeing where they were going and what dangers lay ahead was unnerving.

'Hold on to Mouch,' Genie called out, scared now as water cascaded over the prow and drenched them.

'There aren't any rapids are there?' Renée asked, panic in her voice.

'No. Hell, I don't know,' Rian answered, desperately trying to steady them. 'We've diverted from the main channel I think. Hang on tight.'

A powerful flashlight suddenly flooded the raft. It blinded all three of them. The light moved away wildly as the other raft turned to cope with the fast moving river.

'It's them,' someone shouted. 'I know it is. It's them.'

Genie's heart nearly stopped.

'Jesus,' Rian exclaimed. 'Who the hell?'

'Will they shoot?' Renée asked.

'They don't want us dead.' Genie muttered tersely. 'They'll want the reward money.'

Rian took strength from that. The raft was pitching up and down now as it entered the rapids, a surge of water pushing them forward, squeezing them up against fast moving debris. All he could do to just hold on, likewise for Genie, now holding Mouch tightly, and Renée was lying flat and twisting her hands through the grab handles – just in case.

The powerful searchlight was still seeking them. Rian ducked down beside Genie.

'Start praying.'

'I *am* praying.'

'Good, 'cause I'm crapping myself here,' Renée said. 'Who the hell are they?'

'Bounty hunters. I saw a pair go by earlier.'

Genie and Renée digested this set of facts. Hunters. Hunters meant guns. Big guns. Hunters liked shooting at things.

The river was moving dangerously fast. Genie clung on to Moucher as Renée tried to grab Rian. Suddenly they plunged down into a foaming rush of water, a jagged rock snagged the inflatable and Rian was sent flying.

A shot rang out real close, pinging off a rock. Genie was pitched underwater, churning in the freezing sluice, gasping for breath. Mouch sprang free. Somewhere ahead Renée was screaming as she stayed with the inflatable, rapidly disappearing downriver. And Rian? Where was Rian? Why didn't he come up for air?

'Rian? Rian?' Genie wailed as she surfaced, but there was no sign of him. She saw the Hunter's flashlight approaching and immediately ducked underwater again wondering how long she could hold her breath. All the while she was praying Rian was OK. Please let Ri be OK . . .

'They are right here,' a Hunter was saying, as he reloaded the shotgun. 'I can almost smell the money.'

Rian was reeling, tasting blood. He'd bashed his head hard and swallowed a ton of water. He surfaced, spinning around to get his bearings. He was still moving down river. The flashlight was sweeping the water looking for them and Rian, head spinning with pain, had to dive under again to avoid them finding him.

But where was Genie? Where was Renée? He surfaced again seconds later to look for them and was immediately struck hard on the head again by fast moving timber. He instantly lost consciousness. The river able to do with him what it willed.

Renée tried to untangle herself from the raft. She'd twisted her hand around the straps to keep her in, but now it was on top of her and she couldn't get free. She was being pummelled by rocks and knew if she didn't flip it over real soon she was going to drown.

The hunter with the flashlight turned to his father and pulled a face.

'Can't find 'em again, Pa.'

His Pa swore. 'I told you, Sean, no shooting. They want them alive, you dumb bastard. No shooting.'

'Sorry, Pa. Accident. I swear it. Accident.'

His father attempted to steer the inflatable closer to where the raft was last seen.

'Sweep again. That's my reward money going under and they ain't going to pay up if they drowned.'

Genie and Moucher were sitting shivering like drowned rats on a rock mid-stream, keeping dead quiet in the darkness. The moon was up at last and could be glimpsed through the trees overhead. She realized that somehow they'd taken a run-off channel, the main river was flowing normally about fifty metres away. How that had happened she didn't know, but then not one of them had any river craft.

She watched the two hunters in their inflatable sweeping the water with their flashlight. Where was Rian? She was beginning to panic; she had a terribly bad feeling about him. The hunters wouldn't spot her here, nor could they get their craft near. She discovered her fingers were crossed, she'd been saying a prayer for Rian and Renée and their safety.

You could never count on anything, she realized. Ten grand per head motivated a lot of people in these parts. That was for sure.

The flashlight was sweeping close to her again and she grabbed Mouch and squatted down low behind the rock. Mouch shaking with fear and the cold, but keeping quiet, just as he'd been told to.

Genie heard the inflatable's motor kick in. They were moving off. Either they had given up or were going downstream. Perhaps leaving, in case the gunshot had alerted anyone. But there was little chance of that out here. There was nothing but farmland and trees . . .

Rian hauled himself out of the river and lay gasping on the riverbank spewing out river water. He was in agony.

His head hurt like hell and blood trickled into his mouth. He wanted to yell Genie's name but the hunters might still be in earshot, despite their outboard engine's noise.

He looked downstream for signs of Renée and the raft, but she had disappeared. He hoped like hell she'd managed to flip it over again and stayed put somewhere.

He clutched his head; he felt incredibly dizzy. Shooting pains suddenly overwhelmed him and he had to cough. He felt bad, real bad. He could feel his temperature spiking, a hot flush sweeping over him; his brain was going to boil over. He really needed Genie now. Where was she? He fell back against the mud and sand, groaning loudly as he clutched his head; the world was spinning around him out of control.

Genie pointed to the riverbank. 'We're going to swim? OK, Mouch? Follow me.'

Genie plunged back in, Mouch quickly followed, his doggy paddle pretty good, he wasn't far behind her at all. Clambering out over rocks on the other hand was harder, but eventually Genie got one half-drowned bedraggled hound out of the water and he shook as hard as he could to rid himself of the river.

'Enough already!' Genie exclaimed.

Mouch gave one last shake and then wiped his head on the grass to be sure.

'Rian?' Genie shouted. 'Rian?'

Genie listened. Nothing. She realized that the river made a lot of noise passing over the rocks. He probably couldn't hear. She hoped so. She had images of him lying bleeding someplace and . . .

'Come on. We got some walking to do.'

Mouch was only too happy to walk. Better than being on the river, that was for sure.


Much further downstream, Renée had detached herself from the raft and watched it sink by the dim glow of moonlight.

She'd surfaced to discover a logjam had piled up on a bend and although the water was passing really fast underneath through a sluice, the logs and other debris prevented anything from going any further on the surface. The raft was impaled on a jagged tree branch. Useless now. With it had died her courage and hopes. She really hoped the others were safe; was she the only survivor? She suddenly realized that a life without either one of them would be just impossible. Totally impossible.

She felt guilty; she should have saved the raft.

# REPOSSESSION

Sam Hawksmoor answers our questions!

## What research did you have to do for the story?

In Canada they keep national statistics about missing kids, in the UK they don't. It's shocking – some charities believe as many as 90,000 thousand kids go missing in the UK but no one really knows. Luckily, many are found or return, but the problem is getting worse in this austerity climate.

I read up on the current thinking on matter transference and the law of unintended consequences. That, and a lifetime wondering how teleportation functioned on Star Trek. The Terminator travels naked for a reason. The amount of computer power needed to teleport a pair of socks is IMMENSE. In part two of my story (*The Hunting*) we see just how problematic that can be.

## How close to being real and possible are the events in *The Repossession*?

Right now at CERN in Switzerland they think they have found the God Particle (Higgs Boson), the very building block of life. If true, the reality of transmitting matter is much closer than you think. Finding volunteers might be tricky, however. Failing that, you'd need to do what The Fortress did and keep it very secret.

## Is there a real life inspiration for Spurlake?

The small town of Hope BC is situated at the bottom of a huge gloomy rockface by the southern end of the Fraser River Canyon. I have also spent vacations in Nelson BC and other little former gold rush towns in the beautiful Okanagan. Spurlake could easily exist.

### Are Genie and Rian based on real people?

Genie was inspired by Roxanne – a real girl who is pretty, tough, determined and very bright. Rian by a kid in Coquitlam BC who rescued me one night in a blizzard when my car tipped over. He was 15 then and already taking care of his sick mother and girlfriend.

### What made you want to become a writer?

You don't have a choice in these things. I was writing stories when I was a kid, inspired by music and places I wanted to go to. Luckily none have survived to embarrass me now.

### Do you have anything you do to inspire you and help you write?

I go to the movies every week. I listen to music as I write (classical mostly but contemporary voices too such as Emeli Sandé) and do most of my first drafts in noisy cafés. I don't really like being 'alone' in the attic scribbling. I make sure I go for walks by the water (especially when in Vancouver) and miss the dog (who of course wormed his way into the book anyway). I can be inspired by a person, an object, a memory, or even the weather. I love those moments when suddenly the idea comes and you just have to get it on paper before it all disappears.